Dor S0-ACF-758

SHE WAS HIS WIFE,
HIS WOMAN, HIS MATE,
his companion on the trails as long as there were
trails for free men to ride on; through the valleys
until they were choked with cabbages and people; and up the mountains to the highest peaks,
as long as men felt compelled to seek God. She
was an Indian, but he had not taken her as some
men did to use and then discard. He had taken
her to cherish all the days of his life.

Soon she would bear his child.

Then the day came that turned his blood to ice,
when he returned from his traplines to find his
wife and unborn child brutally slain.

There was nothing to live for now, and nothing
to fill his days—nothing but vengeance, as raw
and unyielding as the pain within his own heart.

Books by Vardis Fisher

Mountain Man

Pemmican

Tale of Valor

Published by POCKET BOOKS

MOUNTAIN MAN

A Novel of Male and Female in
the Early American West

by

Vardis Fisher

A KANGAROO BOOK
PUBLISHED BY POCKET BOOKS NEW YORK

MOUNTAIN MAN

William Morrow edition published 1965

POCKET BOOK edition published August, 1967
14th printing..................September, 1977

This POCKET BOOK edition includes every word contained in
the original, higher-priced edition. It is printed from brand-
new plates made from completely reset, clear, easy-to-read type.
POCKET BOOK editions are published by
POCKET BOOKS,
a Simon & Schuster Division of
GULF & WESTERN CORPORATION
1230 Avenue of the Americas,
New York, N.Y. 10020.
Trademarks registered in the United States
and other countries.

ISBN: 0-671-81823-6.

Printed in the U.S.A.

FOR
Joe
who was one of them

To the Reader

WHAT THE AUTHOR of this novel would like to say to the reader has been so well said by various writers that I am going to let them say it to you. George Frederick Ruxton was one of the sharpest and most sensitive observers of the Rocky Mountains area and its people in the time of this book, or a little before it; and his observations he left to us in his books, chiefly in *Life in the Far West,* published in London in 1849.

On the Indian woman's relationship with whitemen he wrote: "The Indian women who follow the fortunes of the white hunters are remarkable for their affection and fidelity to their husbands, the which virtues, it must be remarked, are all on their own side; for, with very few exceptions, the mountaineers seldom scruple to abandon their Indian wives, whenever the fancy takes them to change their harems; and on such occasions the squaws, thus cast aside, wild with jealousy and despair, have been not unfrequently known to take signal vengeance both on their faithless husbands and the successful beauties who have supplanted them in their affections. There are some honourable exceptions, however, to such cruelty, and many of the mountaineers stick to their red-skinned wives for better and for worse, often suffering them to gain the upper hand in the domestic economy of the lodges, and being ruled by their better halves in all things pertaining to family affairs; and it may be remarked, when once the lady dons the unmentionables, she becomes the veriest termagant that ever henpecked an unfortunate husband."

On the nature of the mountain men a number of perspicacious writers have expressed their views. Just before the time of this novel W. A. Ferris wrote his *Life in the Rocky Mountains,* in which he said: "Strange, that people can find so strong and fascinating a charm in this rude, nomadic, and hazardous mode of life, as to be estranged themselves from home, country, friends, and all the comforts, elegances, and

privileges of civilization; but so it is, the toil, the danger, the
loneliness, the deprivation of this condition of being, fraught
with all its disadvantages, and replete with peril, is, they think,
more than compensated by the lawless freedom, and the stirring excitement, incident to their situation and pursuits. The
very danger has its attraction, and the courage and cunning,
and skill, and watchfulness made necessary by the difficulties
they have to overcome, the privations they are forced to
contend with, and the perils against which they must guard,
become at once their pride and boast. A strange, wild, terrible,
romantic, hard, and exciting life they lead, with alternate
plenty and starvation, activity and repose, safety and alarm,
and all the other adjuncts that belong to so vagrant a condition,
in a harsh, barren, untamed, and fearful region of desert, plain,
and mountain. Yet so attached to it do they become, that few
ever leave it, and they deem themselves, nay are, with all these
bars against them, far happier than the in-dwellers of towns
and cities, with all the gay and giddy whirl of fashion's mad
delusions in their train. . . .

"Scarcely, however, did I ever wish to change such hours of
freedom for all the luxuries of civilised life; and, unnatural and
extraordinary as it may appear, yet such is the fascination of the
life of the mountain hunter, that I believe not one instance
could be adduced of even the most polished and civilised of
men, who had once tasted the sweets of its attendant liberty,
and freedom from every worldly care, not regretting the
moment when he exchanged it for the monotonous life of the
settlements, nor sighing and sighing again once more to partake
of its pleasures and allurements."

Wrote the late historian Bernard DeVoto: ". . . but the
loveliest myth of all America was the far West . . . a lost
impossible province . . . where men were not dwarfs and where
adventure truly was. For a brief season, consider, the myth so
generously begotten became fact. For a few years Odysseus Jed
Smith and Siegfried Carson and the wing-shod Fitzpatrick
actually drew breath in this province of fable. Then suddenly it
was all myth again. Wagons were moving down the trails, and
nowhere remained any trace of the demigods who had passed
this way."

Of the mountain man: "But he was a man. He possessed the
most formidable skill ever developed on this continent. He
possessed, too, a valor hardly to be comprehended. He went

forth into the uncharted peaks and made his way. The Indians slaughtered him in hundreds and he slaughtered them as casually and passed on. . . . This record of him [Bonner's *Beckwourth*] and of his casual hardships, murders, and inattentive violence is quite, quite true."

"There is, perhaps," wrote Washington Irving, "no class of men on the face of the earth, says Captain Bonneville, who lead a life of more continued exertion, peril, and excitement, and who are more enamored of their occupations, than the free trappers of the West." "These," wrote Stanley Vestal, "were the mountain men, a breed of heroes. . . . These mountain men, far more than the soldiers and the statesmen, were the real means of seizing, holding, and settling our vast Far West. They were the men of destiny, whose skill and courage enabled those Americans who followed their trail to conquer a continent. . . . Those mountain men were only a few hundreds in number, hardly more than a thousand all told. Of these the free trappers were the cream, men whose careers illustrated perfectly the principle of the survival of the fittest. To be rated one of the best of these is as proud a title to manhood as the history of these States affords."

Justice William O. Douglas has approached the "wilderness" as a botanist and a poet: "What I had experienced was a symphony of the wilderness. Those who never learned to walk will never know its beauty. Only those who choose to get lost in it, cutting all ties with civilization, can know what I mean. Only those who return to the elemental world can know its beauty and grandeur—and man's essential unity with it."

Lawrence Gilman, the distinguished music critic, says in *Nature in Music*: ". . . M. Pierre Janet, who holds that those who, at different times in the history of the world's civilization, have manifested a strong attraction toward the natural world, have always been persons of a definite and particular type: emotional, subject to exaltation of mood, impatient of hampering traditions, essentially anti-conventional. Mr. Havelock Ellis, in his study of the psychology of the love of wild Nature, characterises all such persons as, in a greater or less degree, 'temperamentally exceptional.' In the strongest and simplest manifestations of the type, these lovers of wild Nature have been persons who were instinctively repelled by their ordinary environment. . . . Chateaubriand, who had small use for mountains except as 'the sources of rivers, a barrier against the horrors of war,' is balanced by Petrarch, who, climbing Mont Ventoux . . . observed that his soul 'rose to lofty contemplations on the summit.' . . . The strongest appeal of natural beauty has always, then, been chiefly to individuals of emotional habit, and especially to those of untrammelled imagination and non-conformist tendencies: in other words, to poetically minded radicals in all times and regions. It is probable that the curious and enlightened inquirer, bearing in mind these facts, would not be surprised to find, in studying the various expressions of this attraction as they are recorded in the arts, that the uniquely sensitive and eloquent art of music has long been the handmaid of the Nature-lover; and he would be prepared to find the Nature-lover himself appearing often in the guise of that inherently emotional and often heterodox being, the musicmaker."

Readers interested in exemplars of Mr. Gilman's concluding statement can find them in the "forest" and "spring" symphonies of the eighteenth century; Handel's attempts to capture in music winds, bird music, running water; Knecht's "Musical Portrait of Nature" and Vivaldi's "The Four Seasons"; and in the tonal landscape-painting of more recent times, such as Debussy's "Après-midi d'un faune," d'Indy's "Jour d'eté à la montagne," MacDowell's "Wandering Iceberg," and many others.

Readers familiar with the history of the American West will be aware that Sam and Kate are drawn in some degree from John Johnston, the "Crow-killer," and Jane Morgan, whose family was slaughtered on the Musselshell. Though these two persons actually lived they are today almost completely lost in legends.

MOUNTAIN MAN

PART ONE

LOTUS

es glowing black with und

1

HE HAD PAUSED to listen to the exquisite madrigal of a Western meadow lark, and had offered to sing with it, choosing as his own, "Give Me the Sweet Delights of Love"; but he had found no bird that would sing with him, though now and then one, like the chat, would try to entice him into mimicry. On his packhorse in a piece of cheverel, the fine soft leather made of kidskin, he had a mouth organ; and a mile and ten minutes later he took it out and looked round him for sign of enemies. He had learned that playing Bach or Mozart arias when in enemy country was not only good for his loneliness; the music filled skulking Indians with awe. At this hour, back home and far away, his father might be playing the pianoforte.

An hour later the object that held his gaze as he sat astride his black stallion, two heavy handguns at his waist and a rifle across the saddletree, was a huge brownish-yellow monster that some men called the grizzly. In a frenzy of impatience the beast was digging into the wet loam, its powerful curved claws thrusting in like chisels. It would pause now and then to poke its face into the hole and sniff, and then would dig again with what seemed to be twice its previous energy. The man on the horse thought the bear was trying to dig out a prairie dog, though why the idiot should ever do that was beyond anyone's guessing: at the last moment the dog would flash up and out, and be off and away, and the monster would sit in doleful frustration on its huge fat rump, as though sunk to its waist in fur. Its small eyes would scan the world roundabout.

Suddenly the man on the horse felt the shock of amazement. It was not a dog's hole the beast was invading but the lair of a badger, and a deadlier fighter than a badger this man had never seen. The man thought he knew what had happened: the badger, eyes glowing black with anger and outrage, had

3

retreated to the end of its underground run and there in the dark, lips snarling, had waited. At last, its blood boiling in fury, it had rushed up the tunnel and with teeth as sharp as needles had seized the bear's nose.

With the emotion of grandeur filling him big and full the man watched the remarkable drama before him. A bear's nose was so tender and sensitive that an assault on it was an affront that filled the big creature with mountainous rage. This brute, weighing, the man guessed, about a thousand pounds, now exploded from its chest a series of wild woofing roars and rose to its hind legs, with thirty pounds of infuriated badger hanging from its nose. Badger claws were striking like lancets at the bear's face and eyes. Having risen, the monster turned round and round, like a great fat man in a fur cloak, its head shaking from side to side, as it tried with feeble gestures to shake off its foe. But the badger had most of its teeth set deep in bear nose, and it was thirty pounds of savage fighting fury.

The man gave a snort of incredulous delight and went on staring.

He had seen some remarkable fights since coming west, seven years ago, but none had made his eyes bug as they bugged now. The bear kept turning and shaking and woofing, or whimpering like a frightened or wounded child; and all the while the four badger feet raked across the eyes and face and down the throat. The grizzly's front legs looked as helpless as they might have looked if they had been broken or the claws had been pulled. The man watching did not fully sense that with all those badger chisels buried in the sensitive nose the big fellow was so filled with astonishment, with bewildered outrage, with confusion and pain, that its will was paralyzed. It could only keep turning round and round, sinking now to four feet, now rising, and all the while pouring out the mournful whimpering lament of a thing whose heart was breaking.

"I'll be damned!" the man said aloud. He looked round him and sniffed for the scent of enemies. He heard a lark singing, and for a moment he thought how strange it was that in the same scene a bird's throat was pure music and two beasts had turned as black as night with murderous fury.

As suddenly as it began it was all over. Into the monster's tiny dull brain came realization of its two powerful paws; with each it seized the badger and literally tore it apart. Like a prince of dignity overwhelmed by disgust, it flung the bloody pieces to the earth, and still crying like a child with a broken heart, it sank soundlessly to front feet and loped softly away into a river thicket.

The man rode over and dismounted. He saw what he had expected to see: the flesh part of the bear's nose was in the vise of the badger's jaws.

It was a Sunday forenoon early in August, in the year 1846. The big man who stood there on the Musselshell, looking with admiration and wonder at a badger's head, was a free trapper, hunter, and mountain man, on his way up the river and over to the Bitterroot Valley, where he expected to take a wife. He was a giant, even among the mountain men of the American West. Without his moccasins he stood six foot four, and without clothing weighed about two hundred fifty pounds. He was twenty-seven years old. Trapping was his trade, the Rocky Mountains and their valleys were his home, and the killing of Indians was only the clearing away of things that got in his path. He admired courage above all other virtues; next to that he admired fortitude; and third among the few values by which he lived was mercy to the weak or defenseless. His passions were love of life, mortal combat with a worthy foe, good music, good food, and that quality of nature which would compel a poet to say, a hundred years later, that its heartbreaking beauty would remain when there would no longer be a heart to break for it. Besides his rifle and handguns he had at his belt a Bowie knife with a honed blade ten inches long. It was a genuine Bowie, not a Green River or a Laos, or other cheap imitation.

He looked at the badger a full minute, paying, in his silent way, his respect to a peerless fighter. He listened, but heard no sound of the grizzly. He scanned the horizons and sniffed the air for scent of Blackfeet. Then, mounting his black stud, he took the path up the river, his gray-blue eyes searching the country around him. His friends and relatives back east might have thought this desolate God-forsaken land, its bluffs eroded and hot, its pine and juniper jaundiced from the heavy lime; but this man loved it, all of it, even the alkali where no plants grew. He loved this whole vast grandeur—the mountains snow-crowned, the valleys berry-laden, the meadows looking like parks that had never heard a mowing-machine, the prairies with their vast herds of antelope and buffalo. It was good for a man to be alive, his belly full of steak and berries and mountain water, a fleet horse under him, a rifle that never missed fire, his pipe glowing, his mouth harp in his possibles bag, a lark spilling sweet music from its tiny bird-soul and a vesper sparrow flitting along the way as though to guide him. God, how he loved it all!

This was Blackfeet country to the north and west of him. Ever since that day, forty years ago, when Meriwether Lewis and Reuben Field killed two of them, in self-defense, on the upper Marias, they had bent their savage wills to the extermination of all white people. This man, so far, had had no trouble with them, but he knew that they were the most vengeful and cruel and dangerous of all his red enemies, and when near their lands, as now, he never for a moment plugged his ears or closed his eyes.

It was already said of him, by other mountain men, and would have been said by eagles and wolves if they could talk, that his sense of sight was that of the falcon; of smell, that of the wolf. His sense of hearing was not so keen. He thought his sense of smell had twice saved his life, but he might have said, if any man could have got him to talk about it, that like the mourning dove, the bittern, the Indian, he had a sixth sense. What he thought of as his sixth sense was in fact only what his five senses agreed on and communicated to his mind, acting together, like an intelligence agency, to sort out, accept or reject, and evaluate the impressions that came to them.

When, a few miles up the river from the scene of the fight, he drew gently on reins and stopped, he did not crane his neck and gawk round him, as a greenhorn might have done, but sat motionless, his senses searching the earth and air and reporting to him. He had seen the rufous breast of a bluebird high in a cottonwood; had heard the soft warning whee-uuuh whistle of the willow thrush; and had smelled the presence of enemies. Five minutes he sat stone-still, all his senses poring over the evidence; and he then was sure that a party of Blackfeet warriors had passed him, not more than ten minutes and two miles back. He touched a heel gently to the beast's flank and moved forward.

After half a mile he stopped again, deeply troubled by something close but unseen. Two birds had given alarm calls; a redwing, hopping about in the river willows, was acting with that agitation that made it tremble and call its alarm, when enemies approached its nest. But this was not its nesting season. An unseen dove was lamenting somewhere ahead of him. But his sharpest realization of something strange and dangerous came through his sense of smell. He was certain that he had smelled fresh blood. Again he went forward, over the low rise of a hill, and looked upriver; stopped, and looked and listened and sniffed; and again moved forward, to come soon and suddenly on the most dreadful scene he was ever to look at.

2

JOHN BOWDEN was a stubborn man. His stubbornness he called will power. In his home town an attorney had said to his face, "You have the most headstrong unyielding intractable contumacy of any man between here and Adam." The wagon train headed for Oregon, of which John and his family were members, was encamped on the Big Blue when Bowden, angry and impatient, said to the overseer that the old map he had with him was right and did in fact, as he had said before, point out a better and shorter route than the one by South Pass and the interminable desert. Why go by the Platte and the Sweetwater, merely because damned fools had been going that way? The overseer, as in former encounters, had refused to listen and had sharply dismissed him, whereupon Bowden had detached his wagon from the train, and with his wife and three children had set forth on one of the most fantastic and dangerous journeys in human history.

With him were his wife Kate, his daughter Lou, sixteen, his son John, fourteen, and his son Robert, twelve. As the other members of the train watched Bowden and his family slowly disappear into the northwest they thought he had gone out of his mind. They thought they would never see him again. The defiant and foolhardy fellow staked his life and his family's on a map that had never been any good, and on his knowledge of the western land, though he had never been more than twenty miles from his dooryard in Pennsylvania. With his family he vanished into Cheyenne land, and then into Crow land, and at last into Blackfeet land, or would have done so if he could have found a ford across the Musselshell. For eight hundred miles into a wilderness of hostile Indians—across a dozen rivers and hundreds of creeks—around great mountain chains and on and on the tenacious and obdurate man took his way, never faltering, never doubting himself, never looking back. He had the luck of an infinitude of fools: not one lone wagon in a thousand could have traversed that vast distance where no wagon had ever gone. That he and his family were not set on by Indians and murdered and scalped long before they reached the Musselshell, or even the Cheyenne River or the Powder, was to become an incredible tale that would be told by trappers around a thousand campfires. How under heaven did he get across the Yellowstone anyway? "I figger," said Windy Bill, "thet he jist looked torst heaven and walked on water." Did no Indians ever see them in that journey of eighty days and eight hundred miles? Indeed, no Indians ever saw them; and the oceans of buffalo, even the wolves, even the grizzlies, fled before them. Not once in eighty days did they see the smoke of a fire, except their own. Bowden had so little knowledge of Indians that he tethered or hobbled his two beasts at night as though he were in his own yard back home, and with the innocence of angels he and his wife and children sank into deep sleep. Kate came to believe that he was guided by a higher power that had told him of a shorter and safer way to the Pacific coast. Before setting out she had heard stories of the hardships en route, and of all the graves along the South Pass trail. There had been hardships but no graves on the path John took.

The fact is that, sulking and brooding, he had only the dimmest notion of what he was doing and where he was. He went so far north that at the end of eighty days he found himself on the Musselshell, only a few miles south of its junction with the Missouri. It might as well have been the Columbia or the Saskatchewan, for all that he knew about it. He had never heard that on Monday, the 20th of May, 1805, William Clark, en route to the ocean, had written of this river as the Shell and the Muscle Shell, noting in his journal that it emptied into the Missouri "2270 miles up" from that river's mouth. Clark had found it to be 110 yards wide and of a greenish-yellow color. John knew only that it was too deep to ford. He saw ripening fruit on the river bottom, and because his rickety and squealing wagon needed repairs he decided to tarry on the east bank a few days. It is hard to tell what he might have thought if he had known that a Blackfeet scout lay on his belly behind a dwarf cedar and watched him. He said he would get things in shape while his family gathered and dried fruit. That he could decide to camp for a week on the very edge of the Blackfeet nation indicates the bottomless depths of his ignorance.

In the morning of the day that Samson John Minard headed up the river, Bowden left his camp and took a game trail through bottomland to look for his two horses. When he did not return after half an hour his wife first called to him and then sent the three children to find him. They had hardly passed out of sight when something—she would never have been able to say what—so alarmed her that she stood rigid and listening. It may be that she heard a scream, or possibly she smelled blood. Seizing an axe, she ran on the path her husband and children had taken and in less than three hundred yards came to a scene that might have turned a weaker woman to stone. In the first instant of amazement and shock she had a lightning image of these things—of her husband bound to a tree and bent forward, the whole top of his head crimson with blood; of her two sons lying on the earth, with hideous redmen bending over them; and of her daughter, also fallen, but screaming nd heart-stricken, as an Indian seized her hair and raised his tomahawk.

Kate turned not to stone but to female tiger. Her fury was such that her strength was multiplied tenfold as she rushed forward and raised her axe. She moved with such devastating speed and her blows were so unerring that four warriors fell before any of them realized that an avenger was on them. At the moment the tomahawk fell on the daughter she buried her axe three inches deep in a red spine at the base of the skull. The two blows were simultaneous. With almost no pause at all she flew to a warrior bent over a son, and she split his skull so deep that the two halves actually sank toward his shoulders. The third, and again the fourth, she also felled with a single blow. It was all over in a few seconds. In the moment when she was returning to her daughter two Indians slashed the thongs binding Bowden, flung him across a horse, and were in flight down the river before Kate could understand what they had done. A half dozen Indians and a scalped and dead or dying man vanished, and Kate Bowden stood, shuddering with rage and tremors and lunacy, her dead children and four dead Indians around her. Her mother-fury turning to nausea, her whole body shaking so terribly that she had the movements of a mechanical toy, she stood, Indian blood over her hair and face and clothes, and so fully sensed the immense and unspeakable horror of it that her conscious mind was blotted out.

The only thing she did for half an hour was to drag the fallen Indian off her daughter.

She was still there, trembling, sick, numbed, and witless, when a man rode into view and sat on his horse forty yards away, looking at her. In the first instant he knew that a war party had passed him on its way down the river.

He had a clear view of the seven prone persons, all of whom seemed to be dead, and of the woman, with blood all over her and with a bloody axe in her hands. He had seen men kill men. He himself had slain and scalped eight Indians since he left St. Louis and headed west. In the world where he now lived the killing of the weak by the strong was the first law of life, all the way from the tiniest gnats and spiders up to the wolf, the elk bull, the grizzly. No day passed in which he did not see creatures killing other creatures. No day passed in which enemies did not look at him and covet his flesh. This was not a country for persons dedicated to the prevention of cruelty by the living on the living.

Sam was not a man who could be easily moved by death and loss but he was moved by the scene before him. It was not the dead warriors; he cared nothing about them. Possibly it was not the sons and the daughter. It must have been the way a mother stood, looking round her and back and forth; the way she bent a little forward and peered at a son, and slowly turned to look at the daughter; the way she knelt and searched the dead faces and bright bloody skulls of the sons, who only a little while ago had thick mops of brown hair; or the way she knelt and looked at her daughter, with the deep tomahawk cleft in the upper face and forehead. So absorbed was she by the grim facts that had desolated her life and soul, so darkened and blotted out was her conscious mind, so depressed was her pulse and her breathing, that she had almost no sense of being left alone in the world, God only knew where.

Sam had at least a faint notion of it all. He supposed that this woman had killed four Blackfeet braves with nothing but an axe, who now was completely helpless before her enemies. Would she kneel there all day and all night, before her dead children? Was she praying? She had dropped the axe and now crawled back and forth, back and forth, between the children. Twenty minutes after Sam came in view she was kneeling by the girl and she seemed to be trying to clothe her; she stripped a thin shawl from her shoulders and laid it over the girl's flanks. In one moment she glanced at the cottonwood tree where her husband had fallen forward. In that moment she understood what they had done to him, but she would understand that only in fleeting moments of insight, and only for a week or two. There would be a few brief flashes in the gathering darkness, when she would know that nothing was left to her but the dead, an old wagon, some bedding, a few utensils, an axe, a rifle. . . .

Turning from her daughter, she saw the big man on the horse. She leapt to her feet, recovered the axe, and began to run. Because he was in the path down which she had come she made a wide detour across river bottom, running with what the man thought was astonishing speed. A few moments later she came down the path toward him, a rifle in her hand, and he felt a vivid flash of horripilation, the bristling of body hair called gooseflesh. The expression on his face changed. Good God, did she intend to shoot him? "Woman, you'd better stop there!" he shouted to her, but she would not have stopped for droves of tigers or rivers of fire. She came on, but at twenty paces from him did stop, abruptly, and with both hands tried to raise the rifle and aim at him. He thought she was shaking too hard to put the sight on a target but he hung his rifle from the saddle's pommel, threw a leg over, and slipped to the earth, both hands high above his head. He advanced toward her and all the while she was trying to aim the gun at him. Failing in that, she threatened him with it.

"Woman," he said sternly, "I'm your friend. It looks like you need one." When she gave no sign of friendliness he again advanced, slowly, trying to look into her eyes; and when twenty feet from her he unbuckled his revolvers and let them fall. He put his arms out wide, his fingers spread. "I'm Sam Minard, New York State. Like I said, you need a friend. We have graves to dig. You have a shovel?"

Holding her rifle with both hands, its muzzle pointed at him, she did not speak. She had so much redman's blood on her face that he couldn't tell what kind of face it was, except that it looked strong, like his mother's. She had blood over one upper eyelid, and when she blinked the red spot flashed in the high sun. Sam was looking at her with wonder and admiration; he would never have believed that a woman with no weapon but an axe could kill four warriors, without herself being touched.

For two or three minutes he looked at her and waited. Knowing that her will had faltered and that he was no longer in danger, he buckled the guns round his waist and went back to his horses. Leading the stud and with the packhorse trailing, he went up the trail to the woman's camp, observing along the way the spots where her husband or children had uprooted firewood. He wanted to ask what in hell they were doing away up here in Crow and Blackfeet land, and where they thought they were going, but he doubted that he would ever get a word out of her. She was wary, like a wild thing; she was lost in blood and horror. What would she do when her dead were buried? Would she let him take her north to the Missouri, to wait for a river boat, or far south to the trail?

He found a shovel in the camp, and thinking one spot as good as another, he was about to dig when she came running toward him, gesturing, like a mute. He followed her and she climbed to a tableland that was high enough to overlook the river and its bottoms, both north and south. She took the shovel from him and marked off three spots. Then, convulsed, it seemed to Sam, by frustration or anguish, she fell to her knees and with a stick made a small rectangle, and close to it another, twice as wide. He understood that she wanted her two sons in one grave. He had seen no tears in her eyes, no sign of the hysterical grief that he associated with women. Now that he was used to her bloody face he saw that it was rugged, with strong jawbones and chin and a fine forehead. He thought her eyes were gray but could not tell, for they were alive with eerie apparitions of light. She had strong hands.

Up here, he thought, was no place for graves, where the soil was meager and the wild winds of wintertime would sweep across in forty-below-zero cold. Still, the soil was drier and rich in lime. So he began to dig, and after a few minutes his face was moist with sweat. She brought blankets from the camp. When the graves were dug he took a blanket and with his rifle across his left arm went to the scene of the massacre, followed by the woman, who had put her rifle away somewhere. Sam spread the blanket at the dead girl's side and gently laid her on it, the mother intently watching him all the while. He folded the blanket over her nakedness and at the same moment drew the shawl away. He then handed his rifle to the woman, and with

ᵉ girl cradled in his two arms he carried her to the grave. So
ᵘch blood had gushed from her horrible wound and down
ᵛer her face that he could not tell what she had looked like,
ᵘt he could tell that she had a full womanly form and he liked
ᵒ think of her as one who had been superlatively lovely. He
ᵉelt and very gently lowered her three feet, to the bottom. In
ᵉ next instant the mother was across the grave from him,
ᵉeeling, and though he could hear no words and see no
ᵒvements in her lips he thought she was praying; and bowing
ᵢs head, he prayed with her. Surely the Almighty was listening
ᵒw. She still knelt, while he placed shovels of earth on the
ᵇlanket, till the tomb was filled. The two lads he buried with
ᵉe same gentleness as the daughter, laying them on a blanket
ᵢde by side and covering them with elkskins that he took from
ᵢs pack. Again, as before, he knelt across from her and prayed.
   He then left her by the graves and went to the dead Indians.
ᵂith skill learned from older mountain men he scalped the
ᵒur, and while tying the scalps together he wondered if the
ᵂoman would go away with him, to rejoin her people, or if this
ᵖot would be her home. In any case he intended to consecrate
ᵗhe graves as well as he could with four outposts; so now he cut
ᵒff the four heads, with no more emotion than he would have
ᵉelt in cutting off the heads of four deer, and took them, and
ᵒur strong chokecherry stakes, to the grave area. The woman
ᵂas sitting by the graves, bowed almost to her knees. Studying
ᵗhe scene, Sam decided to set the four stakes equidistant from
ᵗhe graves, at a distance of about forty yards; but while digging
ᵃ hole it occurred to him that the tough dwarf cedar would last
ᵃ lot longer, as posts, than the chokecherry; and so with the axe
ᵉe went up the hill. It was almost sunset when he had the four
ᶜedar posts set, and with both hands was bringing the heads
ᵈown with terrific force, so that the stakes were rammed up the
ᵗhroats and against the skulls. These four heads would be a
ᵂarning to the Blackfeet, the sons of bitches, and to the Crows,
f they came skulking around. These would tell them to leave
ᵗhis woman alone. The ravens would come and pick the skulls
ᶜlean—the shrikes and magpies and buzzards, the beetles and
ᵃll the insects; and before long they would be four white grin-
ᵉing skulls, facing the four corners of the world.
   John Bowden had set up a crude brush lean-to at his
ᶜampsite. Looking in, Sam had seen bedding, utensils, a few
ᵗools, and some food. Nearby was the rickety wagon. Did she

want him to take these things up to the graves tonight? H
stood in night dusk, looking up the hill toward her; he suppose
she would want to be alone with her grief and loss. Poor thing
poor thing! She was sitting between the two graves, her rifl
across her lap, her right hand laid on the mound that covere
her sons, her left hand on the mound above her daughter
Never had he seen woe as deep as this, or known man or woma
who in one blow from heaven or hell had suffered such
overwhelming loss.

Wondering if she would sit there all night, he took his horse
to the river for water. Somewhere north of him the Blackfee
war party was still racing toward a village of lodges where—i
was always this way—the whole hideous screaming pack o
them, squaws, children, and dogs, would torture and mutilat
this woman's husband, killing him horribly and very slowly
with the fiendish skills in producing agony of which th
Blackfeet were masters. Sam Minard hated the Blackfeet
There was no mountain man from the Rio to the Athabasca
from the Ohio to the Pacific Ocean, who did not detest this re
people. The hatred in some of the men was such a fierce wil
passion that it boiled in their emotions and flamed in their talk
and kept them busy whetting their hatchets and knives. Th
Bloods and Piegans of the Blackfeet nation were the mos
savage tribes in the West; but most of the mountain men hate
all Indians, and placed high among their mountain-man law
the axiom that the only good Indian was a dead Indian—and no
only dead but picked clean by the ravens and wolves.

Securing his horses for the night, Sam went to the woman'
camp to see what she had. A dark night had come. His ea
detected a sound above the sound of tree toads. He listened
Yes, there was a sound, blood-chilling—a wild insane keening
up there by the graves. Again he felt gooseflesh, as he stood
facing her, listening: in his mind he saw her there, month afte
month, year after year, fighting off eagles and wolves and
making her heartbroken jeremiads to God, until at last she
withered and shrank and died, of cold and loss and loneliness
He was afraid she would forget her camp, her bedding and
food, and sinking into stuporous woe, fold over on her lap and
die.

He was to learn that he did not know her.

After going halfway up the hill to listen, and coming back
down, he thought of supper. Ordinarily when journeying

hrough enemy lands he made fireless camps, even in
vintertime; he would eat a chunk of jerked buffalo and roll into
iis buffalo robes. But he had labored hard this day and was as
amished as a winter wolf. He decided to make a fire but first he
would wait for the moon to come up, for he thought he could
lip out to the hills and get a mule deer. Two hours later he
:ame in with a fat buck over his shoulder. Opening it from
hroat to rump, he cut away the choicer portions, including the
iver, loin, kidney fat, and the upper parts of the hams. He built
a fire and brought water from the river. All the while he was
thinking that it would be son-like to take hot steaks or a fine
roast to the mother.

After eating four pounds of venison, a pint of dried
serviceberries, and a quart of black coffee he filled his cob pipe
and sucked flame into it. It was a nice night. He could hear the
wings of night birds and the river's flowing waters. Above him
he could see a thousand stars. Around him he could smell
tobacco smoke, the fertile loam of river bottom, magpie and
crow nests in the cottonwoods, mole runs, moss pads, hot lime
hills cooling in the night, and the embers of aspen and willow in
the fire. He wondered if he should have used two of his robes as
burial shrouds. He was not a very sentimental man; he knew
that in no time at all the dead person or the dead beast was only
a few bones but he knew also that people liked to lay their loved
ones down in the best they could afford. He had two large robes
and several small ones. He guessed he would give one of them
to the woman. Tomorrow if she refused to go north with him
and wait for a river boat, or south to the trail, he would give her
more powder and ball and anything else he had that she could
use. If she was determined to stay here he doubted that she
could long survive in a land where the strongest went down one
by one. She would be all alone with four skulls and two graves.
She would never see a human being, never in God's world,
except a redman on a distant hill, or a mountain man going up
or down the river.

North of her only twenty miles would be the wide Missouri.
Steamboats would chug through its waters as far as the Great
Falls but she would never see or hear them. South of her farther
than she could see, even if she were to stand a thousand feet
above the graves, was rolling hill land covered with scrub pine
and cedar. East of her was the same lonely waste clear to the
junction of the Missouri and the Yellowstone—and west of her

to the Judith Mountains, and Wolf Creek, Arrow Creek, an
Dog Creek. Unless she climbed a tall hill she would never se
the Big Belt or Crazy Mountains, much less such magnificer
massifs of divine sculpturing as the Tetons, the Bitterroots, th
Big Horns, and the Blue. There would be plenty of wild gam
all around her—a few buffalo, many deer and antelope; fifty o
more kinds of duck and goose; squirrels and prairie chicken
and fish in the river; and fruits and roots of several kinds, but n
such luscious wild orchards as she might have if she were in th
Madison or Gallatin valley. . . .

Sam was turning these things over as he puffed his pipe an
thought of her problems. He wished he could stop thinkin
about her; after all, the vast wonderful earth the Almighty ha
made was filled with the dying and the about-to-die. He tried t
force his thoughts to his plan to take a wife, to trap in th
Uintahs this coming winter, to send for a trumpet—to these, o
to speculation on what other mountain men were doing at thi
moment—in what deep impenetrable thicket tall skinny Bil
Williams had hidden from the red warriors, his high squeak
voice silenced for the night; by what fire with its cedar an
coffee aroma Wind River Bill was spinning his yarns an
saying, "I love the wimmins, I shorely do"; in what Spanish
village short blond Kit Carson was dancing the soup danc
with black-eyed señoritas; what tall tales Jim Bridger wa
telling to bug-eyed greenhorns from a wagon train that ha
stopped this day at his post to get horses shod and tires set—Jim
spitting tobacco juice and saying, "Waugh! This here critter is
wore plum down to his quick—I reckon I'll hafta put moccasin
on him"; and in what quiet shelter Lost-Skelp Dan was moving
a calloused palm over the hideless bone of his skull, as if hoping
to find hair growing there. Then Sam's mind turned to Dick
Wooton, who in mountain-man talk was some for his inches: six
feet six and as straight as the long barrel of his rifle, he had once
stood shoulder to shoulder with Rube Herring, and "Thar
warn't a hair's-breadth differns in tall or wide betwixt them."
Even Marcelline, though a Mexican, could easily look down on
the top hair of a man standing six feet—Marcelline, with a
temper ranging from red-hot to white-hot, who despised his
people and abjured his blood, and cast his lot with the white
mountain men. Marcelline was a picture all right, with his mass
of hair half as long as his arm and as black as wet coal, spilling

out from his slouched beaver, to cover the shoulders of his buckskin hunting jacket like a wide mane. . . .

But again and again Sam's thoughts returned to the woman on the hill. He then laid his pipe aside, took a fat dripping roast off the green tripod above the glowing embers, thrust a green stick through it, picked up his rifle and a small robe, and took the path. Slippered with moccasins and as soundless as the wolf or the mouse, he approached the woman until he stood only a few feet from her, and looked down at her bowed head. For two hours or more she had been silent. In her own way she had wept until she could weep no more. She still sat where she had sat when he left her, chin sunk to her breast. One hand touched the daughter's grave, the other that of the sons. The thing that fixed his attention was the heartsick quavering moan she made, when the long deep shudder of grief and horror ran through her. He was not a man in whom pity had a large home but compassion ran deep in him now. For perhaps ten minutes he looked down at her and listened, until the utter bitterness of it, the quivering of her flesh and soul in the loss, was more than he chose to endure. Laying his rifle down and holding the roast with his left hand, with his right he draped the robe across her shoulders and over her lap. He then set the green stick in the earth at her side, with the spitted roast on it. She gave no sign that she was aware of him. After looking at her a full minute he was convinced that she was not. Our Father in heaven, could grief be deeper than that!

Shaken, he turned away and went down the hill. At the fire he put a robe over him like a collapsed tent and took a mouth organ from his medicine bag. His father played the clavichord with dash and clarity, though his hands, almost as large as his son's, easily spanned an octave and a half and sometimes hit the wrong key. Sam had learned to play several instruments, including the horn and flute. When he headed west he had taken only two mouth organs, and he had played them through seven long lonely winters. Tonight, with the robe over him, he played softly, so that he would not start up the night birds, the tree toads and the wolves. Beethoven had imitated the nightingale's song with the flute, the quail's with the oboe, and the cuckoo's with a clarinet. Sam had tried to imitate bird songs—the phoebe's plaintive little voice of a tiny bird-child lost in a thicket, telling its name over and over; the chickadee's and bunting's and horned lark's. Tonight he softly played a few sad old things and a hymn or two, for he was filled with homesickness; or with the yearning that Schubert had felt, who had never found the love he hungered for.

It was the woman on the hill. He flung the robe back, for he didn't want to play down in the depths of fur. He wanted to stand up and shake a clenched fist at that malevolent fate that knocked on the door in the opening bars of Beethoven's C-minor symphony and proclaimed to the world its power over Beethoven's hearing. It was the same unpitying ruthless fate, knocking there in the grand arrogant manner, that had brought savages to this spot, to hack three children to death and take a father away to torture. What was it there, he wondered, looking up at the home of the stars, a divine benevolence or a mindless malevolence? He rolled into a robe but was not able to sleep; he looked up through treetops at the constellations and thought the time was about midnight. Sniffing the odors in the night breeze, he listened; tried to sleep and again listened; and rose at last to sit by the dead fire and smoke his pipe and think. There was something he ought to do. Maybe the woman up there would like a drink of water. Among her things he found a coffeepot and this he rinsed at the river and filled. When a few yards from her he paused to look round him, for the moon was still up. The four skulls looked quite comfortable on their stakes. Out in the moon dusk in the northeast a beast was slinking, perhaps a wolf. She was still there, between the graves, the robe around her, the roast on the green stick at her side. For a moment he thought she might be dead, simply, eternally, of grief. It might be best so. Going softly over to her, he saw that rats or mice had been feeding at the roast. No, she was not dead; the same long shudders were running through her, on every third or fourth breath, and the same unearthly sound of loss and woe followed each shudder.

He sank quietly to the earth and sat by her. Softly he said, "I thought you might want a drink." He had expected no response. All his life he had heard of the riddle called woman, but if she was a riddle it was in man-woman love, not in grief. In grief she was as stark and plain as the face of death itself. Windy Bill might have said that she made a man feel like gone beaver; like what he had once called a stillburn child in a putrefied forest. She made Sam feel homesick for sight of his mother and father, and Christmas around the fireplace.

Bending low and moving forward, he looked around to see if

her eyes were closed. They were wide open. Once more, somewhere in the years ahead, he would see eyes like hers, and they would alter the course of his life. Now he could only feel a stupid and exasperating helplessness. Would she go with him, and take a boat or a wagon train back to her people? He knew that she never would, unless he bound her. She would fight like the bitch wolf when the grizzly approached her lair. If he were to take her a thousand miles away, like the cat she would find her way back—she would return, slinking through the forests and over the mountains, even if it took her ten years. His deepest insights told him that. They told him that all that this woman had in the world was here, under her left hand and under her right.

"You know," he said gently, "I think you're going to need a little house here," and went back to his camp.

3

AT THE BOLE of a cottonwood he untied the end of a long leather rope, and down the tree from twenty feet up came the remainder of the deer. He would eat a big breakfast, for he knew that he would work hard all day. In loin and kidney fat he fried the entire tenderloin, as well as two thick steaks from a ham; and he ate nearly all of it and drank a quart of coffee. Then, while indulging himself with a pipeful, he looked round him at the trees. Either aspen or cottonwood would do. The wood of both was soft and rotted easily but a cabin built of them would stand as long as the woman stood. If he made it about ten by ten it ought to house her all right. He was not a mason, and so would not undertake a chimney, but he would gather stones and lay a foundation, so that the logs would not rot right away; and he would leave a hole at the apex of the roof, as Indians did, to let the smoke out. He had no glass or oiled paper for a window, no planks for a door, unless he were to tear the wagon bed apart. He supposed she would freeze to death when the wild winds of Canada came baying down the skies and the river froze white and solid from bank to bank. But maybe not, for he and other mountain men would bring her blankets and robes. They would take care of her, in their way.

Going up the hill, he looked round him. Where had he left the axe? Among her things did she have a hammer, a saw, nails, a pair of old shoes that he could use for door hinges? Standing at her side, he told her that he was going to build a house for her: did she want it here by the graves or down by the river, where she would be closer to water and firewood, and sheltered from the winds? Did she understand him? he asked, kneeling by her. Was it all right to look among her camp things? She had not touched the water; insects were crawling over the roast.

He found the axe and observed again that it was a good one, though he would have preferred a six-pounder with a blade a good five inches wide. His rifle across his left arm and the axe in his grasp, he went to her camp and thoroughly searched it. He found a few tools in a tall pail; a few nails and bolts and nuts in a small wooden box; some flour, salt, sugar, dried fruits, coffee, tea, and a piece of uncooked flesh that was smelling. He threw it out. He found no tobacco: the woman's husband, he guessed, was not a tobacco man. Well, what kind of man was he anyway?—to bring a wife and children a thousand miles into Indian land, with no weapons but an axe and an old rifle, and a butcher knife with the wood broken off its handle. Rummaging, he found a pair of boy's shoes that would make hinges. Inspection of the wagon told him that there would be enough weathered and cracked boards for a door, if he could tear them away from their bolts without making kindling of them. It looked as if she would have enough bedding for a while, but not enough when winter cold split trees open and froze wolves as hard as river ice. In such cold there wasn't enough bedding in the world to keep a person warm. He had a picture of her, crawling, after the cold came, into her pile of quilts and blankets, taking with her the rifle and axe, wild fruits, a hunk of meat, and maybe some biscuits. She looked robust and able. Out there under the flies and ants were four headless savages, and up north was a horde of them, who had a new notion of what one white woman could do. She didn't seem to have more than a few rags of clothing; he would bring her bolts of cloth and needles and thread, and tanned skins. The Almighty up there in the blue would surely watch over the poor soul and protect her, until she had learned the ways of mountain men and mountain country, and had become part of this vast beautiful land, which to know was to love, was to dig your way into, like the badger and prairie dog, was to sing your soul upon, as millions of birds were doing all over the valleys and hills, and the wolves in their mating song, the elk bulls in their bugling, the moose bulls in their honking. She would learn and would love all the wonderful wild calls of geese and loons and grebes, willets and hawks and prairie chickens. And she would see Sam Minard someday on a mountain summit, shaking his glad powerful fists at the skies and calling on the Lord Jehovah to look down from a heavenly window and see what a fantastic world he had made. A man was a fool who wanted to leave this country, once he had found it. A woman could learn to love its ways. Like the red women, she might learn to trap beaver (he would bring her two or three traps) and break a deer's neck (he would be sure that she always had plenty of powder and ball); and she might grow a small garden, even have wild flowers round her house and over the graves, though it would be a long way to carry water. Doggone it, she might even become the woman of some mountain man—have another child or two, and learn to make buckskin clothing as fancy as a hickory wiping stick, or the finest beadwork of the Crows. That is, if her husband didn't come back. But he would never come back. By this time his agonies were ended and his bones stripped.

So ran his thoughts as for three days, from daybreak till dark, he toiled in the woods and on the hill, building a log shack for a woman who in these seventy-two hours never, so far as he knew, took a drink of water or a morsel of food, though he kept both at her side. Never once had she risen from where she sat, the right hand on her sons, the left hand on her daughter. He had not known that grief could so paralyze the human mind and will. After felling the trees and cutting them in lengths he dragged them to the site with his powerful stallion, one end of a leather rope tied round a log, the other round the tree of his saddle. The logs were about eight inches thick at their larger end. He laid them ten logs high, with a door in the west side, facing the river. The door was an ungainly heavy thing of warped and cracked wagon boards, held together with three slats nailed across them. To the door and to two logs he spiked the soles of a pair of boy's shoes, to serve as hinges. It was, he told himself, the darnedest door ever attached to a house in Indian land; but if you were careful with it you could bring it shut. On the side opposite to the hinges he nailed a strap of leather, to be pulled inside the cabin and looped over a spike, to make the door secure. Through an unchinked crack on the right of the door she could peer out, if anyone were to knock, or shove the barrel of her rifle through and shoot the red bastard, if he was an enemy. Winds and rain and snow would drive in through this and other cracks, in spite of his chinking; but he hoped that she would calk them with rags after he was gone. He had no trowel, nothing with which to plaster with river mud. It was an ugly shack, all right, and it would be a cold one, even with a fire in its center; but until he could buy materials and come again it would have to do. The roof was poles laid side by side across the roof beams, with a pitch of about thirty degrees on either side. Onto the poles he shoveled earth to a depth of six inches. In the exact center of the roof he left an opening fourteen inches across, framed with pieces of wagon board, for the smoke to escape through. It was no mansion but not five mountain men in the whole country had a better house. He had a winter shack a thousand miles south of this spot, on the Little Snake, and it was no better and its door was no better. But his Flathead bride would probably think it a wonderful thing. In warm weather no mountain man worth his buckskin ever crawled under a roof, except the spreading branches of a fir, or a juniper arbor, or a buffalo robe draped across a couple of poles. If you loved the world the Creator had made for you, you did not shut out the blue heaven and its lights, or lie in foul air in a stuffy room, when in a bed outside you could smell the morning and watch its mother-of-pearl light softly touch the hills.

Hoping to shake the woman out of her grief, when close to her during his labor he sang Robert Burns songs, whistled bird and opera arias, and in his deep baritone exploded Bach and Beethoven phrases, all the while watching her to see if he was breaking through; or he talked to her about this and that, saying in one moment, "If you play any small instrument I'll send for it and when I come along here we can sit and play duets"; saying in the next, "When I get my woman over in the Bitterroots we'll come by here and mebbe you'll like to go hunting with us." But she never gave a sign that she heard.

When the shack was finished he carried up the hill all her possessions, except the wagon. Without its box it was a lopsided thing on its sun-baked and wind-dried wheels, the spokes loose in their sockets and the tires half off the fellies.

Thinking that she might like to have it by her house, he looped a rope over the end of the tongue and with his stud dragged the squealing and howling thing up the hill. Lifting first one end of it and then the other, he flung it this way and that until he had it snugly against the north wall, with the tongue ended up and back across the bolster. Her largest vessel, a tin pail, he filled with water and set inside the hut by the door. All her things were in there now, including the axe and rifle. From his own supplies he gave her flour, salt, sugar, coffee; two tanned elkskins as soft as velvet; powder and ball; a couple of large needles and a roll of buckskin thread; a skin pouch half filled with dried wild berries and plums; a couple of fishhooks and a line; and a flat obsidian stone weighing half a pound that she could use as a whet stone. He sharpened her butcher knife. He then went into the hills and returned with two fat deer. Did she know how to jerk meat? Well, he would show her how. He laid a fire about fifteen feet in front of her and built a drying rack above it; and during the hours it took him to jerk most of the flesh he would have sworn that she never once looked at him or the fire. He would have thought she was dead, sitting up, but for the movement of her breathing. Thinking that possibly she heard and understood, even though she refused to see, he told her how to set up the rack, to cut the flesh in thin ribbons, to turn the meat, to care for it and store it. He told her he would leave all this with her, as well as some boiled or roasted hind and front quarters. If she would nod her head just once he would stir up a batch of biscuits. She could believe it or not but he was about the best biscuit maker in the West, except Hank Cady—but Hank, if still alive, was to hell and gone beyond the Yellowstone.

Now and then when toiling and talking to her Sam would straighten and his keen eyes would search the hills around him. He had no doubt that Blackfeet, and possibly Crow, scouts had been spying on him and wondering what he was doing. What brave men they were! Ten, fifty, or a hundred of them could have come here to take him, for he had no friend, no help, within two or three hundred miles; and they would have come to take him, not one of them, or two or six, but ten possibly, or twenty or forty, but for the fact that they wouldn't pay the price. Mountain men had taught them that at least two of them would die, perhaps three, in the assault, and it took a lot of rum, the smell of a lot of loot, including good rifles and plenty of ammunition, to lure them to the risk.

Having scanned the horizon, he told the woman about Hank's breakfasts, for thought of them had made his mouth water. If Hank was expecting an overnight guest he was sure to have on hand a pint or so of the wonderful wild-bee honey, a quart of rendered hump fat, or, better, marrow fat, to use as butter; a dozen wild geese or duck or sage hen eggs, if these were in season; and the finest elk in a thousand miles. His breakfasts of elk steaks dripping in their sizzling hot juices, a gallon pot of coffee, browned biscuits sopping wet with marrow fat, golden honey, huckleberry jam, or an electuary of mixed wild fruits, no mountain man ever forgot. Someday maybe she would go with him and they would have breakfast with Hank. Hank wouldn't run off at the mouth, as Windy Bill did, or Powder River Charley; if he said ten words in twenty-four hours he felt exhausted.

Suddenly Sam turned from a beast he was skinning, and standing straight and tall, looked at the woman, his face a wonder to behold. It was as if there had suddenly entered his mind the words of various wise men, for whom there had been in the human female a natural superiority—her greater compassion, for one thing, that strove to succor the helpless and defenseless; her greater devotion, for another, that could oblige her mother-heart to sit for days and nights by the graves of her children, without food or drink, and probably (Sam would have said) without sleep. The wonder in his face was this larger view of women, to which this woman had brought him. Did she intend to sit here all fall, winter, and spring? he asked her. Would she go with him to find a boat or a wagon train? Did she not think that the Almighty up there, looking at her, would want her to shake out of this, and eat and sleep and go on living? "I'll tell you," he said. "I'll boil a pot of this fat buck and have a cup of broth with you."

In a few minutes he had ten pounds of venison steaming over one fire and a whole loin slowly roasting in the embers of another. When the boiled meat was tender he took to her a tin cupful of broth and a slice of hot loin on a tin plate; and these, kneeling, he offered to her, saying. "You have to eat. These hot deer drippins will warm your innards and make the world look better." He drank broth and ate raw liver and about three pounds of loin. He then filled his pipe and scanned the earth around him. It was foolish to think that this woman could long endure here, if the redmen resolved to take her scalp and weapons; it would be best to spread the word to all the free trappers that she was here, who would then spread it among all the Indian tribes, with the warning that if a redman took her scalp the vengeance of the mountain men would demand ten scalps for every hair of her head. The skulls out there on the stakes were the only language the redmen could read.

While Sam puffed his pipe and looked over the scene his contempt for the red people and some of their ways fanned his emotions until he was in a red heat of anger. The contempt, on both sides, had its beginning in the earliest association of redmen and white, and became a law of their lives as fixed as the redman's death chant or the whiteman's fatalism. The redmen could not understand why the whitemen gave priceless treasure for the pelts of beaver and otter, which for them had little value in a land where beaver were as thick as trees. The whitemen could not understand why the redmen were eager to trade a pile of pelts for a piddling trifle—a handful of blue beads, a piece of glittering metal. "He's like the coon," Windy Bill said. "If it shines he's gotta git his paw on it." Each thought the other fantastically stupid, and his low opinion of the other's mind and values gave zest to slaughter and scalping. If redmen had set four white skulls on stakes mountain men would have laughed loud in the heavens. If Wind River Bill had been here to view Sam's handiwork he would have said, "I reckon that-air will send them heller-skelter torst their tipees." To the pine and juniper hills and the wind rising in the north Sam said he guessed it would, and was satisfied with his labor.

It was time to be off but he was reluctant to go. In a moment of mad male gallantry he had considered digging a well by the shack, but knew that he would have to dig to river level, a depth of a hundred feet. Should he ask her to go on a journey with him, not to be his night woman (he was not a lustful man, nor one to take advantage of the female's helplessness) but to get her mind off her grief. But so far as he could tell, she had not accepted him as a friend. He was not sure that she was conscious of him, or of the wolves howling in the night, or of the flowing-through-mountains sound of the river's waters. He was put out with himself because he lingered: it was the Almighty's problem, not his. The evening of his eighth day here he forced himself to face her; and after looking down at her bowed head for several minutes he knelt and kissed her dusty brown hair, and said, close to her ear, "There's a lot of meat for you in the house. I'm off to get a wife now, but I'll be back soon."

He mounted his stallion and headed south up the river, but four times he stopped and looked back. In this situation a man simply didn't know what to do. If she was determined to sit by the graves and die he guessed she had the right to die alone. No beast, no man, would molest her. His journey lay not over to the Bighorns, the Powder, Tongue, and Wind rivers, but to the Gallatin Gateway, the Beaverhead, and Chief Tall Mountain, whose oldest daughter, blooming into womanhood, was as lovely as the spring song of the bluebird or the alpine lily at the edge of a melting snowbank. A wife, he knew, was a huge armful of responsibility, and responsibility was the disease in man. But he was lonely, and twice as lonely after leaving the woman by the graves.

The fourth time he looked back he saw her come through the doorway and stand by the cabin. She seemed to be looking round her. If the lark at heaven's gate had sung for him alone he could have been no more gladdened. She would be all right! She had only been waiting for him to go away! Dear God, be kind to her! He saw her go over and sink to the earth between the graves. Dear God, be kind to her! Feeling that all was well, he waved to her, knowing that she could not see him, and then rode till midnight, and was thirty miles from her and her gruesome sentinels when he found a thicket in which to hide and sleep. Dear God, he thought, kissing his hand and pretending that it was this mother's cheek, dear God, be kind to her.

4

HE WAS TEN miles beyond the woman's sight when she heard her name called. "Kitty!" the voice said. It was her husband's voice and that was her husband's name for her. Getting to her feet, she looked round her with wild staring eyes and then began to run toward the massacre site. "John!" she called as she ran. After two hundred yards she stopped and looked in all directions, and listened; and called again: "John!" She felt that he was present and not far away. She was staring at the tree where she had seen him bloody and bent when she thought of her children. Turning, she ran back up the hill, expecting to find them sitting by the graves; and when she saw only the two mounds she looked at them, listening, her heart in her throat. "John?" she said. She went to the shack and looked inside. She looked toward the river, and remembering that their camp was down there, she ran toward it, in the ungainly wavering way of one who had had no food and water and almost no sleep for many days and nights. She looked back under the lean-to that her husband and sons had built but nothing was there. She looked round her and softly called: "John?" She listened, but there was only the river's waters. Like a woman waiting for the man who would surely come, she stood by the lean-to for an hour, looking and listening.

She had no weapon with her, not even a knife. It was as if in that hour of utter loneliness and loss she gave up to heaven all weapons and all sense of weapons; for she would now go defenseless to the river for water, to the bottomlands to look for food, to the hilltops to look for her husband. Standing by the lean-to and trembling with hope, her eyes wide open and staring, her ears open to all things between earth and heaven, she went back up the hill and stood by the graves. She had seen but had not recognized the four skulls; and an hour later, when she walked north and east over the hills, looking for her husband, she passed close to one of the Indian heads but seemed not to see it. Her sense of what had happened since that morning was only a faint pallor; it had all been dimmed by sorrow and fatigue and soul sickness. She went almost a mile into the hills, pausing now and then to call softly, to look round her and listen; and then returned to the graves. She would go again, and again—to the lean-to, to the massacre tree; for he would call to her again and again, in the weeks to come. In the dead of night his voice would arouse her from shallow sleep and she would sit up, saying, "John?" He would call to her as August passed and September came in, and the aspens and cottonwoods turned golden.

Now and then she saw him in the distance and ran toward him. She knew that someday she would find him. A rational mind would have seen here a world unlike the one Kate saw.

Standing by the graves, he would have looked north or south and seen the long irregular line of trees that hid the river. In the west, beyond the line, he would have seen hills that looked empty and dead, but for their thin dress of stunted cedar. Looking the other way, to the east, he would have seen the same kind of hills, and sky pallor and thin gray loneliness; and in all directions he would have sensed an expanse of silence and emptiness. Kate saw none of all that, or saw it so indistinctly that it was only the haze upon the clear world in which she lived.

The world in which she was to live her senses did not build at once; it was evoked by prayer and longing and hope, by dreams and visions, and it came into being slowly, out of heaven. For God was kind to her. There had to be this evocation, or there had to be madness that would have thrust her down to the level of beasts. Without her vision she would have wandered away and been killed, by wolf or Indian; or she would have starved or died of cold when winter came. Within a few months the roaming free trappers, having learned her name, would be talking by campfires of that crazy Bowden woman. She would never go home, she would live and die there by the graves. It was enough to make a man feel cut loose from himself and pulled down in deep water like a gone beaver. It was enough to make a man crawl into a deep thicket and cry like a child.

Legend was to say that John Bowden was there. His wife knew he was there; she saw him now and then, always at a distance, always smiling at her, his smile and his eyes saying that he was all right, all of them were all right, and someday they would be together again, with God. The time was to come when she would no longer call to him or run toward him. With a smile she would answer his smile, her eyes saying yes, it was so, they would be together again, they were together now.

Her most remarkable transformation of loss and loneliness enveloped her children. About three weeks after Sam rode away she looked at the graves and thought they needed a loveliness. Up and down the river she searched for wild flowers and found a few, but the plant that caught her eye was a species of sage, with a soft greenish-gray beauty all its own. With the shovel she took up a few of these plants without disturbing the earth that hugged the roots, and set them in holes at the south end of her tiny cemetery. She carried water from the river to give them drink. They flourished, and the time came when she had a garden, there on the barren hillside. The time came when she no longer knew exactly where the graves were. The time was to come when there would pass from her soul all memory of them and all need of them; for her children would no longer be in the earth but above it, smiling at her as their father smiled.

The first vision was in a cold moonlit night, before the fading memory of the graves had completely left her. She had come from the shack and walked over to the graves, to kneel there and pray, when suddenly she was transfixed by the dim heavenly figure kneeling behind a clump of sage, or within it, or of it—she would never be able to tell where it was. This vision was of her daughter. It was not her daughter as she had actually been in life: this girl in the sage, or behind it, was so ethereal, so like a filmy moonglow, so dreamlike, so like a pale and delicate part of heaven, that Kate, looking at her, held her breath and thought how sweet it was to die. After long moments she moved toward it, only to see it fade and pass away, not quickly, but as a moving cloud dissolves and fades. Horrified, she retreated, and as slowly as it had vanished the vision returned, coming out of nothing into an exquisite apparition that was looking at her and smiling, and gently inclining its head, as though moved by a breeze. Kate had eyes only for her until, looking at other plants, she saw her sons; and they were exactly of the same heavenly moonglow radiance, behind a sage, or in it or of it. Like the daughter, they were looking at her and smiling, and gently moving their heads a little up and down.

All night until the moon was gone Kate filled her soul with the three faces. She would have been worse than mad to doubt that her children were there. If she shut her eyes she did not see them. If she advanced too far toward them they simply dissolved into the night and there were before her only the sage plants. But every time without fail they returned when she withdrew and they smiled at her in the same angelic way. They looked to her like exquisitely scented and clothed beings just down from heaven. The eyes of all three smiled steadily into her eyes, not to probe her soul but only to reassure her. "My darlings!" she would whisper to them, smiling, and like them moving her head up and down.

They did not come in the daytime or when there was no moon; and if the moon was only a slice or a quarter, or was wan, they did not come. Her husband came at any time of day or night in any season. She might see him riding a horse and leading a packhorse, going up or down the river; and he always waved to her and she waved to him. She knew that he had a man's work to do. Or he might come at night when she was asleep; in the morning she would find by her door, or just inside it, a leather sack filled with things for her, and in another skin, jerked elk or buffalo. She would find powder and ball, needles, thread, flower seeds, sugar, salt, coffee, flour; and once there was a shining new knife, and time and again there were tanned skins, medicines, such as camphor, aloes, salves, demulcents, baking soda, and a dress or a pair of shoes.

She never fired her gun to frighten away the killers. She came to think of her world as a world without hunters and hunted, though the wolves now and then forced her to take another view of it. It was in early November of her first autumn here that she was awakened one night by piteous crying. Her first thought was for her children; seizing the axe, which she kept by her bed, she rushed outside. There was no moon but it was not a dark night. She listened. The cry came again; it was continuous now, a bleating begging cry of pain and torment, and it was not toward the river but somewhere back of her house. Running toward it, she stopped when she saw the three large tawny forms. On the long journey with her husband and children she had seen the big gray wolf; during the past weeks she had seen these beasts, insolent, fearless, tongues lolling, sharp eyes looking for something to kill.

Convinced that they were killing out there in the night, she did not hesitate but ran against them as she had run against the Blackfeet warriors; and she was so strong and agile, and so borne up by rage, that she was on the wolves and had half severed a head before they knew she was there. The other two then leapt away, incredibly swift, and with a cry wilder than their own Kate chased them into the night. Returning, she saw that the victim was a buffalo calf: the wolves had been eating from the top of the flanks, where they had made a gaping hole to get at the liver, loin, and kidneys. The poor thing was not dead and it was still crying for its mother.

Kate did not know—and God would spare her the knowledge—that the wild-dog family ate its victims alive, if the victims had the stoutness and pluck to keep breathing until the enemy's hunger was appeased. Many a buffalo still walked the prairies that had had a wolf's meal taken out of it. Depending on the strength of his hunger, or his mood, the wolf would rip and tear with its long sharp teeth, usually into the side or back to get at the liver; and often it devoured all the tender flesh along the lower spine before its victim died. Or it might open a hole in the belly. If it had a taste for hams it might eat most of the flesh off a hindquarter. Many a buffalo or elk calf or yearling survived the rending of its flesh and the drinking of its blood, and lived as a cripple, hideously scarred. Kate would never know that this deadly killer which, in a pack, could put the monstrous male grizzly to flight, often teased and tortured, or killed, for the wanton sport of it. Three or four of them would isolate a buffalo yearling from the herd and chase the terrified and bawling creature back and forth in the tall prairie grass, nipping at it, tearing gaping wounds in it, spending perhaps an hour or more in frolic and sport, before the beast's agony was ended.

The calf at which Kate looked was not dead but she knew it must die. Pulling the dead wolf away and kicking savagely at it, she examined the calf's wounds. When she saw that a flank had been torn open and a part of the guts pulled out she smote the forehead a hard blow and put a compassionate hand on the shuddering flesh as it died.

Kate's new world was indeed a world of the hunters and the hunted. She saw hawks strike and kill ducks in mid-air. In the river bottom when looking for roots and berries she saw the nestlings of thrush and wren, bluebird, mourning dove, and lark impaled on thorns in a shrike's old butcher shop. She came to imagine things which she never actually saw or heard, and after a while it became a habit with her to seize the axe and rush into the night, and tremble with outrage while listening and looking. She would hear, as time passed, other animal children crying under the rending teeth, and none more frequently than the rabbit. Her life would be haunted by the scream of the cottontail, seized by a falcon, or of the big hare, overtaken by a wolf.

She would never fully understand that she lived in a world of wild things, many of which were killers—the weasel, mink, hawk, eagle, wolf, wolverine, cougar, grizzly, bobcat—these were ferocious and deadly; but the rabbit, deer, elk, buffalo, antelope, and many of the birds killed nothing, but themselves were slain and eaten by the thousands. In her life in a small

Pennsylvania town Kate had barely known that there was this kind of world. She had known that there were creatures that killed other creatures, men who killed men, for either God or passion; but the world here was one in which to kill or to escape from the killer was the first law of life.

Her female feelings about these things would have astonished most of the mountain men. Windy Bill might have said, "Well, cuss my coup! Does she think Chimbly Rock is a church steeple?" Bill Williams, looking sly and secretive in all the seams and hollows of his long lean face, might have tongued his quid a time or two, before saying, "Pore ole soul. I reckon that woman ain't never figgered out the kind of world the Almighty made." Three Finger McNees would have been laconic: "Why don't she go home?"

The mountain men rumbled with astonishment on learning that Kate sat in moonlight reading aloud from the Bible to her children. It was a very old Bible that had belonged to her mother's mother; and because many verses had been emphasized in the margin with blue ink she had only to turn the pages and look for the signals. When she came to one that had been marked she would read it, her lips moving but making no sound; and if she thought it was something her smiling and nodding darlings would like she would read it to them: " 'I the Lord have called thee in righteousness, and will hold thine hand, and will keep thee, and give thee for a covenant of the people; to open the blind eyes, to bring out the prisoners from the prison, and them that sit in darkness out of the prison house.' "

After reading such verses she would look at her children and smile and nod; and like long-stemmed flowers they would nod and smile. She did not have a cultivated voice but it was clear and strong; ever since they were old enough to understand she had read to her children from the holy book. Sometimes she closed the book and let it open where it would. It might be on a psalm: " 'O my God, I trust in thee, let not mine enemies triumph over me.' " Smiling at them, she would say, "Your father left us some things last night. He is very busy these days; he wants us to wait here, for he will come to us sometime."

In the dark of her senses she knew her husband was not dead, for if he were, he would be an angel here, with his children. She wondered why he rode up and down the river. She would have said he was not trapping, for he had never trapped; he had been a farmer for a while, then a small merchant. Why he never hitched his team to a wagon she did not know; he was doing his work in ways he thought best, and when all things were fulfilled he would come to them.

She knew that, being angels, her children could give no answers, except the heavenly smiles and the gentle assents. In time of full moon, when she could see them most clearly, Kate did not go to bed until the moon was down. For how could she have left them there, kneeling in the sage and smiling at her? Sometimes the moon did not go down till morning, or did not go down at all but just faded away into the day sky; only after her children had slipped back to their blue home did she rise from the buffalo robe that had been left by her husband. If after her children had left her her loneliness was too bitter to bear she would not enter the shack but would stand by it. In such moments she came closest to a realization of where she was—no, not of where she was, for since leaving the Big Blue she had never known where she was; but of her aloneness and helplessness and enemies. She might then step over to look almost curiously at the spots where her children had knelt; it was then that she came closest to an impulse to search the earth for footprints.

But in a few moments it all passed. She would then become conscious of the book in her hands, and there would come to her, infinitely sweet and tender, memory of her three angels, who would be there again after the moon had risen. During the long empty days she had this to look forward to and it sustained her. Her deeper emotions, of which she had no awareness, and which seldom looked out of her features, she revealed in curious ways. Instead of making her bed back in the cabin, away from the door, she made it right by the door, so that she had to step over it; so that, lying in it, she could put a hand out of the ugly little prison and touch the big world. Against a wall at either end of the bed were piled her food and utensils; and there her rifle stood. When she was not carrying water to her plants she might sit on the bed, with needle and skins, and sew on leather jackets or skirts or moccasins. She would look over innumerable times to see if her children had come, or up at the sky to see if the moon was there. Sometimes when coming from the river she would think she heard a son calling, and she would run like a wild woman, trembling in every nerve. Coming to the yard and finding that her children were not there, she would be a tragic picture of loss and hopelessness, too stricken to look or listen.

Or if when reading to her darlings and answering their smiling angel-faces she heard the sound of an enemy—the snarling challenge of a wolf almost at her door or the shriek of a descending hawk—she was instantly transformed into a tigress; and seizing the axe, she would rush blind and screaming against the challenge. No beast was ever to withstand her charge.

It was this sort of thing that spread in legends. In a moonlit night, a year or two after the massacre, Windy Bill was passing by when he heard wild screams and on a hill against the sky saw a woman rushing round and round, the blade of her axe flashing. "I took plum off fer the tall timber," he said. "My hair it stood up like buffler grass and my blood was like the Yallerstun bilins John Colter saw." He improved, or in any case embellished, his tale with each retelling, until what he saw was a witch riding a broom in the sky and shrieking into the winds.

Other men were to see Kate, when passing her way, and to tell tales about her, and the legend of her would grow in an area of more than a million square miles; but while it was still in its innocent beginnings, other legends, to be still more awesome and incredible, were being born, and one of them would enfold the huge figure of Samson John Minard.

It had its origin in his decision to take a wife.

5

THE FREE TRAPPERS were the most rugged and uncompromising individualists on earth. Only now and then did one think of an Indian mate as a wife, even after accepting her in the marriage ceremony of the red people; but Sam Minard had a sentimental attachment to his mother and to an older sister, and under his bluff and reticent surface were emotional channels in which feeling ran heavy and warm. His closest friends were never to know it. Hank Cady, Windy Bill, Jim Bridger, George Meek, Mick Boone, and others who knew him and were to know him best thought that a red woman was for Sam what she was for them, a member of a subhuman species that a man might wish one day to take to bed and the next day to tomahawk. Dadburn his possibles, one of them said; there warn't no human critters except the white. The red ones and the black ones were what the Almighty had in leftovers after making the twelve tribes. Most of the white trappers thought nothing at all of the redman's habit of kicking his old wife-squaws into the hills, to die of disease, starvation, old age, or to fall prey to the wolves.

Sam had a different view of it but he kept it to himself.

Last spring he had seen an Indian lass who took his fancy. Since then he had dreamed about her, and using some thrush and meadow-lark phrases, had tried to compose lyrics to her. The logical part of his mind saw objections to taking a wife. He wondered, for instance, if the physical mating of a girl weighing a hundred and fifteen pounds with a man of his size was the kind an all-wise Father would smile on. Sam was sensitive about his size. His mother had told him that at birth he was so huge that his father, after one appalled look, had said he guessed they'd have to name him Samson. It was no fun being so big and it was a lot of bother. A second objection was her age; she was only about fourteen or fifteen (he thought), and though he was only twenty-seven he seemed to himself middle-aged compared to her. A third objection, he had decided after much thought, was really no objection at all: he suspected that she was not all Indian; the Lewis and Clark men had left white blood running in Indian nations all the way from St. Louis to the ocean.

Sam had been surprised to learn the origin of the Flathead name. Formerly (they had now abandoned the custom) they had hollowed out a chunk of cedar or cottonwood and spent hours dressing it, carving it, and making it buckskin fancy. This cradle or pig's trough or canoe or canim they then lined with cattail down, the fluffy inner bark of old cedar trees, the wool of bighorn sheep; and when it was nicely lined and looked cozy they slapped it on the poor baby's skull almost the instant it was born, and swaddled its head over with tanned deerskins as soft as the underflank of a baby antelope. Laid out on its back, its black eyes staring at the red wise men, the babe then had a feather or wool shawl drawn across its forehead and around. Finally a long flat board, attached at one end to the canim, was forced down on the shawl and the forehead and bound with leather strings, thus putting considerable pressure on the soft bone of the foreskull. The luckless babe was then so securely wrapped and bound that it was unable to move a hand or foot, and did well to wiggle a finger and blink its eyes. In such horrible confinement it remained a year or more, except in those moments when it was unbound and washed clean of its filth and bounced up and down for exercise. The steady pressure on the skull caused the head to expand and flatten, like a big toad stepped on by a grizzly paw, so that the aspect of the upper face became abnormally broad and the skull flat.

The girl of whom Sam was enamored had not had her skull flattened; she was, he thought, the loveliest human female he had ever seen; she was lovelier, even, than the gorgeous alpine lilies, or the columbine with its five white petals in a cup framed by five deep-blue sepals. She was a golden brown all over, but for her hair, eyes, and lips. Her hair and eyes were raven-black, and her inner lips were of a luscious dark pink that he wanted to bite. Whether she was full-grown he had not been able to tell, but she had already had, at her early age, the womanly form, with the kind of full breasts, firm and sitting high, that a man saw on Indian girls only now and then. The quality of her that had most entranced him was what he might have called, had he found words for it, a vivacious surfacing of her emotions, like tossing water spindrift flashing with the jewels of sunlight; and she had a way of looking at a man as though she wished to tease and excite and bewitch him. It had been mighty good to look at and he was now on his way over to buy it.

That would be the most unpleasant part. An Indian chief, whether Flathead, Crow or Sioux, or even the lowly Digger, began to itch all over with avarice the moment he sensed that a paleface coveted one of his females. If it were not for the redman's fantastic love of trinkets and trifles which the whiteman could buy for a song, the cost of a red wife would have been too much for the trapper's purse. Sam had learned that those who said the redman was not a canny bargainer simply did not know him. This girl's father, Chief Tall Mountain, had put her up for sale outside her tribe; this proclaimed to every person who knew Indian ways that the greedy rascal thought she was worth a hundred times an ordinary red filly. The chief would expect handsome gifts for himself. Then there would be her mother, stepmothers, aunts and uncles and brothers and sisters, step-aunts and step-uncles, step-brothers and step-sisters, and so many cousins that she would appear to be related to every person in the tribe, all hoping for nothing less than a fast horse, a Hawken rifle with a hundred rounds, a brace of Colts, a Bowie, a barrel of rum, a keg of sugar and another of flour, a bushel of beads, and a small mountain of tobacco. The dickering would take weeks if you could put up with it. You'd have to let it drag out for several days, for the reason that a part of the redman's joy in life came from prolonging anticipation of what he knew he could never get.

It would be fine if a man could read the price tag and pay it, and swoop his golden-brown doll to his chest and ride away. But the redman, whose life was dull but for warpath and occasional feast, squeezed the last emotion out of everything that came his way. Sam well knew that after he had given presents and renewed the pledge of brotherhood he might have to indulge the old fraud in hours of mysterious silence, while the chief conferred with the more rapacious souls among his ancestors; or Sam might have to sit for so many hours smoking the spittle-saturated pipe of friendship that his stomach would turn, or for days he might have to wait, while the solemn-faced humbug pretended that a few thousand aunts and cousins were coming in from the distant hills.

It would be the same ordeal, no matter what tribe he went to. Around the campfires with other trappers Sam had paid close attention to their talk about Indian women. Some of the stories he found incredible, such as that of Baptiste Brown, a Canadian, who gave almost two quarts of his blood as a part of the bride price; or of Moose Creek Harry, who was tomahawked by his bride on his wedding night. The misogynists among the trappers, such as Lost-Skelp Dan, thought all women the curse of the earth and would not listen to talk about them; but the gallants astonished Sam by the vehemence, sometimes the threats and violence, with which they defended their taste in red women. Solomon Silver swore by the Osages, Bill Williams by the Eutaws, Rose and Beckwourth by the Crows, Jim Bridger by the Snakes, William Bent by the Cheyennes, and Loretto by the Blackfeet. Sam had found different virtues to admire in different tribes. The Eutaws made the finest deerskin leather, and unlike the Crows, Arapahoes, and Blackfeet, they did not steal. On the other hand, they would beg until a man loathed the sight of them. A chief would bring forth all the children in the tribe and they would be crying their heads off and staggering as if with hunger, though there might be enough food stored to last all winter.

The Arapahoes placed hospitality next to valor. They set before a guest the best they had and protected his life with their own. Among this people a man took as many wives as he could pay for, but Sam had decided that one wife for him would be enough. Having met William Bent at Bent's Fort and heard him speak highly of the Cheyennes, Sam had ridden across Cheyenne country. He had been told that the first lodge he entered would be his home as long as he wished to remain, and that lodge had happened to belong to Vipponah, or Lean Chief, who had gravely shaken Sam's big right hand and cried, *"Hook-ah-hay! Num-whit?"* (Welcome! How do you do?) Food and drink had been set before Sam, and after a night in this lodge he had been favorably impressed by the manners of these people. The lodge, in the form of a cone of poles eighteen feet long, set on end with their tops loosely bound so the smoke could pass through, and covered over with skins and buffalo robes, had the fire in its center. No Indian ever passed between the fire and the persons sitting around it. Sam thought it strange that so many of the children had streaks of gray in their black hair, and that the boys to the age of six or seven went completely naked, whereas the girls were clothed from infancy. Lean Chief, observing Sam's appraisal of the marriageable girls around him, explained how it would be if Sam were to bid for one. He would tie his favorite pony to the lodge of the girl's father. If he was acceptable to the father and the girl, the next morning he would find his horse with his father-in-law's horses. If not acceptable, he would find his horse where he had left it, with all the boys of the village around it, hooting and jeering.

Sam had thought of taking a wife from the Crows, before learning that they were the world's biggest liars and most industrious horse thieves. Just the same, they were such a handsome high-spirited people that he had twice returned to look at the girls. He had become amused at the way he was looking at the women in different tribes, and wondered if any whiteman seeking a wife had gone forth to look at French, German, English, Jewish, and other women.

All in all he had found the Indian people to be of middle

stature, with lean straight bodies and fine limbs, their black hair usually flowing loosely over their shoulders, their keen black eyes aglow with the joy of living. Some of them had hair so long that it reached the ground at their feet. Except for those who lived chiefly on fish, they had beautiful white teeth. Practically all the tribes ornamented their garments with porcupine quills, beads, colored stones, feathers, leather fringes, and human hair from the heads of their enemies, dyed various colors. They painted their faces with vermilion, ochre, coal dust, ashes, hump fat, and colorful fruit juices. They wore in their black hair beads, buttons, feathers, shells, stones, and just about anything that gleamed or glittered. It was not unusual to see a squaw with eight or ten pounds of glass beads attached to her skirt, leggins, and moccasins. All Indians liked to sing, but for whitemen the sounds they made were not melodic: their war song would begin on the highest note they could reach and fall note by note to a guttural grunt; but abruptly it was high and shrill again, and again falling, to rise and fall, until white people who listened felt numbed in their senses and chilled in their marrow.

In Sam's opinion there were no handsomer Indians than the Crows. They were a dashing colorful people with above-average intelligence; a few whitemen, like Rose and Beck-wourth, had become chiefs in the Crow nation and had lived with this people a long time. Though the braves had sad-dles they always rode without saddles when hunting wild game, and no other men in the world could match them on a horse. As Windy Bill said, it made a man plain oneasy to see with what fantastic skill they could ride on a dead run, the left heel on top of a ham, the left wrist through a loop of mane, and shoot arrows or guns under the horse's neck; or on a dead run pick up the fallen arrows. But they were a notoriously adulterous people. Bill, who had lived among them, said the men never seemed to be jealous; if they found a wife with a lover they gave her to a brute who was likely to beat the hell out of her. A Crow warrior's highest ambition in life was to lift twenty scalps and to show such skill and valor that he would be allowed to wear in his hair the feathers of the golden eagle, as a badge of courage and rank. One who wore even a single quill was entitled to and received profound deference; one with a half dozen quills was regarded with awe.

On Sam's first visit to the Crows he was smoking a pipe and

for some reason laid his Bowie at his side. He became aware of a Crow standing by him and of what the brave was doing. The sly thief was standing over the knife and had got it between two of his toes, with the robe from his shoulders almost concealing it. He stood immobile perhaps a minute; then, the foot clutching the knife, moved slowly upward into the folds of the robe and a noiseless hand reached down. At this moment Sam rose swiftly to his feet, and seizing the Indian by his throat and bottom, literally pitched him end over end, with the knife spilling from the robe as he sailed through the air. Three years later, when the Crows would change the course of his life, Sam was to wonder if it had all begun in that moment.

After leaving Kate he rode up the Musselshell to the big bend, and then westward nearly a hundred miles before turning south to the Yellowstone. He rode up the Yellowstone until in hazy distance he could see the mark of its deep gorges, and left it to follow a tributary, for Windy Bill had said he would spend the summer here, hidden from his enemies. Sam was still five miles from Bill's camp when he sensed that a horseman was aproaching. Sam halted, his rifle across his left arm, and waited. He was not at all surprised when he heard a bullet whistle past his ear. It was a way mountain men had with one another.

In a few moments Bill came in sight, and he was loud with mock apologies and welcome.

"Wall, wall now, ole-timer!" he said. "I heerd ye wuz under, I shorley did. I heerd a Blackfoot varmint cut ye loose from yore possibles and ye wuz plum gone beaver." This was merely the kind of banter that most of the free trappers flung at one another. They all expected to die violent deaths, and so pretended to be amazed on finding a friend still alive. Sam was grinning in his golden beard.

But Bill did not grin when by the supper fire he heard Sam's tale of the woman up the river. She was gone beaver, he said; god-in-whirlwinds, the wolves would drag the skulls away and the first Blackfoot to come along would lift her topknot. "I feel awful oneasy about thet woman. Why didn't ya bring her along?"

Sam said she wouldn't come; it would break her heart to take her away from the graves. Besides, he had thought he would do a little chirking up and get a papoose for his medicine bag.

With mock gravity Bill looked all around him, as though to see this Indian tribe and that one, and decide toward which

Sam was taking his romantic interest. "I don't see no Burnt-
Thighs," he said, "ner any Broken-Arrers, no Yankataus, no
Pian-Kashas, no Cut-Throats." These were all names for
members of the Sioux nation. "It wooden be a Digger, I doan
expect. Ner a Snake. Jist which one air ye headin torst nohow?"

"The Flatheads," Sam said, refilling his tin plate with boiled
elk.

"Wall now," said Bill, "I think ye be actin real plum smart, I
shorely do. The Flatheads, they ain't no better varmints. They's
the only red people ain't killed a whiteman yit. But one thing,
Sam, I allus figgered, the furder a man is from his in-laws the
longer his marriage will last. The hull doggone tribe will expect
ya to feed them if ye live within five hundred miles."

"I had thought of that," Sam said.

The Flatheads were good honey, said Bill, filling his pipe.
They were scairt to death of the Blackfeet, so would never
come to visit him because they would never dare leave home.
Did he have his sugar plum picked out?

"I saw her last spring."

"She might be some other man's filly now."

"Might be," Sam said.

"Chief's gal?"

"Tall Mountain."

"Waugh! A princess!" said Bill. He fixed his large, rather
bulging pale-blue eyes on Sam's face. He reckoned he had seen
the critter a year or two ago when he was pulling leather for
Pare's Hole. He knocked his pipe out, filled it, listened to the
night sounds, sniffed the breeze coming up the creek, put the
glowing end of an ember to his pipe bowl, puffed a few times,
his bearded cheeks caving in with each puff, and said, "Wall
now, I wish ye luck, I shorely do. As fer me, twenty-six winters
has snowed on me in these here mountains and even a nigger or
a greaser would larn a few things in all that time. I otta could
tell bull from cow. I know deer is deer and grizzly paws ain't a
woman's soft belly and a cactus ain't her lips but I never could
find the tracks in a woman's heart."

He was having trouble with his pipe. He put another ember
to the bowl and puffed hard; and at last he said, "Sam, let me
tell ye. Fer ten year I packed me a squaw, a Cheyenne she war,
and the meanest bitch ever bawled fer beads. I lodgepoled her
on Dead Wolf Crick and traded her fer a Hawken gun. My next
night-love, she war a Crow, and come hell or come high water

thar warn't enough beads and red paint in all of Sublette's packs
ta keep that squaw from cryin. I traded that-air bitch fer a
packhorse. Doan git me wrong, I love the wimmins, but nigh on
three years I put up with that wolverine and she scratched me
till I run blood from a hundred holes. Then I got me a buffler
grass with dew on it—but lemme see—seems like as how the
next was Bird Singin, a Pawnee. And she warn't no better.

"I tell ye, Sam, if she be female, no matter if redskin,
blackskin, or whiteskin, she will torment the life outta ye fer
foofarraw. Day and night she will. I know mountain men as has
tried them all, even the Diggers, even the Snakes, even the
niggers; and I been tole the nigger she is as sweet as Hank
Cady's honey. But I swear by the ole hoss that carried me safe
twenty mile with fifty Blackfeet runnin outta their skins to lift
my hair that wolf is wolf and female is female, and this ole coon
can't stand no more. But a young feller like you, he needs a
dozen or so. A woman's breasts it's the hardest rock the
Almighty made on this ole earth, and I can see no sign on it. I
could track even a piece of thistledown but I never could see no
tracks in a woman's heart. Ye plan to come back this way?"

Sam said he ought to. He wanted to see the woman before
going south to the Uintahs to trap. Bill said he might amble up
the river to see if she was all right: it made him powerful oneasy
to think of a white woman only a wide river from Blackfeet
country and not a friend in three hundred miles. What was her
name?

"Don't know," Sam said. "She wouldn't talk."

"Then she ain't a woman. What should I take her?"

Jerked buffalo or elk; a big warm robe, if he had an extra;
sugar, salt, flour, and wild flower seeds, if he found any ripe
along the way. He would take her a hull pile of stuff, Bill said.

"What's the name yore sugar plum?"

Sam stared at his pipe. He had decided that his woman's
unpronounceable Flathead name would never do but he had
not settled on a new name. Some wild flower, maybe—Lily,
Daisy, Rose—there weren't many flower names given to women.
He might call her Lotus.

Bill did nothing to hide his skepticism. After looking at Sam
a long moment he said, "I didden like the names my squaws so I
give them all the same name. Lucy, it was. There war a gal
named Lucy I liked when I was a kid. Sam and Lotus. Wall
now, ye expect ta have some little Sams and Lotuses?"

"Sure," Sam said with a genial grin. "Two mebbe, one of each."

"Jist right," said Bill. "Wood ticks on my johnny. Ye know, Sam, I must have as many kids as a Mormon bishop. And did ye know them Mormons is all comin out here?"

Sam turned to look at him.

"That's what I heerd, Sam. The hull doggone pligamus shittaree, Brigham Young and all. In a few years we'll be pushed right outta our homes. The Injuns have knowed it all along. Twenty year, thirty, there won't be a buffler left—nothin from hell to breakfast but damn fools plowin ground and plantin cabbages. I ar a trapper an a mountain man but there ain't no future fer my kind. They'll push us inta Canada and then inta the ocean." Bill knocked his pipe out. He looked around him. "Ten thousan, twenty thousan, the hull pligamus mess is headed fer this country and if I wuzzn't a Christian I'd hope they all starve to death. It makes me sick in my boudins jist ta think about it."

"Me too," said Sam, looking round him and wondering where he could sleep. Most of the mountain men whom he knew flung themselves flat on their backs, arms outflung like a babe's, and snored with a violence that put a quiet sleeper out of his mind. Bill began with low rumblings and whistlings and wheezings that climbed steadily to a crescendo of gulping and roaring, and then to a shattering fortissimo. After a few bars that a man could have heard a mile away the wild clamor of frog music in Bill's throat seemed to collapse among his tonsils and adenoids, and he gasped and gurgled and seemed about to die. But like a bullfrog with a bad cold, working out sonata variations on a theme, he would then blow out a few tremendous snorts, strangle until his whole body quivered in the torment, and begin again with the rumblings and whistlings, in another key.

Knowing that he couldn't sleep within fifty yards of Bill, Sam said. "Reckon I'll take a little stroll."

Bill turned on him the knowing grin of a man who had had more than his share of women. "Ye act restless," he said. "Yer lotus gal will take that outta you."

"I reckon," Sam said. With his rifle he moved away into the woods. When Bill was asleep he would slip back for his bedroll and go down the creek a hundred yards. He looked up at the stars. The constellations said the time was about midnight.

6

IT TURNED OUT to be less of an ordeal than Sam had expected. Tall Mountain pretended that fifteen or twenty other trappers would be along any day to make offers for his daughter, each with ten packhorses laden with gifts. Sam smiled at that. The chief feigned astonishment that his brother Sam Minard, Chief Long Talons, had been able to spend so many moons away from this girl, who was lovelier than wild flowers, the sky, the clouds, and trees in their spring dress; for did the bull elk eager to mate with the cow hide in a thicket and sulk in his bull-powers? Sam explained in sign language that he had had to catch a lot of beaver, to trade for a lot of gifts, including the fine copper kettle he had brought for Tall Mountain, bravest and noblest of all warriors, to cook his elk in. Would he have dared to come with empty packhorse to the greatest chief on earth and offer for his most beautiful daughter a handful of cloudberries and a broken knife? The chief conceded the reasonableness of all that, and probed another spot. He said, with words and signs and interpreters, that he had had more trouble than a rabbit in a wolf's den keeping this girl virginal for so long, denying her to other palefaces, who came snorting like studs and with mountains of gifts; turning away immense fortunes that included the fastest horses from the Crow nation, enough rifles to exterminate the Blackfeet, enough kettles to cook all the buffalo on the prairies, all because he so deeply loved his brother Chief Long Talons. His grief had been inconsolable. He had become very ill. For such devotion, patience, forbearance, did he not deserve some special gifts? Brother Long Talons said he surely did, and from his luggage drew forth a two-gallon keg of rum. When Tall Mountain's black eyes saw what it was there came into them the joy seen in the eyes of small children. His bronzed face smiled. He was ready to get drunk.

44

Sam Minard never drank. In such frontier towns as St. Louis and Independence, and at trading posts, he had seen men full of rum and slow on the draw go staggering off—with blood gushing from their wounds. Now, with every amenity and duty fulfilled, he traded ammunition for a tough fleet pony and a buckskin bridle, handed its reins to his black-eyed child-wife, hung a revolver and a knife from her slender waist, and rode off into the south. She had no saddle but she had a robe under her. "Squawhorse," he had said, slapping the beast she sat on. He would teach her English, for he wanted his children to speak English. "Squaw hitch." He touched a packer's knot on the packhorse. "Saddletree—stirrup—horn—latigo." He had decided that blood from a Lewis and Clark man was running in her veins, and he hoped that man was John Colter. While he studied her complexion she had looked at him with sober childlike interest. Like all Indian girls, she heard that the pale men were cruel to their women; perhaps she was wondering how far from her people she would be when he knocked her senseless and tossed her out. But she responded to his words with open lips and a flash of her teeth.

"Lotus," he said, tapping her gently. "Mrs. Lotus Minard."

Her open lips said, "Lo—"

"—tus. Lo-tus. My golden-brown biscuit."

"Bis-kit?"

"Biscuit. My Injun filly. My wife."

Around them had stood hundreds of Indians, their black eyes staring. Cocking her head at her sisters in the manner of a bird, she had said, pointing to Sam, "Lawng Tallongs."

"Chief Long Talons and Princess Samson Minard. It'll be a hell of a day for both of us if you turn out to be Delilah. Delilah Lotus, that's you."

"Sam," she said. She knew his white name. "Tall." Her people on his first visit had asked him what he was; he had held his hand about six feet four inches above the earth and had said. "Tall."

As he rode south from the village, with Lotus trailing him, he was thinking that for a few days they would be safe in Flathead land. These Indians not only had never killed a whiteman, or robbed or deceived one, so far as whitemen knew; they were noted for their courage, prudence, candor, and piety. Their children were taught never to fight, except in self-defense

—or, as the Indians put it, never to go hunting for their own graves. A tenet of their faith forbade them to seek vengeance.

How, Sam wondered, riding along the eastern flanks of the Bitterroots, would Lotus want to train their children? Most Indian fathers were sentimental fellows who doted on their sons, crooning to them and telling them tales of valor; but they had little patience with one who showed cowardice or rebelled against tribal disciplines. Sam had seen a six-year-old Crow son in a screaming tantrum, in midwinter, and had looked on with amazement as the father poured pail after pail of ice water over the shrieking and shivering lad. He had seen mothers set naked babes only a few months old outside in the snow, and leave them for ten or fifteen minutes; when the infants were brought into the warmth of the lodge they had waved their arms and howled with delight. Hank Cady had once said, in one of the rare evenings when he uttered more than ten words, that he could forsee the time when white children wouldn't be worth knocking on the head. Well, Sam Minard's would be wonderful, a boy and a girl, and he would love them like the old dickens.

He gave his Lotus the first of many surprises when he dismounted, took a Don Giovanni stance, and burst into baritone song. Pretending that she was Donna Elvira's maid and that the horse she sat on was a window ledge, he serenaded her, giving to the aria all the soul he had. If she had a voice he would teach her to sing. He again astonished her when they stopped to make camp. She had supposed that her lord would smoke his pipe while she gathered wood for a fire, fetched water, and prepared supper for him; but Long Talons lifted her off her pony, held her to him a few moments with her feet ten inches off the earth, his lips kissing in her black hair; and then made a fire and set out a supper of dried buffalo, stale biscuits, and a pot of coffee—a hell of a marriage feast, he told her, but there would be better tomorrow. He opened a tin of sugar, and touching a fingertip to his tongue to moisten it, touched the sugar and again his tongue. He then took her hand, touched her finger to his tongue and to the sugar and kissed the sugar off her finger. When he looked at her eyes there was such childlike wonder in them that he had to smile. While he was setting the food out and she was wondering what kind of man this could be who did the labor of women, she looked round her and saw bushes black with berries. Seizing a cup, she hastened away and returned with the cup brimming. Sam poured half the berries into her tin plate and half into his own and sprinkled sugar over both.

"I see you'll make a good wife," he said; and again astonished her when, bending low, he turned her face up and kissed her berry-stained lips.

Blessed Eros, it was good to have a bride in your arms and be riding away over the world. It was good to be for a few days in friendly country where a man could sleep. He was more than two hundred miles from the Blackfeet, four hundred from the Crows, six hundred from the Eutaws. After they had eaten she stared at him, fascinated, as he washed the dishes in a cool mountain stream. For most Indians the only dishcloth was a dog's tongue. He hobbled the beasts, piled bedding against a tree, leaned against the bedding, filled and fired his pipe; and then, looking over at Lotus, said gently, "Come to your man." She must have understood his eyes, if not his words, for she moved over until he could take her arm and draw her down at his side. He snuggled her comfortably against the robes, put his strong left arm around her, and looking up at the sky, said, "Look down, Almighty One, and see your Adam and Eve here in the garden. She fed me the berry-apples but I don't kallate we will sin till she gets used to me." Looking round at her face, he said softly, "Poor little Lotus-Lilah, left all your people to go with me. I'll be a good husband." That was not what he wanted to say; he guessed he was not much of a gallant. She would look up to meet his eyes but he could read nothing in the black depths. His left arm drew her a little closer, his left cheek sank to the lustrous warmth of her hair. His temple moved down till it touched her temple. Then he held his breath, for he could feel her pulse beating against him, at a hundred throbs a minute. Putting his pipe aside, he sat up straight, and taking her hands, laid them, backs down, across his big left palm. He then studied the lines. As a youngster he had known what some of the lines were supposed to mean. It looked to him as if the lifeline had been chopped off at the shoulders, but in another line there were two children, and that was good. He brought her hands to his bearded mouth and kissed both palms. Then he turned toward her, and framing her face, tried to look deep into her black eyes but it was like looking into a bottle of black ink with a light under it. He patted her knees, again put his left arm round her, and taking up his pipe, filled it from a deerskin pouch. It was while he was tamping the tobacco that she moved swiftly away from him and returned with a glowing ember.

A few minutes later he again put his pipe aside and took his mouth harp. In turn he played and sang. "Au clair de la lune," a French chanson of the eighteenth century; "The Troubadour's Song"; "Green Grows the Laurel" but in the middle of this he broke off to tell her that far south, in Kit Carson land, they were calling it lilacs. He would play a phrase, sing it, and play it again; and all the while she intently watched him, like a child determined to understand.

> "Flies in the pemmican, skip to my Lotus
> Flies in the pemmican, skip to my Lotus,
> Flies in the pemmican, skip to my Lou!"

She gave him a marvelous smile for that: she knew the word "pemmican."

"You know, Mrs. Minard, I think I'll send for a banjo."

"Ban-jo."

"Banjo." While pretending to strum an instrument he made banjo sounds with his lips. When he left home the only banjo he knew was the long-necked fretless instrument, used in black-faced minstrel shows, English ballads, and popular Irish and Scottish tunes of the day. A letter from his brother David said there was now a banjo with five strings and frets in the fingerboard, and that the playing style was changing from chording to a developed solo. That all sounded good.

> "Hey, git along, git along Josey!
> Hey, git along, Jim along Joe!"

She smiled at him. He brought her hands to his lips and kissed them, both backs and palms, and then the fingers. He thought they were getting along all right. When the moon rose above the trees he pointed and said, "Moon."

"Moon."

"A Mozart moon." When the moon was round and melon-ripe, like the one up there, he wanted to make his mouth organ sound like a French horn, so that he could play a horn solo; he wanted to express the music in winds, the murmuring lullabies in flowing water, the exquisite bird arias, the great lovers'-sighs made by trees—for the Almighty, his father had told him, had the finest orchestras and the most magnificent symphonies in the world. It was his father who had told him that Knecht's "Musical Portrait of Nature" had fertilized the soil for Beethoven's Pastoral Symphony. On the pianoforte his father had striven to paint tones—to evoke mental images with auditory impressions; on his mouthpiece Sam could do a fair imitation of the flute, cello, and oboe, but he failed completely when he tried to bring forth the round golden bell-tones of the horn.

"What fun we'll have," he said, squeezing her. "No taxes, no policemen, no government, no neighbors, no preachers—only the four of us, eating and sleeping, playing and singing." He turned and lightly kissed her forehead, cheeks, lips, but she gave no response. He had thought that Eve was the same in all women. Did she know that some of the finest singers on earth were birds? On their long ride south they would hear them, the meadow lark, the hermit thrush, the wood thrush, the grosbeak, the oriole. He guessed he would have one more pipeful and they would roll in. Standing, he looked at the bluff above them and at the country roundabout, to be sure that the only approach an enemy could make was from the front. He then sat, and while he smoked and looked at his wife her gaze moved over his face, as though to fix it in memory, or as though marking the differences between red faces and white. He supposed she did not know what to make of whiteman music, or of his kissing, for the redmen did not kiss their women. Perhaps she was wondering when he was going to take her, with the brutal and savage passion with which most of the males of the mammalia took their females. Poor little Lotus! She would have a few more days of peace.

Yes, it was a Mozart moon. September was almost here; at this season the nights in the high northern mountains seemed to have been lifted off the glaciers. But he had plenty of bedding. Putting his pipe away, he rolled her into a buffalo robe as though she were a doll. Raising the part on which her head lay, he dragged pine needles and twigs under the fur so that she would have a kind of pillow, though he was not sure that the red people used pillows; and he put the revolver and knife within a fold of the robe, within swift reach of her hand. If enemies came, he said to her, he would get four and she must get two. He now wrapped a robe around him and lay at her side, with the rifle between them. A thousand stars were out, and the moon among them looked like a round golden note from a French horn. Sam was not a religious man in the sense of creeds and churches but he felt a powerful affinity to the earth and to the heavens and to all the living things around him, except the professional killers. He looked at the moon and the stars and began to talk.

He told his silent and listening bride that the Almighty had created a beautiful world and that the Rocky Mountains, the cordilleras of the continental spine, or Stony or Snowy Mountains, as some men called them, were the marrow, heart, and soul of it. He had not seen them but common sense told him that by comparison the Andes were only foothills and the Alps were for children to climb. This conceit made him grin in the robe. Together they would explore the Gallatin and Madison and a hundred other valleys; the Tetons, the Bighorns, the Green River, Columbia, the Blue, the Big Belt; and a thousand peaks that any man alive and joyful wanted to reach the top of; and the rivers and lakes and the high white cascades against the snowlines. Why any man would willingly live in a city, with its infernal stinks and noises, he would never know. Why a man would live back there among the hummocks called mountains, east of the Mississippi, when he could come west to God's finest sculpturings, both Greek and Gothic, and be his own lord and king and conscience, with no laws except that the brave survived and the cowardly perished, and no asylums for crazy men who could no longer look at city life without shrieking— and no churches except this in which she lay, no priests except the larks and wrens and thrushes, no bible except this land's language for those who could read it. This was the life he loved. This was where he would live until an arrow or a bullet found him, and when that hour came he would be content to let the wolves strip his bones clean and leave them upon this great map of the magnificent. . . .

The girl lying at his side understood only a few of his words but she understood the emotion, for in its essence his mood was her mood. She was thrilled by both felicity and fright when his hand moved over to touch her, to squeeze her arm, or (once) to spread out flat on the robe over her navel. Strong emotion she understood, for her own people, all the red people, were supercharged; but she did not understand a man, white or brown, who for hours would do no more to his woman than talk to her. She would never know that for the pure glory of it a romantic man was falling in love.

The next day her astonishment and wonder continued to grow.

He tarried in friendly land, turning aside from his straightest course to camp by a mountain lake. He looked at the cold high-mountain water and told himself that he needed a bath. In his sly but human way he wanted to see his wife with no garments on her. He sniffed at his arms but the only odor there was the smoke essences used to tan buckskin. Like all the free trappers, whose lives depended solely on their alertness and courage, he had many times saturated his leather clothing in the smoke of burning cedar, sage, and stinkbush to overcome the human scent. The odor of smoke, tanned skins, and beaver pelt was about the only odor he had. But because he was a bridegroom and liked the smell of human hair and skin, freshly washed, he wanted a bath.

After tying the horses and placing his weapons where he could swiftly seize them as he stripped off his clothing. He knew that his wife was watching him; he supposed she was wondering if he intended to strip her down. Poor frightened doe, did she think her hour had come for rape? He made a sign to her to take her garments off and in a few moments she stood naked; but he had already plunged into the cold waters and was swimming. Then he stood, treading water, looking over at her, with water running down the strands of his long hair. After she entered he swam to the shore, and using sand for soap, scrubbed himself. He then plunged in again and swam like a bull buffalo compared to his wife, who swam high and swift like an antelope. Standing in water to his waist, Sam watched her. As though to show off her skill she swam thirty yards to his left; turned with such ease that she seemed to be on a towline and swam to his right; and then came straight toward him. He could have been no more enchanted if she had been a mermaid. She stood before him, the water almost to her chin, her black hair down her back in a wet tangled mane, her wet face as grave as a child's as black eyes looked up at him.

"You swim a lot better than your man," he said. "I hope you shoot that well."

Moving close to her and reaching into the water, he put his right arm under her knees and his left across her back and brought her up. He waded ashore and stood in full sun, holding her dripping body, looking at the beauty of her bronzed Indian skin; at her breasts, which he thought perfect; at her lovely throat and shoulders; and at last at her eyes. What he thought he saw in her eyes he had no words for. It was as if he had lived for twenty-seven years within the prison of self, without communicating a single time to another living soul, to find now, in the miracle of this moment, that he was not alone. He guessed that was what love meant. Still holding her with one arm under her knees and the other under her back, he raised her, so that his lips could touch her, from her knees to her lips. Kissing over her, he moved her back and forth with such ease that she seemed to be weightless. He tossed her with a turning motion and in mid-air caught her, with his fingers now spread against her thighs, and against her chest just below her breasts; and he put his lips to her thighs and up her back to her nape and her hair. He tossed her again and with spread hands caught her at her waist and set her on her feet. With a tentative timid forefinger she touched him gently on the upper muscle of his powerful right arm. She had not known that there were men with such strength. She now would have been only a little surprised if Mick Boone had told her that he had seen this man, to whom she had been sold for good or ill, take two Indians of average size by their necks and smash their heads together with such power that they both dropped dead; that Sam could put a palm with fingers spread against her belly and lift her to arm's length above his head with the ease with which most men would have lifted an infant; and that he could go under the belly of any beast in her father's herd and with hands grasping his legs below his knees could put all four feet of the horse off the earth. Her eyes said that she knew he was a mighty one. She was looking at his hands.

Taking the mouth organ from his medicine bag, he played here and there in a few things, trying to find what he wanted; and having found it, he began to dance, solo, back and forth across the lakeshore sands, and a bronzed girl, glistening with melting diamonds, her black mane covering her whole back, stood still and looked at him. He would never know whether the wonderful melody went like the hermit thrush's song into her mood. For him it was like the scent of warm melting wild honey; like the spring song of the bluebird; like an armful of alpine lilies. He then put the harp away, sniffed the atmosphere and listened, and heard only the sweet low note of the water thrush. He then walked over to his bride.

What he did astonished and frightened her. Bending over and putting his left arm behind her knees, he lifted her; straightened; gave her an upward thrust with his left arm and right hand, so that in the next moment she sat on his left shoulder; and walked over to her clothes. There he let her slide down to his left arm, and as she sat, like a big golden bird, staring at him, he looked at her eyes and smiled. Adam and Eve were measuring the wonder of one another. He then uttered words which, once spoken, he would find ten times as hard to say again: "Lotus-Lilah, I reckon this white nigger loves you." She was his wife, his woman, his mate, his companion on the trail as long as there were trails for free men to ride on; through the valleys, until these were choked with cabbages and people; and up the mountains to the highest peaks, as long as men felt compelled to seek God.

He set her down and they began to dress. He thought she was surrendering to his maleness but he was not ready to take her, not yet. There was a huge emptiness in him to be filled, and so little of it that could be filled with sexual passion. When they were both dressed he turned to her, where she stood waiting and looking at him, and putting his arms across her shoulders under her hair, he held her close to him, murmuring down at her, "Mine, all mine." Then, putting hands under her arms at the shoulders, he held her straight out, at arm's length, and looked at her. With her feet still off the earth, her wonderful black lustrous eyes looking at him, he fetched her close against him, from her toes to her face, and pressed his bearded mouth into her hair.

"Well," he said, releasing her, "I reckon we best be on our way. You won't be eating bitterroots for a long time." The bitterroot, which her people called spetlem, and boiled until it was like a fondant, was far too bitter for the whiteman's taste. Because she and her people had not lived sumptuously, in the way of the Crows, he was eager to cook feasts for her on the long journey south. He hoped to get grouse for supper.

"You like grouse?" he asked her. "Geese? . . . Quail?" He tried to imitate the calls of these birds. The song or talk of the prairie chicken was so startling and in ways human that it gave a man a queer feeling; and the quail and white-winged dove could lift the hair on his neck. He imitated the cries by pinching his nostrils and honking and whistling, and by fluffing his hair to make feathers and flapping his hands to make wings. He made her laugh for the first time. That for him meant that his marriage was getting along.

7

SAM HAD NEVER thought much about love. He had had good parents. He had never as a child felt unwanted and unloved. His father, a rather ineffectual giant whose chief passions were music and philosophy, and who was sometimes found reading Descartes and Locke and Tom Paine when he should have been tending his small general store, had far more interest in Descartes' effort "to attain to the knowledge of all things" than he had in the family larder. Sam took his love of music from his father; his practical sense in a world where a man had to adapt or perish, and his love of adventure and freedom, he took from his English mother. His father was French and Scotch with generous measures of still other peoples: he had, Sam had concluded, so many strains in him that they were constantly at war with one another. But he loved learning while his mother loved life. Daniel Minard had a library, small but excellent, and a hankering to write a book someday. Sam thought he might write a book, if he ever left the West and went back home. Some of the mountain men were about as illiterate as a man could be—such as Kit Carson and Jim Bridger, neither of whom, it was said, could read or write. Some were educated. Some had written books about their adventures in the West.

At nineteen Sam had told his parents that he guessed he would go out beyond the Mississippi and take a look around. He had intended to stay only a year or so but in the frontier town of Independence he had been fascinated by tales of Kit Carson and other mountain men. Then one day he threw a bully over his shoulders with such force that he broke both the man's arms, and fled from the law, as many young men had before him. Long before his first vision of the Tetons he knew that the free trappers were his people and that these mountains would be his home.

On his way out he had gathered all the tales he could of the men who had gone before him. There was Edward Rose, who, if still alive, was an old cuss now. Negro, Cherokee, and white, Rose had worn (said those who knew him) the most fiendish expression this side of hell, his face scarred with old knife wounds, a crooked lip pulled into a perpetual snarl, and eyes as cruel and cold as the falcon's. Most of his nose had been chewed off; he had an ugly brand on his forehead that some enemy had put there with a red-hot iron; he had buckshot and bullets in both legs; and like Jim Bridger, he had for a time carried an arrowhead embedded in the flesh of his back. About thirty-five years ago he had come west and joined the Crows and had become a powerful chief, and because of his reckless courage in battle against the Crows' red enemies his name had been changed from Cut-Nose to Five-Scalps. Jim Beckwourth, who had also become a Crow chief, said Rose was killed about the time Hugh Glass had his dreadful fight with the grizzly. But there were those who said that Beckwourth was the biggest liar in the West next to Bridger.

It was Caleb Greenwood, squawman, mountain man, and scout who had changed Beckwourth's life and made him the Devil's own brother. As the story came to Sam, Caleb and a few companions had unwittingly killed a couple of Crows, and still had the two wet scalps when half the Crow nation surrounded them. To save the lives of his men Caleb had convinced a Crow chief that Beckwourth was a Crow—that when a band of Crows had been captured by the Shi-ans Jim was a Crow boy among those captured. Years later when Beckwourth and Bridger were fleeing for their lives Beckwourth was captured and taken to a Crow village. Having seen him with Greenwood several Crows recognized him as a brother; and so all the older women were summoned and told to examine this man, to see if they could identify a lost son. An old crone who had inspected almost every part of him said at last that if he had a mole over his left eyelid he was her son; when the lids were pulled down like two small rubber awnings, as pure as gumption there was the mole. During the next hours Beckwourth almost died under the welcome; the enraptured hugging and squeezing of him by scores of shrieking sisters and aunts and cousins had made him feel, Jim said, as if he had been rolled over and over in a ton of fresh *bois de vache*. But he survived it to become a famous Crow chief, and for years had his choice of both women and horses, their only recognized form of wealth. It was said that he became enamored of a girl warrior, who had sworn never to roll under for a man, but to give her life to the extermination of her people's enemies. Jim boasted that he had won her but no one believed his story, for even Jim Bridger said that as a liar he had no peer. It was a sad day for him when, growing weary of women and horses, he wandered away; on his return to the Crows he was promptly poisoned, so that they could keep his brave heart, the house of his phenomenal daring.

Sam hadn't even seen Rose or Beckwourth, or a dozen other free trappers haloed by legends; but he had met Kit Carson, the most famous man of them all. Kit had served as scout for an explorer, and so many pages had been written about him back east that the greenhorns had made him a national idol. Sam had seen this Scot and Kentuckian twice and had looked hard at him. In an average group of mountain men Kit looked more like a boy; he stood in his moccasins only about five feet eight inches in height, and weighed, Sam guessed, no more than a hundred and fifty pounds. He had sandy hair, bowed legs, freckles, and steady steely-blue eyes. It was said that he had killed a lot of men and lain with a lot of women and been in a lot of fights. When only a lad his family had taken the trail of Daniel Boone, and when only nine Kit had seen his father killed by a falling tree. At sixteen he headed west. When in an accident a man's arm was crushed, all the men with him said they didn't have the nerve to saw it off. Kit, only a youngster, said he would saw it off if they would hold him, and with a dull old saw he went through the bone of the upper arm, cauterized the wound with a red-hot kingbolt, and said he guessed the man would be all right.

Such tales about him had made Sam look at him hard. It was also said that Kit was a romantic cuss who didn't think that woman, white or red, was something to embrace and then kick into the nearest river. Kit's taste ran to the blackeyed Spanish and Mexican lasses, in the Taos area, for whom kissing a man or stabbing him was all the same thing. Sam had seen some of the señoritas and had thought them bundles of vanity and violence. He preferred his Lotus, and by the end of a week it would have taken a lot of big spacious words to express the full scope of his feeling for her. She was mother, wife, daughter,

trail mate, and angel, and the soul of his medicine bag. He had
been teaching her to handle both rifle and revolver and to throw
the knife. She was an apt pupil with all weapons, and English.
In the vacuum where for seven years he had known only eating
and killing and dodging his enemies he now enthroned her and
she began to fill him; and his emotions enfolded her as she
enfolded him, until on awaking she would be the first thing he
would think of, and the last before falling asleep. Heaven help
the man, white or red, who ever dared touch her.

Possibly he was afraid that man would, for during these
blissful golden autumn weeks with her he never let her out of
his sight for more than a few minutes. He found to his
astonishment and delight that the sexual embrace had
endeared him to her. Before that, she had stood off, as though
to measure the depths of his villainy; after that she would come
up to him, shyly, and look up at his eyes. At night he would lie,
naked, on his robe and hold her, naked against him. He would
let her lie on her back down his chest, belly, and thighs, the top
of her head just under his chin, her toes barely reaching his
ankles. Sometimes they would fall asleep that way, with a robe
over them. He called her his golden bottom, his twin apples, the
house of his son, and a score of other foolish endearments, while
his big hands moved tenderly over her. Sometimes he would sit
with Lotus on his lap and look for a full minute into her
wonderful eyes, and she would look into his blue-gray eyes, her
gaze moving from one to the other, back and forth. Sam would
look and never say a word, as a man might try to look through
an opaque pane into heaven. Sometimes she would tickle him
in his beard or over his chest; and though her face was sober he
could see laughter in her eyes.

"Love me?" she would say.

"You doggone right I love you."

"Supper?"

"Loin steaks and strawberries."

Looking into her eyes, he would think of Loretto, who had
come west a few years before Sam—a hot impetuous Spaniard
who had ransomed from her enemies and captors, the Crows,
and taken as his wife, a beautiful Blackfeet girl. A year later he
and his wife and their baby were with Jim Bridger and his men
when they came on a band of Blackfeet; and the girl,
recognizing a brother, handed the babe to Loretto and fled to
his arms. Then the Indians moved swiftly away, taking the

protesting and weeping girl with them; and Loretto, the babe in his arms, went crying after them, begging his wife to come back. A Blackfeet chief then advanced to meet him and said his life would be spared if he would shut up and go away. That was the price of his life but not of his love. He lived and waited for the moment when he would see her again; and the truth of his abiding love for her became a lovely legend all over the West. Most whitemen found it strange that a whiteman could love an Indian girl, and made the matter agreeable to their prejudice by saying that a Spaniard, after all, was not white, but a cousin of the red people. Did Loretto ever see her again? The legend said he did not. Sam hadn't thought much about the story before he held his Lotus close to him and felt the living wonder of her; after that he thought about it every time he looked into the lights and the melting liquid-black of her eyes.

In a high mountain meadow they found ripe wild strawberries, and on a hillside a young fat barren elk cow. The supper tonight would be a feast. There wouldn't be cream for the berries or sourdough bread and wild honey or hump fat for butter but it would be a feast just the same. Taking her in his arms, he said, "Drink to me only with thine eyes and I will pledge with mine." Yes, she said, and then did something that surprised him. From the berries she chose one of the largest and ripest, and this she crushed across his lips. She then crushed a berry over her lips, and standing tiptoe, looked up at him and said, "You drink?"

"I'll be doggone," he said, and looked across her hair at the sky. Then he kissed her. "Mmmm!" he said, loving the scent of the berries and the taste of the kiss. He kissed her again. He had tried to teach her the meaning of the word "what" by taking an object, saying, "What?" and naming it. She now looked up at him after the second kiss and said, "Lotus. What?"

He pulled his bronzed forehead down in thought. A fruit, he said. It was the fruit the lotus people ate that made them drunk. He turned to the berries. "Lotus. What? This."

"Ohhh," she said, sucking the meaning into her. She thought the lotus was the wild strawberry. She stood looking at the berries; he supposed she was telling herself he had named her for this delicious fruit. She seemed deeply pleased.

Knowing that he could not always be present to protect her, he spent many hours teaching her to shoot and throw the knife. Most Indians did not have rifles, and the few who had rifles never allowed their women to touch them. The recoil and the sound of the explosion frightened her at first but she was determined and apt; after fifty rounds she could hit an object the size of a man's head at fifty yards. The heavy revolver she could never master, but she practiced daily with the knife. It was James Black who began making the knives—who hardened and tempered the steel with a method he never divulged to any man. After James Bowie with a knife made by Black ripped open three assassins who had been hired to kill him the knife became known as the Bowie; and it became so well-known and widely used that schools sprang up in which fighting with the Bowie was taught. Sam on his way west had spent time in one of these schools. The real Bowie had a guard, and a razor edge on top of the blade from the point back about two and a half inches. For throwing, a knife was machined and balanced to turn over once, twice, or three times in a certain distance. Sam had had his knife balanced to turn twice in thirty feet; at that distance he could drive it through a man's heart. He taught his wife to throw it, because in his opinion it was the best weapon in close fighting; you could throw it faster than you could get your rifle up, and you could rip open three men while trying to shoot one. He said he would get her a Bowie at Bridger's post and a lot of other things. They would be in debt but the next winter he hoped to get four, perhaps five, packs of beaver. Did she know how many pelts were in a pack?

A pack, he tried tell her, in words and signs, had ten buffalo robes, fourteen bear, sixty otter pelts, eighty beaver, a hundred and twenty fox, or six hundred muskrat. Four packs of beaver would be three hundred and twenty and that should be seven hundred dollars at a post or rendezvous. She knew the word "rendezvous" and she asked if it would be six moons.

"More than that." He pulled all her fingers and thumbs out straight, and starting with a thumb, said, "This thumb is October; forefinger November, big one December—except it isn't very big," he said, and kissed it. "This is January; the little one is February, as it should be. This other thumb is March and the forefinger is April. About seven and a half moons." He turned his thumbs in and held up his eight fingers.

From the Bitterroots they had gone southeast to the continental divide and had crossed it just north of Henry's Lake. From there they went to Pierre's Hole and climbed the backbone of the Teton range and looked east across what would be known as Jackson Hole country. On the eastern flanks of this range, high against the spine, were more wild flowers than Sam had ever seen in one spot—whole acres, whole hillsides, with such a wealth of color and scents that he could only stand and stare. He knew only a few of them—the asters, paintbrushes, pentstemons, gilias, mallows; none of them for him was as lovely as the marsh marigold, which he called alpine lily, or the alp-lily, with their yellow centers and six creamy white petals; and the columbine. But he loved them all and marveled at the beauty of this mountainside. Among the flowers, as if to set them off, were the ferns, the leathery leaves of myrtle, the mountain laurel, and various berry plants, including the huckleberry. And the huckleberries were ripe.

Sam gathered a few of the loveliest flowers and intertwined the stems in her black hair. Someday, he said, he would make her a mantle of the mariposa lily, white, lilac, yellow, and red. While she gathered berries he went down the mountain to a spring, to fill the coffeepot, for they would have their supper on the summit, with the Almighty's magnificent sculpturing all around them. This, he said, was the greatest elk country in the world, and yonder only a hundred miles the buffalo were so thick they turned the prairies black. He stood a few moments looking into the northeast; up there a long way was a sad and lonely woman and he guessed they ought to go see her.

It was dark by the time he came in with the loin, liver, and a hindquarter of an elk. In a natural room, high and fragrant, formed by dense evergreen tangles, he made a fire and set on the coffee and steaks. Lotus had gathered two quarts of berries. The huckleberry, Hank Cady said, was the finest in the world; every autumn he gathered gallons and decocted his delicious jam, using wild honey and a little sugar to help inspissate the fruit. Remembering how Hank used berry juice and hot marrow, Sam now fed his wife as though she were a bird: he opened a hot biscuit, poured melted marrow over it, sopped it then in huckleberry juice, and presented it at her lips. He would then take one, and shutting his eyes tight so that he would have no sensation but that of taste and smell, he made murmuring sounds of pure joy. The warmth brought out the full marvelous scent and flavor of the berry. Other delicacies Sam prepared for her, in the warm scented room under the fir boughs. Over a morsel of raw liver, well-heated, he sprinkled a very little pepper, then poured hot marrow over it and plopped it into her mouth. Imitating him, she would close her eyes when she chewed. He would kiss her lips when they were moist with marrow fat or berry juice.

They spent two nights and a day here, feasting on wild game and wild fruits, and then descended to a beautiful lake and went past the majestic blue-gray granite towers of the Tetons. Two days later they were at the southern edge of what would be known as Yellowstone Park. That was the area of John Colter's hellhole and hot bilins, steaming vents and spoutings and mudpots. In a geyser basin they could be safe all fall and winter; the red people seldom ventured close to the huge vomitings of hot water or to that part of the lake where hot springs boiled in the cold depths. The journey north to see if the woman was still there would be an extra eight hundred miles but a mountain man thought little of that. There wasn't much to do before the snows of winter. Besides, he thought the woman might come to her senses if she were to see another woman. As they entered Crow lands they both steeped themselves and their garments in the smoke of woods with a strong incense, such as cedar, sage, and buffalo bush; and Sam put his music and his songs away and no longer talked above a whisper. As his manner changed, so did hers; she became as noiseless as the weasel.

After they had gone north past the Bighorns and come close to Blackfeet country, Sam put away his pipe and built no more fires. They would now eat jerked elk, roots, and dried berries. Lotus's people, like the Shoshonis, had long been preyed on by the Blackfeet and lived in chronic fear of them. Sam had told himself a thousand times that he must never fall into their hands. The Crows, the Cheyennes, even the Sioux might ransom him, but the Blackfeet squaws would dance round and round him like shrieking things out of hell, and piece by piece hack the flesh off his bones. He knew with what hellish glee Blackfeet warriors would make off with his wife, if they ever got hands on her. So he became as wary as the wolf, and Lotus became more hunted animal than human being.

Smell of the Blackfeet always made Sam think of John Colter. Had there ever been another such race with death as his? Surprised with a companion by five hundred warriors in the Three Forks area, when trapping, John had not resisted. The fool companion had been shot full of arrows. John was given a chance. It was a mighty slim chance but it was a chance of a kind, and Sam could imagine with what eagerness the man had seized it. There he was, stripped naked, defenseless, five hundred howling savages around him, his companion lying dead in his blood. Even his moccasins were taken off. He was told that he could run for his life, with the five hundred at his heels. Colter had not only to run barefooted; he had to cross a wide area that was densely studded with cactus, whose thorns were as sharp and stout as needles. Sam had crossed the area over which John ran, and had examined the thorns. He supposed that a man running not only for his life but to escape torture would hardly be aware of the spines driven into his naked feet. What had the soles of Colter's feet been like after three hundred yards?

After three miles Colter had glanced back and seen a gloating buck only a hundred yards behind him. Calling on what had seemed to Colter to be the last of his strength, he had tried to run faster, and soon began to hemorrhage, the blood bursting from his nostrils and spilling down over him. At the end of another mile a backward glance appalled him: now the red warrior was only forty or fifty feet behind him and was in the act of hurling his lance. In that instant Colter made his decision. He stopped short and turned. Possibly his body, red with blood, unnerved the Indian, for he seemed to make only a feeble effort, then stumbled and fell; and in the next moment Colter was on him and with the lance spiked him to the earth. At least two hundred of the howling savages were still swiftly advancing, spears flashing in the sun. Blood still spilled over him but Colter now ran with the energy of despair and came at last to a river. He plunged in. His life was saved by the fact that he came to the river at a large eddy, covered over with driftwood. He dived and swam; came up a moment to gulp air, and dived and swam again; and so kept swimming under and coming up until he was a hundred yards from the shore. He then found above him a huge cottonwood trunk with a lightning wound in the underside of it. By lying on his back he could put his face up in the cavity of the wound and breathe. For hours he lay under that tree, while above him went the baffled and shrieking warriors, leaping from driftwood to driftwood, and insane with rage because they had lost their fleetest runner and their prey. After Colter was convinced that they had gone he cautiously left his hiding place and looked round him. He did not leave the eddy until the blackest part of the night; he then swam quietly downriver several miles and sat on the bank to consider his plight. The soles of his feet were filled with thorns. He had no clothes, no weapons, no food, and he was at least a week's journey from the nearest whiteman, on the Roche Jaune River. But because he was John Colter and a mountain man he made it, with nothing to eat in seven days and nights of torture but a few roots.

It made a mountain man proud just to think of him. It made him proud to think of Hugh Glass, who, torn open front and back by a grizzly and left to die, had crawled a hundred miles on his hands and knees, with maggots swarming in his wounds. There were so many to be proud of. There was Jedediah Smith, as intrepid an explorer as Meriwether Lewis; Jed, who carried a Bible in one hand and a rifle in the other; who prayed in one moment and blew his foe's head off in the next. In an encounter with a grizzly his head had been seized by the monster's mouth and huge chisel-teeth had raked furrows in flesh and bone and torn one ear almost off. Jed had had the ear sewed to his skull with a crude needle and buckskin thread.

It was a riddle, Sam thought, listening to the night sounds and moving a hand caressingly back and forth over his wife's thighs—it was a riddle how the grizzly managed to get so many heads in its mouth. There was Lewis Dawson on the Rio de las Animas Perdidas: in his fight with a bear his companion's gun had missed fire three times; three times a bitchdog had attacked so furiously that the bear had turned to chase her; and three times the beast had returned to maul Dawson. Three separate times it had Dawson's entire head in its mouth, and his wounds, like Jed's were stitched together with leather thread. But one big tooth had gone through the skull, and after three days the brains began to leak out and Dawson died in delirium.

How will I die? Sam wondered, and sniffed the night air for scent of Blackfeet. How would Lotus die? He was sure that neither of them would die in bed. Few whitemen in this land had sense enough, when eyes and trigger finger began to fail, to pack their possibles and get out. Tom Fitzpatrick might die in bed but how many times had he come within a hair of going under? He hadn't turned gray overnight for no reason at all. Tall, grizzled, hard-muscled, Fitz had been one of the biggest and best of them, until that day in 1831 when his hair turned white; most of the flesh wasted from his bones and, too weak to stand, he had been found by two half-breeds crawling along a creek bottom. One day when alone on the Big Sandy he had come face to face with a band of Gros Ventres and had raced for his life until his horse fell dead under him. He had then crawled into a hole in a mountainside and filled the entrance with stones and leaves, and had remained there until almost dead of hunger and thirst. Crawling out, he had headed for Pierre's Hole but while crossing swift waters on a raft had lost his rifle, pouch, and knife. Defenseless, he had had to climb a tree and sit in it all night, when attacked by a pack of wolves. There were no words, Sam supposed, to tell how much a man suffered, whose hair and beard turned from brown to white in a few days.

When they came to the big bend of the Musselshell, Sam and Lotus gathered a pile of dead cedar boughs and stripped off their clothing. Sam then fired the pile and they stood naked in the heavy smoke, holding their garments in their hands. It is possible that Sam overrated the redman's sense of smell, because his own was so acute; but his years in Indian land had convinced him that often the redman could smell an enemy when he could not see or hear him. He had concluded that the whiteman had a strong body odor, of which he was unaware. After all, was the mountain goat conscious of its odor? Or the cougar and the wolf? With the wind coming from the beasts, Sam could smell a pack of wolves five miles away. He had got to know the body odor of all the mankilling beasts, and of such birds as the horned owl and red-tailed hawk; but it was the odors of red people that had been his special study, until now, by odor alone, he could distinguish between Blackfeet and Crow, and between these and the Cheyennes and Eutaws. When he saw the four warriors the woman had chopped down he would have known by their body smell that they were Blackfeet, even if he had not known by the shape of their moccasins or by their hairdress.

After he and Lotus had saturated their pores and garments with cedar incense they turned their moccasins inside out and smoked them, for there was no part of man with a stronger odor than his feet. If their path were found a score of Blackfeet warriors would go down on hands and knees to sniff at the footprints of horse and man.

8

When on a late September day they looked over at the woman's shack there was no smoke or sign of living thing. After staring for a full minute Sam said, "I don't see hide or hair of her but I feel she's there." He went down to the river trail and followed it to the lean-to. Nobody had been there in a long while. On the path leading to the river he saw her tracks and took the path up the hill. She had been sitting just inside the hut, on her bed. He was never to forget how she looked, the moment she came in view, standing there by the shack, the rifle in her hand, her body bent forward, eyes staring and ears straining.

"It's me," he said in a loud voice, for he was a hundred and fifty feet from her. "It's Sam Minard, your friend." For two or three minutes they looked at one another and nothing more was said. He thought she had a very crazy way of staring at him. Putting a hand behind him, his fingers motioned to Lotus to go back down, for he suspected that the woman had seen her and recognized her as Indian. He then advanced, slowly, until he stood before her and looked down at her gray hair. He thought it had turned gray since he saw her last. Father in heaven, how she had suffered! "I'm your friend," he said, and looked over at the sage plants, and the wild flowers by the graves. The wetness of the earth around them showed that she had watered them within the past two or three hours. Nowhere was there any sign that she had made a fire.

Still moving slowly, lest she become terrified and scream, he set his rifle by the wall and took the gun from her hands. "I guess you fired this since I left," he said, "because it isn't loaded now." She had not yet looked up at him. Thought of her sitting with an empty gun before her enemies filled him with such pity and pain that he placed a hand lightly on her graying head and kissed her hair. "I'm your friend," he said, his voice low and gentle.

Then he took his rifle and went back down the hill. He couldn't stand any more of it; he was afraid he was going to break down and cry like a child. To hide his emotion from Lotus he said they would go out and get a couple of deer, but even after they had come in with them and he was slicing liver for her he felt sick clear down to his guts. The trouble with deer and antelope, he said, to make talk, was that they didn't have the full-bodied chewing of beef. He guessed it would be all right to make a fire here; the skulls were still on the stakes, the Blackfeet had scouted this area perhaps a dozen times. They had read the warning. They would never strike here, not now. The woman up there, she looked as if she hadn't eaten a thing since he left her; she was scrawny and gray, and so full of sorrow that it made a man want to cry just to look at her.

His rifle within reach, he knelt to slice venison, and Lotus brought wood for the drying racks. The larger intestines he cut into lengths about eighteen inches long, and turning them inside out, took them to the river and thoroughly washed them. With a hatchet he laid open the spine and the shoulder and thigh bones to get at the marrow, for he intended to have boudins tonight. Lotus came over to see what he was doing. She hadn't got used to the fact that he liked to cook and had a gourmet's interest in food; she invariably looked astonished when he gave a cry of delight over some delicacy. She preferred a slice of raw liver to his warm golden biscuits, dunked in hot marrow fat; and the serviceberry to any other berry. But when he was feasting and exclaiming she had learned to smile and exclaim with him, and to say, "It's all free," after hearing him say the words a hundred times. She hadn't the slightest notion of what a whiteman meant by the word "free." Boudins she did like, and she watched with fascinated interest as he prepared them.

When he heard a meadow lark he stood straight and tall and listened. Its song was so much finer than the meadow lark's back east; this he took to be a sign that these mountains were a better home for a man than the hills of New England. The purple finch had a marvelous warbling song that was continuous; the orchard oriole's welcome to springtime was almost as fine as the bluebird's; the hermit thrush in the high cool canyons sang as he imagined the angels must sing; but this solitary vocalist of the prairies and fields, with its yellow vest and black cravat, was his favorite of all songbirds. He listened until it flew away.

"I wonder," he said, "if she ever hears it."

He now put the marrow and the tenderest part of the kidney fat in a frying pan and melted them. The choicest flesh of the tenderloins he minced, using his hatchet and knife, along with a portion of liver, two kidneys, a cupful of brains, and a pound or two of hindquarter taken close to the bone; and all this minced meat he mixed with the rich marrow and suet greases, sprinkled the compost with salt, squeezed over it the juice of a wild onion, and stuffed the whole of it into several lengths of the intestine, with one end tied off. When the boudins were ready for cooking each was about ten inches long and tied off at both ends. It had taken him an hour to prepare them for slow broiling or roasting; he now turned to the biscuits and steaks, but paused every minute or two to glance round him and listen. Lotus meanwhile laid slices of flesh on the drying racks and kept up the fires.

A man and woman in love, preparing their supper, was the most beautiful thing in life. Didn't she think so? No taxes, he told her for the twentieth time; no policemen, no laws; the odorous abundant earth turning over in its garden of good things, round and round, its face following the sun like a child its mother. He was mixing biscuit dough. Rib steaks and a large roast were laid out, ready for the fire. He hadn't left her much flesh to dry, had he? he asked, looking at the slaughter he had made of two carcasses. Tomorrow they might find an elk, though this was a long way from elk country.

When the supper was almost ready, the roast and steaks brown and dripping, the boudins gently simmering in their hot juices inside the gut-sleeves, the biscuits ready to bake and the coffee to set on, he said he guessed they ought to go up the hill and ask the woman to eat with them. He supposed she wouldn't but they ought to ask her anyway. The rifle over his left arm, his right arm gently across his wife's shoulders, he went up the hill; and the moment Kate heard their footfalls she reached for her gun. With Lotus behind him now Sam went forward, knowing that her gun was not loaded; and Lotus followed, peering round him, for he had told her the story of the woman and she was curious. Sam called her attention to the graves and their flowers, and black eyes looked back and forth from the graves to the woman. She knew that the mother who stood there, looking so frail and alone and frightened, had three slain children buried under the withered flowers.

Taking his wife's hand, Sam said to Kate, "We're your friends." He watched her face, hoping to be able to tell if she understood him. "We have a fine hot supper down by the river. We wonder if you would come eat with us." Before he was done speaking he knew that she would not; the way she sat and everything in her face told him that she wanted them to go, that she wished to be alone. She looked terribly thin in her huddle of clothes, and very white and tired and old.

Kate's next response amazed him. Apparently she had been only dimly aware of Lotus, if at all, and now she saw her as an Indian; for she screamed, and the cries of the loon, the bittern, the hawk, the grebe, all together, were not as blood-curdling as this woman's cry. In the moment of the scream she ran frantically to her bed just inside the cabin and began to paw in it for the axe. Her cry had been so dreadful, so unhuman in its hate and fear and desperation, that Sam was unnerved, almost shattered; his bronzed face turning a shade paler, he seized his wife's arm and moved swiftly back. The woman had found the axe but had got entangled in something and was struggling to get up; and because she was so weak, so desperate with fear, she screamed again, and in all his life Sam had never heard such a sound. He moved back again, back and back, until he and Lotus were almost a hundred yards distant; and there he stood, shaken and unbelieving, his eyes fixed on the creature (she could hardly in that moment have been called a woman) who crouched at her doorway and peered, the axe in her grasp. "Almighty God!" he said. He felt nausea all through him. He felt that he was going to cry like a child. And he was trembling, clear down to his moccasins.

Sensing at last the pathos of it, the ghastly woe of it, the broken mother-heart of it, he took his wife's arm and went down the hill. The supper had been spoiled for him. All the beauty and sweetness of the earth had been turned bitter for him in that moment when he grasped, in full measure, the loneliness and nightmares and stark insane wondering of a mother there with her dead children. He ate one of the rich boudins, a steak, a hunk of roast, and a half dozen biscuits; and he drank a quart of strong black coffee; but he was hardly aware that he was eating. He then folded one of the deerskins flesh side in, making a bowl of it; and in the bowl he put a skin of boudins, a piece of roast, a steak, and a few biscuits. He told Lotus to remain here, alert, hand on her gun, while he went back to the woman. If the woman were somehow to get away from him and rush at Lotus with the axe she was to shoot her, if she had to, or climb a tree, if she could. With his rifle he went up the hill with the hot food, and over to the woman, who now sat between the graves; and he set the skin of food right before her, turning the folds back so that she could see what was there. He did not speak and he did not linger. He supposed that she would recognize the food and that she would ignore it or throw it away. What could he do or what could any man do that was any good for her? Was there in the whole world anything that could break through such grief as that? Perhaps the Almighty could do something for her; perhaps he was doing it in the only way that it could be done. Sam's guess was that she would sink deep into sorrow, and from sorrow into death.

But he did not understand her. He might reasonably have asked, What man could? He would never know of her frenzied assaults on the killers that invaded her small world, or that she had totally forgotten her people. If he had known about her visions in the sage garden and her reading and talking aloud to her dead ones he would have thought only what Bill was to say, that she was as crazy as a loon with three eagle babies in its nest. Kate on her side would have found it hard to understand the redmen and the mountain men, who month after month shot thousands of healthy beautiful animals and took only a few pounds of flesh, leaving the remainder to the wolves and vultures; who found delight in waging savage war against one another; who caught and killed lovely creatures, such as beaver and otter, for no more than their skins. She could hardly have understood Sam Minard—for on a high mountain spine he would beat his chest in a raging storm and call on the Almighty to look down on the world he had made.

The next day Sam and Lotus brought three deer from the hills and built fires and jerked nearly all the flesh; and this Sam put in skin pouches and took to Kate's door. He wanted to touch her hair a moment, with palm or lips, before going so far away from her, but her attitude told him that she wanted him to get out of sight. And so without saying another word to her he took his wife and headed up the river. The cottonwood and aspen were putting on their yellow cloaks, the chokecherry its scarlet; the river, done with its goaded spring torments, was a broad flowing of clear waters, borne down from the highest mountains. It was a beautiful day. A meadow lark was singing exquisitely in two octaves; mourning doves and owls foretold the coming of rain. When, having passed the big bend. Sam saw the far blue mists of mountains south of the Yellowstone, he told his wife that yonder were the Wolf and the Rosebud summits, and the northernmost summits of the Bighorns.

The ebullience of his emotions, spilling all day long into spontaneous enthusiasms, or into song, was new to her. Her people were emotional but they didn't exclaim with delight over such things as flowers, the swift sudden dive of a dabchick, the strange dusk-sounds of the snipe's tail feathers, the juicy ripe flavor of a wild plum, the wing markings on what he said was a swallow-tailed butterfly, a badger's footprints. After they swam the Yellowstone they were out of Blackfeet country, and she thought her man seemed to feel that he had no enemies. He would burst into song. He would shout at her to draw her attention to the things around her. "There!" he said, pointing to the blue-and purple belt of peaks lying east and north of the Bighorns. She looked, and saw only mountains and mist and distance. A map of the whole vast sweep of it was in Sam's mind—the Yellowstone, Bighorn, Wind, Powder, Green, Snake and a dozen other rivers, and all their valleys; and the Little Snake, the Yampah, the Uintahs, and a hundred more. He had decided to stop long enough to say hello to Bill Williams, if he could find the sly lean old codger, holed up in some thicket between Medicine and Bald mountains. From the Bighorn River, which he had been following upstream from its junction with the Little Bighorn, he turned east; and pointing to two peaks, he said to Lotus, "Somewhere between them, if he isn't dead yet." Bill was not dead and he was not asleep. Early in the morning two days later Sam was walking and leading his beasts, as he pushed his way through tangles and thickets, when suddenly a high shrill voice cried, "Do ye hear now? I wuz nigh to givin ye hell, I was. If I didden think ye wuz a Blackfoot after my topknot I'm a lyun nigger, I shorely be."

A moment later there he came, tall, cadaverous, gangling, a rifle across his arms and his right hand on the trigger guard, his bright almost glittering gray eyes peering out under shaggy brows. The face Lotus saw had a long thin nose, lean bearded cheeks, and a narrow forehead with veins standing out in the temples. He had a high-pitched, almost whining voice that made some men think he was crying. Around his waist hung a lot of contraptions, including a queer-looking bullet mold, an awl with a deerhorn handle in a sheath of cherrywood, hand-carved by him, and a vial made from the tip of an antelope horn in which, in season, he carried his castor bait. Bill had begun life as a Methodist preacher in Missouri, but (according to his story) every time he appeared at the church door the roosters shouted, "Hyar comes Parson Williams! One of us goes inter the kittle today." One morning when preaching at his fervent best a girl in a front seat got his mind so mixed up that he kallated he wasn't born for preaching. He took his gun and headed west.

"Wall, tie up my boudins!" he said, ambling over. "If it ain't Sam Minard. And who is this here red filly?"

"My wife, Bill. Mrs. Samson John Minard, the most beautiful woman in the world."

"Wall now," said Bill, squinting his small keen eyes at the girl. "If this nigger sees good she doan look bad a-tall. Where fer be ye headin?"

"Uintahs. I need four or five packs, for I have a wife to support now."

"They cost, I've heard. Ye best spend a night with me, I reckon. I have some of Hank Cady's huckleberry preserves and the best buffler hump ye ever tasted."

They spent the night with Bill. After supper the men and the girl sat by a small fire and Lotus looked at Bill most of the time, for he was spinning tall yarns and his facial mannerisms fascinated her. If Sam asked a question that touched Bill's emotions the sunken face would turn grave, the eyes would narrow to slits of light, and Bill would knock the pipe out and fill and light it before uttering another word.

"Ivar Carlsson, ye say? That be a sad tale, Sam. We wuz huntin lass spring, it was over on Shields River. Wall now, I dotta knowed better, I'll be dogged if I shooden. That time a year the Blackfeet is all over the place. I tell ye, Sam, Ivar wuz as full of arrows as a porkypine, with one stickin plum through both cheeks, another stuck deep in his meat bag, and six or seven in his hump ribs. I tuk them out but it was like butcherin him almost; but he war a mountain man—waugh!—and he never give off more than one little grunt; and I'll be dogged that wuz when I cut the arrow outta his boudins. That one was so deep I could feel the pint against his backbone. Of course the one stuck through his cheeks I jist whacked the head offen it and pulled it back out; but the one in his meat bag it was plum buried too, and that doggoned one in his boudins. I had to slice him open so I could git inside. . . ."

Listening to Bill's high-pitched words, Sam's mind went back to a blizzard three years ago, when he had spent a night with Bill on the headwaters of Bear River, near Sublette Mountain. About forty feet from their fire had stood Bill's old grayed-over and grizzled pack mule. Its guts filled with Western bunch grass and cottonwood bark, it stood, half dead with cold and age, and sound asleep over its picket pin, its limbs drawn a little under it, its rump in the blizzard, the stark bone of its back arched in the driven sleet, the whole weathered skinny carcass wavering a little from side to side, as, disturbed in its slumber, it opened its eyes a narrow slit to survey the storm. Now and then Bill had looked round him with piercing intentness at the driven white winds but always in the end his gaze came back to his faithful mule; and at last he had risen to his creaking legs and said, "I'll be dogged iffen I doan think I'd best put a robe over Balaam. It ain't as warm here as it wuz in Moab and he do seem to be shiverun powerful hard."

"Ivar live?" Sam asked at last.

"I'll be dogged if he didden. But didden ole Hugh Glass live? It takes a lot, me boy, ta kill a mountain man."

For breakfast Bill gave them what the mountain men called French dumplings. After mincing buffalo tenderloin and hump with marrow and hump fat, and rolling it into balls and covering these with flour dough, he simmered and fried the dumplings in marrow. Sam swore that he had never eaten a better breakfast. The hot biscuits he spread with Hank's huckleberry preserves, and with biscuit filling one cheek and dumpling the other he listened to Bill's yarns and drank two pint cups of hot black coffee. He smoked two pipes before bringing his beasts in.

"Bill," he said, falling into mountain-man argot, "ye git down our way this fall we'll set up sich a doggoned feast it'll make ya give up cookin."

"Wall now, I spect ye would. How about Christmas dinner?"

Sam would not expect him for Christmas or for any other time. He knew that old Bill Williams was a loner who never visited any man, but took his solitary way from hideout to hideout.

"Watch yer topknot," Sam said when he was ready to take off.

"Watch yourn," said Bill.

Three and half years later, when the mountain snows were beginning to melt, Bill was found sitting upright against a tree, frozen stiff, a bullet through his heart. His rifle was gone but across his lap was an old broken gun that his assassin had left in its place.

9

THE STORM foretold by the doves and owls came in shocking fury when they were still in the foothills of the Bighorn Mountains. The moment the first drops kissed his cheeks Sam stopped and dismounted and stripped off all his clothes. He knew that this storm would be a champion. Seeing what her man did and knowing the reason, Lotus slipped off her horse and did likewise. The leather garments of both Sam put inside a rainproof pouch. The mountain men told stories of greenhorns dressed in leather and caught in heavy downpours who had then ridden into hot sun, only to find an hour or two later that the leather on them was tighter than their own skins. It had to be cut off. Looking up to study the sky, Sam was sure that this would be one of the Almighty's finest thunder-symphonies.

As they rode along, both completely naked, with the first large raindrops caressing their skins, Sam began to sing, howling into the storm his admiration of the Creator, whose genius had wrought such marvels. Of a storm in Beethoven's pastoral symphony a musician had said that it was more than a storm; it was a cataclysm, a stupendous convulsion of all the powers; but for Sam it was nothing compared to what he had heard in these mountains. Beethoven had hardly done more than whisper among the aspens. Sam's spirit in such hours as this needed stronger music than any Beethoven or Bach or Vivaldi had dreamed of. He shouted his head off, knowing that once the conductor got the hang of things he would open with a prelude that would shake the earth. He thought of Blake's words, that music exults in immortal thoughts; but at its greatest reach, when the heavenly instruments flung down the grandeur of their thunders, music was a lament over what Thomas Browne had called the iniquity of oblivion—the lonely finality of death and the eternal night of the grave. But he was young today, and in love, and his naked bride was close behind him. He strove to improvise his mood, pouring forth wild baritone harmonies that dissolved into the winds. As the lightning's voice roared in awful grandeur, like a gigantic orchestra of drums and percussion, the sheets of fire set whole areas of sky aflame, and Sam became so intent on trying to become a part of it that for a little while he forgot the girl behind him. When he turned to look at her he knew that the storm was sounding the depths of her primitive emotions, for he could tell that she was singing. Lotus could not hear his words, except now and then, but she could see his imperious gestures, like those of a man using a pine tree for a baton; and she knew that he was lost in wild raptures. At first he had been concerned with the blandishments of the early raindrops and with tuning up his throat, but when the first crashing chords came he opened his soul to the sky and sent it forth on wings. If Lotus had had knowledge of whiteman's music she might have thought her man was improvising a rosalia: he was singing, "Rejoice, O My Heart!," climbing from key to key until his voice cracked and he doubled over coughing. He was a handsome figure—a big golden fellow on a black stallion, wet with rain, his hair flowing out into the wind that was rushing over him, his arms gesturing to the horns to come in, or the strings, as in fancy he herded the harmonies into overwhelming crescendo. Bushes and trees along the way were in such convulsions of frenzied joy that now and then one tore its roots free of the earth and went off into the sky and the thunders like a huge shaggy bird. "Hear! Hear!" Sam shouted, drenched now, his hair sopped and matted, the rain moving in a thin cool envelope down over his whole body and over the glossy pelt of his horse. The rain was also stirring the innumerable scents of the sweet earth, so that all the harmonies of rain music were infused with fragrance. It occured to him that an opera house ought to be drenched with sweet essences, instead of with the bad breath and body odors of a thousand overdressed creatures. Remembering again that his wife was behind him, he turned to look back; and her wet face and hair, her eyes shining like two black jewels, and her lips parted across white teeth were all such a picture of female loveliness that he stopped, slipped down, and went back to kiss her. "It's beautiful!" he cried in her ear, and kissed the wet ear. Then he kissed her wet leg that was next to him, and drawing the wet foot up, he kissed it.

The storm, he thought, was close to the climax of its overture. Lightning was now setting whole patches of sky afire; thunder was crashing in such chords that the earth trembled; but for him all this was only a potpourri of the themes, moving from allegro to vivace. He hoped it was so; no thunderstorm could be too violent for him. He now threw his arms wide, to embrace the whole wet world around him; again kissed his bride's leg and her foot; and bursting again with tempests of song, returned to his horse. His girl-wife, fascinated, soaked, and shivering a little, looked at his broad naked rain-swept back and wondered in her innocent Indian way if he was actually a man, or a spirit. He frightened her but in his presence she felt safe from enemies; for what a fountain of energy and courage he was, bellowing praise to the Great Spirit as he rode on and on in the deepest and darkest and wildest rainstorm his wife had ever known.

They rode on and on in the heavenly music of falling rain, and the whole atmosphere of earth was darkened to night. Lotus knew it was not night. Somewhere ahead the sun would be shining, and indeed it was shining just around and beyond the blue-and-purple belt. After riding for two hours in a downburst that seemed eager to wash all the mountains into the rivers they came to the outriding scarves and skirts of it, with sunlight making jewels of the countless raindrops clinging to trees and grasses. In this wonderland that was half rain mist and half sun glow they rode for another hour, and then were out of it. The storm was behind them, sweeping in a vast gloomy darkness across the Beartooth Pass. When Sam stopped, Lotus was the first to reach the earth. He went back and from the packhorse took their pouch of clothing; but then glanced at his wife, and finding her as supremely lovely as a caltha lily washed by rain and caressed by sun, he set the pouch aside and took her up, one arm under her knees, the other against the small of her back, and set her against his chest, with his lips to her shoulder. Then he held her away, so that she could turn her head to look at him; and for a few moments they looked into one another's eyes, without smiling.

"You know," he said, "I think we should have a feast."

She tried to look round her, for berries and roots.

After kissing over her body he set her down and looked off at the sun; it was an hour and a half high. After putting on his leather clothing he dug into a pack for dry cotton cloth to wipe his weapons. One reason he liked a storm like the one that had just swept over them was that then it was safe for a man to ride unarmed; no brave ever skulked around in such a deluge, but cowered in his miserable leaking tent while the sky raining dogs and cats scared him out of his wits, and every blast of thunder made him shake like a sick dog.

Dressed, they rode again, now in pale golden sunlight, with Sam's nostrils sniffing out the scents. He was as hungry as a wolf in forty-below weather and for his supper wanted buffalo hump and loin, though this was not best buffalo country. He might have to settle for elk steaks, or even antelope or deer. But on entering a grove of aspen he saw the kind of grouse that the trappers called fool hen, for the reason that these chickens seemed to have a little sense of enemies. He dismounted and ran among them with a long stick, knocking their heads off. They were plump and fat. Thinking that they would need at least eight for supper and a half dozen for breakfast, he kept after them, among the trees and up the hillside; and when he returned to the horses he had eleven. He saw that Lotus had hitched the beasts to a tree and gone. Was she after berries? No, she was after mushrooms, and in a few minutes she came in with a gallon of them. "Waugh!" cried Sam, looking at the white fat buttons. What a feast they would have! They would spit the chickens over an aspen or cherry fire; and under them in a kettle he would catch their juices, to use in basting them and to fry the mushrooms. While he was gathering firewood, Lotus, with revolver and knife at her waist, explored the thickets; returned with a quart of large ripe serviceberries; again disappeared, and came back with a dozen ripe red plums, wild onions, and a handful of fungus that she had stripped from a rotted tree stump.

"And what be that?" asked Sam, staring at the mold. He knew that Indians ate just about everything in the plant world, except such poisons as toadstools, larkspurs, and water parsnips. It was a marvel what they did with the common cattail—from spikes to root, they ate most of it. The spikes they boiled in salt water, if they had salt; of the pollen they made flour; of the stalk's core they made a kind of pudding; and the bulb sprouts on the ends of the roots they peeled and simmered.

Lotus was looking at him to see if he was pleased. To show her how pleased he was with such a resourceful wife he put his mouth organ to his lips, an arm round her waist, and began to waltz with her. The elder Johann Strauss's waltzes had been sweeping over Europe like an epidemic for years; in a letter last spring his father had written Sam that the younger Johann was even better, and was the rage of all the capitals. Sam found the three-fourths time just right for him, when in moccasins, with no floor but the leaf depth of an aspen grove. Around and around he went, his right arm controlling his wife, his left hand holding the harp to his lips. "Wall now!" he said, pausing at last; and lifting her as if she were a child, until her face was even with his own, he kissed her. "What a fine supper we'll have."

But the fungus bothered him. He knew that Indian women boiled tree mold and moss with buffalo beef, as white women boiled potatoes and cabbage; but he had found them tough and tasteless. A brave would open the end of a gall bladder and use the bile as a relish on raw liver; and warriors with an overpowering thirst for rum would get drunk by swigging down the contents of as many gall bladders as they could tear out of dead beasts.

Lotus went hunting a third time and returned with a few of the succulent roots that had saved John Colter's life. These Sam tossed among hot embers; later he would peel them and slice them and simmer them in grouse fat. He set on a pot of coffee. When the supper was ready he spread a robe for them to sit on, with their backs against an overhanging precipice of stone. The rifle at his side, revolver and knife at his waist, and his gaze on the only direction from which an enemy could approach, he rinsed his mouth with cold mountain water and began to eat. What more, he asked Lotus, did any fool want in this world? She asked what "fool" meant. "The King of England," he said. "The President of the United States. All fools, because money- or power-mad." They had never tasted such grouse. They never would. The world, he said, before sinking his teeth into half a breast and tearing it off, was full of vanity and vexation of spirit, as the Bible said; as well as of persons who didn't have enough get-up-and-gumption to go find their food, after their mothers had painted their nipples with aloes and tucked their breasts away. Feeding flesh and juices and hot mushrooms into his mouth, he told his staring wife that in no restaurant on earth could such fowl be found, or such mushrooms, or such odors of heaven in a place to eat, or such paintings as the magnificent sunset yonder, with two rainbows through it. Tomorrow they would have buffalo loin basted with boss; mushrooms simmered in marrow and hump fat; hot biscuits covered with crushed wild currants; and they would before long have buffalo tongue and beaver tail, and flapjacks shining with marrow fat like golden platters. Waugh! What a life they would have! It was a fine world, and they would eat and sing and love their way right through the best of it, like Breughel peasants on their way to heaven.

Pulling handfuls of grass to wipe his greasy beard, he turned to see how his wife was doing. He had eaten his third bird and taken up a fourth; she was still with her first. "Good?" he asked. Her eyes told him that it was good. What, he wondered, watching her, did the red people know about cooking? If hungry, they simply tore a beast open and shoved their heads in, like wolves; and after drinking the pool of blood in the bowl of fat under the kidneys, or burying his famished red face in the liver, as likely as not the Indian would then yank the guts out, and while with one hand he worked the contents of the gut down and away from him, with the other he would feed the gut into his mouth like a gray wet tube, which in fact it was, his eyes bulging ferociously as his ravenous hunger choked it down. As cooks the squaws—or the few he had observed, anyway—were filthy, by white standards. For the Indian nearly every live thing was food, including the flies and spiders and beetles that tumbled into the buffalo broth, or the moths and butterflies and grasshoppers, or even a chunk of meat that a dog had been chewing at. Sam would have said that he was not squeamish, but his appetite was never good when he sat at an Indian feast. After he had paid for his bride his father-in-law had set before him the boiled and roasted flesh of dogs, and though Sam had heard that Meriwether Lewis had preferred dog to elk steak or buffalo loin he had had to gag it down, as though he were eating cat. Well, there were white trappers who thought the cougar, a tough muscular killer, the finest of all meats.

Sam was aware from time to time that his wife was studying him. He did not know why. He did not know that Lotus felt there must be some fatal lack in her, or he would have ordered her to do the cooking and the chores. Among her people the husband was lord and king; he hunted and made war and beat his wife and that was about all that he did. Sam baffled her. At the beginning she had been suspicious of him, and a bit contemptuous, but his extreme gentleness in the intimacies, his thoughtfulness, his daily gathering of flowers for her, his making for her magnificent mantles to hang from her shoulders, his way of touching her and hovering like a colossus over her needs and welfare, had reached down to what was in all women, and found warmth and a home. He had fertilized and nourished in her an emotion that, if not love, was the next thing to it. She had even learned to like his cooking, as she had learned to like his embrace. When he looked at her now, holding his fourth bird, his eyes twinkling, she flashed a smile at him that parted over perfect teeth, wet with fool-hen grease. He ate five of the birds and she ate two, and they ate all the mushrooms and roots and berries, and drank a two-quart pot of coffee. With grass he wiped his beard and said he guessed he ought to shave the damned thing off, and then he filled his pipe.

When she felt round her for grass he watched her. Throughout the journey he had covertly watched her to see if she ate bugs. The Indians of some tribes, notably the Diggers, ate every insect they could find; it was a wonder, whitemen said, that there was a beetle or stinkbug or longlegs left in all the desert of the Humboldt. The Diggers seemed able to exist for weeks, months, even years on nothing but dried ants and their larvae. Sam had seen the miserable starved wretches in their filthy coyote skins plopping live ants, moths, crickets, and caterpillars into their mouths. He had watched squaws build a fire around a hill of big red ants, thrust a stick into the hill, hold a skin pouch at the top of the stick, and catch every ant in the hill, as they crawled up in three or four solid lines to escape from the flames. He had never seen a Flathead eat a bug; their food was chiefly small game, fish, roots, and wild fruits. He also watched his wife for signs of illness. All the trappers had heard the tale of the missionary who had told Indian people that their way of worshiping the Great Spirit was wrong. The Indians then sent four chiefs to St. Louis to learn the right way, and there they had sickened on whiteman's food and died. Lotus looked to Sam like a picture of perfect health, though one morning after drinking a cup of coffee she had slipped into the brush to vomit, and had returned looking faded and foolish.

"Smell it," Sam said, and drew in a long breath. What was it? Besides the odors of food and tobacco and coffee he could smell aspen and its berry bushes and grasses; geranium on the stone ledge above him; catnip in the palm of his left hand; and something that he was not able to identify. Rising, rifle across his arm, he began to prowl in the woods around him. Lotus saw him through the trees, sniffing, turning his head this way and that; bending low to peer at something on the ground; and at last falling to his knees and going on all fours like a beast. On returning he said, "Funny I didn't smell it before. Hank says when a man marries he loses half his sense and his enemies soon track him down." He was sniffing at a finger. "Crows," he said. "The Absaroka. This is Crow country. Over there they made a fire and burned some hair in it. That don't look good to this coon."

"Crow," said Lotus.

"A war party," said Sam. He brought his stallion in and staked him as a sentinel only fifty feet from his bed. Then he went east a mile or two over the path the Crows had taken, to scout the area. He and his wife had been in Crow country several days; most of the mountain men trusted the Crows but Sam trusted no redman. He was worried but he tried to hide his mood from Lotus.

The next morning at daylight they headed south, and about noon he saw a wolf and suspected that buffalo were not far away. A few minutes later he sat on a hilltop, overlooking a herd. Seeing among the big shaggy beasts some deer and antelope, he knew that packs of wolves had surrounded the herd, to drag down the young, the sick, the wounded, the old, and the stragglers. It was a habit with deer and antelope to seek safety in buffalo herds. This was a large herd, and as Sam studied it he was again impressed by the orderly manner in which a big herd, even a hundred thousand head, moved across the miles. On the other hand, a herd would stampede at no more than a shadow. The old-timers like Bill Williams said the herds put vedettes out, in the way of an army, to give the alarm if enemies approached—four or five young bulls that, on scenting the foe, would rush pell-mell straight for the herd.

The cows and calves would then move to the center and the bulls would surround them. In April and May, during calving time, the bulls went round and round the cows, to protect them from the wolves. In old age the bulls became abject victims of terror; all alone on a vast prairie a bull would give a feeble bellow when he saw wolves approaching, and the wolves would answer in concert.

While wondering if he was within rifle sound of Crow warriors it occurred to him that possibly this was the first herd of these beasts Lotus had ever seen. He turned to look at her face. What he saw there so riveted his attention that he could only stare. She was so lost in contemplation of the tens of thousands of beasts, making the prairie black as far as she could see, that she was unaware of him. Well, good Lord, she should see one of the big migrations, when a herd was a full hundred miles across, and extended to such depth that a man could only guess at the number. Williams and Bridger and other mountain men said they had seen herds of at least a million beasts, with ten thousand wolves around the circumference.

Did she like buffalo better than fish and rabbit? Did he dare have tenderloin for supper? It was his favorite meat. Mick Boone was extremely fond of moose, if it was taken in its prime. Bear Paws Meek was a beaver-tail man; he swore that a tail, properly seasoned and expertly basted with wild goose oil, was the only food he would ask for in heaven. Cady preferred elk.

Sam examined his rifle and they rode forward until they were about three hundred yards from the nearest beasts. Again he studied them. He wanted a fat tender one and a swift clean kill. A buffalo, unless shot through the heart or brains or spine, took a lot of time to die. While sitting and watching he told Lotus his favorite story of a greenhorn. An especially choice lubber, callow and green, had fired eight or nine pistol balls into a bull and had then stood, nonplused and bug-eyed, while blood poured from the beast's nostrils. A practical joker had told the numskull to slip up from the rear and hamstring the bull. He could then cut its throat. Accepting the suggestion, the city tenderfoot had crept up behind the bull and stabbed at one of its hams with a knife. In that instant the beast exploded with fury, its nostrils spouting blood and foam for thirty feet. For some inexplicable reason the tenderfoot had seized the bull's short stiff tail, and the bull then whirled round and round at such speed that the man clinging to its tail was flung off his feet and laid out on the air; and round and round he went, his eyes popped out like glazed marbles, his voice begging for help. Then the bull dropped dead. The thing that had scared the daylights out of him, the greenhorn afterward confessed, was his fear that the tail would pull out or break off.

Telling Lotus to be alert, Sam left her and slipped forward, until he was only forty yards from a young barren cow. He shot it through the heart and was cutting its throat when Lotus came forward. Sam rolled the beast over to its belly and pulled the four legs out like broken braces to prop it. He made an incision from the boss to the tail and skinned the heavy hide back both ways. Entering a side, he cut the liver free and drew it out. Laying it across the cow's back, he sliced off several morsels, offered one to Lotus on the point of his knife, and plopped one into his mouth. As Lotus chewed her black eyes smiled at him. When going to a pannier for his hatchet Sam had to kick a coyote out of his path and chase a dozen into the distance. Coyotes were a worse nuisance than flies when a man was butchering. They would come in close, while the wolves, farther out, trotted back and forth, drooling. If you threw a piece of flesh to a coyote the idiot instead of eating it would make off with it, and the wolves would pounce on it and tear the meat from its jaws. It sometimes looked as if the coyote was the half-witted lackey of its larger and more ferocious cousin. Both beasts were also a camp nuisance. They would slink into a camp and chew saddles and bridles and leather clothing, and had been known to eat a part of the moccasins off a sleeping man's feet.

Pausing every few moments to look round him for enemies, Sam chopped the ribs in two along both sides, and the spine in two, back and front, so that he could lift out the choicest portion of the tenderloin. That ought to do them for supper, he said. Lotus had been looking round for edible roots, and came in with an armful of lupine and two dozen mushrooms. Sam looked hard at the lupine. The camas root he had eaten, after it was pounded into flour and mixed with water to make flat dough-cakes, which were then baked over hot stones. The onion bulb, or poh-poh, made into a thick jelly, was even more tasteless than the camas, or the skunk cabbage, mixed with the inner bark of pine or hemlock. He preferred cakes made of sunflower or buffalo and blue grama grass seeds. He had never eaten the lupine root.

Lotus went off again and returned with a quart of the blue-purple chokecherries. Sam made a face at them, for they puckered the hell out of a person's mouth. Knowing how he prepared mushrooms, Lotus made incisions in their plump bellies, stuffed inside each a blob of marrow fat, and set the buttons on their backs in an inch of hot hump fat. When they were turned to a nice golden brown and the steaks were hot and dripping and the sliced lupine roots were sizzling in a platter of fat and the coffee was steaming Sam looked up at the sky, for this was his way of saying grace before a meal. Every time he feasted he thanked the Giver of the earth's fantastic abundance.

"No taxes," he said. He had uttered these words so many times that Lotus now said, "No taxes."

"No jails."

"No jails."

The steaks were as tender as young Canada goose. The mushrooms melted in his mouth. Even the lupine tasted fine.

"Good?" he asked.

"Good," she said, gravely nodding.

Sam chose a fat golden mushroom and offered it to her on the point of a green stick. She opened her mouth in a pucker, sucked the mushroom in, and closed her eyes. He fed her choice morsels of steak, knowing all the while that she was abashed by these little gallantries. Instead of feeding their wives delicious morsels the red husbands as likely as not kicked them away from the fire and left for them only the scraps of the feast. Still, most of the squaws were fat, and Lotus, it seemed to him, had gained ten pounds since her wedding day.

Sam had cooked the whole tenderloin and half the liver. Raw liver and rose hips, the older mountain men said, were enough to keep any man healthy, if he also had pure water and air and a hard bed. Some of them ate a lot of yarrow, including its white flowers when it was blooming; as well as the onion bulb, the thorn apple, pine nuts, watercress, and viscera besides liver. Sam had watched red women in the Snake River country shake chilled grasshoppers off sagebrush into baskets, in cold September mornings, and roast them in pits and pound them into cakes, as well as crickets, mice, snakes, wood ticks, and ants. He had seen them thicken soup with these things, and though Bill Williams said they were all fine Sam had refused to taste them. Just the same, Bill could outwalk any man in the country, and go for two or three days and nights without food, sleep, or rest.

After they had eaten and Sam had smoked a pipe they both set to work on the buffalo hide. Stretching it flat on the earth, fur side down, with knives and stone chisels they took off every last particle of the flesh and fat. While Lotus boiled this flesh and fat into a thick gelatinous soup, Sam opened the skull and took out the brains. He then turned the task over to his wife, for the reason that no man seemed to have a woman's intuitive skills in making fine leathers and robes of the skins of beasts. Sam sat back, rifle across his arm, and smoked another pipe while drinking another cup of coffee.

What a beautiful evening, and what a wonderful life it was! He hoped he would live to be a hundred years old.

10

NEVER HAD SAM been so happy as on this long journey south; he would never be as happy again. He so loved them that he found delight in telling her the name of every mountain range, peak, river, creek, valley, and landmark they passed, or could see in the distance—Yellowstone, Powder River, Meadowlark Lake, Sun River Creek, Tongue River, Rosebud Creek, Papoose Peak, Black Panther Creek, Absaroka Summit, Little Goose Pass, South Pass—he loved them all, for in his soul they were like the call of the French horn in a Mozart concerto.

Side by side when eating or sleeping or riding Sam told her about the men he had met since coming west—Three-Finger McNees, a tall slender man as straight as a lodgepole, with coarse black hair and beard, a grave mien, and one eye cocked off at an angle of forty-five degrees from the other. He was a tough critter in a fight—and so was Lost-Skelp Dan, a muscular scowling giant who kept putting a hand back over his hideless skull, as though to brush his hair. Lord, how he hated the redmen! It was Dan's ambition to scalp a thousand—and he didn't take off a mere topknot, but the hull thing, as Bill would say, clear down to the ears and halfway to the eyebrows. She would see Jim Bridger soon; except Kit Carson, he was about the most famous of them all, unless it was old Caleb Greenwood or Solomon Silver or Moses Harris or Jim Clyman. Not all of those were free trappers. The free trappers were a clan of their own, and man for man could lick any gang on earth or in all the spaces beyond.

Jim Bridger was probably the biggest liar in the whole pack. Though it was said that he could neither read nor write, and talked as if he had found his English in an Indian tepee, he dearly loved to spill his chin music and spin his yarns, especially if greenhorns were listening. He loved to tell the lubbers from back east that he had once run for his life with three hundred tall Cheyennes after him; that he came to trees and clum, and fell down and clum other trees; crawled out on a limb and found it as full of redskins as a blooming chokecherry with honey bees; fell plum to the ground and clum other trees, till his hands were gummed over an inch deep with sticky pine sap. But he kept running and came at last to a canyon that narrered and narrered and closed down to a pinch that a spider couldn't get through; and there he was, with three hundred red devils swarming over him, and arrers falling as thick as pine needles in a hurrycane. At that point Jim would stop. The bug-eyed greenhorns, mouths agape, cheeks twitching, would stare at him; and in a hoarse whisper one would ask, "What happened, Mr. Bridger?" In a weary old voice Bridger would say, "They kilt me."

Another of Jim's favorite talks to novices was about a panther, which he called a painter. He was hunting elk on the flanks of Battle Mountain, when suddenly out of a thicket came a painter, to study him with cold green eyes, while the tail moved back and forth. Jim had felt awful oneasy; jist lookin at the critter made him shiver and shake, for he kallated that the painter was sizing up his dinner. "Nice ole feller," Jim said to him, and made like he was dying to stroke and pat him. But with a flip and a flop and two somersaults the painter was right in front of him, his mouth open four feet wide. His teeth were as long as Bowie knives. There was nothing to do but reach into the mouth and down torst the tail and grab it, and quicker than a wink turn him inside out. He was then headed in another direction, and figgerun that Jim had jist took off, he sailed out of sight. "When one of the greenhorns said, 'Aw shucks,' it kinda dawned on me that he thought Jim wasn't exactly telling the truth."

He guessed maybe she had never heard of old Caleb Greenwood. Caleb said the bravest of all the red people were the Crows, but then he was prejudiced, for he had married one, named Batchicka. She was not a mere winter squaw, as so many red women were for whitemen, but a fine year-round work-plug. The truth was that Caleb had loved his wife and his five sons and two daughters.

One son and one daughter they would have, Sam said, patting his wife's belly.

The Caleb-Batchicka relationship had touched Sam's sentimental soul. In his late seventies Caleb became almost blind, and when all the Indian medicines failed him he asked his wife to take him to St. Louis. For weeks she had shot buffalo and jerked the flesh, dried fruits, gathered roots, and made leather clothing for all of them. Then, with her husband and all the children but the oldest son, she had climbed into a canoe and headed down the river. In Siouxland they were attacked by a horde of shrieking warriors, most of whom plunged into the river and swam toward them, bent on plunder; but when Batchicka laid open the skull of one with a canoe paddle the others went howling to the bank. Learning somehow that her man was blind and helpless, the braves so admired the woman's courage that they gave her safe passage down the river. In St. Louis, Caleb had had growths removed from both eyes and had come with his family back up the river. Now somewhere in his eighties he was kicking as hard as ever.

Sam wondered what the white people back east, with their turbid feculent rivers and garbage dumps, would think of Caleb's love for a squaw, or Loretto's, or his, or Kit Carson's for Maria Josefa Jaramillo. After telling Lotus about Caleb and Batchicka, Sam felt a bit choked up. Slipping down, he put his arms around his wife as she sat on her horse; and she looked down at him with strange and wonderful things in her eyes. He looked up to meet her gaze (this had become a habit with them) and they looked into the eyes of one another, without smiling or speaking.

If he went blind, Sam said, in words and signs, would she take him down the river?

"Yes," she said.

"Make pemmican?"

"Yes."

"Kill my enemies?"

"Yes."

"You love me?" She knew the words but she didn't know what love meant.

"Yes," she said.

Sam hugged her, his face pressed to her belly. "I love you," he said, and mounted his horse.

When they came to a beast that had been killed Sam examined it, with Lotus at his side. He said he could usually tell the kind of killer. The wolf nearly always attacked buffalo, elk, deer, and antelope in the flank or ham; the mountain lion seized the throat of larger beasts, and wrenching the head around, broke the neck; the grizzly left the marks of its terrible claws. Of them all, the wolf for its size had the strongest jaws and teeth. Whitemen, he told her, had a small dog called a terrier; it would attack a wolf or a whole pack of wolves. He had once seen wolves literally tear a terrier in two, as he had seen a grizzly tear a badger in two. Whitemen had a larger dog, part staghound, part bull, that could kill a wolf, or even two or three, in a fight. The wolf was such a powerful beast that it had been known to drag an eighteen-pound trap, attached to a forepaw, for twenty-five miles in a few hours—and at the end of that time had enough stamina left to outrun a man and disappear.

With boyish pride in all the things he had learned in seven years Sam halted to show her a scent post and the furrows in the earth left by claws. After voiding its urine against the tree the wolf had scratched the earth, in the foolish way of the dog family. There was its run, he said, pointing; it was always in fairly open country—the bottoms of canyons, dry ravines, the lowest saddles across divides. The only unfailing scent-lure for a wolf was the scrapings from a scent post, taken far from the wolf run where the trap was to be set. Unfamiliar wolf urine caused a male wolf to tremble with excitement and run round and round, sniffing and snapping, and stepping at last on the hidden plate of the trap. Sam told her that while he was gone from her this winter, wolves might bivouac her and try to bring down her horse. He would show her how to trap them. She would kill a rabbit and wet her hands in its blood; she would cut the rabbit in small pieces and scatter it over an area as large as her father's village; and in the center of it she would set the trap just below the level of the snow and put a thin covering of snow over the plate.

Sam talked to her about these things after they had gone to bed, trying to foresee all the possible dangers. He would build a corral for her pony but if she did not watch out the wolves would sneak into it to chew the leather hobbles, or to hamstring the beast and bring it down. For an unknown reason the wolf had a great fondness for horseflesh. Folding one of her small hands into a big palm and sniffing the night air for scent of an enemy, he would talk to her until she fell asleep. His sense of kinship with all the wild things of nature was so strong in him that he wanted his wife to share it; to know the ways of the water ouzel, sandpiper, kildeer, and flicker; the songs of birds, such as the plover's, the two notes of which were the two g's on the flute stop of a pipe organ; or such as the meadow lark's, for it seemed to him that in the lower of two keys it stated the theme and expressed it again in a higher key. With his mouth organ he tried to imitate the songs of birds, and at last, thinking of himself as a man with many blessings , he would fall asleep.

He did not want Lotus ever to know about a whiteman's cities and way of life. Even a trading post was so crowded, and so rank with human odors, that he was glad when his exchanges were made and he could get away, alone and free, into the vastness. The big trapping companies had so debauched the red people with rum that drunkenness, which Sam abhorred, was rife at the post; red warriors were sprawled everywhere, their black eyes out of focus and their rum-sotted minds busy with evil plots. Sam had heard that some of the company traders put narcotics in the rum and that the drugs filled the redmen with such wild lunacies that on one occasion they roasted a trader alive on his own fire, thrusting a sapling through his body and suspending it from two tripods, so that it could be turned over and over in the flames like a haunch of venison. Sam had seen stone-drunk braves dragged by their heels out of trading posts and scattered over a half acre of ground, until it was literally covered with them. He had seen haughty warriors sitting under sun shelters, which their old limping discarded wives had been forced to build for them—sitting, half drunk, with their young beauties, while the old crones hustled around, trying to steal more rum for their lords, or with their bodies buy more. In front of each arrogant red prince stood a tripod, on which were his shield, bow and quiver, medicine bag and pipe. The Indian male was so innocent and gullible that when giving him rum in exchange for pelts the white trader could let three or four fingers slip down into the cup, to displace that much liquor; or he would actually put melted suet in the cup to the depth of half an inch and let it harden before pouring rum in. As the redman got drunker the whiteman would dilute the rum, until at last it was one part rum and ten parts river water. Sam had watched drunken warriors gamble at the game of Which Hand, until one owned all the horses and clothing and weapons, and the other sat stark-naked, wondering what else they could find to wager.

To impress his wife with the way thousands of immigrants were pushing into the Western lands, to overrun the homes of the red people, Sam had wanted to show a few landmarks, such as Independence Rock in the lovely valley of the Sweetwater, a river that at first was not *Eau Douce* but *Eau Sucrée*, because a packload of sugar had been lost in it. The great granite table was two thousand feet long and almost two hundred feet high, and would eventually have, Sam supposed, at least a hundred thousand Mormon names chiseled on its top, eighty thousand of whom would be polygamous wives. But he had decided to go far west of the Rock, for he was on his way to Bridger's post. He had wanted to show her Scotts Bluff, after telling her the story of another brave man.

A party of trappers coming down the Platte had capsized their canoe and lost practically all their supplies, including their powder. Defenseless in enemy land, they had given way to panic. One of them, a man named Scott, had become too ill to walk, and the others, pretending they were only going over the hills to find food for him, abandoned him on the river bank. What had been his thoughts after he realized the cowards had deserted him? Even after the fleeing party had overtaken an armed group of whitemen they did not mention the sick man they had left to die, but said that Scott had died and they had buried him. The next year some of the men in that armed group came back up the river and found the skeleton. It was plain to them that Scott had crawled on his hands and knees for more than forty miles, in a pathetic and desperate effort to overtake the cowards who had left him. Hugh Glass had crawled farther than that, with maggots swarming in his wounds—digging in the earth for roots, chewing on old bones, all the way to Fort Kiowa on the Missouri, his soul burning on the one thought of vengeance. Would Sam Minard ever dedicate his life to vengeance? He could see no likelihood of that, but he was not looking very clearly into the future.

When they came to the Oregon Trail Sam halted for an hour and looked east and west. Most of the Indian tribes now believed that before long swarming masses of humanity would overflow this magnificent land and drive the red people from their homes. Did they also foresee that hundreds of beautiful rivers and creeks would be polluted? Now a man could lie on his belly and drink the pure waters of any of them, except those in alkali wastes, like the Humboldt; but there were no pure waters where man pushed up his cities and scattered his filth. What an unsightly country it would all be someday!—with its unplanned mushrooming cities, the stink and belching dark of thousands of smokestacks, the paralyzing poisons of sewers and clutter of vast junkyards. He guessed the few men who needed space and freedom as they needed air would move north to Canada; and again north, until on the whole earth there would be no broad clean land to go to, but only the litter and stench and ugliness that the swarming billions would make of the earth.

Going over to the Trail, he looked curiously at the wheel ruts. Within the past week a wagon train had squealed and churned along these ruts, with dusty unclean women clutching their whimpering children under the canvas tops, their eyes staring past the bent backs of the drivers at the country ahead. Week after week and mile after mile they pushed on and on. Arriving at Bridger's post on Black's Fork of Green River, Sam learned that the Mormons hadn't come, and was feeling relief when Bridger said, "They kallate next spring. They're on the Meesouri now, ole Brigham and his thousan wives, holed up fer the winter."

"All the Mormons?"

"The hull shittaree, thousans and thousans."

"Going where?"

"Only God and Brigham knows."

"And all with more than one wife?"

Look alive, said Jim; had any but the bosses had more than one, in the Bible or anywhere? Brigham, they said, had fifty mebbe; the one next to him mebbe forty-five, and the next forty, and so on down to the corporal, who mebbe had two.

A man could never tell when Jim Bridger was serious.

That was a fine filly Sam had, he said, his strange eyes (they looked gray but flecked with tiny pieces of bright steel) sizing up Lotus. At this post Sam bought on credit, against next spring's beaver packs. He bought a fast horse for his wife; and a good rifle and a Bowie, and plenty of powder and ball, as well as cooking utensils, a half dozen three-point blankets, awls, needles, and thread; for he would be away trapping and she would be making leather clothing for the three of them.

"Ya mean ya intend ta leave her alone?" asked Jim, narrowing his eyes at Sam.

"In the cabin on the Little Snake," Sam said.

"All winter?"

"She'll have a fast horse," Sam said. "She shoots well. Besides, no red varmints ever go away down there."

How did Sam know he hadn't been watched in his journey all the way south? How did he know how many red devils had smelled along his tracks? By God, he would think it over, Jim said; you never could tell where the red varmints would show up, or when. After Sam was ready to go, and Jim had told him to watch his topknot, Jim said again, "You better think it over." The words troubled Sam, for he knew that in all the West there was no man more Indian-wise than Jim Bridger. But he looked at his wife and thought, she'll be all right.

With Lotus on her new pony, a strong spirited sorrel with a blazed face, and with two laden packhorses, Sam headed into the southeast. It was desolate country, with mountains in the far distance. It was yonder on a branch of the Yampah, that Henry Fraeb and Jim Bridger had built a post; and it had been there only five or six years ago that Henry and four of his men had been killed in a battle with the Sioux. Possibly Jim had this battle in mind when he told Sam to think it over. Sam had been twice to the Uintahs to trap; so far as he knew, no Indians ever came as far south as the Little Snake in the wintertime.

When they came close to the mountains Sam and Lotus killed four deer, jerked the flesh and rode on. He had seen his wife looking back now and then, back into the long misty distance out of which they had come. Was she homesick for her people? Did she wonder why her man came so far to find trapping? He had tried to explain it to her: there was good trapping in areas up north but it was staked out by the older men. There was a cabin away down there, plenty of game within rifle reach, and an abundance of food for her horse. In the cabin she could be warm and safe and busy with her needles. Little Snake country was almost a no man's land: west beyond the mountains were the friendly Eutaws; northwest were the Snakes, but far away. The Blackfeet were to hell and gone a thousand miles up north, the Crows, Cheyennes, Comanches, and Arapahoes all far away. A war party from any of these tribes might kill her for her horse and weapons but he was sure that none would come away down south after the heavy snows fell. And he was sure that no scouts had seen them on their long ride down. Trapping in the Uintahs would be very good and fast; he might come out with five packs, even six. Back in there he'd not have to watch for enemies day and night, and so could get a lot done. Lotus had said she wanted to go with him and help him but he felt that he ought to be firm; as a husband he'd be no better than a Digger if he took a pregnant wife to the high mountain meadows and subzero cold, with no place for a bed but the earth under a fir tree. He was deep in debt now; he had a wife and would soon have a child. It was time to strap on his medicine bag and go.

The cabin to which he took Lotus was about like the one he had built on the Musselshell. On the wind side of it he now put up a small corral and a storm shelter for her pony; with her help he gathered a lot of meadow grass for the horse and this he piled against the cabin where the coldest winds would strike. He dragged in a lot of firewood. Every day he gave her lessons in firing her gun, and before long she could ride into the hills and within two hours bring back a deer. They jerked enough meat to feed her until the following May. He told her, over and over, never to go far from the cabin after the deep snows came. A piece of chinking in a wall he shaped so that she could remove it in an instant, and thrust her rifle barrel through. Again and again he pointed to the mountains in the west and said he would be there, working hard in every daylight hour and until long after dark. He would be thinking of her all day and dreaming of her all night.

After a week or two at the cabin he learned that she was pregnant; he put her right cheek against his beating heart and held her close. God Almighty, now he would have a son, to ride the swiftest and shoot the straightest of any man in the mountains! When would it be born? He counted off the months: in May perhaps, or June: somewhere along there. This night he held her nightlong and the next day he looked round him for other things to do, to make her cozy and safe. Possibly in sunny weather she would like to sit by the doorway and look into the west where he would be; so he brought a piece of thick log for her to sit on. They were sitting on it one evening when, abruptly, she rose and sat on his lap and looked steadily and gravely into his eyes. Her gaze was so searching that he was troubled. Did she think he intended to abandon her? Surrendering to a great gush of tenderness that poured through him and warmed him all over, he drew her close and murmured promises and endearments in her ear. "I will never leave you," he said. "Not in all the years of my life—never, never. I will come back," he said over and over. He would return with many packs of fine pelts, so that next summer they could pay their debt and have money to buy things for the following winter, and for their son. In all the languages he knew he told her that rather than doubt his return she should doubt that the sun would rise or the snows fall. He framed her face and kissed her forehead, eyelids, cheeks, lips, and the leather jacket over her breasts. Looking into her eyes, he said, "I love you, I need you, I will never leave you." With a quick impulsive movement she touched her lips to the point of his nose and said, "I love you." His heart leapt. Had he, then, after all, won this strange girl from a strange people? He said he wanted to take with him a lock of her hair, and from the back of her head, above the nape, he took a lock, and kissed it and held it to his lips. He stretched it out and thought it two feet long; her hair when down hung below her waist. Round and round a forefinger he wound the hair, and kissed it, and pressed it to her lips; and then tucked it away under his leather shirt. She had watched him as though a little astonished. Had an Indian husband anywhere in the world ever taken a lock of his woman's hair, to cherish through a long lonely winter?

He told himself a thousand times that she would be all right while he was away. Indian women, unlike the white, did not have to have doctors and nurses and a ton of medicines. The child would not be born before his return. She would be all right. He would come riding in from the mountains with both packhorses loaded with pelts from their manes to their tails. The cabin had no windows; he had fixed the door so that she could bar it; and he told her over and over, a dozen times, always to carry the knife in her belt, a revolver at her waist, and keep her rifle within reach. He had told her what the woman on the Musselshell had done with an axe. Lotus had a good axe and she must keep it always just inside her door. He thought it would be safe for her to fire her gun any time the wind was from the north; but she had plenty of jerked meat, and flour, dried fruits, roots, coffee, sugar; she had plenty of wood, plenty of bedding, and more than enough skins to keep her busy. The nearest Indian was two hundred miles away. She would be all right.

Nevertheless, during his last days and nights with her he did not act like a husband who thought his wife would be all right. Her courage had deeply touched him: hardly more than a child, and a long way from her people, she had given him no sign at all that she was afraid. He had also been moved when, seeing her at last for the remarkable person she was, he understood what an ordeal it must have been for her to go with him. He would then take her to his lap and hold her, and debate with himself whether she should go with him or stay here. But then he would see her seven or eight months pregnant in the high cold mountains, and riding a horse out not long before her child would come; he would see her with no roof over her, alone all day while he walked miles and miles on his traplines; and he would convince himself again that it would be best for her to remain here. Trying to follow him from trap to trap, she would wear herself out. It would be bad for the child. She might become sick. . . . He was still debating the matter back and forth when the November morning came that he had set for his departure. It was snowing, a deep quiet storm, in which nothing was visible but the millions of swirling flakes as big as dollars. He saddled his stud and the packhorses and hitched them to the corral. He then went to his wife, who had been standing in the doorway, looking at him and at the storm into which he would disappear. There was no sign of mountains and river now.

He shook snow off his leather coat, slapped across his belly and thighs, and said the Almighty had more ways of making the earth lovely than mortal man could have thought of. He was trying to be cheerful but he felt the loneliest he had ever felt since saying good-bye to his people. He stood by her and together they looked up at the marvelous dusk of flakes. Then he took her in his arms and kissed over her hair and face; bent to kiss the leather over her belly; and held her close for a full five minutes.

Then suddenly in an instant he took his farewell, as he had taken it from his people, and was gone. He was on his stallion, with the packline in hand, riding away into the snows. Lotus stood looking after him as long as he was in sight, and long after he was gone. For more than an hour she stood there, looking into the gloom. Was she thinking that he had abandoned her, in this strange lonely land almost a thousand miles from her people—that she ought to leap on her pony and head north, to the Bitterroots and home? Whatever she was thinking or feeling, there was little sign of it in her lovely face. A white girl of her age might have broken down and run crying after her man; this girl, after looking for an hour at the gloom into which her husband had vanished, went to the corral to hear the breathing of her pony. She glanced down at the knife in her belt, the revolver at her waist; and then with a start thought of her rifle and hastened into the cabin to get it. She carefully examined the priming. She looked up the river, the direction from which her enemies would come, if they came. She then crawled between two poles and went over to her horse, and leaning the rifle against her with the stock between her feet, she looked at the pony's quiet eyes. She put her right hand under its jaw and to its right cheek, and her right cheek to its left cheek, and stood there while the storm turned her and the pony and the cabin and everything a pure mountain-winter white.

PART TWO

KATE

11

IT WAS LATE April in 1847 when Sam Minard came down from the mountains. Peltwise, he had had a full winter; he had found more top-quality beaver in one group of streams than he had ever found before. From the first week of his arrival he had trapped but his finest pelts had been taken in February and March. He had trapped all day long, every day of the month, and even in nighttime when the moon was full. Of first-class pelts, called a` plus, and pronounced by the mountain men plew, he had two and a half packs; of inferior pelts he had almost three packs; and he had about fifty otter.

A typical day for him had run like this. At daylight he had stirred in his blankets and robes, back under the low branches of a pine, and had crawled out until he could stand. He came out of bed fully clothed. He had had no such feasts as he had had on the journey with his wife; his meat was jerked venison, lean elk, beaver tail, muskrat, together with flour and coffee. Sometimes a whole week passed with no fire. He was simply too busy. Working over the graining blocks and stretching frames took a lot of time. Every day he had to move his horses to spots where they could find forage, either along streams or in mountain meadows, where they could paw down through three or four feet of snow to old grasses. He spent hundreds of hours at the tiresome and painstaking task of dubbing—that is, of removing with pieces of sharpened elkhorn or obsidian the fat, flesh, and blood from the pelts. He walked hundreds of miles back and forth on the streams, setting his traps and bringing the pelts in. Once in a while he made a fire and roasted a couple of beaver tails and made a pot of coffee. He took time to fill his pipe now and then. He had thought a great deal about his wife and had worried about her; he had had dreams about her that troubled him. As spring drew near his worry became so chronic that he almost burst from the mountains to learn if she was all right.

When at last he fought his way out, along streams, over elk snowpaths, or over paths which he had to break for his beasts, he tried to think of something at the posts which he could buy for her. If she was like most Indian women she would want brightly colored cloths, beads, ornaments, and ribbons for her hair; he hoped she would prefer a handsome saddle, with bridle and trimmings to match. He had a picture of her dressed like a Crow warrior in the finest embroidered buckskin, with long tassels and fringes, and a gorgeous headdress, with its mass of feathers floating behind her in the wind. Their son would be in a saddle on her back, standing up, his bright fearless eyes fixed with astonishment on everything he passed. By the time he was four or five he would have his own pony and would learn to ride like a Crow; and he would have his own saddle, the finest, and his own buckskin clothing, with the prettiest beadwork the squaws could make. Sam liked to think of his son riding like a Crow not only because the Crows were the best horsemen in the world; they made excellent weapons and were the most formidable fighters on the plains. At leatherwork and embroidery there were no women to match the Absaroka—that is what the stupid French called them, the *gens des corbeaux*, the Absaroka, the Sparrowhawk people. The Crow warriors were so brave that they went boldly against any people who invaded their lands, including their ancient enemies, the Blackfeet; and they seemed to feel friendly toward the whitemen because the whitemen also loved to slaughter the ferocious Bloods and Piegans. The Crow nation boasted that it had never killed a white person or a friend of the white people; Sam was thinking of this boast as he followed the windbreaks down the canyons.

He was to think afterward that he had had a sense of it miles before he reached the cabin. He called it his enemy-sense. His enemy-sense would have prompted him in any case to make a wary approach. As mountain man and fatalist he had known all winter that his wife might be killed while he was away; that she *could* be killed—and indeed that he might be killed, by man or beast. Riding toward her, he told himself that he might be ambushed for the pelts he carried; there developed in him a feeling that Indians had been through this country since he rode away. His guard was up, his senses were alert, and a nausea of loss and loneliness was sinking from his mind down through him, when a mile from the cabin he drew on the reins and then sat, feeling. He didn't like it at all. He secured his beasts in an aspen thicket and went softly forward on moccasined feet, the rifle barrel across his left arm. On a hill above the river he came within sight of the cabin. There, well-hidden, he peered out, and held his breath. He could see the corral but no sign of the pony; the cabin, with its door wide open, but no sign of his wife. He was beginning to feel desperately ill. He felt that she was not there, and if she was not there he prayed to God that she had gone back to her people. If she was a red warrior's captive she was now a slave in some village, beaten and cursed by the old shrews of the tribe. If she was a prisoner he would find her, if it took all the years of his life. . . .

His gaze searched the aspen hillside that sloped down to the cabin from the east; and the river bottomlands to the south and the north. He looked everywhere for a snowtrail. Convinced at last that his wife was not there, and with grief and rage rising in a hot flood all through him, he went forward, but instead of approaching directly from the west he flanked the cabin and came in from the east, a soundless stalker among the trees. When a hundred yards from the cabin he paused and tried to feel the situation. He prayed that she was in the cabin and alive but logic told him that Indians were more likely to be there, waiting for him. He went forward again, until he came to the rear wall, and put an ear to a seam between logs and listened. Then, his rifle cocked, his finger on the trigger, his knife loosened in its sheath, he slipped around a corner and along the north wall. He was peering round the northwest corner, for a glimpse of the doorway, when with a start that shook him clear to his feet he saw the objects before him.

In an instant of recognition that convulsed him worse than illness or nightmare could have done Sam knew what had happened. He was holding his breath. He felt faint. There before the open door and scattered roundabout were the bones of his wife. Without moving, and without feeling now, for he had been completely numbed, he looked at them and all around them for perhaps five long minutes. He saw bones that had been picked clean by crows and magpies; and when he advanced, at last, he saw, a hundred feet distant, the skull. The scalp had been so completely taken that there was only a little hair across the nape. He went forward until he could look down, and then stared at the eye sockets, at the holes that were the ears, at the marks of hatchet or knife in the bone of the skull. Then swiftly he entered the cabin. There was nothing in it. The murderers had taken everything.

Still drawing only half breaths and still feeling faint, he knelt among the bones and saw what until this moment he had missed. As gently as if reaching for a butterfly he picked up an object, set his rifle by the wall, and laid the object across a palm. It was the skull of a baby. He now saw, on looking round, that scattered among his wife's bones were the bones of his child. He took up one after another to look at them. His first glance had told him that his wife had been dead no more than ten days or two weeks. Sick with grief and remorse, he was telling himself, over and over, that if he had come in two weeks ago she would now be alive: she had been sitting there, on the log he had placed for her; the dear faithful thing had been looking across the river and into the west, for sign of his coming; she had been sewing leather clothing, looking and sewing, sewing and looking. Her rifle had stood by the wall at her left; her knife was in its sheath and the revolver at her waist; and the pony staked on the river bottom had surely been out of sight, or it would have given an alarm. She had been so intent on trying to see him, or on pushing the needle through leather, that she had not heard the soft footfalls; and around the corner had come a red killer and he had been above her before she sensed his presence. With one blow he had almost severed her head low on the neck. He had scalped her and stripped her of everything she had on; and she had lain there, dead, with the baby, his son, kicking and dying inside her.

Lord God Almighty, this vengeance would be his! His deeply tanned face drained to a sickly gray, he looked north and northeast, knowing that the killer had had to come in that way. In a few minutes he would find a sign of him and he would know from what tribe he had come.

Sam gathered every bone he could find—a few had been dragged fifty yards or more from the cabin; and he then sat on the earth, and putting them all in his lap, looked down at them. After a few minutes he knew that his eyes had blurred. He had not known that tears were so hot. He could recall no moment from all his years when he had wept. He pressed the skull of Lotus to one cheek, his son's to the other, and sat, trying to think of what he should do. But he knew what he would do.

When at last he gently put the bones aside and rose to his feet he was dizzy with rage so blindly murderous that he reached for his rifle and failed to find it. He struck at his eyes but they were clogged with grief. Never before in his life had he felt such dreadful loss and loneliness. He stood, trying to see, and began to wipe at his eyes; and when he could see, and had the rifle in his grasp, he stood still, letting his fury grow, until it filled his whole frame and made him ache to be on his way. As he sensed more deeply his loss and the fantastic cowardice of the killer he could think only of vengeance. The years before him became as clear as they would have been if he had had a time-map; but first he had to gather what remained of his wife and child, and then search the area to determine which tribe was guilty.

While walking here and there, around the cabin, over to the river and back, he realized that there had been a light snowfall since his family was slain. Seeing a mark like a shadow, he would reach into the snow and bring up another bone. From the thicket he brought his beasts and took from a packhorse a blanket; within this he put the bones, and wrapped and tied the bundle, and made it secure behind his saddle. He found a needle that Lotus had dropped. Had she been making a jacket for him, a shirt, or moccasins, or something for the child, at the moment the tomahawk fell across her neck?

From what tribe had the killer come? Sam thought he must be from the Comanches, the ferocious varmints who had cut Jed Smith down with knives and hatchets. Round and round the cabin he went, inside and out, sniffing, but he could detect no Indian odor; nor could he find any sign in the cabin or around it. So he took their snowtrail up the river, and at the junction of the Little Snake with the Yampah he sat on his horse and looked round him. From this point the path went up the Snake. He hardly knew what to make of it: if it had been the Comanches they would have struck off to the east, south of Battle Mountain. He kallated it was not the Comanches after all.

He knew it was not when, after a journey of two days up the river, he came to an Indian campsite that had been protected by heavy trees from the recent storm. It was on a U-bend of the stream, and on three sides it had such dense windbreak and snowbreak that the ashes of their fire had been undisturbed by wind and storm. A few moccasin tracks were in the clay under a high bank. Sam did not know the moccasin print of the

Comanche but he knew that of the Crow as well as he knew his own. These prints seemed to have been made by Crows but this he found so incredible that he studied them with extreme care and searched round them for corroborating evidence. There could be no doubt of it: the redmen who had camped here had been Crows!—the Crows, who boasted that they had never harmed a whiteman, or his friend!—the Crows, who with the mountain men waged war against the Blackfeet. Sam was remembering now that for two or three hundred miles he had ridden with Lotus through Crow country; perhaps the one who had tried to steal his Bowie had trailed him; or perhaps it had been a war party of foolhardy youngsters, eager to count a coup and kill. Because there had been no trace of his snowpath of last November and no sign of him anywhere they had not known where to look for him, and so had slain his wife and fled with her horse, weapons, bedding, and food. One of them had her scalp, and would have it, until Sam Minard found him and cut him wide open, and flung his cowardly liver to the wolves. He would find that killer before he died, so help him, God!

Over on his right, as he took his way up the river, were mountains, with peaks that rose eleven thousand feet above the sea. As he approached the mountains Sam studied their snowy summits and the forests blanketed with white, wondering how high up those flanks he could climb; for he wanted to swear an oath of vengeance, somewhere high above the earth. The snow up there in the pale sky haze might be fifteen feet deep but on the north side it ought to hold him. He would hide his beasts and fur packs in the foothills, and with his rifle and a little food he would climb as high as he could.

From the base of the peaks it was only a few thousand feet to their summits but it might take a man a week to get there. While wondering if he should be so romantic and foolish Sam thought of the lovely flowers that would now be blooming on the southern slopes, below the snowline. He would climb at least that far. And when at last he stood far up, in a night world, silent but for the winds, with the scent of flowers around him, he held fragrant bloom to his face, remembering the hours when he had put lupine and columbines and roses in her hair, and hung a mantle of flowers from her shoulders. What a lovely thing she had been when her eyes looked out from the wreath that framed her face and her lips smiled!

Half the night he waited for the golden lamp to rise out of the

gray murk of the east. He was ready when his moment came.
Standing on a crag of wind-swept precipice, his rifle at his left
side, he looked up at the stars and the blue-gray of the first
morning. When half the golden lamp was in sight he spoke. He
asked the Almighty Father to look down on him in his trouble
and his grief. Never in his life had he raised a hand against the
Crow people, but had been their friend, yet when he was gone
they came like wolves in the night to kill his wife and child.
They had known that this girl was a whiteman's wife. They had
known that she was alone, a thousand miles from her people
and a long way from her man. She never had a chance to
defend herself. There she sat, a baby in her, sewing on a shirt
for her man or her child, or looking into the west for sign of her
man; and without a moment of warning they had chopped her
down. And there she had lain in the yard, dead, with her baby
dying inside her—there for the wolves and the magpies and
ravens.

He paused there, wondering if he had said enough. There
was more that he had wanted to say—to say that in the holy
book it said that vengeance was God's, but that in this case it
was Sam Minard's; to say that he intended to make war,
singlehanded and alone, against the whole skulking cowardly
Crow nation; to say, "From where I now stand until the day I
die I swear upon the bones of my slain wife and child that I will
kill every Crow warrior that crosses my path!"

That was it. That was what he had wanted to say. Was there
something else? There had been words from Job, that his father
had read at breakfast one morning—that his eyes did shine, and
were like the eyes of the morning, or something like that. He
had intended to shake his clenched fist at the Crow nation and
hurl into the listening night such words of power and fury as
would make the peaks tremble. But after coming to the flowers
and remembering the flower-hours, and her eyes and smile, a
gentleness of the morning or of heaven had touched him; and so
he stood on the crag, his face to the morning sky, and became
aware of himself as a man who had sworn a terrible oath of
vengeance. Never had he really hated any man, or wished to
kill any man, but this had been forced on him, and only the
coward would blanch from it and turn back. The eyes of the
morning, that was all he would need, and a little help from
divine justice in the right places. And so he stood, the male on
the mountain peak, making his vow of vengeance; and eight

hundred miles north the female knelt in her tiny graveyard, before the angelic faces of her slain ones, and uttered a prayer to the same Father.

The sun was an hour high and the atmosphere a pale golden above the white when Sam turned down the mountain. He had gathered a whole armful of the lovely alpine lilies. On his way down he tried to lay his plans. He would take his pelts to Bridger and pay for the things he had bought; and the remainder he would take to the Laramie post, for that was close to Crow country. He would buy a faster horse if there was one, for there would be times when he would ride for his life. He would buy another Bowie, for there might be times in close fighting when he would need to lay their bellies open, right and left. He knew well that as soon as he had killed a few Crows every warrior in the nation would dedicate himself to his death. He would need a few of the toughest hides to make moccasins for his horse, to be put on when he approached an enemy camp; and he would need twice as much powder and ball as he had ever bought before.

As he went down the mountain flank he came to other flowers, creamy white with yellow centers, that he thought almost as lovely as the lilies. To make a basket he stripped off his leather shirt, and inside this he carried a bushel of flowers. On returning to his hidden beasts he took the bundle from behind the saddle, opened it, and literally wrapped and smothered the bones in flowers. The hair on the nape of the skull he kissed. Then, tenderly, with large clumsy hands, he folded bones and flowers within the blanket and made the bundle secure behind his saddle. During these moments he was thinking not of Loretto but of Milton Sublette, who in a fight with the half-breed John Gray had been stabbed so mortally that his associates, thinking he would die, had left him in the care of Joe Meek. Milton had got well and soon thereafter he and Joe had fallen into the hands of a party of hostile Indians. They would have been killed but for a chief and his lovely daughter, who in the dark of night had helped them to escape. Smitten by the girl, Milton not long thereafter had married her. Leaving her in the mountains, as Sam had left Lotus, Milton had gone east on a business trip and had died on his return journey; and within a year or two his wife was shot down by the Bannock Indians. This Indian girl, Meek had said, was the most beautiful woman he had ever seen. But not, Sam told himself, as beautiful as Lotus.

While riding northwest to the Bridger post Sam decided that if he were to live another year, much less five or ten, he would do well to map a plan of attack. This thought led him to a long and careful appraisal of the nature of his enemies. There were some curious advantages on his side. The whiteman was far more adult than the redman, who, in fact, was only a child in his emotions—impulsive, hotheaded, and by turns craven or reckless. The whiteman, faced with danger, decided instantly and acted swiftly; the redman was in some measure inhibited by his burden of superstitions, and had to wait on medicine men and propitious signs. The whiteman had no boss, no chief. The redman was the servile creature of ritual and ceremonial—he spent a part of his life in such monkey business as touching the earth with the bowl of his pipe and then turning the stem upwards to invoke medicine magic. Even so, the redman thought the whiteman as brainless and vacant as the fool hen, as slow as the turtle, and as gullible as the antelope. Why, he asked, did the whiteman put the centers of logs in his fires, instead of the ends? Look! There they were, hours later, with the centers burned out and the ends lying on either side of a dying fire. It was true, Sam had decided, that the whiteman was buffalo-witted in some ways.

Well, one fact to keep in mind was this, that if sixty redmen faced an enemy every single one of them would figure that if one and only one of his party was killed he would be the dead man. If two were killed, or three or five, he would be one of them. It was for this reason that the warriors of most tribes would turn and run after one or two or three had been killed. The whiteman, on the other hand, figured that if only one of sixty were to die the odds were fifty-nine to one in his favor. He was likely to think the odds greater than that, for the reason that he did not look on himself as an average fighter.

On arriving at Bridger's post Sam was so sunk in brooding and plotting that he carried a part of his pelts in, asked for a reckoning, and turned to leave. Jim's strange eyes had been studying him. Jim called out, "I doan see hide ner hair yer wife."

Sam turned. "She's dead."

"How thet happen?" asked Jim, showing no astonishment.

"Crows."

Jim took a few moments to consider that and then followed Sam outside. "Sartinly not the Crows, Sam." Bridger had in mind that Beckwourth and Rose had been Crow chiefs, and that a number of the free trappers had taken Crow women. His eyes said he didn't think the Crows had done it.

"The Crows," Sam said, cinching up his packs.

"I jist can't believe it. Did ye find plenty sign?"

"Plenty."

To change the subject Jim said, "Black Harris wuz here. Says a million Mormons is comin through this summer. All back there on Misery Bottoms gitting their wagons ready."

Sam was no longer interested in Mormons and Brigham Young and his wives.

"Heerd anuther thing," said Jim, trying to get Sam to talk. "Lot of the boys are meetin up at Laramie bout now. They might know if the Crows done it. There's Powder River Charley—"

Sam said, "For what I have coming give me credit. Watch your topknot, Jim."

"Jist a minute," said Jim. He walked over to Sam and looked at Sam's eyes. "Yer kinda young. Ye intend ter go inter the Crow country?"

"Right through the middle of it," Sam said.

"I wooden do that, Sam. Ye intend ta fight the hull nation?"

"The hull nation."

Jim was still looking at Sam's eyes. He put forth a gnarled hand and said, "I reckon, then, I best give ye a handshake, fer I doan spect I'll see ye agin."

"I figger you will," Sam said, and clasped the hand.

From Bridger's on Black's Fork he rode east and north to Green River; then east and north to South Pass, the Sweetwater, and the Oregon Trail, which he followed east to the Laramie post, where he would trade for supplies and, if lucky, a fast horse. On this long ride he tried to lighten his mood by singing songs, but the only one that would rise from his depths was "Sorrow, Sorrow, Stay." He couldn't sing "To Celia" any more, or "When Laura Smiles" or a dozen others, for there rose before him the picture of his girl-wife on that long sweet journey south, and he would reach behind him to touch the blanket that enfolded the bones and flowers.

A few of the free trappers were at the post; after their long lonely winter they were eager to swap talk but Sam did not want to talk. Lost-Skelp Dan came over to him. Dan was a big man; he stood a good six feet two in moccasins and weighed two hundred and twenty. He had large full pale-blue eyes that were cold and mean but that had a light touch of warmth when he looked at Sam. Dan had heard that Sam's wife had been killed, though how he had heard it Sam was never to know, for no rider had passed him on the Trail.

Dan wanted to express sympathy but he was clumsy and tactless. He did manage to say at last, "Sam, ever need any help, jist holler."

"Thanks," Sam said. He would never holler. What he wondered was whether Crows at this post had talked about the death of Lotus.

Mick Boone was there and Mick had also heard about it. All the trappers knew that Mick had one of the fastest horses in the West, a big strong bay with the lines of a racer. Mick first asked Sam if he would join him in a drink. Sam thanked him and said he never drank. "Bad habit," Mick said, and put on the queer smile he had when self-conscious. It took him a few moments to get the words out. He said he figgered as how Sam might like to use his bay for a while.

Sam looked into Mick's brown eyes and said, "I couldn't take your bay."

"Not a thing to stop you," Mick said. "If ya aim to ride plum through Crow country—and I figger ya do—you'll need a fast horse or ya might never reach the other side."

"You might be right," Sam said.

"I'll change the saddles," Mick said.

So Mick took the stud and Sam set off on the big bay. The news would spread fast that the Crows had killed Sam Minard's wife and unborn child, and that after declaring war on the whole nation Sam was showing what kind of business he meant by riding clear across, it, alone. When he rode away into the north Sam was not thinking of that. He was again thinking of the nature of his enemies. The vast plains-and-mountains area, which they claimed as their own and fought to hold, lay chiefly upon the southern drainage of the Yellowstone—upon its tributaries, the Bighorns, the Rosebud and the Powder and the Tongue. The heart of the Crows was the valley of the Bighorns, though they claimed the lands lying in all directions from these rivers, to a considerable distance. Sam had heard it said by some of the older trappers that the Crows had the finest bodies of all the redmen; that they were the handsomest; and the ablest hunters; and the most expert thieves; and that of all the red warriors they were the deadliest shots with the whiteman's weapons. The American Fur Company had built four, the Missouri Fur Company two posts solely for their convenience in trading.

It saddened Sam to think that these people had made him their enemy, for he had been a little enchanted by them. Four hundred Crow lodges on the move was a remarkable spectacle in rhythm and color—the warriors in their richly ornamented robes, with floating and flowing fringes and feathers and headpieces; and with the principal squaws in really elegant mantles and cloaks of birdskins, spangled over with beads. Standing upon the mother's backs were a hundred papooses, in cradles as richly ornamented as the mothers' garments, the children swathed tight but standing, their bright black eyes expressing joy in life. Behind the procession or ahead of it or on its flanks were hundreds of ponies under huge burdens, as well as hundreds of dogs so covered over with camp litter that almost no part of them was visible. From a distance it looked as if a prairie of brilliant colors was flowing in a gentle wind.

Well, it was by their own cowardice and brutality that Sam Minard was their enemy now. Mick, like Bridger, had acted as if he doubted that the Crows had done it. But Sam knew the print of the Crow moccasin. The Cheyennes, Arapahoes, and Comanches all had an inside straight edge on their cowskin moccasins, and the point so turned as to give the wearer the appearance of being pigeon-toed. The Pawnee moccasin looked for all the world as if the Indian had placed his foot in the center of a piece of buckskin and then pulled all the edges to the top of the foot, in front of the ankle, with the rear part brought up behind the leg and tied round with leather string. The Crow moccasin, like their clothing, was so expertly tanned and made that its print was skin-smooth in every part of it, with no sign of the little bulges and irregular seams that marked most of the others. He had examined with the utmost care a dozen footprints. To one who had made a study of the prints of different tribes the Crow print was as plain and as unlike any other as their manner of cutting their hair—the Cheyennes and Eutaws wore their hair in long loose locks, cut off close above the brows so that vision would not be obscured. The Pawnees and Kansas shaved the front and back, leaving only a topknot at the crown, which was so stiff with grease and grime that it stood up straight and barely wavered in a wind. The Blackfeet usually confined their hair in two long braids; the Crows, more artistic in hairdress than any of the others, arranged their hair to harmonize with their elaborate and colorful headdress.

Maybe Mick and Jim hadn't made a study of footprints. Maybe they didn't know that the Crows were more nomadic than any other tribe. It was not unusual for these skulking thieves to be seen a thousand miles from their central village, for with their faster horses they could easily outrun their pursuers. Most of the red people occupied settlements that were more or less fixed, in the center of which might be a big lodge of buffalo skins painted red and tattooed with the secret and magic totems of the tribe. Not far from this central station there might be a scalp pole, from which the scalps, some dried and shrunken, some still wet and bloody, flapped in the winds. The scalp pole was the visible measure of a nation's heroism. Near it was another pole from which hung the medicine bags with their strange and potent contents. Sam, like most of the mountain men, had made a study of totems, because from the nature of the totem could be inferred the character of the people—the eagle, wolf, bear, fox, serpent, wolverine, hawk— though Sam had concluded that the choice of totem was largely determined by the kind of country the tribe occupied. The skins of totems were often to be seen stuffed and set up in conspicuous places for worship. All the tribes Sam had visited seemed to be, in the way of small children, fond of strong bright colors, particularly red, yellow, vermilion, and blue. Sometimes for black as a medicine color they used the scraped-off powder of charred wood, mixed with gunpowder, if they had it. Whitemen had laughed themselves into exhaustion when told the story of the brave who smeared his entire body with gunpowder and moved close to a fire and exploded. This was the same reckless warrior who had eaten buffalo tongue at a time when it was taboo to him, and had so paralyzed the whole village with terror that to save his people and himself he had thrust and pulled his tongue out so far that the roots of it were almost in the front of his mouth. At the same time he had bellowed with such rage and pawed the earth into such dust clouds, as he snorted and heaved, that he had cast off the malevolent spell and returned his people to safety and calm.

Few things had more astonished Sam and the other trappers,

or brought from them more vigorous expressions of contempt, than the redman's fanatical devotion to a mysterious and intricate system of ceremonial and magic. The Indian's world was so overrun by evil spirits and wicked powers that there were times when he was immobilized: he could not shoot a rabbit or make a fire or put on his war paint without first engaging in his mystical and propitiating grunts and gestures. There was his pipe, which he passed in solemn supplication to all the directions and to every conceivable thing, including sun, moon, winds, and sky. He had many symbols attached to his lodges, utensils, and war tools. No hunting party, no war party, no journey could be undertaken, no lodge could be built or buffalo robe made, and no planting could be strewn in its furrows or harvest gathered, without first going through his interminable childish rituals. This gave to enemies an advantage they were quick to seize; now and then a band of warriors was attacked when by magic and conjuration and thaumaturgy it was simply helpless and useless and not able to fight.

Sam was thinking that now and then he might catch a few of them without their medicine bags, and find it as easy to knock them over as to knock over fool hens. His grief was so hot and his hatred so black that he did not care if when he fell on them they were not prepared to fight; he intended to shoot them and knife them and knock their heads off, as undisturbed by their cries as a wolf seizing a rabbit. Looking round him at the miracle of spring, listening to the arias of bluebird and meadow lark, gathering early flowers to press into the blanket, and thinking, over and over, of the joy with which he had looked forward to riding north with his wife, he actually turned pale with suppressed furies, and promised himself that a dozen scalps would dangle from his saddlebags within a month. To show his contempt he might even collect, and display, an assortment of their medicine bundles, such as the stuffed heads of wolves, or the skin, claws, teeth, and feathers of various birds and beasts, whose virtues the absurd creatures believed they had assimilated. Still, Windy Bill had said that they were no more ridiculous than those white people who partook of different sacraments.

Above all, Sam wanted them to know who was about to strike, when they heard his cry; who had killed a warrior, when they found the flesh and bones. So he decided, while riding along, to leave his mark on every dead brave—a mark that the whole Crow nation would recognize as his mark. The whole nation would also know his battle cry. He wished he had a trumpet. If only he could drive the whole damned Crow people into mourning or lunacy! That would be a sight to ennoble the heart, equal to Napoleon and his ragged army hurled back from Moscow. A Crow when mourning and lamenting a slain or mortally wounded warrior hacked at nearly all parts of his body, and sometimes cut off one or more fingers: what gouts of blood he would make flow! In what rivers of blood he would avenge his wife and child! How the men, women, and children, the whole nation, all of them, would set up a wild dismal howling and quavering and shrieking that would curdle the blood of a loon or a wolf. If ten braves came forth to take him, as a war party had once gone forth to take a Blackfeet chief, with none and nothing ever returning except the moccasin-carrying pack-dogs, what an infernal sky-filling bedlam of rage and frustration the Crow nation would be! It overjoyed him to think of it. It would be like the time Jim Clyman told of—of a camp gone wild and stark mad with woe after looking on a scene of slaughter: how the women and children had torn at their flesh and screamed, with all around them the frenzied howling of dogs, the insane neighing and braying of horses and mules, the mournful hooting of owls, and over it all the horrible sickening stench of grief and sweat and dung and warm blood and mingled coyote and dog odors.

The Crow war whoop, *"Hooo-ki-hi!"* that had raised the hair on Sioux, Blackfeet, and Cheyenne and made the gooseflesh swarm down their backs would be stilled in a lot of throats. A lot of braves now strutting in their gaudy war paints and battle dress would count coup no more. Coup, which in this land was pronounced coo, in the French way, was the highest heroism an Indian warrior could aspire to: to count coup he had to strike an enemy with his quirt or bow or knife or coup stick *before* he attacked him; or he had to take from the enemy all his weapons; or he had to slip up afoot and steal the horse of an enemy tied to his own lodge. There were a lot of ways to touch coup, all of them devised to show more than ordinary courage. After a warrior had counted coup he had the right to wear an eagle feather in his hair, and another thereafter for each coup he made. If he were so clumsy or frightened while attempting a coup that he received a wound he had to wear a feather painted red. Sam had seen a Crow chief with seven feathers in his hair. Against one of such valor he doubted that he would ever have a chance; to bring him down the nation would send only the young warriors who were the bravest, fleetest, and deadliest, or the most adept in stratagems, such as tracking and ambush.

Let them come, the cowardly unspeakable murderers of a lone woman and her unborn child! Let the chief send those who were battle-hardened; who had waged war against the Lacota or Sioux, the Striped-Feather-Arrows or Cheyennes, the Tattooed-Breasts or Arapahoes. Let them all come! Let even the Pine-Leafs come! A legend said that Pine-Leaf when only twelve years old lost a brother in battle, and thereupon vowed that she would never marry or do a woman's work until she had killed a hundred of the enemy. Sam did not know if she had killed any or what had become of her; or indeed if such a girl had lived. And there was the squaw named She-could-be-dead, whose man had been slain; she then became as crazy as two wildcats with their tails tied together: mounting a pony and armed only with bow and arrows and knife, she had gone forth alone against the Cheyennes. Nobody seemed to know what became of her, but in legends there she was, riding—riding—riding forever, at great speed across the plains and ravines, her bronzed face smeared with red ochre, her arrows, tipped with lightning, flashing into the foe's breast. Sam had heard at least a dozen stories of the furious intrepid assaults of red women whose men had been killed. Now and then, a tale said, one of them returned from the warpath, her face as black as night as a sign that she had triumphed over the enemy. His weeks with Lotus had acquainted him with the spirit and daring of the Indian girl.

He wished, while riding along and making plans, or pausing to target-shoot with his revolvers, that he had a good knowledge of the Crow tongue, so that he could hurl abominable and shocking insults at the moment of striking. Powder River Charley spoke the language as well (he said) as the Crows themselves; he liked to make fun of them by translating what he had heard them say: "In the mornin this ole woman her garden when she come and to it got was all pulled up. This ole woman it was. What I wonder is this, come and to it got was all pulled up. What I wonder is this, said she. All the time critters none whatever git to me truly, this what is it that me has got to? The tracks small were they when looked at them she. Bad critters thought she bad. This ole woman this night she laid down she prayed. When mornin come then the garden in she hid. Them there bad men them she wanted to ketch. Time passed. Passed more time. Moon come, moon sick, moon gone. This which she hid in the garden what she took back this ole woman there was nuthin there was nuthin. This ole woman over there food she puts away in holler tree. Then come time this ole woman was not there she wherever she went to. In the garden always there is none no none. The food she stored in the holler tree its eater did she kill? Doggone don't ask me."

Charley would sit by a campfire and suck at his pipe and roll his pale eyes from face to face; and say, "There that and this here wind comes on him it falls it kills him. When close to it he run and came. When fast he went he was under it fast when this wind it come crashed was he." That, he said, was word-by-word translation of Crow talk. He would knock his pipe out, refill it, and say, "Now over there ten sleeps some bad ones there are. Sleep they do not. Hate you they do kill you they will skelp you ghosts like these warriors are slinkin no sound to make none there their knifes they take out all aroun your neck off they chop ole woman runnin she comes but save you she cannot her head chopped off it will be."

"Doan they never stop fer a breath?"

"They never seem to. They talk like children talk. And let me tell you, don't never call them Crows. They think you call them that because the Crows they steal from bird nests and they say they never steal not ever never."

"They're doggone liars," someone said.

"The Apsahrokee, that's what they are. The Sparrowhawk people."

From Charley and others Sam had picked up a few words and phrases. *Xatsi-sa,* which he pronounced Zat-see-saw, meant, "Do not move." *Di-wap-e-wima-tsiky,* which he rendered as Di-wappi-wimmi-tesicky, meant, "I will kill you." Riding along, he recalled that phrase and strove to master it and fix it in mind. But what he needed was words of insult and contumely, that would freeze their marrow and glaze their blood. He now rememered *Bi-i-kya-waku,* which meant, "I will look out for me"; and *Dara-ke-da-raxta?*—"Don't you know your own child?" Then there came from one of Charley's garrulous evenings *K-ari-c,* meaning, "Old women." Charley had called it Ka-ree-cee, or something like that. He would hurl it at them. He would crush the bones in their necks, drive his knife through their livers, and kick them so hard in their spines that their heads would fall backwards and across their rumps. If only he could call them sick cowardly old women crawling in the sagebrush!

The redmen had a child's fondness for insulting words. Sam had heard the story of Jess Danvers who, with his five or six free trappers, was crossing the plains from one river to the next when suddenly, with no warning at all, his party was surrounded by Sioux warriors crawling toward them sagebrush by sagebrush. The Indians were less than two hundred yards from Jess when a chief stood up and, making a sign of peace, approached Jess and his men. As he drew near he made more signs of peace and told Danvers that he and his men, the long-knives, had been burning the wood off Sioux land and killing their game and eating their grass. The old rascal, stuffed full of guile, said he knew that Jess had come to pay for these things—with his horses, weapons, tobacco—with everything that he and his men had. He was Chief Fierce Bear, whose tongue was short but whose lance was long; he preferred to speak with his weapons rather than jabber like a woman. With hostile gestures he again said that the long-knives had robbed his people blind and would now pay with their horses, weapons, tobacco, everything they had. If they were not paid at once his braves would get blood in their eyes and he'd not be able to control them. In that case they would take not only the horses, weapons, tobacco, and all the clothing but they would take their scalps and possibly their lives.

By this time Danvers was so choked with rage that he could barely speak. He said, in signs and words, and with furious gestures, that his heart was big and the hearts of his men were big, but not toward those who threatened while pretending to be friends. If they were to give their horses and weapons it would be to brave men, and not to a band of cowardly limping bent-over squaws, crawling on their bellies like snakes in the sagebrush. He and his men were not French engagés, or toothless old women eating bugs, or sick dogs and coyotes, but fearless warriors with rifles that never missed fire and knives that were always driven straight through the heart. The creatures yonder in the sagebrush, crawling on their bellies and with sand in their eyes, looked to him like sick old women hunting *les bois de vache*. Waugh!

Chief Fierce Bear then took his turn at insults. He said that

Danvers and his men had killed so much of the game, cropped so much of the forage, and burned so much of the wood on Sioux land that the children were so hungry and feeble they could not stand; the women shook with moans and laments all day; and not five horses in the whole nation could rise to their feet. He and his warriors had loved peace; they had never killed a man; but if he and his braves were to be treated as if they were sick coyotes, and if they were to be robbed, it would be by brave fighters and not by coughing and sneezing palefaces. He and the men with him were the bravest on earth; they had only scorn for long rifles and knives in the hands of womanish creatures who had turned pale the first time they faced a foe and had never got their color back. He would say again, and for the last time, that the blood in his men was hot and their honor was crying for vengeance. The horses, weapons, tobacco, all these were to be delivered at once.

According to the tale told by trappers, Danvers and the chief swapped insults for an hour or more, and then, backing off, each returned to his men. The battle commenced at once. Danvers was shot through the lungs and suffered so from hemmorhage that he could only stagger around, unable to use his weapons or to speak, able only to stand helpless while he exploded torrents of blood from his mouth and nostrils. Only one whiteman escaped to tell the story.

Sam's mind again wandered to Windy Bill and Bridger and Charley and their tales; and suddenly out of campfire and tobacco smoke and evening odors there came as sharp and clear as his mother's farewell these words:

Old woman's man her children their ghosts there in the blackest night they are in the sagebrush they are crying.

Those words, known to every free trapper in the mountains, had surely been sent down by the Almighty, for the woman on the Musselshell. Sam looked north across Crow land. How was she now? After he had taken a few scalps he would go up to see.

12

By the time he reached the middle fork of Powder River Sam had become as wary as an Indian. Just ahead were the southern foothills of the Bighorns. He was undecided whether to swing west and go down the Bighorn Valley or straight north between the Bighorns and Powder River, and on to Tongue River, which had its source in the Bighorn Mountains. After hiding his beasts in a thicket and making a fireless camp he considered the matter. What he wanted to know was where most of the Crows were at this time of year. Too lazy, or maybe too restless, to cultivate the soil, they were a wandering people, always on the move. While eating stale jerked meat and thinking, Sam heard the warbling aria of a purple finch. Lord, hearing bird song put hot grief all through his blood and bones; how many times on the long journey south had they stood together, his arms to her shoulders, while listening to this singer, or the robin, the vireo, the vesper sparrow, the lark?

Taking his mind off song and putting it on vengeance, he wished his first triumph might be the death of a chief. That would be a coup to raise the hair of the nation. He had heard that one of their boldest younger chiefs was River of Winds, whose medicine bundle was the weasel, the ferocious killer of the gentle prairie dogs. He had an image of the Crow people, the whole five or six thousand of them, shaking in a national convulsion as they filled the sky with their blood-chilling mourning-howl. It was the women who shrilled the loudest; their infernal noise was so wild and savage that they turned a whiteman's blood to water. When with their hideous incantations they tried to terrify the evil spirits they silenced even the wolf. Sam had once seen a large village in which was a mortally wounded warrior: instead of allowing the poor devil in his agony to lie on the fur side of a robe and die in such peace as

118

he could find the women had dragged him all over the place, while blood flowed from a dozen wounds and dogs lapped it up; while with beating of drums and pounding of kettles and blowing on reeds, and flinging piercing yells and shrieks at the sky, they made his last hour on earth a perfect nightmare. They were frightening the evil spirits away. Sam had no doubt that they had; if the squaws were to enter hell all the creatures there would flee before them.

This evening as on every evening since leaving the Laramie post he examined his weapons. On stone and soft leather he had honed his knives until they could mow the hair on his arms. His revolvers and rifle were oiled, loaded, and in perfect order. His wiping stick, used to force the ball down the rifle barrel, was of tough hickory and the best he had ever seen. He didn't intend to use his rifle in close fighting, or his handguns either. In a close fight you couldn't shoot fast enough or straight enough. Jim Bowie had taught them all that with a knife you could lay open three assassins before you could shoot one. A man's heels, knees, fists, and elbows were faster and more deadly than a gun in close quarters. With a blow of his heel driven by powerful leg muscles Sam could break a man's spine. With his two large hands on a throat he could in an instant so completely shatter the neck that the head would fall over toward the backbone. He felt able to take care of himself in a close fight with as many as four or five redmen, if he had the advantage of surprise; but he thought it might be smart to call on Powder River Charley. He didn't like Charley the way he liked most of the mountain men; he felt that this tall, sly, awkward-moving trapper had been born with larceny and murder in his heart. Charley seemed always to be boiling for a fight, as though his honor had just been impeached or his mother insulted. Three or four of the trappers had pale-blue eyes that looked half popped out but none had such bulging ferocious eyes as Charley. The moment you met his gaze there was a change in his eyes; they seemed to swell and to move a little out of their caves and to fill to overflowing with the lightnings of challenge. But Charley might know which Crow warriors had gone south to the Little Snake.

He had his own private hideaway back in the Bighorns, with a sheltered foothills meadow that gave forage to his beasts; there were excellent trapping streams all around him. He was in Crow country—he was right in the middle of it—but he was their friend; he had had two or three Crow wives, though still a youngish man. Charley had known such white Crow chiefs as Rose and Beckwourth, and he was a friend of John Smith, one of the most eccentric of the mountain men. It was said that Charley and John used to forgather on a Sunday to sing pious songs and make reverent gestures toward the Father, though Windy Bill said they were the most sanctimonious pair of hypocrites and the meanest varmints and the most inexplicable mixture of caution and foolhardiness, of good will and venomous hostility, to be found in the mountains. It was said that Smith had lived for a while with the Blackfeet, then with the Sioux, then with the Cheyennes, taking wives in all three tribes. It was also said that he could turn the air to a sulphur blue cursing in English, Spanish, and four Indian languages. Sam had never seen the man.

While thinking about Charley there came to Sam the one tale of the many told about him that he liked best. Riding into camp one evening leading a packmule, Charley had wanted to unpack the beast close to the fire; but when he pulled on the leather rope to bring the mule forward, the mule, most stubborn of all critters, laid his ears back and sank toward the earth at his rear end. Charley had then wrapped his end of the rope twice around his waist, and like a horse in harness he had tried to surge forward and take the mule with him; but the mule, if he moved at all, moved backwards, with his rump drawing closer to the earth. Charley by this time was getting up the insane fury for which he was famous. Dashing back to the sulking mule, whose eyes by this time had turned yellow with hate and whose ears had been laid out flat, Charley seized an ear and sank his teeth in it; and then with wild howls of rage in both English and Crow he grabbed the nostrils with thumb and fingers and tried to tear the nose off. With a moccasined foot he delivered a blow at the beast's ribs, and so wrenched his big toe that he screamed with pain and fury; and then smote the mule's ribs with both fists. By this time the beast had sunk to his hind end and was sitting like a creature determined to sit forever. Charley ran back ten paces, swung, rushed at the mule, and with all his might heaved himself against it, trying to knock it over. By this time several men were shouting encouragement to Charley, who, with a badly sprained toe, bruised hands, a slobbering mouth, and bulging eyes wild with bloodshot, was looking desperately but blindly round him, as though for a crane or derrick. He next worked at right angles to the beast, both right and left; surging forward with the rope, he would yank the mule's head around and try to topple him over; and then run in the other direction and try to spill him that way. But the mule by this time had his rump flat on the ground and his front feet spread. If Charley had left him alone he probably would have sat there for hours.

After all his furious and futile effort Charley was so possessed by insane rage that he turned his eyes, bloodshot and filled with sweat, on his rifle. Seizing it, he ran cursing to the beast, thrust the muzzle against the skull, and pulled the trigger. The forelegs collapsed; the mule then rested on its belly, with its big bony head laid out on the earth.

About noon Sam slipped into Charley's hideout. Charley, like all mountain men who spent a part of their time hiding and watching for the enemy, had heard Sam coming and was waiting for him, concealed, left elbow on left knee, rifle cocked and aimed at the sound. Sam was only fifty feet from him when Charley stepped forth. Then in his awkward loose-limbed shuffling gait he came forward, his eyes bugged out with suspicion and welcome, his tongue saying, "Wall now, if it ain't you. I thought mebbe you was one of them Whigs and danged if I can stand a Whig. I heerd you got rubbed out down on Santy Fe."

The words revealed to Sam a part of what he wanted to know. He had never been down on the Santa Fe and Charley had no reason to believe that he had. According to Sam's reasoning, the words said that Charley knew that Sam had been far south and that this past winter he had possibly been killed. Who could have told him that, except the Crows?

"Who said I was on the Santy Fe?"

"I don't rightly recollect," Charley said. "Wall, doggone your buckskin, git down, git down, and smoke a peace pipe."

A woman had come forward from her hiding place in the trees, a Crow, with narrow forehead, high cheekbones, eyes too close together, heavy lips and chin. She looked young but overfat, unclean, and stupid.

"Where ya off to?" asked Charley, looking up at Sam, who still sat on his horse. "And cuss my forked tongue, ain't this Mick Boone's bay?"

"You might be right," Sam said.

"I heerd Mick loves this horse moren himself."

"Just borrowed it," Sam said. He thought it best to force Charley to do most of the talking. Dismounting, he put his rifle in its buckskin harness, led the bay and packhorses over to trees and hitched them, and turned, his pipe and tobacco in his hands. "All right, let's have the pipe of peace."

Charley was no fool. His intuitions were quick and sharp. Sensing the double meaning in Sam's words, he must have decided to lay his cards on the table, for he now said: "Heerd ya had a woman. Where is she?"

Sam was tamping his pipe. He now met Charley's pale-blue gaze and the two men looked into the eyes of one another a long moment. "Who told you?" Sam said.

"Don't recollect that neither. Mighta been Bill, mighta been Hank."

Sam looked up at the squaw, who was ready with a live ember. Both men sucked flame into their pipes and smoke into their lungs; blew streams of smoke out through nostrils and between lips; looked again into one another's eyes; and pressed the burning tobacco down in the bowls. Deciding that it was useless to fence with this sly treacherous man and not much caring whether he learned a lot or a little, Sam said: "Dead. The Crows killed her." In that moment Sam looked at Charley's eyes but Charley was suddenly busy with his pipe.

Then for an instant he met Sam's gaze and said, "Crows? Ya mean the Sparrowhawks? I find that onreasonable, Sam." After half a minute while both men smoked, Charley said: "Who tole you?"

"Moccasins."

During the five minutes they had been sitting by the fire, smoking and sparring, Sam had observed the position of Charley's weapons and of his squaw. At his waist Charley had a revolver and a knife; his rifle was about eight feet behind him, leaning against camp trappings; and a wood hatchet lay within reach of his right hand. On sitting, Sam had not loosened his knife in its sheath: if he had to fight he did not intend to use a knife. He had been aware from the first that he might have to fight, for it was well-known over the whole Crow country that Charley was a friend of the Crows and an unpredictable man. He could blow hot and turn murderous in an instant.

The squaw stood at Charley's right and a little back. Her right foot was only eighteen inches from the hatchet.

"It wasn't only my wife," Sam said. "My unborn son too."

Charley again tinkered with his pipe. It was all his sense of the proper could bear to hear a whiteman call a red Injun his wife. But the son! Half-breed children were, for him, a species of animal only slightly above the greaser. With a thin smile in his beard that was close to a smirk Charley said, "Jist how on earth could ya tell it was a son?"

"The pelvic bones," Sam said. He had been keeping his eye on the squaw. He knew that she had never taken her black gaze off him, and he wondered if she had a knife hidden in her leather clothing. Charley was puffing at his pipe and looking at Sam. Sam decided that he might as well say what he had come to say.

"I figgered you might know who it was," he said.

"Wall now," said Charley, taking the pipe from his yellow teeth. "Doggone it, Sam, how would I know? It was the Rapahoes, if ya ask me."

"It was the Sparrowhawks," Sam said, using that word instead of Crows so that Charley would not boil over. "I expect I'll take my vengeance and I thought they just as well know it. I thought mebbe you'd like to tell them. You can tell them this, if you want to, that if the ones who did it will come out and face me, three at a time, all of us with no weapons, I'll leave the others alone. If the chief won't send the murderers out I intend to make war on the whole nation."

Charley took the pipe away from his teeth and left his mouth open. "The whole nation. Jist you?"

"Jist me," Sam said.

"So that's why ya have Mick's bay."

"Mebbe." Sam rose to his feet. "I figger the sooner you let the chief know the better it will be. I don't intend to give him much time for medicine and powwows."

Charley stood up. "Wall now, Sam, ain't ya a little onreasonable? The Sparrowhawks are good fighters. Ya know that. I figger ya will be gone beaver almost before ya git to the Yellerstone."

"I might be gone beaver before the next Canada geese come over but there will be some bones for the wolves to pick. And don't forget to tell the chief that I'll leave my mark. I don't want anyone blamed for what I do."

"A mark," said Charley, looking at Sam. He seemed fascinated. "And what," he asked softly, "will the mark be?"

"I'll take the right ear."

"The right ear," said Charley, staring.
"Besides the skelp," Sam said.
"Wall, I'll be doggone," said Charley.

13

IT WAS FOUR redmen that he saw sitting by a campfire after dark, three days after he had left Charley. Sam had sensed the presence of Indians an hour earlier and had hidden his beasts in a thicket and gone forward as the wolf goes—among whitemen of the West the scout was known as the wolf. On each foot he had three moccasins of different sizes. He thought a small war party was there by the fire, on its way to another tribe to steal horses and take scalps; or that it was returning, with a scalp or two at its belt. The warriors would be smoking their pipes and thinking of themselves as very brave men. Perhaps they had feasted on buffalo loin. If their bellies were full they might be a little sleepy. . . .

As soundless as the wolf, Sam went forward. When a half mile away he could tell that the party was encamped on a small stream that flowed down a hillside through an aspen thicket. To the left was a tableland, from which he hoped to get a clear view of the camp. On reaching this he was delighted: the four warriors, sitting by a fire, were in plain view, in a small clearing by the streambank. It was a poor campsite for men who expected to see the next sunrise but they probably thought there would be no enemies in this area so early in the season. The mountain men would be heading for the posts with their packs; the redmen would be feeling only half alive after the long cold winter.

Sam stood in full view of them but he knew that in the dark they could not see him. He wished that somehow the Almighty could let him know if these were the men who had killed his wife and child. Wondering if Charley had taken the message to the chief, he studied the physical situation below and around him, until he knew the nature of the soil and plant life. It was still early spring; the old grasses and weeds along the stream and above the patches of snow were sere and whispering, like a million insects. It would not be easy to make a soundless approach through such grass but the soil was in his favor, for it was moist and soft. His three layers of moccasin skin would sink against it as if it were cotton.

To learn if there were more than four of them Sam became a man who, to the impartial observer, would hardly have seemed human. He had drawn on his five senses for all the information they could give him and was now like a man intently listening, though actually he was consulting what he thought of as his danger sense. His physical posture was exactly that of the wolf when it felt itself in the presence of an enemy and stood stock still, trying to measure the danger.

Sam now doubled back a mile and scouted the area east and north of the camp. He thought it unlikely that there were other Indians within miles of this spot but the men who had accepted the unlikely as fact were all dead. He went two miles east by north, striding swiftly but softly along the crests of aspen-covered hills. Time and again he stopped to listen and sniff. After two hours of reconnoitering he knew the direction from which these warriors had come and the direction in which they were headed. He knew they had no horses, no dog, no fresh scalps, and that they were the kind of party that had killed his wife. If only the one who struck Lotus down were there!

He came back down the hills and took a position south of the camp. His revolvers he had hidden near his horses; his rifle he now set by a tree; and he adjusted the Bowie's sheath on the left side of his belt, two inches forward from his hip-bone, so that he could seize it instantly. Then he went forward. For two hundred and fifty yards he followed a buffalo path along a stream. A strong breeze was blowing against him; the odor of the campfire and of the four men around it was in his nostrils. How well he knew that Crow odor! A hundred yards from the men he stopped, and stood a few moments, sensing. One of them seemed to be lying on his robe. The other three still sat and smoked, with dying firelight playing over the face of the one on the north side. Sam wished that he was the one lying down. The warrior facing him seemed to have no sense of danger; he did not peer into the dark or listen or glance round him. Sam knew he could advance no farther as long as the man sat there. He would have to wait.

While waiting he again went over his plan. At the instant

when he was ready to strike the first blow he would give the dreadful Crow battle cry; with all the power of his lungs he would explode it in their ears. A sliver of moon had come up. It cast a little light but not much. There was a little light from the fire but he could no longer see the Indian's face. An hour later the last of the four had lain down. Again Sam went over his plan: when six feet from the man lying on the south side he would give the cry, with enough rage in it to arouse the dead. At the same moment he would paralyze the man with his right heel. The next instant he would smite with his clenched fist the man on the east side; and swing and bury his knife in the man on the west side. The man on the north side might by that time be on his feet. Sam's plan was to seize him by the throat and with one powerful wrench snap his spine. He figured the whole thing would take no more than seven seconds.

He began to move forward. Against the moist earth his moccasins made no sound but he had to move with extreme care when thrusting a foot forward through the dead grass. He supposed that the four of them were now asleep. They were dreaming dreams of murder and bloody scalps and young women wildly acclaiming them. When thirty feet from them Sam paused to study their positions. Then he crept forward until he stood almost above the man on the south side. He took a few moments to settle his big tensed body into quiet. Then he soundlessly inhaled air until his lungs were filled and in the next moment exploded it:

"Hooo-kii-hiiii!"

The sound shattered the night. The man next to him had no time to move before a tremendous blow paralyzed him. The man on the east was struggling to sit up when Sam drove his fist against his windpipe. A moment later the twelve-inch blade went all the way through the chest of the man on the west side, who at that moment was on his knees, reaching around him. The man on the north was on his feet, as Sam had expected him to be, and was making a move to flee when Sam's huge hands closed round his throat. Sam heard the neck snap and released it, and at the same moment with a thrust of his foot struck the man in his belly and sent him plunging for fifteen feet.

His next move was to draw the knife from the man and plunge it through the heart of each of the two he had knocked unconscious. With the skill of one who had studied the work of professionals he took the four scalps and cut off the right ears.

He looked at the dead men but none of them seemed to have Lotus's Bowie. Then he hastened to his rifle. There he waited. If there were other warriors in the area who had heard his cry they would come slinking and skulking, their black eyes like jewels in the moonlight. But no warriors came.

Settling the scalps and ears in the forks of a tree, Sam took his rifle and went to the bodies, to see if on them or in their trappings there was any sign of his wife—her scalp or a utensil or a weapon. He could find none. Taking each by an ankle, he dragged the corpses into position, side by side, and flung their weapons across them. If other warriors found these bodies before the wolves got to them they would see that the right ears had been sliced off close to the skulls. They would know that Sam Minard had left his mark.

Returning to his horses, he rolled into a robe for three or four hours of sleep. His last thoughts before the night closed over him were of his wife, whose bones, in the blanket behind the saddle, were within reach of his hand.

14

THE NEXT MORNING after eating a hard dry breakfast he patted the blanket over the bones and said, "Don't you worry, Lotus-Lilah, I'll get the son of a bitch." He felt such contempt for his enemy that he shot a deer in the heart of their country and roasted the loins and both hams. Three days later he met Wind River Bill close by the Yellowstone. Bill said he had been up to see how the woman was. He guessed she was all right. All winter he had felt powerful oneasy about her, for he had figgered she would be dead hump-ribs before spring; but doggone it, there she was, lugging water up the hill to her plants and sitting by the graves long after dark. Were the four skulls still on the stakes? Doggone if they warn't. Jist looking round up there had made Bill feel as the Indians felt when ole Belzy Dodd yanked his skelp off. Had Sam heard that one? Dick Wooton told it. Belzy had a head as bald as a buffalo skull after thirty winters in the blizzards. He covered it with a wig.

One day at Bent's Fort when a lot of sneaky Rapahoes were snooping around Belzy rushed among the Injuns making loud and blood-curdling whoops and waving in all directions with his weapons. At the top of his war tantrum he yanked his wig off and shook it at them. Every last redskin fled in terror because he thought that with one stroke Belzy had scalped himself.

When Bill asked Sam what in the doggone creation he was doing with four new scalps Sam told him the story. After staring at Sam as a few days earlier he had stared at Kate, Bill reached for pipe and tobacco. Tamping tobacco into his pipe, he said, "Ya kallate to sterminate the hull doggone nation?"

Sam said dryly, "Only as many as I have time for."

"Doggone it, Sam, you shorely ought to reconsider. Thar muss be two thousan them Crows and thar ain't a devil as hisses won't be after yore skelp."

"That's how I figger it," Sam said.

"Godamighty!" Bill said. He now was staring at four ears hanging on a leather string. "Cuttin their ears off, Sam? Why, doggone it, ya might as well cut their balls off. Ever see a wasp nest laid open?"

"Many times," Sam said.

"That's the way the hull Crow nation will be, I shorely think so. How many have ye kilt?"

"Only four but I'm not through."

Bill puffed his pipe and looked at Sam for half a minute. "Whyfor ya cut their ears off?"

"I want them to know you didn't do it. That's my mark."

"Wall now, that's mighty nice of ye, Sam. I shorely wooden want them two thousan devils after me. Tell the truth now, how long ye figger to live?"

"About fifty years."

Bill pondered that a few moments, his eyes full and incredulous. "Why didden ye tell the chief ta send the killers out?"

"I told Charley to tell him but he won't do it."

"No, he never would. This is what he'll do." Old Twenty Coups, Bill said, would call all the braves into a big powwow and he would say to them, "Brave warriors, the bravest on the hull earth, one sleep, two sleeps, is a bad one; sleep he do not and hate he do and kill he do; like a ghost he is; a sharp knife he is and his gun is shore as shootin. Ye gotta raise his hair; let not the sun set nor the moon rise before this varmint is dead and skelped and cut up in little pieces." They would cut Sam loose from himself, they shorely would. The chief would call for volunteers and all the hottest bloods would step forth, eager to kill Sam Minard so they could wear an eagle feather as long as an elk horn. There was another thing that had just occurred to Bill, that itched him like wood ticks on his johnny. The Blackfeet, who already hated Sam, would be out to take him, alive, so the squaws could squat all over him, dropping their urine and dung; and so they could ransom him to the Crows for ten times a king's ransom. God alive, he could see a thousand Blackfeet warriors after Sam, he shorely could. Was Sam keeping in mind the fact that the Crows were the best shots in the country with bow and arrow?—that in fact some of them could shoot straighter with it than most whitemen with a rifle? And there was another thing: had Sam ever seen the way the Dakotas and Assiniboins hung from the ceilings of their lodges? They cut through the muscles on their backs and chests and pushed leather ropes through the holes; and by these they were lifted off the ground, and by God they hung there for days and nights and you could hear their screams for miles.

Yes, Sam said, he had heard about it. He knew that Bill was trying to suggest the hazards and horrors but Sam did not want his brotherly concern or any man's. He changed the subject.

"You think the woman on the Musselshell is all right?"

"I shorely do, Sam." She was wearing, Bill said, the same clothes she wore last fall; she looked stooped and seemed to be turning white; but all afternoon he watched her carry water up the hill. He expected that she was as crazy as a hoot owl but would get along. He expected that she would live a lot longer than Sam Minard.

"Anyone heard of her man yet?"

"Ner hair ner hide. He was gone beaver long ago."

"The red devils haven't bothered her?"

"I didden find a sign anywheres."

Sam said, "I expect I better go up and see what I can do. I have some things for her."

When the two men parted, one to swim the Yellowstone and ride north, the other to go up the valley of the Bighorn, Bill put forth a hand, as Jim Bridger had done. He squeezed Sam's hand and said:

"Watch your topknot."

"Watch yours, Bill."

Before Sam reached the river he surprised two Crows chasing a bull buffalo and shot one off his horse. The other fled. Sam took the scalp and right ear. Wall now, he knew as well as Bill or any man that the chief would call his braves to a council of war. He would tell them that a terror was loose in the Sparrowhawk nation. Sam thought that possibly the old chief himself, as brave an Indian as ever went forth to battle, might take the warpath, though it was more likely that he would choose ten or fifteen of his bravest and pledge them never to rest until the enemy was dead.

Maybe Sam Minard's days were numbered.

As the mountain men put the story together from Charley and others, the chief took his medicine men into his confidence and they agreed on the warriors most eligible for the honor. Because, like most primitive peoples, the chief counted by his fingers, the number he chose was ten. After a second powwow it was raised to twenty, but only to the shame and distress of every Crow brave: how absurd to think it would take twenty great warriors to bring down that clumsy and cowardly killer! The chief told them that any one of them could easily do it—old man that he was and full of winters, he could do it; but he wanted to give as many as possible a chance at the glory and two eagle feathers—for there would be two. Hundreds of warriors had clamored to be chosen.

The twenty picked for the glory were bold but not equally bold; wary but not equally wary; and skilled in hunting and war but not equally skilled. Wily old Twenty Coups knew that no two warriors were ever the same. His plan, therefore, was to call on all the skills of his people. Night Owl had so assiduously aped his totem that he was known as the ablest of the night hunters; it was believed that in pitch-darkness he could see as clearly as the owl. The chief knew this was not so but it was good for his people to think it was so. Red Feather was possibly the ablest strategist among the younger men; he had the cunning of the serpent, the craftiness of the fox, the resourcefulness of the wolf. Will Win was, in the chief's opinion, the best tracker in the nation; he had such a powerful sense of smell that on hands and knees he could follow the scent of man or beast across geest or a talus slope. Mad Wolf was a reckless one and might be the first to die, if any were to die. Ever since his initiation into manhood he had wanted to go alone to take Blackfeet scalps. Medicine Bird was as expert as any with bow and arrow and had one of the fastest horses. Coyote Runs was the fleetest warrior in the nation; in a race of a mile or two, over hill and down, there was no other brave who could touch coup on his flying heels. Eagle Beak was of those men born and dedicated to the profession of killing; he had counted coup at seventeen, and by the age of twenty-two had scalped two Blackfeet and three Cheyennes. The chief thought he had no warrior who could go in a straighter line to the enemy. Wolf Teeth was one of the most skilled horsemen in a nation whose horsemen were the best on earth; with only a foot and a hand showing to his enemy he could, while his horse was on a dead run, hit an object the size of a man at a distance of a hundred yards. First Coup was a sullen and grimly tenacious brave who as a boy had, with incredible intrepidity, repeatedly risked his life to touch an enemy, before cutting him down with tomahawk and knife.

Those were nine of the warriors chosen. There were eleven more, all with special talents.

Twenty Coups, the mountain men learned, called his people into meeting, and after the evil powers were propitiated and blessings invoked, he told the multitude that a dreadful killer, a paleface and a mad dog, had vowed to kill every Sparrowhawk brave he could find. To justify his bitter malevolence he was telling this absurd and outrageous lie, that a party of braves had gone a whole moon down, where the Little Snake flowed north, and had killed the mad dog's wife and unborn child. His medicine men had told him that the Cheyennes did it, urged on by the Arapahoes, who lived on coyote bones and bugs. The Sparrowhawks had always been friends of the palefaces, had fought side by side with them against their common enemies. This thing, this terror, was mad; he was the dog when it slobbered and drooled and clicked its teeth; he was like the hundreds who had flung themselves off precipices because their women and children by the tens were dying of the paleface diseases. He left his mark as a taunt and a challenge by cutting off the right ear.

They would not go as a war party, the few who were chosen, but singly and alone. Every one of them would have an equal chance to bring the mad dog down. The one who brought in the scalp and the right ear would win two eagle feathers; the one who brought him in alive would be made a chief. If this mad thing fled in craven fear, if it crawled into a dark cave to tremble there like the rabbit, or for any other reason was difficult to find and kill, the chief himself would go forth and find him. The honor, the heroism of an entire people were at stake. All the palefaces from the great salt water to the big blue, from the mountains far north to the rivers far south, would be waiting and watching to see how long it would take for a Sparrowhawk warrior to touch coup on this mad evil and bring its scalp in.

Even while the old man was haranguing his people a messenger came in with the terrible news that The Terror had slain another brave, just south of the Yellowstone; and two days later had killed a war party of three as they sat by their fire. These bodies, like those of the four, had been laid parallel with one another, their bloody skulls to the west; and from every skull the right ear had been sliced off. The chief was so outraged that his face turned the color of the red clays along the Yellowstone and his old body trembled. But for the arthritis in his joints and the blindness in his eyes (sun blindness and snow blindness) he would have put on his war paint and gone forth. His braves were not what they had been before the whitefaces came with their diseases and firewater. He must have felt as all leaders feel when, looking sharply at their people, they sense in them a moral degeneracy that portends the end of the nation.

He went ahead with the rites that would insulate the twenty warriors from harm. He personally saw that each of them had his medicine bag, his best weapons, and his choice of a horse from the large herds. At the encampment on Tongue River he bade farewell to each of them as he rode away, alone, into the southwest. The braves were garbed in their most colorful raiment, with a long headdress streaming like a banner in the wind. They were twenty handsome young men—twenty of the finest warriors from one of the most remarkable of all the Indian nations—all dedicated to a single and irrevocable mission. Rarely in human history had twenty such superb fighters gone forth to bring down one man, every one a specialist in certain skills, every one hoping that he would be the lucky and famous one. Within a few weeks news of the vendetta would reach trappers and traders as far away as the Rio and the Athabasca.

Jim Bridger gave the news to old Bill Williams. Bill's long thin sunken face, looking as if it had been covered over with poorly tanned leather and was about to crack open in its deep dried-out seams, turned unusually grave. His small pale eyes with the abnormally small pupils looked into the north country, where at that moment, he had no doubt,—Sam Minard with naked knife was slipping up to a Crow. The wrinkled bloodless lips sucked at a corncob pipestem. He took the stem away from his broken teeth and said:

"Ya said twenty?"

"Charley says. The best in the hull doggone nation."

"How many has Sam got so far?"

"A few. I heerd only yisterdy he got the one called Mad Wolf."

Bill sucked at his pipe a few moments. "Wonder if he'd like some help."

"I reckon not. He figgers to do it alone."

"He jist might at that," Bill said, and went on smoking.

Jim Bridger at his post on Black's Fork had been telling everyone who came along what Sam proposed to do. He knew most of the men in the West, for he had been a partner in the Rocky Mountain Fur Company, and after that had been with the American Fur Company, until he built his own post. Possibly no man in the West had a fuller knowledge of its mountains, rivers, valleys, passes, and trails. Thinking of Sam and the mad impossible task he had undertaken, Jim would recall that hour in 1832 when a redman shot an arrow into his back. The head of the arrow had remained in his flesh and bone for more than two years; it was then dug out with a knife by Marcus Whitman, a missionary to the red people. Jim shivered a little when he thought of all the stone arrowheads that would be speeding toward the flesh and bones of Sam Minard.

When Three-Finger McNees came to the post and heard the story he fixed one eye on Jim while the other seemed to be looking off to the Bighorns.

"You say he got Mad Wolf?"

"So I heerd."

In a hand-to-hand fight, McNees said, Sam was a match for any five redmen, and for any two white men, with doggone few exceptions. He was a holy rip-snorter. He would take care of himself unless they ambushed him or crawled up on him when he slept. Had the old chief put on his war paint?

"They say he's clum his hoss fer the lass time. It's the young bucks tryin ta take Sam off of the bay." Mebbe they would, mebbe they wouldn't, said Jim, who like all the mountain men was a realist. Today you were here and a-snortin with funk like a bull with his tail up, and tomorrer you were gone. If McNees saw Sam he might tell him that there was now a better rifle than the one he had; and the Colt revolver had been improved. As for the rest of it the mort, the note sounded on a horn at the kill, would be ringing over the hull damn land.

Did any man know where Sam was pitching his camp? Right in the Bighorns, Jim had heard.

After shooting Mad Wolf while the reckless idiot was creeping up on him, apparently determined to make a coup, Sam had crossed the Yellowstone and gone north to see the woman on the Musselshell. He rode right up to her door, said, "How are you?" and in that moment observed that her hair had turned white. By her cabin he set food, buckskins, a pouch of flower seeds, and after staking his horses on the river bottom he gathered stones from the area roundabout and piled them a few feet from the graves. He said he didn't know if she understood him when he spoke to her, or even if she listened. She had seen his wife last fall. Well, the Crows killed her and the baby that was in her and all he had now was their bones. He was going to build a stone cairn and put them in it. Having told her this, he waited, hoping that she would speak, but she was as silent as her dead ones. She was sitting between the graves, with her Bible on her lap.

On the river bottom this evening Sam smoked and brooded, and tried to see himself more clearly in life. Now and then he wondered if he was making a fool of himself. But when he thought of the vivacious Indian girl who had been his wife, and of the depths of his longing for a son, and when he contemplated again the bitter black cowardice of the killers, the old rage boiled up in him and he was eager to be off to the warpath. The next day he laid the stones, chinking them with river mud. It was harder than he had thought it would be to immure the bones—to say farewell to them, to touch them for the last time. He guessed he was a pretty sentimental fellow. He wondered if the mountain men would have laughed if they had seen him pressing his lips to the skull of his wife; holding the skull of his son in his two hands and pressing it to his cheek; and reaching in to touch them a last time before putting in the last stone. He looked over at the woman and her Bible, wishing that the bones in there could be blessed and delivered into the care of the great Giver who had set the rainbow as a guerdon to innocence; wishing that Beethoven's choral finale on the "Ode to Joy" could be played softly, forever and ever, by this cairn, and for this woman and her children.

God in heaven, what a thin unwashed ragged forlorn poor critter of a thing she was, with nothing but her Bible and two graves! Life was a riddle, damned if it wasn't: less than a year ago he had been holding his darling close and dreaming dreams—and now both darling and dreams were entombed in a pile of stones. Less than a year ago he had been singing madrigals with the birds and now he was on the warpath. A year ago this woman and her husband and children had been making the long trek to what they believed was fabulous land, an Eden or a paradise, their hearts and souls big with hopes and visions; and now four of them were slaughtered and she was lost by two graves among four whitened skulls. It was not the Father's fault if His children were damned fools who couldn't make decent use of the wealth and beauty He had given them, or get along with their neighbors. Perhaps the Almighty had long ago rued that hour when He put Adam and Eve on a planet with larks and thrushes and mockingbirds, water ouzels and geese and squirrels and blue jays and the whole diapason of music; because all these things seemed so much more in tune with land and water and sky. Sam hoped that someday he would laugh again and sing and play his music. Someday, perhaps. Meanwhile he had his own private war, and a lesson to teach as only killers could be taught.

"I'm going now," he said, standing by her and looking down at her white hair. "I'll be back before long." He bent low to touch his lips and his fingers to her hair, and then he was gone. Kate did not look up. She did not turn once to look after him as he rode up the river and disappeared.

15

HE WAS RIDING up a long mountain flank of aspen when he sensed it. At once he stopped to get his bearings. He did not recognize this area but a man could not know every one of the thousands of aspen hillsides. There were mountains south of him and across the southwest; he knew them by sight but he was on a strange trail. All redmen except the cricket-eating Diggers and the fish-eating tribes on the lower Columbia were experts in the art of ambush. It was in ambush that one small immigrant train after another was perishing.

Turning, he rode back down the trail at a fast gallop. After four hundred yards he swerved sharply, and leaving the buffalo path, headed for a summit, hoping there to be able to overlook a wide area. In this he was disappointed; and so he sat, unable to see more than a few hundred feet, and sniffed and listened. The bay raised his ears to the direction from which they had just come. Sam was wondering what had warned him; there were so many things in nature that give signals—the kingfisher, red-winged blackbird, wren, bittern, chipmunk, ground squirrel, magpie, crow—the wild world was full of them and a man had only to learn their ways. Something had told him that he was in the presence of an enemy. Because he had hidden his packhorses and was on a very fleet horse he chose one of his favorite stratagems. He would make a run for it until he found a spot he liked; and so, going at full speed, he descended from the summit and took another path, his eyes looking for a hill with jutting ledges. His was the cougar's trick, which he had observed three separate times.

The cougar—or panther or mountain lion—usually stalked his prey at their watering holes. If the hole happened to be on a stream that flowed close to an overhanging ledge of stone, the beast would crouch on the ledge and wait; and when the animals were drinking he would leap to the back of deer, antelope, elk, buffalo, or wild horse. Leaping to the shoulders, he would sink his claws deep into flesh and at the same moment reach for the throat with his long powerful teeth; and if it was one of the smaller beasts he might with a swift movement seize the head and wrench it backward, breaking the neck.

Sam was looking for a vantage point where he could leave the path, leap off his horse, and advance swiftly to meet the enemy. After two miles of forcing the bay at top speed he saw it. The trail rounded a hill. Barely past the point was a forest of trees. Rushing off the path and a hundred yards into the woods, Sam leapt down, and leaving his lathered beast to recover his wind, he ran forward and stood behind a tree. He was not surprised when no Indian came in sight. He now hastened through the woods and up the hill. On hands and knees, crawling swiftly, he went forward to a bluff above the path and looked down. Back there on the trail, two hundred yards, was a Crow warrior, the paint on his face glinting like gold in the noon sunshine. He sat on a tall sorrel pony, looking and listening. Having no doubt that this was one of the twenty, Sam watched him through a lattice of leaves. He could have shot him off the horse at that distance but on thinking it over he decided to walk out in plain view and give the man a chance.

The moment he was in full view he gave the Crow war cry and raised his gun. But he did not fire. His sharp eyes were watching the enemy's movements; it seemed to Sam that the redskin was deaf or paralyzed. He would have sworn that for a full ten seconds the fool sat there, his black eyes staring at the giant who stood a hundred feet above him and two hundred yards away. Sam could imagine how the eyes shone, with a gem of light in their center; and the tenseness of the clutch on the gun, and of the thighs clasping the pony. Suddenly the Indian came to life and brought his rifle up; in that instant Sam fired and the pony fell. Almost at once the redman was on his feet. Again with electric suddenness his long rifle came up but Sam had ducked down and back to reload. When ready he shot up into full view and the Indian's gun in that moment exploded. In the next instant Sam fired and saw the man stagger. Sam dropped to his knees to reload. Knowing that this young warrior had momentarily lost his nerve and fired wildly, Sam doubted that he was one of the twenty: more likely he was a green youngster who had taken a gun and slipped away to find glory.

Running to his horse, Sam mounted and rode into the forest above the bluff. The pony was dead and the warrior had disappeared. There was nothing to do but watch and wait. If, as Sam imagined, this was a youngster, eager to cover himself with honors and an eagle feather, he was alone; but if he had been scouting for a war party the three shots would bring it in. While waiting, Sam wondered if he would not soon be weary of this night-and-day stalking; if he should have gone to the old chief and demanded the right to meet the killers; or if he should have gone back to his people for a visit. He had considered all these alternatives and rejected them; reconsidered and rejected again, for the reason that all the red people were fantastic liars and cheats. Anyway, the chief would have sworn by all his dead ancestors that none of his braves was guilty.

There was still another matter, Sam told himself as he sat in tall grass, looking out and down. The Crows were now claiming broader lands than they had ever occupied—all the country that bordered the Musselshell on the south and east. This included the woman and her graves and the cairn. So far as Sam could tell, it included lands claimed by the Blackfeet. If these implacable enemies, with their age-old feuds, were to go to war they might, when their blood got real hot, murder the woman; if they did that, half the mountain men in the country would march against them, and there would be enough blood to turn a river red. If there were only good trapping spots close to the woman he would live there and watch over her and someday take her back to her people. But there were no good beaver ponds within two hundred miles of her.

While looking down at a dead horse and waiting he also dwelt on the fact that warriors from other tribes would now try to capture him, knowing that the Crows would pay a fabulous price for him. Windy Bill had been emphatic about this two weeks ago when they puffed their pipes after breakfast and drank black coffee.

Sam, he said, would look worse than a stillborn child in a putrefied forest after they were done with him. Old Jake Moser's nephey he had trapped on the Heely—wall now, the Comanches had wanted him, and so the Rapahoes they caught him, and when the squaws were done with him you cudden a-tole if he was man or coyote. Some people they were good at one thing, like sailing the sea; and some at another, like being a lying politician; but the Injuns they were the best on earth at torture. Bill could jist see the squaws slaverin as they looked at Sam, he shorely could. If Sam were fool enough to let the Blackfeet take him alive they ought to open his skull to see if there was anything in it.

"I don't figger they'll take me," Sam said.

Had any man ever, who was taken? "Sam, I wisht ya would think it over, I shorely do."

Bill had proposed that twenty mountain men should ride into the Crow village on the Tongue and demand the murderers from the old chief; they would tell him that if the killers of Sam's wife were not handed over the mountain men would bring the Blackfeet and the Cheyennes against them, and the Sioux for good measure. Sam had refused to consider the proposal; this, he felt, was his own private feud. He felt that no life but his own should be risked. Doggone it, Bill had said, the

Blackfeet would be trailing Sam day and night. As for himself, he'd rather face a grizzly or ten bitch wolves than a Blackfeet squaw with a knife in her hand.

Sam hoped that the Blackfeet would not be on his trail, for he had dreamed of spending a winter in their beautiful country: of hibernating during the months of December and January, like the bear; of eating and sleeping and communing with the creator's infinite, while playing a few themes from Corelli and Bach and Mozart; of enjoying the pure heaven of being alone, far from policemen and tax collectors and all the parasites who made up any government. Bill Williams had once said there actually were damned fools who spent a good part of their time in wanton romping with women; and other damned fools who thought it the supremest pleasure to stand at bars swilling gin and rum; and still others who thought the good life demanded a neighbor within thirty feet on either side. Nearly all the mountain men agreed with Bill. They were all rebels.

Convinced after two hours that no other Crows had been in the area, Sam went down to the horse. It looked like a very ordinary pony but you never could tell about an Indian pony. A trail stained with blood led away to a thicket. Warily Sam followed it and soon came to a man lying on his face, stone-dead. Or a youngster, Sam saw, after turning the body over: not eighteen, perhaps not more than sixteen: a good-looking boy who had slipped away and gone forth to take Sam's scalp. Poor dead young one! He had a rifle so old that it looked like one the first voyageurs brought down from Canada; and a stone hatchet with a broken handle.

For a full five minutes Sam looked down at the brave youth, thinking that his son would have been much like him. He did not take the scalp or cut off the ear. If he had had a shovel he would have buried this brave kid; if there had been stones in this area he would have built a cairn. The most and the best he could do was to heave the body to the fork of a tree, eight feet up; there, on its belly, the corpse hung down, both head and heels, but it would be safe from the wolves. The old musket Sam tied to the tree just below the youth. If the Crows found this dead son they would know that Sam had hung him in a tree and they would know why.

But there was something that they would never see and never know. It was in Sam's face and eyes after he had gone fifty yards and had turned to look back.

16

His killing of the Crow boy chastened his male aggressions a little; but two days later he killed Wolf Teeth, without knowing who the man was; and a week after that he killed Coyote Runs. He sensed that he had an unexpected advantage in the fact that the hotbloods sent out to get him were competing with one another and taking foolhardy risks.

It was while thinking one day of the pathetic form hanging grotesquely in the tree that Sam recalled an experience that had haunted his dreams. It had been two years ago. He and two companions, looking for beaver ponds, had surprised six Blackfeet warriors riding down a ridge. Because members of this tribe had recently killed one of their friends they gave the mountain man's dreadful war cry and charged. Their first three shots toppled three redmen from their ponies. Reloading while they raced after the survivors, they fired again, aiming at the horses because of the distance; and the three beasts stumbled and fell. Two braves leapt up and fled. The third had a broken leg and was crawling away like a wounded badger when the white men overtook him. The Indian then struggled up to his sound leg and drew a knife. An expert with a Bowie, Sam at that moment had hurled his blade and knocked the Indian down. Leaping from his horse and rushing to the fallen man, Sam had drawn the knife out and plunged it through him, in the region of his heart. Gouts of blood had spouted from the wounds and from the mouth and nostrils.

Sam had then raced after his companions, who were pursuing the two Indians. They lost them and returned to the dead horses. Fifteen minutes passed before one of them looked over at the warrior with the broken leg. His cry of amazement had brought Sam to his feet. The man through whom Sam had twice driven his knife had managed to sit up—even had managed to find his knife; and there he sat, a hideous figure, his whole chest red with the gore that streamed down from his mouth. The thing that had held Sam's attention was the Indian's eyes, staring at him through a red mist; they were filled with the deadliest hatred Sam had ever seen. But even more terrible to look at than the eyes were the hands, washed with warm blood and trying feebly to close nerveless fingers around the handle of a dagger. After a few moments the Indian had made a chilling sound, as from agony, mixed with the choking gurgle of blood in the throat; and as blood burst in a red vomit from nose and mouth the head sank forward, and the body, and the warrior was still.

There was nothing in a man that Sam admired more than courage. More than once since that hour Sam had awakened from a dream about this man and had been too disturbed to sleep again; more than once he had been troubled, as now, by contemplation of man's or beast's helplessness before an enemy. Nothing else in life went into him so deep, or with such pain and pathos; nothing else drew from him such a cry of pity to the Creator. Man to man or beast to beast, when both were in fighting fettle, was one thing; to be helpless before a merciless enemy was another thing. He knew, he never for a moment forgot, that the Blackfeet tortured their captives with fiendish ferocities that few whitemen could have imagined. It was true that no one could believe, without having seen them, how savage the squaws could be. Were they mothers? Did they feel tenderness when cradling their babes? How was a man to reconcile such hellish cruelties with a courage, sometimes a valor, that brought cries of admiration from their enemies?

Around campfires during the long winters tales were told of the red people's nature and doings—such as the wager between a Sioux and a Cheyenne, both from a war-loving people. They had met unexpectedly one day, at a time when their nations were not at war, and the Sioux had challenged the Cheyenne to a game of hands. In this simple game one of the two players took a small pebble, and putting both hands behind his back, clasped the stone in one of them. Bringing his hands into plain view of his opponent, knuckles up, he asked him to choose the hand that held the stone. This was a favorite game with Indians; they were such inveterate gamblers that they would wager everything they had, including their horses, weapons, women, and sometimes their lives.

The Cheyenne won everything the Sioux had, and that brave, sitting stark-naked and wondering what else he could wager, offered his coveted scalp. He wagered it against everything he had lost. It was the wily Cheyenne's turn with the stone, and behind his back he took so much time changing his mind and moving the stone from hand to hand that his opponent cried out with impatience. Suspecting a trick, he demanded to see the stone, for sometimes a brave's medicine was big. The Sioux took the stone and examined it. He could see no erosion caused by magic, but asked nevertheless that a bullet from his medicine bag be used instead. It was the Cheyenne's turn to suspect a trick; he stared hard at the piece of lead as he turned it over and over in his hands. Though it looked all right he tested it with his teeth and he smelled of it. His sly mind was telling him that the Sioux was dull and unimaginative and could be deceived; and so he kept the piece of lead in his right hand as he examined it, and it was still in his right hand when he put his hands behind his back. It was still in the right hand when after five minutes of anguished searching of his wits and his magic the Sioux said it was in the left hand. The Cheyenne had guessed that the stupid fellow would get hooked by the notion that the bullet would be slipped over to the left hand.

Without the slightest trace of fear the Sioux had folded his arms across his naked chest and bowed his head. Without the slightest feeling of mercy or pity the Cheyenne had taken up his knife and stood above him. With his left hand he seized the long hair and pulled the scalp taut, while with his right he cut through hair and skin to the bone, all the way around the skull. If the Sioux flinched the Cheyenne did not see or feel it. The customary way of scalping, both red and white, was to put a foot on the prostrate enemy's neck or face and with a powerful twisting jerk snap the scalp off. The Cheyenne, without benefit of foot on neck, had to snap the top-knot back and forth and at last with a swift movement jerk it off. The Sioux rose to his feet, blood streaming down over him. He had seen men scalped who lived; he knew that his skull would heal but that forevermore he would be a bald and disgraced one. He wanted vengeance.

So he demanded that they meet again for another game of hands, after two moons. Feeling immeasurably superior, the Cheyenne readily agreed. He foresaw another triumph. He stipulated that they should bring to the rendezvous their finest horse and their finest weapons. They would meet on Owl Creek, at its headwaters, in two moons. All the time the two were making their agreement the Sioux stood with blood streaming down his front and back, and the Cheyenne openly admired his bloody trophy, which he held by the long hair.

They met again in two moons, the Sioux's skull as bright and smooth as sun-baked bone, the Cheyenne unable to keep the gloating out of his face. But either luck or cunning was against him this time; he began to feel after several losses that his opponent had stronger medicine; and with all the magic taught him by the wise men he prayed for and strove to summon, in moments of intense concentration, a power that could defeat the bald eager man who kept guessing right four times in five. But he lost his horse, his weapons, and every piece of leather on him; and he sat as his opponent had sat, two months earlier, stark-naked, with nothing left to wager but his scalp or his life. If he had wagered his scalp and lost the Sioux would have been satisfied, but the Cheyenne, like his people, was a proud haughty one. Besides, he now thought his magic was working, and so resolved to wager his life against everything he had lost and everything the Sioux had brought with him. The impassive Sioux accepted the proposal. The Cheyenne lost. That moment, Sam had thought many times, must have been about as intense and electric as any moment had ever been between two enemies. How many whitemen would have run for their lives? The Cheyenne merely stood up and faced the Sioux. Had he begun to chant the Indian death song? The story said only that the bald Sioux faced the Cheyenne and drove his knife through the Cheyenne's heart.

It was a man's country out here, and not for tall boys called men. Sam had never known an Indian and had never heard of one who had begged for mercy. Mercy was not a word in their language. A white captive who begged for mercy—and most of them did—aroused in their captors such contempt that they could not devise tortures fiendish enough to degrade him. Every mountain man knew that if he were luckless enough to be captured the only way to face the red people was to hawk phlegm up his throat and spit it in their faces. They might then torture you and they certainly would kill you but they would admire you and they would treasure your scalp.

Sam looked squarely at the fact that he might be captured someday. Few whitemen in Indian lands had lived to be as old as Caleb Greenwood and Bill Williams. Twice captured by the Blackfeet and twice escaping from them, Jeremiah Flagg had said, "I spect it's time fer this ole coon to git back to his tree." He said there had been a time when he could smell a cussed redskin ten miles toward nowhere but now couldn't smell him unless he could see him.

It was terribly beautiful country covered with violent life. The beaver was a gentle fellow who lived on bark; the milk-givers ate leaves and grass; but the flesh-eaters were all killers, and man was a flesh-eater. Sam had observed that most of the flesh-eaters were savage in their love-making. A favorite with some of the red people was the soup dance, in which the men and women in two lines faced one another across a distance of thirty or forty feet. A girl would coyly advance with a spoon (of buffalo or mountain sheep horn) filled with soup. This she would offer to the man of her choice and quickly withdraw, with the man pursuing her until she reached her line. He would then retreat, dancing to music, and she would come again; and still again; and from those watching there would be laughter or hoots of derision. When whitemen participated they substituted kissing for the spoonful of soup; but the Arapahoes, with whom, it was said, the dance had originated, rubbed noses, though now and then a couple would try kissing and seem to like it. The girls sometimes but not always wore a hair-rope chastity belt, with the ends tied around their waist.

A story was told of Kit Carson in one of these dances. A huge French bully had proclaimed himself the favorite and guardian of all the more attractive girls. Half drunk and with his lusts boiling, he had chased a girl into an adjacent woods, and after catching her had been so eager that he had slashed with his knife back and forth at the chastity belt, opening deep wounds in the girl's thighs and belly. She had then drawn a hidden knife and stabbed him and run away. According to the tale Sam had heard, Kit then challenged the bully to a duel, killed him, and took the girl, Singing Grass, as his mate, changing her name to Alice.

Sam had learned that most of the flesh-eating males were brutal to the females. Possibly the cats, big and little, were the most ferocious of all, though no more cruel than some of the men, red or white, when filled with passion and rum. The way his Lotus trembled under his touch during the first days had told him things he had never read in books. The red lover was sometimes worse than the male bobcat: at one of the posts during trading time Sam had watched drunken braves mating with their women—had seen a Cheyenne cover one of his wives and then in a senseless fury stab her repeatedly with a long knife. He then embraced her a second time, after she was dead.

Weariness with killing had turned Sam's thoughts to love, and to John Colter's hell. Why not spend a winter there? He could go deep into that steaming and exploding area and no Indian would dare follow him, for they thought that evil spirits were working their magic there. They thought a geyser spouting its boiling breath fifty or a hundred feet into the sky was an especially large devil showing off his powers. All the tiny hot-mouth poutings were, Sam supposed, the puckered lips of little devil-babies. It was a fearful land tucked away in the basins among densely forested mountains. No buffalo were there, but deer and elk were, rabbits and grouse, and ducks and geese on the lake. He could build a fire without having to feel anxious; soak himself in hot pools; eat hot food, play or sing, and think of his wife. He could study the loveliness of coruscant glitters and winkings of light in a coppice when a breeze was on it; and the empyreal elemental fires in the sunsets; and the fugues as choirs of birds sang around him. If tax collector or policeman or political boss ventured in he would chuck him headfirst into a big boiling mudpot.

Yes, he would go there, to recover his poise and nourish his powers; but first he would go up to the woman to see if she was all right. He wished he could persuade her to come with him, for it chilled his bones to think of her alone in another winter, under the howling megalomania of the Canadian winds and the wild subzero blizzards. The mountain men might even move the graves down there, where she would always have heat and hot water and shelter, and lifelong security from her enemies.

17

HE RODE, by night, through Crow country, and four days later sat astride the bay on a hilltop, looking first at the cairn. Then he saw the woman sitting between the graves. God in heaven, would she spend all her life over the bones of her dead? Was this a typical mother? Before her tragedy imploded into his being he had never thought of the differences between the human male and female. While looking over at this lonely woman and thinking about her he recalled a dream about Lotus that he had dreamed many times. She had lain naked on his thighs and belly, as though on a big thick mattress of meat, her chignon of black hair snuggled against his throat, a slender bronzed hand reaching up to play with his beard. His beard had lain down over one side of her face like a covering of horse mane. She had liked to run fingers through his whiskers and yank gently at the hair over his chest, possibly, he had thought, because the redmen were so hairless. Then she had moved up through hair to his mouth and had kissed him.

Now, looking over at the woman, he felt a surge of tenderness; in memory emotion flowed in lightning heat all the way south over the path they had taken, and to the cabin, and to the pitiful armful of bones that was all that had been left of the vibrant thing he had loved. He was hungry for woman but he had no hunger for the woman with white hair sitting by the graves. If she was anything for him she was a mother image, or female-with-little-ones image, like the grouse with her lovely darlings, or the female mallard webfooting it across a lake, with seven or eight soft little balls of fluff and down in her wake. This was a large soft hour for Sam Minard, goose-down-lined, geyser-warm, antelope-eye gentle, mountain-lily white and tender, as he looked at the woman. Sentimental softening of his will and senses had not moved in such a deep current since he last reached in to touch the immured bones, his soul enfolding all that remained of one who in his dream of her and his plans for her would have been wife and mate and straight-shooting warrior at his side.

Sam then rode off into the hills. Had this woman learned how to jerk flesh, catch fish from the river, dry wild fruits? Or did she sit there the whole time, except when bringing water to her small elysian garden? Suspecting that he knew little about the human female and her ways, he tried to summon a clear image of his mother and of other mothers he had known, in their pattern of living. His mother had worked hard for her children and work was about all she had had. This woman had time and that was about all she had. She would have years and years of time and she would grow old there and die, and like his wife, be eaten to her bones by wolves and ravens.

He returned with two fine deer, gutted but with the hides still on, and went over to the shack. The woman had seen him coming, and now actually looked over at him as he drew near. Bill had learned her name and now all the mountain men knew her name; and so Sam said, cheerfully, "How are you, Mrs. Bowden? How have you been this long time?"

Dismounting, he untied the deer, and taking each by a hind and foreleg, laid them on their backs, open bellies up. Looking round for stones to prop them, he saw that the northwest skull was not the one he had put on the stake. He walked over to have a look at it. Some mountain man had killed and beheaded an Indian and had brought the skull here. "Looks like they're watching over you," he said when he returned to the cabin.

Because she had risen to her feet he went over to her. He simply stared at her and she stared at him; after a few moments his gaze moved over her face and he saw that it was starvation-thin; and down over her body, noting the details of her garb. On her feet she had the tatters of a pair of shoes; her ragged dress looked to him like the one she had worn the first day he saw her. Her hair hung in uncombed snarls; her face and hands looked as if they hadn't been washed for years.

He went over to a pannier, saying, "The Crows don't have feet as big as mine. Mebbe some of these will fit you." He offered them to her but she did not take them. Again he looked at her eyes. He had never seen such eyes. He had not known that in human eyes there could be such glittering and chilling lights. Something like horror ran along his nerves as he looked into Kate's eyes and saw that they had no memory of anything not fenced in by this river and its hills.

He went to the door of the shack and looked in. It was bleak with the first chill of autumn. He turned to look at her plants. She had quite a garden of sage and wild flowers, but the flowers were now withering in the freezing nights. Facing her again, he said he wished she would go with him to the region of bilings, where she could be warm in any kind of weather. He and Bill and some others could take up her loved ones and carry them down there and bury them by the hot waters of a pool; and she could have a much lovelier garden, almost the year round. But he knew after a few minutes that his words were not entering the small bleak world where she lived. He sensed that in strange ways that he would never understand it was a wonderful world, where a mother lived with her children, and the angels and God. He framed her thin tired face with his big hands and lightly kissed her forehead and her hair.

"I brought you some things," he said, speaking cheerfully, doubting that she would understand a word. From his packhorses he took sugar, flour, coffee, salt, raisins; a roll of buckskin inside of which were pepper, needles, thread, matches; a roll of cotton cloth, inside of which were pencils and a notebook; and a buffalo robe. Here were pencil and paper, he said, holding them in full view of her stare. He thought she might like to write letters back home. Every time a mountain man came by she could hand the letters to him, and he would give to her the mail that came in for her. Sam had had the notion that she could be won back to a sense of the realities if she were to write and receive letters; but he knew, good Lord, he knew that she was far below that, or above it.

He dressed out the meat, jerked most of it, roasted one tenderloin for himself and the other for her, and the next morning turned back up the river. He had not gone far when he stopped to think. Why would a woman, even a mad-woman, carry water all day long up a hill to water such a plant as the sage? Concluding that there must be a mystery in it, he decided to go back and spy on her. What did she think about all day long, what did she dream about all night? The pile of wood he had laid by the south wall she had never touched; all around the cabin there was no sign that she had ever made a fire. She had never brought river mud to daub the hut—she must have almost frozen to death during the past winter, when temperatures dropped to thirty or forty below zero and winds colder than ice smote the walls. The more he thought about it the more incredible it seemed that she was still alive. On his way down the river he searched the bottoms but found no spot where she had dug for roots, no berry bush from which she had taken fruit.

Hiding his beasts in a thicket, he went up the hills and turned north. Approaching behind one juniper and another, he drew within sixty yards of her and sat to make himself comfortable, and to observe her and wait. Peering between cedar branches, he had a good view of her and her yard. She was sitting. It looked to him as if she was sitting between the graves, and she seemed to be talking but he could not be sure of that. The sun was sinking; it would be dusk soon, and then night, with a full moon two hours before midnight. How simple it would be for a Blackfoot from the west, a Big Belly from the east, or a Crow from the south to slip in here and take her scalp and everything she had! He knew that redskins must have been tempted to the verge of frenzy. He knew that only fear of mountain-man vengeance stayed their hands. It had become a law of this country that if the redmen of any tribe were contemptuous or brutal toward any mountain man, or any person whom mountain men were protecting, word of it would go forth all the way to the San Juans, the Big Blue, and to Oregon's Blue Mountains and beyond; and a summons to a rendezvous and vengeance. The vengeance would be so dreadful that survivors would turn gray with fear and flee to the remotest hills. Sam thought it unlikely that any buck would ever be fool enough to take the scalp of this defenseless woman.

Because the wind was coming his way, down from the Bear Paw Mountains, he filled and kindled his pipe and breathed in the aroma of Kentucky tobacco. There was nothing much to see; she just sat there, and an hour passed, two hours, and she still sat, as though waiting for something or someone. When deeper dusk came he could barely see her. In the breeze moving over him he could smell her and the shack with its big pile of unclean bedding; he could smell the bleached-bone odor of the skulls and of all the deer bones mountain men had scattered roundabout. Putting his pipe away, he went on a wide detour and approached from the north. As she sat she faced the south by southwest. Taking his time, he slipped forward until he came to the shack on the north side; he then peered round the northwest corner. There she sat, between the bones of her children. He looked back to the hour when he had buried her loved ones; he saw the scene again and knew that her daughter's grave was on her right, within reach of her hand; the grave of her sons on her left. The riddle was why she spent so much time there. For an hour Sam watched her and she did not move half an inch either way. He sensed that she was waiting for something but there was nothing before her that he could see, except a dozen sage plants that she had brought from the river bottom, and scrub juniper farther out, and the night dark of river trees.

About ten o'clock the moon came out of mountain dark; it looked like a round piece of cardboard with pale paint smudges on it. But it cast a lot of light. He saw that at once there was a change in the woman; she moved a little and seemed to sit a little higher; she took something up from her lap; and then to his utter amazement she began to speak. Like a man who now found himself in a strange eerie place, he glanced round him and up at the night, and listened. Her back was to him but by the way her arms moved he knew that she had something in her hands that she was looking at. Her voice was surprisingly strong and clear. He heard the words, "The wilderness and the solitary place shall be glad for them." Straining forward, he heard: "The Lord meant you, and you, John, and you, Robert—the wilderness and the solitary place, all around us here, it is for us. All this is glad for us, my darlings; you make it more pleasant in the sight of the Lord. John, my darling, Robert, my darling, and my darling daughter, do you all hear me? . . ."

Sam heard her. He was rigid with astonishment. The moon had risen the height of four tall men in the sky, and Lou and John and Robert in the cocoons of their moon-gray sages were nodding softly, like flowers, and smiling, with heavenly radiance like a silken halo around them.

Sam advanced from the corner, and stared and listened. In his wonderment he now realized that this woman had some education; he thought she had the accents of a schoolmarm. But he could see nothing to talk to. Soundlessly he advanced until he stood just behind her, and his amazement grew as he stared and listened.

"We're in the wilderness and solitary," the woman's voice said, clear and strong. "We don't have much but we've always been poor people; all our people have been poor people as far back as anyone knows; but our Lord, he said to his disciples, 'Blessed be ye poor, for yours is the kingdom of God. Blessed are ye that hunger, for ye shall be filled. Blessed are ye that weep now, for ye shall laugh. . . .'"

"Almighty God!" Sam said under his breath.

On her right the image of her daughter, so delicate that it seemed to have come from subdued light and the softest kind of cloud silk, moved as the breeze moved, and nodded gently and bowed, like flowers, and smiled and listened to her mother; and on her left the two sons, looking like pure soul divested of all its dross, smiled and nodded. Sam stared until his eyes ached but could see only the sage and the withered flowers. After an hour he slipped back to the north side of the cabin and there he pinched himself to be sure that he was not asleep and dreaming; looked out to the distant hills like piles of night dark; at the tree line of the river—at all these to see if they were still familiar, for he was feeling uneasy and queersome. Everything looked as it had always looked, except this woman. He now returned to his position behind her and looked down over her head to see what was in her lap. Never would she know that this tall man stood almost touching her and stared at her gray hair and at the Bible in her hands. His eyes searched the earth before her and the plants, but except the plants and the woman and the cedars and the river trees he could see no sign of living thing.

To her dear ones and her darlings she was now saying, "Repeat after me the words, 'Glory to God in the highest, and on earth peace, good will toward men.'" She told them that most men seemed not to want peace, but mothers wanted peace, for the good of their children. Sam strained his ears but could hear only her voice and the flow of the river and the cries of night birds. He saw that here and there in the book she had put slivers of paper; she would lift pages, fifty or a hundred at a time, and move from one slip of paper to another; and then pause to read, " 'For ye shall go out with joy, and be led forth with peace; the mountains and the hills shall break forth before you into singing.'" A little later she was telling them that the Lord called on the heavens to sing and the earth to be filled with joy, and all the mountains to burst with song. She was saying, "Until he comes we will be solitary in the wilderness."

Sam slipped fifty yards out into the night, so that tobacco smoke would not reach her, and filled his pipe and smoked. There had been strange music in her words, strange soothing caress, as of a wild mother's hand; he did not want to let this tenderness go from him. The mountains and the hills would break into singing? For him the earth had always been singing. Here in these mountains were fugues, arias, sonatas, the thousands and millions of them interweaving the harmonies of one another; and there was the other side of it, in Thomas Hood's lines:

There is a silence where hath been no sound,
There is a silence where no sound may be.

There was that kind of silence in the pathetic youngster hanging from the tree crotch.

Suddenly there came to Sam an impulse to get his organ and at a distance from her, unseen and unknown, play soft music. So he went to his baggage and returned; and lying on his belly behind a mound of earth, with the night breeze moving across him and toward her, he made low musical tones, while wondering what he should play. His instrument was not generous enough for Bach's organ music. The things that flooded his soul were the love songs he had sung and played for Lotus. "Have You Seen a Whyte Lily Grow?" He played that. He played a tender Mozart minuet, the soft notes floating away on the breeze to that dear mother's ears. Almost at once she began to sing. The sound of her voice in mezzo-soprano song was so electrifying that for a few moments Sam was put off his music; he could only listen in astonishment and gaze up at the night sky, knowing that the Creator had a hand in this. The woman did not move or turn to look round her. He thought she was singing hymns; he began to improvise, mixing snatches from serenades, Corelli phrases, the themes of thrush, lark, and warbler, in a pleasing assonance all his own. After a while he understood that what he played did not matter at all, as long as it was in harmony with her mood, the moon, and the night. With her back to him she was singing to her children, and Sam was playing softly to the stars and his mother and Lotus. He kept the notes low, for he did not want to alarm her; the whole lovely thing would have been shattered if even a faint suspicion had broken through to her mind. He blew out just enough music from "The Mellow Horn," bird arias, the theme so often repeated in Beethoven's violin concerto, and other musical tidbits, to keep her singing. For two hours or longer she sang in a fair soprano, with a marvelously clear bell-tone now and then ringing from her throat; and the moon rose to the zenith and a thousand stars came out.

When at last Sam slipped away into the night he wondered if his playing had been a kindness: if there was no music tomorrow night, the next night, and for weeks or months, how would she feel about it? Well, doggone it, he would return as often as he could, to play what she surely must think was heavenly music. She would hear it and she would sing to her children: deeper happiness than that there was none, for mothers anywhere.

18

BECAUSE IT WAS impossible to enter the geyser basins on
horseback up the Yellowstone or over the Yellowstone
Mountains Sam had to go south and up the South Fork and past
Hawks Rest and down the Yellowstone to the lake. Across
timbered mountains, black and beautiful with health, he
followed the east side of the lake, going north, and then the
north side, until he came to steaming springs. It was a marvel to
all who had seen this coastline, for out in the cold lake were hot
springs, some of them a hundred yards out; and there the hot
and cold waters mingled, and steam rose from the surface. At
the lake's edge a man could find water of any temperature,
between icy cold and almost boiling. Before going to the area
on the west side of pouting and hissing paint and mud pots Sam
stripped off and plunged in. He had known no experience more
exhilarating than swimming back and forth through extremes
of hot and cold. It was such a delightful and thrilling surrender
of his senses to the caresses that, floating on his back and
looking up at the blue, he said to the Creator, in Bill's language,
"No man alive ever made a bath pool like thissen!" What was it
the woman had read from the holy book? "The wilderness and
the solitary place shall be glad for them." How glad he was to
be here, solitary, alone, and safe in the wilderness!

This evening he was entertained by the mudpots, which he
thought of as mud mouths: they took him back to the blond
neighbor girl, named Nancy, who had puffed her cheeks at him
and then slapped them with both palms, pretending that her
face had exploded. Another of her impish tricks had been to
puff her cheeks as far out as she could and then insert a small
reed between her lips. It was, she gravely told him, a puncture;
as she forced air out through the reed her cheeks slowly
collapsed, her blue eyes all the while soberly watching him.

153

The hot mud mouths puffed their lips out and up; and sometimes the lips parted and a burst of hot steam-breath shot up; and sometimes the lips were expanded to astonishing fullness, without parting, like thin gray rubber or a toad's throat. Now and then they sucked back and forth, as Nancy had sucked her lips in and pushed them out.

Sitting on warm earth among the mudpots, he tried to write a letter to his parents. Unlike the great explorers Lewis and Clark, who had come through the rocky mountain land before Sam was born, or famous scouts like Bridger and Carson and Greenwood, Sam had had twelve years in good schools. With note pad on his knees and brows perplexed, he wrote the salutation; and then for ten minutes wondered what to say and what not to say. Should he tell them that he had taken up arms against an entire Indian nation and next spring would be on the warpath again? No, he would not worry them with that. Should he tell them that he had married a lovely and loving Indian girl, who only a few months later had been struck down by a pack of killers? Should he tell them that he stood chance of being dead within a year? No, he would tell them only pleasant things. He recalled how one morning his mother had looked out at a wide-spreading apple tree with five bushels of ripe apples on it and said, "This is the first time I ever thought of an apple tree as a mother." His mouth watered as he remembered the sound fragrance and the juices bursting past his lips as he sank strong teeth in those apples. Waugh, if only he had one now!

Well, he would tell them that the more he looked round the world the plainer became the glorious truth that the Creator was a great artist in all fields. His paintings, which included sunsets and mornings, mountain lakes in pure jeweled radiance, and the firmament with two rainbows across it after a rain, were Rubens and Rembrandt on canvas as big as worlds. What sculptor would dare set his puny and trifling creations beside the Tetons or the Black Hills or the Wind River range, or the vast acres of ruga in the lava flows over by the Snake? The Creator had more bird musicians, playing their arias with flute, piccolo, harp, and tiny horn, than any man could guess at—in any moment of the twenty-four hours there were millions of bird throats singing. In His stupendous orchestrations the Creator could overwhelm a man with His mastery of counterpoint in rivers and winds and thunders, or with the variations in His cosmic sonatas. Sam would tell his father he

ought to be out here, for he remembered the man's deep
emotion when he listened to the conclusion of the second
movement of Beethoven's Third or the F-minor sonata. If only
he could hear the music in this wild land—the horn calls of the
loon, coot, crane, helldiver grebe, or the incredible music of the
snipe's tail feathers at dusk!

He would tell them that snow was falling in winter blankets
on the forests now but that he was sitting on hot earth, with hot
water boiling out all around him. If they were here they might
be looking at small puffs of steam above a stone basin and a few
moments later see a million gallons of boiling water hurled a
hundred feet into the air, to fall downward in streamers and
mists as still other millions of gallons exploded from the world's
hot insides. Deep warm fog in subzero weather would envelop
them. He would try to make them understand what a divine
loveliness it was when, in heavy snowstorm, the millions of
flakes, many as large as oak leaves, descended into the
atmosphere above one of the steam vents; how, looking up,
they would see the millions of them coming down; how
they would see them vanish by millions, as in the winking
of an eye they melted and fell in big fat raindrops; how they
would marvel at this enormous chamber of heat within a
circumference of pure white snow. In a hundred or two
hundred steps from hot earth they would find snow six or eight
feet deep. In only a few seconds they could walk from thirty-
degrees-below-zero cold into such warmth that they could
stand in comfort with all their clothes off. They could lie in a hot
natural pool and see trees so cold that they were bursting open.

He would spend the winter here, alone, thinking of his wife
and son, without having to keep his eyes skinned, as Windy Bill
would say, day and night. The snow all around him except in
the hot places might be eight or ten feet deep; but the grass was
tall and his horses would paw the snow away to find it. He
would get two or three elk before the heaviest snows came, he
would jerk some meat and hang up some hindquarters; and he
might go south to the Big Snake where he would find whole
mountainsides of berry bushes bent under their fruit. Like the
red people, he might gather some acorns, pine nuts, chestnuts,
hazelnuts; and of berries the service, elder, choke, thimble, as
well as big juicy yellow currants and rich wild plums. Away
down south beyond the San Juans was a tall sage plant, the
seeds of which Indians pounded into flour. Jim Bridger called it

chia; he said bread made of it was so strong that when washing his hands a man had to be careful or he would pull his fingers off. The Creator had put an abundance of food in the land and there was no tax on it. Had they ever heard of wild broom corn and balsam root? If they would come out for a visit their son would set before them such feasts as they had never known; and they could take home a bag of pemmican made of buffalo tenderloin, hump fat, huckleberries, and arrowroot jelly. Tongue in cheek, he would tell them that they might wish to sample red-ant cakes, made of the terrible big red ant, mixed with camas roots and onion bulbs. Or for breakfast with their pancakes they might like a hash of grasshoppers, or rattlesnake broiled on cedar embers, or a paste of castoreum. That was the orange-brown stuff from the beaver, with the strong wild odor, which trappers used as a lure.

Above all, he would ask them to imagine the kind of winter he was spending, with its pure mountain streams, its deep white snows, its millions of acres of forest that an axe had never touched; its abundance of food, its cathedral quiet when the birds were hushed, its hot baths and chambers—all as free as a mother's love for her child.

After writing the letter he wrapped it in buckskin to keep it dry and safe from mice.

He lingered a few days at the delightful hot springs by the lake and then crossed a low mountain range to the geyser basins. He was now in dense forest that lay before him in all directions for a hundred miles. Under a huge pine just south of the geyser that would someday be known as Old Faithful he made his camp. When it became cold enough to keep meat with jerking it he brought in both elk and deer, and the choicest portions he hung from branches of trees, loosely shrouded in buckskin sheaths. He had plenty of salt, sugar, coffee, tobacco, a fifty-pound bag of flour, a thousand rounds of ammunition, seeds and nuts and dried fruit, perfect health, and a mountain appetite. What more, he would have asked the philosophers, did any man want? And all of it was free.

It was in his thankful moods, induced by thunder's magnificent orchestrations or the witchery of high-mountain snowstorms, that he would climb to the spine of a range and stride along it, flinging his arms toward heaven and pouring song from his throat. The wonder of being alive and healthy and free was for him such a miracle that only in song could he express his gratitude. "Thank you, thank you!" he would cry, his red face and golden beard turned up to the storm. Then he would go on long strides, singing into the thunder or the snow, or with his feeble music try to be an instrument in the cosmic harmonies. An empyrean glissando in the rolling chords of thunder might abash him for a few moments; but soon he would be exploding his loud cries in his effort to develop his theme of joy-in-life over the theme of death-levels-all; and he would try to build his own crescendo, as though he were a bassoon or a French horn, all the while waving his arms to bring in other instruments, the whole ten thousand of them, for the celestial finale.

Once by a slim chance Bill had seen this red-bearded giant striding against the skyline down a mountain's back, and had said later to Hank Cady that he figgered Sam had been teched by the death of his wife. For there he was up yonder like a buffler bull full of mush and molasses, bellering his head off. Had Hank ever seen the likes of him? Hank said in his slow, over-deliberate way that he spected Sam was just happy. He hadn't ever knowed a man loved life like Sam.

Sam was writing a lyric in the only way he knew, or a paean of thanksgiving, for he thought that life was indeed a "wilderness of sweets" and his transports carried him now and then to bel cantos so wild that most men would have thought them pure lunacy. Sam was enraptured, enchanted, fascinated by the simple fact of being alive and healthy, with no clock to watch, no boss over him, no taxes to pay, no papers to sign, nobody to give an accounting to, except the Creator, whom he was glad to thank morning, noon, and night. He would have said that in an ideal world every man should have at least ten thousand acres on which to stride and explode and feel free. That was a puny spot, that many acres, but a man could turn around on it. He had heard McNees say that at the rate babies were being born all over the earth the time would come when no man could find room to stand on and blow his nose.

It was Bill who told Kate about Sam Minard. He told her that Sam strode up and down all the mountain spines in the west, singing into the heavens and praising God. Thereafter Kate always saw him when she looked for him. She would look off in the direction of the Big Belt or Bear Paw Mountains, though from where she stood she could see none of them; and there in the sky was a stupendous range, and Sam striding along the crests, looking as tall as pine trees, a gigantic figure with flaming hair and beard, and a voice that could be heard halfway around the world. It got to be a habit with her to stare at him in the far blue mists and to listen to his singing.

One of the best cooks among mountain men, Sam's specialty was steaks. He had learned that steaks broiled over embers absorbed the flavor of the wood; and so he had used all the kinds of wood he would find: pine, fir, spruce, and cedar he did not like, for they were too strong; aspen and willow were better, alder was fair. The flavors of woods also appeared in tanning. Those squaws did the best tanning, in both odors and textures, who had the best wood for it. Sam could smell a piece of leather and usually tell what wood had been used. He wouldn't wear leather for which the wood had been the poplar, willow, aspen, birch or plum.

It took him five or six hours to broil ten pounds of elk steaks and to make two pans of biscuits. It was the steaks that took so much time, and digging the fat out of marrowbones. The embers had to be just right, and he had to hover over the meat, lest it absorb too much of the wood odor. Here in the geyser basin he had some pepper beans, which he powdered in a mortar. For butter on his biscuits he used marrow. He had wild honey, which he had robbed bees of; when his meal was ready he feasted on juicy dripping steaks, biscuits sopped with marrow fat and honey, and coffee. While eating he would look out to watch the geyser blow. He could have felt no safer from the redmen if he had been encamped at the entrance to hell. His chief problem was his appetite; he had to have three big meals every day, and if they were all hot meals, most of his time was spent cooking. The livers he ate raw, or warmed through and seasoned; and every day he ate a handful of rose hips, for the reason that Bill Williams said every mountain man should. He also ate uncooked the livers from trout and grouse; they were extremely tender and savory.

One of his chief joys in wintertime was to walk in deep snowstorm when there was no wind but only the loveliness of movement and design, light and shadow, as the countless flakes like tumbling moths came down in such density and in such dodging, weaving, swirling grace that he found it amazing that no two flakes ever seemed to collide. They reminded him of the fantastically intricate dance of gnats when thousands of them in a tight swarm moved for hours in a pattern so complex and yet so perfect that no one man could believe it possible who had not seen it. He marveled at the flight of birds. He had watched red-winged blackbirds passing over him in early morning, on their way to feeding grounds, and he had guessed their number in the hundreds of thousands, possibly in millions, for they had been flying at a speed of twenty or thirty miles an hour, yet had darkened the sky above him for thirty minutes. All of them darted and bobbed and dipped and capered like birds out of their minds with joy, yet he had never seen two of them touch one another. He would lie on his back in soft new snow a foot deep and gaze at the myriad flakes until his senses swam, and never once had he seen a flaw in the constantly changing and infinitely complex pattern. It was as if every flake had eyes. He could never foresee where one would come to rest, for until the very instant of touching snow, earth, or water it was weaving and dancing and changing its course, yet it came to rest as if it had found the inevitable and perfect spot for its soft little cargo of frozen water. He would rise and walk again, and in the gentle wonderful world of white storm and dusk he would see wild things—his neighbors, the rabbits, birds, deer, weasels, bobcats—all acting as if they were as glad and thankful as he. A deer, ears pointed toward him, would stand and gaze at him, its coloring blending so perfectly with the storm's gray dusk that it hardly looked alive; and then it would move soundlessly away and vanish, like a patch of slightly darker dusk dissolving into the storm. The rabbits were gentler, the birds tamer, in a deep storm; all wild things seemed to feel the grace of benediction. The melting flakes reached down over his face like tiny cold fingers; the snow on his golden hair sopped it and turned it curly. He felt the damp against his moccasined feet, the chill down his spine.

The geyser, to which he came now, was larger and angrier than the one by his camp. It exploded its furies only once in a while. He was lucky, for as he approached the geyser he heard the hissing and rumbling up its hot throat, and after a few minutes saw, first, a prelude of belchings, as of a throat being cleared, and then the immense quantities of boiling water vaulting upward, to spill downward like shattered waterfalls. The geyser then seemed to pause, as if gathering the forces in the depths of its belly, and then vomited even more sensationally, with the steam devouring the storm over a wide area. Hot water fell downward in tumbling piles of vapor and flowed in steaming rivers toward him. This colossal eruption in the depths of a snowstorm was, Sam told himself, as beautiful as anything he had ever seen or heard. A man just about had to believe that Beethoven had seen it. Dropping to his knees, he swept the snow back and put an ear to the stone crust. He thought he could hear monstrous rumblings and heavings of subterranean waters, as though the whole earth might burst open in one self-consuming vomit. No wonder the redmen fled this spot. Sam backed away from it and into the storm, and watched, entranced, until the last furious puffs and snorts had been blown out of the throat and the underground angers had fallen back into the belly's gurglings.

In cupped palms he gathered hot water and drank it. Two or three hundred miles south were the soda springs, by the Oregon Trail, from which he had drunk. He liked those waters and their catharsis but these in Colter's bilins tasted of alkali and bitter salts.

After he had rubbed his horses down and eaten a big supper he spread his bed on earth that fire had warmed, and lay, snugly enfolded, and wondered about his future. He suspected, in these deeper moments of calm, that he had been a bit of a fool to fling a challenge into the beautiful white teeth of a whole nation; for as long as the vendetta endured he would have to be vigilant twenty-four hours a day, the whole year round. He had no wish to spend his life in a blood feud but he could think of no sensible and honorable way to withdraw. The red people loved feuds and warpaths and undying hates. They wouldn't want him to ask for peace. And there were the Blackfeet and Cheyennes, possibly even the Sioux and Arapahoes, all determined to capture him. And every scalp he lifted would boost the ransom.

It was not that he was afraid; he was as much a stranger to fear as the human male can be. It was not that he would feel sorry for himself if he fell under the redman's weapons. It was that he knew a simple truth, that men who loved life were not men who liked to kill. He would never be able to put out of memory the shocked and paralyzed youngster who had looked at him or the ungainly pathetic body hanging from the tree. Besides, he wanted to trap and hunt, cook and eat and sleep, without having to be watchful every minute. He'd not mind too much staying on the warpath another year, if the hot-blooded idiots would then wipe their knives and go home. They would never do that. He had begun to think that most men in the world wanted nothing more than any enemy whom they could hate and plot against. He did not pretend to know why this was so.

He hoped the next summer to ride over to visit his father-in-law. He might take a gift of four or five gallons of rum; like all the redmen, Tall Mountain had an enormous thirst for it. Living in an area meager with game and pelts, he did not have much to trade that white men wanted. He would be transported to a red heaven if Sam were to make a long journey to see him—a white son visits his red father, and rides two hundred miles right through Blackfeet country!

During this winter of reflection, with its many marvelous storms, there were tasks to keep him busy. He had garments to make. Because his hands were so large he was not nimble with needle and thread. Bear Paws Meek, fat and jolly and tobacco-stained, had large hands but he had a pianist's mastery of them. There was nothing dainty or artistic in Sam's sewing; he punched holes through the leather with a bone awl, thrust the needle through, and pulled the leather thread through one hole after another, to make his moccasins and leggins, trousers and jackets. While sewing he would wonder what kind of people they were back east and over in Europe who clamored to buy the scalps of the red people. Would they also be eager to buy testicles? He also made during this winter several pairs of moc-casins for the bay; he expected next summer to be pursued not only by Crows but by war parties from the Blackfeet and Cheyennes. In certain dangerous situations two or three layers of leather over the stone hoofs of a horse were the difference between life and death. If he were to outwit the warriors the old chief sent against him he would need to be master of warcraft and woodcraft—equal to Kit Carson in the first and Jim Bridger in the second. He was pretty sure that he had got Wolf Teeth; two years earlier he had seen this brave showing off on his pony, and had marveled that a man could ride with such grace and skill. It was said that some of the Crow warriors could hit flying birds with a rifle; that some were so noiseless they could slip up to the sleeping wolf and take it by the tail; and that some could devise phenomenal deceptions in ambush. Sam was not at all sure that he would be alive when the next frosts came but he was a fatalist; a man, like the buffalo or elk bull, could only do his best, and when his time came let go his grip on life and slip under.

As spring approached he put his weapons in perfect condition. A knife got dull and needed a lot of fine honing. He had two Bowies, so that in a tight place he could lay enemies open with both hands. In a buckskin pouch he had pieces of obsidian and filing whetstone, which he had saturated with hot goose oil to make oilstones, and hard and soft leathers. One knife, his finest, he kept wrapped in soft oiled leather; the other was his hunting and kitchen knife. His rifle and revolvers he kept spotless. He was not the kind of shot with a revolver that Bill Hickok would be a few years later, or with a rifle, as a man named Carver would be; but he felt that he was a match for the Crows, for the reason that his nerve would be steadier. The redmen in a crisis were notoriously bad shots. Bridger said it was because for the redman a gun was big medicine and all medicine was magic. If you were using magic you didn't have to pay much attention to sights or wind drift or buck ager. Buck ague or buck fever the mountain men called buck ager; they meant the trembles and willies, when a man suddenly faced a charging grizzly or bull moose. The redmen, as Sam had sized them up, were pretty good fighters when running, or riding hell-bent in a pack, because the heat of battle and the presence around them of their own kind brought their courage to the fusing point; but alone, man to man or man to grizzly, without war cries and wild commotion, few of them had the heart for it. Now and then one preferred to fight alone for the glory of it. It was these, Sam knew, who would be sent against him.

During this winter, when he lay snugly warm in the dark midnight of another dead day, he faced the possibility of capture and so thought of the squaws. Tom Fitzpatrick said they were red women, not squaws, but Sam knew that *squa* was the word for female among the Massachusetts Indians. Most mountain men thought them too cruel and ferocious to be called women, much less ladies; for look at the way some of them beat their dogs. When the squaws of most tribes went for firewood they used dogs, with their travées or trabogans; the dogs of the Crows looked to Sam like a cross between wolves and rawboned shaggy mongrels. They looked mean and evil and they were lazy. When harnessed to the trabogans they were a sight to make the whitemen die laughing; they sank back on their haunches like balky mules, and with tongues lolling and crafty eyes half closed they simply sat. The squaws then would run shrieking at them, and the dogs would slink away toward the woods; but after the trabogans were loaded with wood the dogs sank not to their hams but to their bellies, and like the mother grouse protecting her young, pretended to be wounded. It had looked to Sam as if some of them had feigned sickness. Ungovernable furies then seized the squaws; screaming and wailing, they would grasp heavy cudgels, and running up to the dogs, almost knock their heads off. Sam had never seen his Lotus angry, or brutal with any creature.

Sam had dug a bath hole in the earth, into which and out of which hot water flowed; and in the hole he soaked himself every day. What a land it was! All over its broad breast there were hot springs; Bridger said it was possible to travel a thousand miles and have a hot spring at every campsite. Since Sam had learned, with the Indians, to bathe in cold water, winter and summer, it was a delightful luxury to lie half asleep in a hot pool; and this, with the sumptuous meals, the magnificent mountain-winter all around him, the crisp purity of the air, and the wild things in the silence and aloneness, made him unwilling to leave the basin. With Lotus and his son he would have been content to live here forever. It seemed to him that in wintertime most people suffered a wintering of their emotions. And one other thing he had learned: that the folk in cities never got a chance to know themselves and one another: in this land, where enemies honed a man's wits and the forces of nature kept him trimmed of physical and emotional fat, a person had to learn what he was and what he was not.

It was late April before Sam reluctantly saddled and packed his beasts, hung a revolver and knife from his waist, mounted the bay, and sat for ten minutes looking around him. He then went over to the lake and down the west side to the headwaters of Snake River, and followed the river to the broad valley of the Tetons. On one of the streams flowing past those magnificent sculpturings he expected to find Wind River Bill.

19

"WALL NOW, I'll be cussed fer a porkypine!" Bill cried as Sam rode up to his cabin door. "If it ain't the Crow-killer hisself I'll be hog-tied and earmarked. Sam, whar in hell have ye bin?"

"Out and around," Sam said.

"Dog my hide," said Bill, staring. "We had it figgered you wuz dead and tuk. We bin awful oneasy. Have ye heerd they are callin ye The Terrer?"

"Hadn't heard that," Sam said, dismounting. He was looking round him when back in a recess he saw Zeke Campbell squinting at him. Zeke, Sam had no doubt, was the most taciturn man in the world; he had seen him a dozen times and had never heard him utter a dozen words. His usual affirmative was an almost inaudible grunt; his negative was a cold stare through the smoke from his pipe. In size and strength and agility he was only average. The most unusual thing in his appearance, for Sam anyway, was his hair; his beard so completely covered his face that only the forehead and the small green eyes were visible. Zeke even had hair all the way down the bridge of his nose. His hair was of a bronze color; when it was full of sunlight the man's face looked hidden behind a thicket of golden wires.

"How are you, Zeke?" Sam said. Zeke grunted.

Bill said, "I smell selfer." He came up to Sam and breathed in. "I spect ye've bin in the bilins," he said.

"How's trapping?" Sam said.

At once Bill looked downcast. Soon a man would starve to death, without he dug his fingernails off, and even then he would get ganter and ganter. Between him and Zeke they had only about five packs, though they had worked like two coons climbing greased poles.

Any extra tobacco?

164

Wall now, they did have plenty of that. Bill went to a hidden cache and returned with a few inches of twist. "Fill yer pipe, Sam, and rest yer hinder. Tell us what ye have been up to in the bilins."

This evening Bill cooked a supper of lean elk roast, beaver tail, muskrat broth, and coffee; and after the men had eaten and filled their pipes they sat by a loud-talking fir-and-cedar fire and wondered aloud about this and that.

"I wunner," Bill said, "about ole George." He meant Bear Paws Meek. George had gone into the Bear Paws Mountains, all alone, smack dab into the middle of Blackfeet country. Was George tired of life?

George was a smart coon, Sam said.

"Many's the smart coon ended up in the pot," Bill said. "He might as well a-set down at Three Forks and blowed his bull whistle. I figger George is gone under, I shorely do."

He doubted that, Sam said. George had been up that way twice before and had come back.

Bill scratched through his thick hair to his unwashed skull. He and Zeke, he said, had had a close shave last fall. In fact, two. One was the Cheyennes. Zeke was up Bull Elk Creek on a trapline and Bill had just brought in a fine buck and was skinning it when suddenly four red devils appeared out of nowheres, with so much grease and coal dust smeared over their faces that at first Bill had thought they were niggers; but his second glance saw their headdress, his third, the scalps. Wall, doggone it, if there was one thing the whiteman knew he must not do in such a situation it was to reach for his gun. Bill said he was bent over, with skinning knife, and he just remained bent over and let the knife fall, his mind wondering how he could warn Zeke. As sure as varmints Zeke at any moment would come back and walk right into his own funeral. Bill broke off in the story, filled his lungs with strong tobacco fumes, and exploded smoke from two hairy nostrils. His mind, he said, was thinking like a horse loping but there was nothing in it. He had never had such an empty mind in all his born life. He knew, of course, that the red killers were asking theirselves if he was alone or if mebbe two or three men were back in the brush looking torst them. "I tell ye I was plum scairt, I shorely wuz."

He figgered, Bill said, that his hump fat was as good as gone. His rifle was six feet from him; his revolvers were hanging over a limb not far from his rifle; and his knife lay at his feet. He was trying to remember some prayer to say when suddenly there was an explosion that sounded like the bursting of twenty rifle barrels. The redman closest to Bill fell almost on top of him but Bill didn't wait around to see if the varmint was down for good. In the instant he heard the shot he knew that Zeke had let daylight into the soul of one of them; in the next instant he had plunged his knife into the belly of another; and in the third instant the other two took to their heels like antelope in a high wind. They kallated that a hull war party had descended on them. Zeke had had time to reload and he dropped the third. The fourth then took to wings and when they last saw him he was ten miles above the Tetons.

Their other close shave was with two Crows. Bill guessed that these two had it figgered that he was The Terrer, for at the moment when they came in sight of him he was standing on the humped back of a log in a beaver pond and looked a foot taller than he was. He guessed that one or both of them belonged to the twenty old chief had chosen to bring in Sam's topknot and ears. They had him dead to rights, for like the fool he had been ever since he left his mother's knee, he had stood his rifle against a tree and had gone toad-hopping from log to log, looking for a floater stick that would show where a beaver trap was hiding in the deep water below. It was Zeke who again saved his life.

Through a cloud of smoke Sam looked over at Zeke. Though safer in pairs, the mountain men usually trapped alone. A lone trapper never for a moment put his rifle more than a few inches from his grasp. But no matter how wary they were they died violent deaths, one by one, year after year; there was never a rendezvous, at Pierre's Hole, or Brown's, or Laramie or Union or Bent, that they did not look round them to see which faces were missing. Bill was now looking at Sam. He guessed Sam knew that he had killed five, mebbe, six, of the twenty sent out to take him, and that the others were waiting for him to come out of Colter's bilins. He had heard from Charley that these braves had met in a secret powwow and had cast lots to see which of them would have the first chance at the Terrer's scalp. The lot had fallen to Eagle Beak.

"Don't reckon I ever heard of him," Sam said.

Wall now, if you put a few rattlesnakes, a wolverine, a bitch wolf, a falcon hawk, and a nest of hornets in a pot and stirred them well and then pulled out an Injun, it would be the one who had sworn to cut off Sam's ears and scalp, and cut out his liver, before the first currants were ripe. Charley said Eagle Beak had slain two Blackfeet before he was old enough to know what a woman was for.

"The first currants are ripe about July," Sam said.

There was a long silence. Zeke puffed his old smelly pipe and stared at Sam under two brows that looked as tough as bedstraw. Bill was also studying the Minard countenance.

Where was he headed for? Bill asked at last.

The Musselshell, Sam said.

In Bill's mind was a map of the route Sam probably would take—the path up Dog Creek and then over to Buffalo Fork; from there over to the Du Noir and up it to the South Fork and down it all the way to the Bighorn. He would then be south of the Musselshell at its big bend. Still, Bill reflected, sucking into his lungs a man-killing mixture of strong old tobacco and kin-nikinic, Sam might not take the well-worn way, knowing that killers were on his trail. As likely as not he would go over to the Badlands and ride right through Wind River Valley.

"Wonder if she lived through the winter," Sam said.

Bill said he had taken a fresh head and put it on one of the stakes, for he figgered that fresh sign of the whiteman's hatchet might be good medicine. She had acted awful disarted and skeared but she allus had. When he rode up early one morning she was gathering wild-flower seeds. He had talked to her but she had paid no heed and she hadn't tried to pint her gun at him or anything. Did Sam kallate ever to figger her out?

"I don't kallate I'll ever figger any woman out."

How woman, made of man's rib, could be so different was a riddle; old Bill Williams, he said a woman's breast was like the hardest rock and there was no trail on it that he could find. This crazy woman's breast seemed to be all butter. Any woman's was, Sam said, for her children.

"And fer nuthin else, I guess. And white gals, they're too much like pictures."

"I reckon," Sam said, quietly smoking.

"Ever heerd hide or hair uv her husbun?"

"Heard he was alive but I doubt it."

That was Abner Back, Bill said. Abner said the husband had escaped and was on the warpath; Crazy Bode, that was what they were calling him, a terror as bald as Lost-Skelp, hiding somewhere by the Great Falls.

Sam had taken from a leather pouch a note pad and a pencil; he said he wanted Bill to write a letter for him to the Crows.

"Doggone it, Sam, I can't write. You knowed that. But what's on your mind anyhow?"

Sam said he wanted the rest of the braves to come on, so they could get it over with. He would send them a few choice insults. With note pad and poised pencil Sam waited.

Wall now, Bill said, he might think of one or two he had learned. Bill spoke the syllables and Sam wrote them down. The first one said: *Ba wara pee-x-ee buy-em*. As nearly as he had been able to tell, Bill said, that one meant, "Once in a while I'll cut your balls off."

If that was what it meant, Sam said, it was almost enough in itself; most men seemed to be horribly sensitive to an attack on that part of them. Did he have another one as good?

Bill searched a mind that since he came west had paled under the snows of many winters. Why didn't Sam say, simply, that he intended to wipe them out one by one, or in litters and batches, and send their topknots to the Blackfeet? That was fine, Sam said; how did he spell it out?

After Bill had pronounced the words over and over Sam had this on his note pad: *Dee wappa weema sicky hay keeokoh*. He said there seemed to be a lot of *pa* and *ma* in that one, and gave the paper to Bill, who could give it to Charley when he saw him, and ask him to read it to the hull nation.

Bill said it all reminded him of a Mormon. This fool from a wagon train of greenhorns had taken his holy book and a man to interpret, and had gone to the Cheyennes to make Mormons of them. Seems the Mormons believed the red people were one of the lost tribes of Jews, or something like that, and this preacher went over to tell them the good news. A fool of uncommon size, he stood on a tree stump facing three hundred warriors, their hair glistening with buffler fat, his face boyish and simple and rosy-red; and he told these red devils that they were lost Jews whose ancestors millions of moons ago had somehow crossed to South America. He told them they would all go down to hell and fry in hump fat eternally if they didn't wash off their war paint and come every Sunday to hear Brigham Young preach the gospel. What then happened to that pore greenhorn was enough to make white women give up having babies. He was tuk away and spitted and roasted like a goose, and his holy book's leaves made some of the brightest flames in the fire.

The Indians didn't look like Jews, Sam said.

"They shorely don't," Bill said.

"I thought their chief belief was a lot of wives."

Wall now, Jim Bridger he had talked to Brigham; he said Mormons were a special people, like the Jews once were. Sam said he reckoned all people thought they were special people.

After trapping with Bill and Zeke for two weeks Sam said he guessed he would be gone, to see if Eagle Beak wanted a hugging match. He would leave his packhorses and pelts with them, and if his topknot was lifted out yonder, Zeke and Bill could have the pelts and horses. When Sam turned to leave, the emotion in Bill was running deep. He managed to say at last, "I figger ya jist hafta git it over with."

"For them," said Sam dryly. He mounted the bay and turned for a moment to say good-bye. Zeke and Bill stood side by side, looking at him.

"Watch your topknots," Sam said, and raised his right hand in a good-bye salute.

"Watch yourn," Bill said. He felt like crying a little.

Zeke was silent.

20

SAM HAD so abandoned himself to a delightful winter of hot baths, hot meals, mountain climbing, music, and deep sleeps that his wariness was not what it had been. He made a conscious effort to shake himself out of his notion that all was well, and to realize, after entering the Wind River desolation, that he was in Crow country and was a hunted man in the lands of five nations and ten thousand enemies. In Crow villages the squaws were still gouging themselves with sharp flints and wailing at the heavens, because of the dead braves The Terror had slain. What a day it would be for Sam Minard if he ever fell (wounded perhaps) into the clutch of the Crow women! How they would spit their mucus in his face and empty their bladders and bowels over him! There was nothing the inflamed and shrieking lunatics would not do; they would hack testicles off, tiny piece by piece; dig eyes out with sharpened hawthorn sticks; skewer the end of a tongue and pull it out and slice it off in thin slices; run knife points along gums where they met the teeth, and slice the gums down and back—the frightfulness of their cruelties and obscenities, said those who had been captured and had escaped, could be known only to those who had suffered them. Sam was telling himself these things. Were these human females and mothers? It made a man look back to his own mother and wonder if he had ever really known her.

He did not intend to be taken alive. He had told Bill that, and Bill had filled his pipe and said that a lot of men said they would never be taken alive but had been taken. If they took a man by surprise and he found a rifle barrel against his back, or if he looked up from his supper or his skinning to see a dozen warriors with drawn bows or knives, hope would rape his mind and paralyze his will, and he would surrender and begin to pray for escape.

Sam rode straight into the heart of Crow country, his thoughts now and then leaping into the north, where the bones of his wife and child were in a cold cairn and a woman sat by two graves. Before long now he would travel only by night; his camps would be fireless and his food cold, until he reached the Yellowstone. His sole task in the next few days was to leave his mark across Crow country.

It was his seventh day out after leaving Bill and Zeke. He was riding along Wind River Canyon when he came to large hot springs just north of Owl Creek Mountains. He wanted a hot bath, but knowing that he would be a fool to linger here a moment, he headed north and east to the foothills of the Bighorns. The desolate country he was now crossing would become, before many years passed, the site of famous battles between redmen and white.

He rode through the late afternoon and the dusk and most of this night, never for a moment doubting that he was being trailed. Now and then he turned abruptly off the path and hid, hoping to surprise his enemy. But this Crow was not to be tricked. Maybe it was Eagle Beak or maybe it was Night Owl. Sam didn't like it at all: he had allowed himself to be outmaneuvered, for he was now in eroded hill-country, with steep ravines, deep washouts, grotesque stone bluffs: there were countless places where an enemy could hide and look across sights at him—from a ridge, a pile of stones, a cave, a few stunted trees. He was reminded of an old mountain man's words: "When ye is trailed in open country ride backwards, then ye can see what's behind ye and yer horse will see what's ahead." His gaze searching the landscape in pale moonlight, Sam told himself he had better get out of here. He had been across this part of the Wind River desolation only once before and was not familiar with it; in the north he could see piles of mountain or of cloud, but to the east or west he could see only the fantastic wastelands carved by winds and water. The ground was so stony and pitted that he would risk his horse if he tried to outrun a foe; and there were no good places where he could hide and wait.

It was about two hours before daylight. He had just ridden up out of a ravine and reached the crest of a hill when he felt the sudden sledge-hammer blow of it. In that fraction of a moment he knew all that any man could have known about it—that he had been shot and the bullet had gone through him, or the bullet had smashed his rifle, or had struck the carved hawthorn handle of the Bowie. In that split instant he reached a decision that was practically reflex action: dropping the bridle reins, he pitched forward, headfirst, like a man shot from his horse; but it was a planned falling. His horse would stand against great provocation when the reins were down. His life, he knew, would depend on his lying in such a position that he could see, if with no more than the corner of one eye, the bay's head. Against an unseen foe who could be no more than a hundred or two hundred yards away this looked like the best of his chances. And so in the moment of striking the earth and sprawling on it Sam flung himself half around, so that with his left eye he could look up at the bay and watch the signals. They would be better signals than those of kildeer or red-winged blackbird. To anyone standing in the area and looking over at him he appeared to be a man who had plunged headfirst off his horse and was now dead or unconscious. Both hands were under his lower ribs, by design, one on the right, the other at the left of his breastbone, with palms outspread against the earth; his rump was humped up a few inches, as though he had jackknifed; his head was jammed back between his shoulders and turned down to one side. One leg lay straight out, the other at a right angle against it. His mind in these few moments had been working at lightning speed.

He knew now that a Crow who was a master of stealth had flanked him on the right and a little ahead of him; and out there, laying his gun across a stone or a hummock, had taken steady aim at Sam Minard's torso and fired. Since Sam had almost instantly pitched off like a mortally wounded man the Indian would have little doubt that he had shot him through; but on approaching he would be as wary as the wolf. He might wait half an hour before making a move. But Sam was fairly comfortable and full of ironic contempt for himself: what an idiot a man was when he hung guns around his belly and thought he was safe! Because his self-esteem had suffered such a shock he told himself that he might catch a few winks of sleep while the red devil was deciding whether his enemy was dead or feigning. The bitter flashes of mirth came and went in him, for he knew that he stood a good chance to be dead within an hour. There might be a dozen Indians out there. Or if there was only one he might come within a hundred feet of Sam and shoot him again. He was not so sure now that his pitching off headlong had been the best plan; it might have been better to have made a run for it, though in that case the Indian would have shot his horse from under him. If it was a brave not fully seasoned in battle he would not shoot a second time; as softly as the wolf he would approach, step by step, gun reloaded, knife drawn; or in his deadly soundless way he might approach with only tomahawk in one hand, knife in the other. He would not know that Sam was watching the head of the bay, or that the movements of eyes, ears, and the whole face would tell him as surely as Sam's own eyes could have done the moment the Indian left his hiding place and started forward. The bay's eyes, his ears, his nostrils, the position of his head, and the visible sensation through his whole body would tell Sam in every moment what the redman was doing and how close he was.

Sam would have said that a full hour passed before a sudden movement in the bay's head told him that the enemy had become visible. Sam now considered leaping up with his rifle and making a duel of it but he was not sure that his rifle would fire. Even so, his enemy would have the advantage of the first shot. If the Indian was as cool as ice—and some of the red warriors were—the second shot would mark the end of Sam Minard.

Or if the second shot dropped his horse and the Indian had confederates Sam would be as good as dead.

He decided that his best chance was to play as dead as gone beaver.

The bay's ears, eyes, nostrils, and whole face told Sam that the redman was advancing. Sam could hear no sound of feet. He had not expected to. His right eye was buried and could see nothing, but the upper part of his left eye had a clear view of the horse's head, neck, and shoulders. The ears were now up and forward; the eyes were standing out a little in anger and fear; there were spasms in the nostrils and the neck muscles. By the direction of the beast's gaze Sam knew that the Indian was coming in from the right and front. He felt a wish to examine the handle of his Bowie and the stock of his rifle, for he felt sure that the bullet had struck one of them. He could feel no wound, he had no sense of bleeding. What a lucky fool he had been! But as Jim Bridger said, a man got real big luck only once.

Sam did not dare to make the slightest move, for the Indian's eyes were almost as keen as the hawk's. Knowing that the foe was slowly coming in and that the slightest movement would fetch a bullet into his back, Sam barely breathed. When he saw the bay's eyes open wider for a moment, then return to their normal position, he knew that the Indian had paused. In fancy Sam could see him there, crouched, silent, peering, listening. What a hero homecoming he was dreaming of, when, waving The Terror's scalp, he accepted the shrieking acclaim of his people! It was because the hero would want a perfect scalp that Sam knew he need not fear the tomahawk—for the hatchet, as old Gus Hinkle loved to tell the greenhorns, spiled the skelp.

For about five minutes (the horse's eyes told him) the Indian stood and looked and listened. Sam knew that the redskin was studying the prone body for signs of breathing. He must have decided at last that his foe was not feigning, for the bay lifted his head suddenly a good three inches, flared his nostrils, and opened his eyes wider. These told Sam not only that the Indian was again advancing, but advancing more swiftly. That was good. Perhaps he was now coming at a fair walk, eager to lift the scalp and possess the horse. He knew that the Indian would stop again, when only twenty-five or thirty feet away, and again study the body for signs of breathing. If he saw none he would again advance, hoping to seize the bridle reins. If the horse backed away the Indian would pursue it, if he had no doubt that Sam was dead. Sam had his hands in such a position that he could draw a small breath without movement; it was his abdomen and not his diaphragm that moved a little in and out.

As he waited he could recall no time in his life when he had been more tense and anxious. He tried to relax just a little, for when the moment came to move he would have to move with what mountain men called greased lightning, which was almost as fast as the cougar's speed when it leapt from the ledge to the shoulders of moose or elk. What disturbed Sam most was the fact that his enemy was behind him; it gave him a touch of gooseflesh. His left eye, strained and smarting and staring upward, and winking fast to keep the tears away and its sight clear, watched the bay's head. He figured that when the foe was fifteen feet away, or surely no less than ten, the horse would bug his eyes and perhaps snort a little, and back off two or three steps. That was the moment when Sam would make his move, for in that instant the horse's movements and its compulsion to flight would rivet the Indian's attention.

Staring up, Sam saw that the bay's eyes were growing a little wider all the time. They were an exact measure of the Indian's movements and of his distance from Sam. But there were other registers in the handsome sensitive face of the bay—in the ears, the nostrils, in the nerves down the cheek, and in the neck. What a picture he made!—standing guard over his prone master, and staring in fright and anger and astonishment at the noiseless slinking creature in war paint and headdress, coming forward.

The sudden low snort came a little sooner than Sam had expected. The horse jerked his head up a good six inches and his eyes bugged with a mixture of ferocity and terror. In the same instant he backed off two swift steps. And in that instant Sam moved. His whole body shot backwards about three feet, propelled by his hands and arms; and all his muscles turned hard and tense for the leap that followed. In the moment of moving backwards he also came to his feet, his lungs filling with air; and he exploded a dreadful screaming cry that in the dry atmosphere could have been heard for two miles. It was such a fearful screech of rage that the Indian, only a few feet from the horse, his hands reaching out, was stricken; and before his nerveless right hand could raise his knife Sam's powerful grasp was on his throat and the bones in his neck were snapping. As the bones snapped Sam's right foot came up and with tremendous power struck the redman in his loins, sending him in a reeling spin. An instant later Sam was on him, to cut off the right ear and the scalp, and it was when drawing his knife that he learned that the little finger of his right hand had been shot away.

After a second glance at his hand Sam turned away without taking the scalp and went to his horse. The beast had backed off about sixty feet, and there he stood, nostrils twitching, his whole body trembling, his bulging eyes looking at his master. Sam went up to him slowly, gently, saying "It's all right, old feller, it's all right"; and voice and hands tried to soothe him. Gentle palms caressed the head and neck; stroked down the flat hard cheeks; and down the forehead, a forefinger softly patting just above the upper lid of the eyes. Standing to the left of the head, Sam put his right hand under the chin to the right cheek, as Lotus had done with her pony that farewell morning; and while he stroked the cheek he searched the horizon around him and talked all the while. "You saved my life, old feller. Do you know that? You're bettern the wren and the road runner and the magpie. . . ." Looking over the horse, Sam saw that he was covered with sweat. So he went on talking and patting, until the bay no longer trembled and had a normal expression in his eyes; and not until then did Sam look at the stock of his rifle. A piece of it had been shot out, along with his finger. The bullet had taken his finger, hit the stock, deflected, and plowed a furrow across Sam's stomach and up his ribs. Two inches back of a rib it had torn out a piece of skin and flesh as big as his thumb. Drawing his leather clothing up, he studied his wounds. They were nothing at all. He would have a long scar across his side and he guessed he would call it his lotus scar. He would fill the wounds with tobacco, and with balsam sap when he came to spruce trees. For a few moments he looked at the bloody bone stub of his finger and wondered if he ought to try to draw skin over it. He guessed not.

Going over to the Indian, he tried to make out the features but they were lost in hump fat and red ochre. The Indian braves, he was thinking, were only boys at heart; they simply must smear themselves with rancid grease and dance through a clutter of rituals and shriek like lunatics to get their blood up. Was this Eagle Beak? In any case it was one of the twenty. Sam looked into the medicine bag; pieces of the totem should be in it—teeth, claws, tail, beak, or something. There was a beak. Sam studied it and thought it might be the beak of the golden eagle. Had he slain the most deadly one of all his enemies? He hoped he had.

All the while scanning the world around him, he took off the moccasins, thinking that Kate could use them; took the scalp and shook blood from it, and hung it and an ear from a saddle string; chewed tobacco and rubbed its juice in his wounds and over the bone stub; and then mounted the bay. Farther north in Crow country he would hang the medicine bag above a well-traveled trail, for all the passing braves to see. Glancing over at the dead warrior, he thought it a pity to leave such a brave man to the vultures and ravens.

He sat, the rifle across his left arm, and looked round him. It was God-forsaken country all right, if it could be said that the Almighty had disowned any of His handiwork: as far as a man could see in all directions it was ravines, gullies, washes, eroded bluffs, alkali lime wastes, with only stunted plants. He didn't suppose that the bones of Eagle Beak would ever be found away out here. Curious to learn how he had been so neatly ambushed, Sam rode in the direction from which the bullet had come. He found the exact spot where his foe had knelt and fired, and guessed the distance at two hundred yards. It was a fair shot at that distance. He remembered that most Indians preferred gut shots. A good gut shot might take time but it always killed, whereas a shot in the rib cage might not be mortal, unless it struck the heart or exploded the liver.

Sam now perceived how his enemy had got close to him. Below was a deep ravine that ran forty yards east, swung sharply to the south for about a mile, and then to the southwest. Two miles back Sam had crossed the head of this ravine. Eagle Beak, on his trail, had ridden swiftly up the ravine, to wait for him. Sam felt hopelessly stupid. Only a fool would ride up a long ridge, with a deep ravine parallel to his line of travel. He might as well walk naked into a Crow village and climb into the pot and tell the squaws to pour boiling water over him.

Descending into the ravine, Sam found the Indian's pony in a thicket of scrub juniper. It was a fine horse. The twenty picked warriors had had their choice from large herds. Near the horse was a bedroll. Feeling over it, Sam could tell that inside were ammunition and a skin of pemmican. There was no saddle. After tying the roll across the pony Sam mounted the bay, and leading the pony climbed out of the ravine. The redman's rifle he left by the stone where it had been fired.

He was hungry but his thoughts were on the Musselshell and back with the dead warrior. On his way to the Yellowstone he killed five more warriors, three of whom, their horses and equipment said, belonged to the twenty. He was a little tired of killing these people; it was too much like knocking over fool hens. Two of those he killed were mere boys, with poor weapons, shaky trigger fingers, and a childlike belief in magic. Perhaps he ought to go visit his father-in-law. He might find another Lotus there.

21

HE WAS THINKING of all this while riding across wolf country. During the deep winters in northern latitudes wolves roamed over the frozen world, looking for deer, elk, moose, even for mountain sheep and goat, that had become feeble from hunger and got stuck in the snow. When spring came, wolves looked for dead animals that had been buried by snowslides. The grizzly and other bears, ravenous with hunger after the long sleep, also searched along steep mountainsides, where the avalanches of melting snow swept down, uncovering the tender shoots of early plants, and animals that had died during the fall and winter. Sometimes wolf and bear met on these feeding grounds.

In the southern foothills of the Bighorns four big gray prairie wolves, the mother and father and two children, had found several deer that had been smothered by a snowslide. They had eaten and were making a cache of the remainder, at the base of a sheer ledge that rose above them, when with a movement as swift as any in the animal world the bitch turned, at the same time lifting her head and pulling her lips back to show her fangs. A deep warning growl came up her throat. The father wolf, alerted, looked over at his mate. The two youngsters also sounded a warning. Then all four, backs arched, ears forward, fangs clicking, looked off to the left, where an enormous male grizzly had risen to his hind feet, to have a better look around him. He had smelled the dead flesh. There he stood, a monster, his small eyes peering, his front furry paws hanging loosely. But for his sensitive sniffing nose he seemed to be in an attitude of prayer. Because the wolves were a hundred yards away it is possible that the bear did not see them, for like the buffalo's, his eyesight was poor; but he smelled the meat and he thought he knew where it was. Sinking soundlessly to all four feet, he moved forward in an easy rolling gait of fat and fur. The wolves watched him come on and warned him with growls and snappings, and backs steadily arching higher. Even if the grizzly had seen the four of them he would not have paused. This male weighed eleven hundred pounds and was afraid of nothing on earth that he had ever seen, though he did try to keep sensibly out of sight when he smelled men and gunpowder. His only plan was to find the flesh and eat, and then stretch out for a siesta in the warm sun.

When sixty feet from the wolves he heard them and his dim eyes saw them. He then did what a grizzly bear usually did when faced by something whose nature and purpose he was not sure of. He rose to his hind legs, his front paws again in that curious attitude of prayer. He saw the four wolves—they now stood abreast, facing him, backs arched, mouths open, teeth snapping. He smelled the animal anger in them but he also smelled the flesh and he was too hungry to be prudent.

When the bear sank again and stood on his four enormous paws he seemed to consider his position for a few moments and then moved forward; and four wolves shot toward him like four gray lightning flashes. If a man's eyes had been watching—and from the ledge above a man's eyes were watching—they could not have followed the incredible speed and agility and grace of these four wild dogs. As the father wolf shot past on the bear's right he snapped savagely at the sensitive nose; and on the other side the mother wolf snapped at it; and though the grizzly in a flash raised a paw and swept an area, long curved talons extended, the wolves not only were gone from his reach but had rushed past his flanks and turned and leapt to his back. Both mother and father had fangs over two inches long, and jaws so powerful they could crack the leg bones of an elk. Both nosed into the deep fur and sank their teeth in the upper flanks; and when the bear, astonished and burning with anger, made woofing sounds and awkwardly rose to his hind legs, the two wolves clung to him, fangs buried. The youngsters, obeying the knowledge that lay deep in their instincts, flashed forward the moment the bear reared, and tried to bite and tear through fur and hide to his ham tendons. The grizzly was covered over with tawny gray furies determined to kill him.

Most bears are by nature placid, good-natured, and friendly. If this grizzly had any power of thought in his small dark skull he must have wondered why he should be attacked merely because he wanted food. All the first sounds he made were of astonishment and wonder; then came exclamations of pain and anger; and when the parent wolves dropped from the back and gouged at the hams, eager to chew the tendons in two, the grizzly exploded with a roar of rage that shook the mountain, and sinking again to four feet, turned swiftly round and round, his front paws sweeping across great arcs but never touching his foes. It was now that the wolves showed their amazing agility and daring. Not a dog among them, not even the young ones, but knew that if the bear's powerful paw struck them they would be ripped open from shoulder to ham. Yet with superlative courage they took their chances. The four of them were marvels of speed and light as they flashed in and struck, flashed out, burned in a lightning instant, and struck again. Never once was one found in the way of another. Time after time the bear's long deadly claws came within an inch or less of striking dog flesh; but not once during the fight was wolf touched by fang or talon. The bear was so goaded, so out of his mind with fury and frustration, that he set up a bawling roar that became louder and louder, until the hills roundabout echoed it. For twenty minutes the savage fight continued, and not for a moment did any of the wolves pause in their lightning attack. The grizzly's fur was too deep, his hide too thick and tough, for the dogs to be able to hamstring him. Besides, he kept turning, or standing up and coming down, or shaking himself like a monster in a great fur coat, or striking out with both front paws. Now and then the parents shifted their attack to his flanks or underbelly; and the father in an act of superb courage faced the monster and struck and furrowed the sensitive nose. This brought from the bear a cry that must have been heard for miles.

The man on the ledge was wishing that a piece of great music could be played above this struggle—the tempest in the sonata in F minor, or—yes, indeed!—the choral in the Ninth.

As suddenly as it began it was all over. The bear had had enough. He turned back the way he had come and moved off in a rolling-gait lope, whimpering like a spanked child. After fifty yards he looked back across a shoulder. Then he did something that would have moved any heart but a wolf heart: he stopped and rose to his full height and looked back at his exhausted and snarling enemies, his small black eyes bright with wonder, red drops falling from his nose. After a few moments in which he saw little and learned nothing he came down soundlessly, and in his rolling gait went over the hills and out of sight.

On the ledge above the four wolves a tall man shook a clenched fist at the sky. Almighty God, what a fight it had been! He sang a few triumphant bars in his loudest baritone and then addressed himself to the four dogs who, mouths open and sides heaving, looked up at him. "Hyar, fellers! Shore as shootin that war no fight for greenhorns! I salute you, wild wolves of the mountains! This here critter knows a good huggin match when he sees one and that was just about the best he has ever seen." To the panting wolves still staring up he said, "Hyar!" and waved a hand at them. "Good-bye, brave warriors! Keep your teeth sharp, and good luck!"

Sam had a lively admiration for the big gray wolf. He thought it the most intelligent of all the wild beasts—in tracking, in dodging enemies, including traps, and in loyalty to his own kind. He knew there were stories of wolves that devoured one another when half dead with hunger, but no mountain man had any proof of it. The human animal would eat his own kind, but not the wolf. On the contrary, a wolf family would fight to the death to protect one another, and that was more than most human families would do. No other beast, and only a few of the birds, would do that. He liked the clean deadly way in which they fought. Around campfires mountain men raised the question, Which of the beasts in the Rocky Mountains was king? Now and then one argued that the grizzly was, and he was, beast for beast; but twice now Sam had seen wolves put a grizzly on the run.

He knew all the wolf calls. Some men said there were five, some, six. Sam could identify only five. There was the high-keyed rasping whine the parents made when warning or commanding their pups; the hunting call, a loud deep-throated howl in two or more keys, followed by sharp barking; the shrill eager yelping when in pursuit of prey; the announcement that the prey had been brought down, a deep growl exploding up the victorious throat; and the mating cry in midwinter, which was the chilling howl in the frozen white nights.

As far as Sam could figure it out, the Almighty had made the world only for the brave and the strong, both male and female; and though Bill Williams said a woman's breast was a hard rock on which he could find no trail, and though some of the mountain men agreed with him, Sam thought the female of both man and beast had her special virtues. He liked best of all the way some of them would fight to the death for their children—and what female, he wondered, had ever fought more magnificently than the mother on the Musselshell? Not all mothers would fight, or even most of them. The buffalo cow, the big strong lubber, would beller her head off and bug her eyes out, or make short charges at the wolves determined to bring her baby down. She would fall behind with her calf and then have to make the choice of leaving it or going with the herd. She always went with the herd. So did the elk mother, and so, Sam had heard, did the caribou mother. It was only a few of the flesh-eating mothers that really fought for their young.

The bitch wolf would fight till she died. Or the wolverine, the bobcat, the badger, the weasel, the bear, the cougar, and many more. These were all natural fighters. But the most remarkable courage, for Sam, was shown by some of the feathered mothers, who actually had nothing to fight with. He had seen a grouse mother fly into the face of a wolf and try to strike it down with her wings; and in the next moment he had seen that mother torn into pieces, while her downy little ones scattered to the undergrowth. He had seen the avocet spread her wings, open her absurdly long bill, and rush on her long spindly legs at the enemy, only to die as suddenly as the grouse mother. He had seen a horned lark with a leg and a wing broken rush from her nest at an enemy, half walking and rolling and fluttering on the good leg and the good wing. What the poor crippled creature, little more than a handful of feathers and song, had thought she could do against a coyote Sam could not imagine; or why the Creator had put such courage in creatures that had nothing to fight with. God had built into the osprey hawk knowledge of how to carry a fish in flight, so there would be the least possible wind resistance; into the shrike mother the knowledge of how to spread her wings in hot weather, to protect the babies in her nest; and into the red-tailed hawk the sense of how to execute, in mid-air, a deft maneuver when the falcon came down to strike—the redtail suddenly turned over on its back and presented its talons. But he had not built into the meadow lark, one of his superlative musicians, the sense not to build its nest on the ground, where every coyote, bobcat, weasel, and wolverine could easily find it.

Reading nature, for Sam, was like reading the Bible; in both, the will of the Creator was plain. Or so anyway it had seemed to him since coming west; his experiences had run the gamut from the tenderest to the most savage emotions. One day he had looked down from a ledge on three baby redtails in a nest with a dead squirrel: one baby hawk, no larger than his brothers but more aggressive, was so determined to have all the squirrel that when the other two strove for a part of it he struck them fiercely with talons and beak, and then, seizing one by the tail, upended him and pushed him over the rim of the nest and down. One morning he had lain in daylight dusk in a kind of tent he had made and watched the marvelous flight of two swallows flashing back and forth just above him, as they looked over his interior to see if it was suitable for a nest; and another time he had observed the amazing mating dance of the sage cock. The birds had returned to their strutting grounds, to which they came year after year; and while the plainly dressed hens looked for insects and seemed not to care at all for wooing, the handsome males showed themselves off in dance steps. A cock would take six or eight quick steps and half turn, his wings drooping, his spiked tail spread to its fullest width, his proud head high and back, his chest puffed full of arrogance. He looked as if he were showing off the pure snowy whiteness of the feathers around his neck. As he danced, repeating his steps and half turn, feathers parted and small bare areas of his body became visible, looking like gray leather; and his air sacs, for all the world like two eggs nesting in white down, alternately filled and collapsed. As the air sacs collapsed he uttered a kind of gobbling or plopping sound and raised his wings, holding them high an instant and letting them fall. This part of his act he usually repeated three times, and then danced again. His gutturals were in a series of three and at the end of the third the cock voiced a high flutelike sound that carried to the farthest hen in the area. When thirty or forty cocks were dancing and strutting the mountain men thought it one of the doggonedest spectacles they had ever seen. But whether it was the loon

treading with both feet and wing tips at high speed across the
waters and uttering his insane yell, or the hummingbird poised
on wings that moved too fast for the human eye, while with her
long bill she thrust deep into the throat of her baby and
pumped food into its stomach, or meadow lark or purple finch
or bluebird or wood thrush pouring upon the golden air their
liquid notes, or the water ouzel diving twenty feet to stroll
along the bottom of a pool, or the snipe's tail feathers making
fantastic music at dusk, or the harsh symphony from the music
boxes of a hundred frogs and toads, it was all for Sam a part of a
divine plan and he loved it all. What made him most unhappy
were the hours he had to give to sleep, in a life that was short at
best. He thought that possibly the Creator had given sleep to
His creatures so that they would awaken with the eyes of
morning and a fresh discovery of the world.

Sam was thinking these thoughts as he rode down the
Musselshell and came close to Kate's shack. He was in a more
sentimental mood than was usual for him—deep gone in mush
and molasses, Bill might have said if he could have looked into
Sam's soul; for Sam was thinking of the bones in the cairn and
his arms were filled with flowers. His first sight of the woman
was halfway up the hill with a pail of water; he sat and
watched her around her plants and flowers, and his thoughts
went out to all the wild mothers he knew.

"Hello, Kate," he said after riding up to her yard. He had
hoped that her name would make her look at him but she gave
no heed at all. She looked thinner, she looked older. There was
a lot of white in her hair now and deep seams all over her face.
He thought she was not yet forty but she looked eighty. Instead
of moccasins—he and other men had brought her a dozen
pairs—she still wore her tattered old shoes, bound to her feet
with leather strings. Her garments were cotton rags covered
with patches. But her sage looked nice and her flowers looked
eager and strong.

He wondered if she would ride his packhorse and go with
him down the river to meet a steamboat, but he knew she would
not. When her pail was empty she went back down the hill and
the moment she was out of sight Sam looked into the cabin.
Nothing had changed. The bed was still just inside the door,
and over by the north wall were a few things including a pile of
skins. He saw no rifle or axe or knife. She seemed not to know
that there were enemies in the world, perhaps because she had

sunk so deep into loneliness and sorrow, or had entered so fully into heaven. The time would come, he supposed, when she would forget to eat, or to wrap herself against the cold.

By the river he ate a dry lunch and washed it down with river water. On his way in he had seen a few buffalo and now kallated that he ought to get one and jerk a pile of beef. He guessed he ought to gather a bushel of berries and dry them for her, for the time was again late August and the serviceberries were ripe. Before coming here he had picked up his pelts at Bill's spot and had gone to Bridger's to buy some things, chiefly on credit. It took a lot of pelts, with sugar a dollar a pound, coffee a dollar and a quarter, blue cloth four dollars a yard, and rum twelve dollars a gallon. He had found a five-gallon keg of rum by the Trail, cached by Mormons or other immigrants; he hoped that Mormons had left it, for they were not supposed to drink rum, or coffee, or tea. Though washing soap was a dollar and a half a pound he had brought a pound to Kate. For his father-in-law he had a copper kettle, and for his sister-in-law he had blue cloth and vermilion and assorted beads.

The next day he gathered berries and spread them on a robe in the sun to dry. He shot a young buffalo and brought it to the river bottom. He then went up the hill and over to the cairn; he had removed a stone and thrust his armful of flowers back over the bones, and now, reaching in, he clasped the skull of his wife and looked at Kate. She was watering her flowers. "My mother raises flowers," he said, wishing he could make her talk. "Yours are just as nice." He meant the Indian paintbrush, pentstemon, and aster. Patting the skull and pushing flowers down on it, he drew his arm out and walked over to Kate. Would she come down to the river and have supper with him? Did she want to learn how to jerk flesh? Had she written a letter to her people that he could send out for her?

She took her pail and turned down the path and Sam followed her. He watched her at the river dip the pail full and turn back, and he followed her halfway up the hill. Then he turned to the task of drying the meat. From the loin he put aside steaks for his supper and breakfast, and sliced the flesh of hams and shoulders. The slices he laid in piles and cut down through the piles; jerky should be not more than two or three inches wide, and from four to six inches long. Green saplings above a fire he covered with slices of flesh, and set up a second rack, and a third. In a smaller fire he laid a part of his steaks and basted them with hot fat. Pore ole critter, she was nothing much but hide and bones. Could he get her to eat a steak and a hot biscuit? He would have given a year of his life to bring a smile to her face; he would have trembled with joy if he could have made her talk. His mouth watered, his eyes smarted in the smoke of four fires, his body clothed in leather itched in the heat. But there was a feast to look forward to, and lo, what heaven it would be if Lotus were here!

The afternoon waned, the sun sank, and it was dusk, and down the hill came a dreadful sound. Sam thought at first that he heard a wolf scream; then, that it was the cry of a buffalo or elk calf under wolf teeth. But no, God no, it was the woman! He couldn't see her but he could hear her unearthly blood-chilling lament, and he had a picture of her, there by the graves, bowed, snarls of gray hair falling over her face. Knocking the fires down so that the meat would not burn, Sam took his rifle and ran up the hill. Yes, there she was, as he had imagined her, bowing low and rising—sinking in what seemed to be a long shudder, and rising with gasping sobs. In all his life he had never heard sounds of such utter sadness and loss. They made him feel weak and furious and helpless. After running back down the hill to take care of the meat he stood among the fires and looked back and forth at drying racks and listened. He could not put away the thought that it was his presence that had touched her off to this bitter lament out of grief and fear. My God, did she think he was an Indian? He thought of that quiet and delightful evening when he had played for her and they had sung together, but now her voice was wild and piercing and full of such horrors as only a heart-stricken mother could feel. He looked west, where the Blackfeet lurked, and south, where the Crows waited for him.

Removing the layers of meat and covering the racks with raw flesh, he laid a choice steak on a large cottonwood chip and went up the hill. The woman was still bowing and rising. Kneeling before her, Sam said he had brought her a fine hot steak, knowing that it would do no good to say anything; he held the hot meat so that its aroma would rise to her nostrils. Would she look at it, please? Would she take at least one bite? He felt an impulse to shake the hell out of her but it passed in an instant. He stood up, looking round him and trying to think of something to do. There seemed to be only the presence of death here; the silent cairn was full of it, the shack, and this woman. He bent over and said in her ear, quietly, "I also have sorrow, Mrs. Bowden. My wife and child, the Indians killed them too; and they are there, their bones, in that pile of rocks. But no matter what our grief we have to go on living." He straightened and looked at the sky, wondering what the Father thought of a woman like Kate. Sam then faced her, laid the chip and steak down, took her arms away from her face, set the steak on her lap, and returned her arms. It was like moving the arms of a dead person who had not yet turned rigid.

He went back to the fires and tried to eat but his appetite was no good. Up the hill he could hear the woman crying. The odor of hot steak was rising to her nostrils and she was crying, for she did not know what hot steak was and she was afraid of what she did not know. A man *had* to listen to a lament like that, as he had to listen if his mother spoke, or the Almighty. It was one of the deep and eternal things. Sam filled his pipe and sat, rifle across his lap, listening and thinking. He had aroused some terrible fear in her; she knew he was with her, yet did not know, and her lament was a prayer to God to send him away. The poor lonely thing! he thought, puffing and thinking.

After he had jerked all the beef and put the meat in buckskin bags, and put out the fires and looked after his horses, he sat again and smoked. Then he took his rifle and harp and went up the hill, and came in behind the hummock where he had lain and played. He began softly, with the Ave Maria; and then played back and forth, from one tender thing to another, trying to make the music sound as if it were in heaven or came from there; and he was overjoyed when suddenly he heard her singing. How beautiful it was! For his own sake and for the bones in the cairn he played a few things that he had played for Lotus, and sung for her; and he played old hymns and Corelli and Schubert, softly, so that the music reached her and faded, and reached her again, as though the Creator were closing windows and putting some of the musicians to bed. After two hours he figured that if the music faded away gradually she would feel all right about it.

At midnight she fell silent. At daylight Sam was awake and the first sound he heard was her footfalls on the path. He watched her go to the river and return. The heavy pail bent her over, and she looked very frail and thin and old. Carrying water to flowers that bloomed above graves was, he supposed, what people called ritual. It seemed to be symbolic. It seemed to be deeper than the conscious mind. When she came again Sam rolled out, and with his rifle, and a hundred pounds of jerked flesh over his shoulder, he went up the hill while she was at the river; and the first thing he looked for was the steak. It was there, with the appearance of something that had spilled from her lap when she stood up. He turned and watched her come up the hill, bent forward, her shoulders looking pulled out of joint. Her face seemed bloodless and drawn, as from famine, fatigue, and want to sleep.

He had set the meat inside her cabin by the bed, where she could not fail to find it. He remained in this area until October, when the first snow fell. He put fresh stakes under the white skulls with their fringe of hair; gathered more wild fruit; and brought deer from the hills. With deer flesh and berries he made pemmican for her. With her old shovel he put three inches of earth on the cabin's roof, and banked earth all the way around it, to the top of the first log. He brought river mud and used it for mortar to fill the cracks. When he could think of nothing more to do he packed his horse and saddled the bay, but even then stood, undecided, looking up the hill. There she was, a bent old mother in ragged shoes and tatters, carrying water to flowers withered by frosts and needing no water now. Not sure that he would ever see her again, who had become a precious part of his life, he went up the hill, leading his beasts, for a good-bye look at these familiar things. Framing her sad face with his two big hands, he kissed her forehead and her gray hair.

"Good-bye," he said. "I'll see you before long."

He was to see her again a lot sooner than he expected to.

22

AT THE BIG bend of the Musselshell he took from a cache the keg of rum, the kettle, and a few other things, and then sat on the bay and looked west and south, wondering if he should take the safer way over the Teton Pass or the more dangerous way by Three Forks. Storm determined it. It was snowing this morning, and all the signs said it would be an early and a long hard winter. If he went by the pass it would take twice as long and he might find himself snowbound up against the Tetons or the southern Bitterroots. By far the easier route was by Three Forks, where John Colter had made his incredible run to freedom; where the Indian girl who went west with Lewis and Clark had been captured as a child; and where beaver were thickest in all the Western land. It was there also that more than one trapper had fallen under the arrows or bullets of the Blackfeet.

It was a foolhardy decision but mountain men were foolhardy men.

For a hundred and fifty miles, with snow falling on him most of the way, he went up the river, and then followed a creek through a mountain pass. He was leaving a trail that a blind Indian could follow. Straight ahead now was the Missouri; on coming to it he went up it to the Three Forks, the junction of the Gallatin, Madison, and Jefferson rivers. He knew this area fairly well. Lewis and Clark had gone up the Jefferson River, which came down from the west, but Sam planned to go southwest and cut across to a group of hot springs in dense forest. The snow was almost a foot deep now and still falling, but he had seen no tracks of redmen, only of wild beasts, and he had no sense of danger. Just the same he hastened out of the Three Forks area, eager to lose his path in forested mountains. He might have made it if pity had not overthrown prudence. He had gone up the Beaverhead, past a mountainous mass on his left, and hot springs that would be known as the Potosi, and had then ridden straight west to a group of hot springs deep in magnificent forest, when suddenly he came in view of a mountain tragedy that stopped him.

Two great bulls of the wapiti or elk family had been fighting and had got their horns locked, and a pack of wolves was circling them, while turkey buzzards sat in treetops, looking down. Sam saw at once that it had been a terrific fight; the earth was torn and the brush trampled over half an acre. The two bulls looked evenly matched, each with a handsome set of antlers, and beautifully muscled shoulders and neck. Sam had sometimes wondered why the Creator had put such an immense growth of bone on the head of elk and moose; their antlers were about all their necks could carry, much less handle on a run through heavy timber, or in a fight with another bull. It was not an uncommon thing to find bulls dead with horns entangled in dense underbrush, or interlocked, as now. These two had their rumps up in the air to the full length of their hind legs but both were on their knees and unable to move their heads at all. Any moment the wolves would have moved in to hamstring them and bring them down, and feast in their bellies while they still breathed. If Sam had found one bull dead and the other bugling over him he would have thought it all right, but to find two magnificent warriors unable to continue their fight, who deeply wanted to, was such an ironic miscarriage of the divine plan that he was outraged. He would set them free if he could, so they could resume their fight.

Sam looked round him and listened. Thinking that he was many miles from danger, he secured his horses to a tree, hung his rifle from the saddlehorn, and walked about a hundred feet to the bulls. He went close to them to study the interlocking of the antlers. The astonishing thing about it was that bulls were able to do it; Sam had heard men say that they had taken two antlered heads and tried for hours to get the horns inextricably locked. These two sets were so firmly and securely the prisoners of one another that it looked to Sam as if he would have to cut through two or three bones to set them free. He had no saw but he had a hatchet. While considering the matter he walked around the two beasts, studying them with the practiced eye of one who knew the good points of a fighter. Yes indeed, they were well matched; he thought there was not thirty pounds' difference in their weight; their antlers had the same number of points and in clay banks had been honed to the same sharpness. They had been in a great battle, all right; their eyes were bloodshot, their chin whiskers were clotted with the stuff that fury had blown from their nostrils, and both had been savagely raked along ribs and flank. What a handsome pair they were! Sam patted them on their quivering hams and said, "Old fellers, ī kallate I'll have to chop some of your horns off. It'll hurt just enough to make you fight better." He again studied the antlers. So absorbed by the drama that he had been thinking only of the two warriors, he glanced over toward the horses where his hatchet was and turned rigid, his eyes opening wide with amazement.

Seven Blackfeet braves had slipped soundlessly out of the forest and seven rifles were aimed at Sam's chest. Seven hideously painted redmen were holding the rifles, their black eyes glittering and gleaming with triumph and anticipation, for they were thinking of rum and ransom and the acclaim of the Blackfeet nation. Why in God's name, Sam wondered, hadn't he smelled them? It was because the odors of elk and battle had filled his nostrils. In the instant when he saw the seven guns aimed at his heart, at a distance of eighty feet, Sam had also seen a horde of red devils around his horses. He knew that if he moved toward the revolvers at his belt seven guns would explode.

Slowly he raised his hands.

He had turned gray with anger and chagrin. This was the first time in his adult life that he had been taken completely by surprise. A Blackfeet warrior over six feet tall, broad and well-muscled, with the headdress of a subchief, now lowered his gun and came forward. He came up to Sam, and gloating black eyes looked into enraged blue-gray eyes, as red hands took the knife from its sheath and unbuckled the revolver belt. Guns and knife were tossed behind him. The chief then hawked phlegm up his throat, and putting his face no more than twelve inches from Sam's and looking straight into his eyes, he exploded the mouthful into Sam's face. A tremor ran through the whiteman from head to feet. In that moment he could have killed the chief but in the next he would have fallen under the guns. Other warriors now came over from the horses, all painted for battle. They began to dance around their captive, in the writhing snakelike movements of which the red people were masters. Sam thought there were about sixty of them. He stood immobile, the saliva and mucus dripping from his brows and beard, his eyes cold with hate; he was fixing the chief's height and face in his mind, for he was already looking forward to vengeance.

After a few moments the chief put aside his dignity and joined the dance. It seemed that all these warriors had rifles and long knives and tomahawks. In a victorious writhing snake dance they went round and round Sam, their black eyes flashing their contempt at him; and Sam looked at them and considered his plight. Now and then one gave shrieks of delight and redoubled his frenzies; or one, and then a second and a third, would pause and aim their guns at Sam, or raise knife or tomahawk as though to hurl it. Sam stood with arms folded across his chest. In the way he looked at them he tried to express his scorn but these shrieking writhing killers were children, for whom the only contempt was their own. Not one of them had paid the slightest attention to the bulls with locked horns, or cared with what agonies or humiliation they died.

When at last the Indians made preparations to take their prisoner and depart they still paid no attention to the bulls. With loud angry curses and then with signs Sam made them conscious of the two beasts; and they spat with contempt and said, with signs, that they had plenty of meat and would leave these to the wolves. Their insolence filled Sam with fresh rage. He was now less concerned for himself than for two helpless fighters who had a right to another chance—who in any case were too brave and too noble to die with wolves chewing into their bellies and with buzzards sitting on their horns. Speaking in tones that rang with anger and with angry signs, Sam told the chief that he should shoot the two bulls or chop a part of their horns off, or he should crawl off like a sick old woman and die with the rabbits. After appearing to give the matter some thought the chief went to the beasts and looked at their horns. He shouted then to his warriors and several of them ran over to him; he spoke again, and they put muzzles at the base of the skulls and fired. The two bulls sank to the earth, locked together in death.

Sam had been hoping that the Indians would break open the keg of rum and drink it here but the wily chief had other plans. One plan was to humiliate and degrade the whiteman until he was delivered to the vengeance of the Crows. He would not be delivered with all possible dispatch; he would be taken north to the principal Blackfeet village, where the squaws could shriek round him and hurl dung and urine on him, and with the voices of ravens and magpies caw and gaggle and screech at him; and where the children, emulating their elders in ferocities and obscenities, could smear him with every foul thing they could find and shoot arrows through his hair, as he stood thonged and bound to a tree. Such thoughts were going through Sam's mind. He expected all that red cunning and ingenuity could devise, though he imagined that they would not seriously wound him, or starve him until he could not walk, if they expected to collect a huge ransom. It would be childlike contempts and indignities all day and all night.

These had begun when the chief exploded in his face. As soon as they had him manacled with stout leather ropes the other warriors vied with one another in heaping abuse and insult upon him. With leather thongs soaked in the hot waters of a spring they bound his hands together; and around the leather between his wrists was tied the end of a leather rope thirty feet long. A huge brave took the other end of the rope and made it secure to his saddle. Mounting his horse, he jerked the rope tight, and with pure devilment kept jerking it, after taking his position in the line. About half the warriors went ahead of Sam, about half behind, with the chief at the rear, riding Sam's bay and leading the packhorse. Now and then one of the redmen, eager to torment the captive, would leave his position in the line; and breaking off a green chokecherry branch, he would slash stinging blows across Sam's defenseless face. With blood running from brow or cheek Sam would look hard at the painted face, hoping to fix it in memory and telling himself that these were the fiends who had slaughtered the defenseless family of the mother on the Musselshell. He had the face of the chief in memory; the red varmint had a scar about three inches long above the left eyebrow, and another scar just under the left chin. If with God's help he could ever free himself he would hunt down that face. In some such manner as this, he supposed, they had taken Jesus to the hill; but Jesus had carried a great burden, under which he had fallen again and again; and when he fell they spat on him and kicked him and cursed him. The one who had slashed at Sam's face had been rebuked by the chief, but his boldness had given ideas to other braves; and hour after hour as Sam moved through heavy snowstorm one man after another dropped out of line to hawk and spit on him or hurl snow in his face or make murderous gestures at him. After a while the braves seemed to understand that it was all right to show their contempt if they did not wound him; and so by turns they hawked and spat and shrieked, or hurled snow, mud, and pine cones at his face. In their black eyes was a clear picture of what they wanted to do with him, for they knew not only that he was the Crow-killer but that he was the one who had scalped the four Blackfeet warriors and impaled their skulls on the stakes around the cabin.

It was the snowfall that worried Sam more than the insults. This storm looked like the real thing. If winter was already setting in and there was to be three or four feet of snow in the mountains in the next week or two, as there sometimes was this far north, what good would escape do him, with the snow too deep to wade through? It would be a dim future for him if it kept snowing, and they meanwhile weakened him with starvation and cold.

Why the red people so loved to torture their helpless captives was a riddle to all the mountain men. Sam thought it was because they were children. A lot of white children tortured things. Windy Bill said he could tell stories from childhood that would curdle the blood of a wolf. Sam had never heard of a whiteman who tortured a captive. Once when a wounded redman was singing his death song Sam had seen Tomahawk Jack pick up a stone to knock the helpess Indian on the head, and had heard Mick Boone let off a howl of rage as he struck the stone from Jack's hand. "Shoot him decentlike, if you wanta!" Mick had roared. "He ain't no coyote." Sam had once seen a whiteman kick a wounded Indian in the belly and head; he had seen another scalp a redman while he was alive and conscious; but deliberate torture for torture's sake he thought he had never seen. Torture for the redmen was as normal as beating their wives. The wolf ate his victim alive but he was not aware of that. The blowfly hatched its eggs in the open wounds of helpless beasts, and maggots swarmed through the guts of an animal before its pain-filled eyes closed in death. The shrike impaled on thorns the live babies of lark and thrush. The weasel and the stoat were ruthless killers. A horde of mosquitoes as thick as fog would suck so much blood from a deer or an elk that it would die of enervation; and sage ticks, bloated with blood until they were as large as a child's thumb, sometimes so completely covered an old beast that it seemed to be only a hair bag of huge gray warts. But the red people tortured for the pure hellish joy of seeing a helpless thing suffer unspeakable agonies. It was chiefly for this reason that mountain men loathed them, and killed them with as little emotion as they killed mosquitoes.

If he could have done it Sam would have struck all these warriors dead and ridden away with never a thought for them. As it was, his mind was on escape and vengeance. These redmen knew, all the red people knew, that if ever a mountain man was affronted, when helpless, and treated with derision, contempt, mockery, and filth, the mountain men would come together to avenge the wrong, and that the vengeance would be swift, merciless, and devastating. Sam had no doubt that this chief knew it. There could be only one thought in his mind, that this captive would never escape from the Blackfeet or from the

Crows, and that mountain men would never know what became of him. The chief would take his captive to his people, so that they could gloat over him and see with their own eyes that he was not invincible after all—that he had been captured by the Bloods, mightiest of warriors, boldest and most fearless and most feared, and most envied of all fighting men on earth. Sam thought that he might be slapped, spat on, kicked, knocked down, but not severely injured; that some of the squaws might squat over him; that children might drag their filthy fingers through his hair and beard and pluck at his eyelids and threaten his privates; and that dogs of the village might howl into the heavens their eagerness to attack him. He would be given, once a day, a quart of foul soup, with ants and beetles and crickets in it, for the red people knew that some of their food made white people gag, and this kind they took delight in forcing on white captives. For as long as he was a prisoner that would be his fate. Then four hundred warriors in full war paint and regalia would march off with him in the direction of the Crow nation. On arriving at the border between the two nations they would encamp and kill a hundred buffalo, and feast and sing and dance, while scouts went forth to tell the old chief that his enemy was bound and helpless. For days the wiliest and craftiest old men in the two nations would haggle and dispute over the size of the ransom. The Bloods would demand many kegs of rum, many rifles, a ton of ammunition, at least four hundred of their finest horses, and piles of their beaded buckskin. The Crows would give no more than a tithe of what was demanded. The Bloods knew that. They would ask for a hundred, hoping for fifty, prepared to settle for twenty, even for ten, plus the privilege of watching the torture of Sam Minard.

Well, if it kept snowing this way they could not take him to the Crows before late spring. If he was not able to escape he would have a long winter of starvation and cold and insults. Sam did not for a moment intend to be delivered to the Crows. He did not believe that the Creator would allow a man to be taken and tortured and killed for no reason but that he had sought vengeance for the murder of his wife and child. The holy book said that God claimed vengeance as His own. In Sam's book of life it was a law that man best served the divine plan who made a supreme effort to help himself.

Sam intended his effort to be supreme. Now and then, while

trudging along, he looked down at the elkskin that bound his wrists. If he got a good chance he could chew it in two but he knew that when he was not marching his hands would be bound behind him. To sever tough leather rope when his hands were behind him would be impossible, unless he could abrade it against something hard and sharp, such as stone, a split bone, or wood. During the nights he would have one guard, or possibly two. He would have to eat what they gave him to eat, no matter what it was, and preserve his strength as well as he could. He would do his best to sleep a good part of each night. He would act as if resigned to his fate. If only they would make camp and open the rum!

The day of his capture they moved without pause until almost midnight. All day long a heavy snow fell. While walking in the deep wide trail made by those ahead of him Sam tried to look through the storm to mountains roundabout. By branches on trees he knew they were going north. He supposed that this war party would traverse mountain valleys and passes west of the Missouri until they came to the big bend, where, he had heard, they had a large village on Sun River, and another over on the Marias. They might take him all the way to Canada but he doubted that they would, for if they did it would be a long journey to the Crows. By the time dusk fell he thought he had been walking about five hours. He was hungry. When his bound hands reached down to get snow for his thirst the savage on the horse ahead of him would jerk at the rope and try to shake the snow out of his hands. He was a mean critter, that one. Sam would clench the snow in his palms to hold it but the moment he moved hands toward his mouth the watchful redskin would jerk at the rope with all his might. Sam said aloud to him, "I reckon I better fix your face in my mind, for somewhere, someday, we might have a huggin match." When a third or a fourth time the Indian jerked the rope Sam in sudden rage swung his arms to the right and far back, hoping to break the Indian's grasp on the other end. But the other end was tied round the saddlehorn. To punish Sam, the Indian kept jerking at the rope, and rage in Sam grew to such violence that it took all his will to restrain a forward rush to seize and strangle his foe. I'd best calm down, he thought; for if he got weak and fell he would be dragged along like a dead coyote. His time would come: he refused to think of alternatives: his time would come, somewhere, and he would hear bones crack in this Indian's neck, and he would see the black eyes pop out of the skull, as though pushed from behind.

When at last at midnight the party made camp Sam was tied to a tree and put under guard. Snow was still falling. The snow where he was to stand, sit, or lie during the remainder of the night was about eighteen inches deep, a third of it new snow. If the storm broke away it would be a bitter night. He did not expect them to give him a blanket or a robe; he would be surprised if they gave him food. They would want to weaken him some. He would sit or lie by the tree all night, with the storm covering him over, and at daylight he would march again. The man assigned to guard him had a large robe (it looked to Sam like one of his own), on a part of which he sat, with the remainder up over his shoulders and head like a great furry cape. He had a rifle across his lap and a long knife at his waist. Under his fur tent he sat, immobile, sheltered, warm, his black eyes never leaving Sam's face, save now and then to glance at his hands. Sam wondered if this would be his only guard. If so, and if the man dozed, Sam could chew at the bonds. He knew that it would take his strong teeth an hour or two to chew through the tough wet leather, and he knew that two or three minutes would likely be all the time he would have. About fifty feet beyond him and the guard the party had pitched camp and built fires, but Sam could see no sign of rum-drinking. Possibly they would not drink until they came to the village.

About an hour after the first fire was built he saw a warrior coming toward him with something in his hands. As the redman drew near Sam saw that it was one of his own tin cups or one just like it, and that the cup was steaming. The Indian proffered the cup and Sam took it, knowing that this was his supper; and after the Indian had gone away he looked into the cup and sniffed at its steam. He didn't know what was in the cup but his grim humor imagined that it was a stew of coprophagous insects. There was almost a pint of it. All through the soup he could see what looked like hairs and small bugs, but with both hands he put the cup to his mouth and gulped the contents. Two or three small pieces of half-cooked flesh he chewed. Ten feet from him the guard ate his supper, his eyes fixed most of the time on Sam. Sam set the tin cup aside. With snow he washed the beard around his mouth.

Under him he felt the wetness of melting snow; his rump and

thighs itched in wet leather. If he had to march day after day in deep snowpaths and eat only this thin slop he would need sleep, but how could a man sleep with melting snow under and over him? Before morning he would be chilled through. One thing was now plain to him: when a man faced torture and death he was forced to do some thinking. Looking up through the lovely swirling flakes, he told himself that if the Creator was all-mighty there was justice in the world; and if that were so, there would be justice here, for him. He suspected that this was a childish thought but it comforted him. It comforted him to reach emotionally across the wintry desolation to the shack where Kate sat, talking to her children, with the snow falling white on her gray hair. While thinking of her, alone and half frozen and facing a bitter winter, there came a flash of recognition that made him pause in his breathing: in this war party were some of the braves who had slaughtered her family. The brute who had jerked the rope was one of them. They knew they had in their power the man who had set the four Blackfeet heads on the stakes. What a struggle must be convulsing their wild savage souls, as they wavered between avarice and blood lust! How they would have loved to drink the whiteman's firewater, while with insane shrieks they hacked his flesh off in little gobbets and filled his wounds with the big red ants!

Having now, it seemed to him, seen his plight in clear terms, Sam faced the question whether greed or blood lust would win. He saw now all the more reason why his escape, if he were to make one, should be as early as possible. It would be fatal for him if they took him to one of the larger villages, because there the squaws would tear the floor out of hell and blood lust would win. He studied the guard before him, praying that the villian would fall asleep. This hope was dashed when about two in the morning two fresh guards came to relieve him. The crafty chief was taking no chances.

Of the two savages who now sat and faced him Sam could have said only that they had black hair and eyes. Each had a rifle across his lap, a knife at his waist. Sam knew there could be no escape this night. In two hours other guards would relieve these two, and at the first gray of daylight he would march again. He probably would have to walk from daylight till dark, with no more than a cup or two of stinking soup to nourish him. The only thing to do was to try to sleep.

He pushed his legs out and lay back, his face turned to the golden bark of a yellow pine tree. He closed his eyes. Even if he could not sleep with snow melting under and over him he could relax and doze and that would be good. He thought an hour had passed when he felt a presence close to him. He smelled it. He smelled an Indian strong with the Blackfeet odor but he did not open his eyes and stare, as a greenhorn would have done. If a savage had come over, eager to thrust a knife into him, he would need in his black heart only the most trivial excuse. He could say to his chief that the paleface had opened his eyes and leapt at him, and in self-defense he had struck. Telling himself as a warning that the redman was emotional, high-strung, impulsive, Sam allowed nothing in his face and posture to change, as a guard, drawn knife in hand, bent over him and studied his face. In his mind Sam had the picture. He could have leapt with his incredible speed and even with bound hands he could have broken the man's neck, but that would only have brought on slow torture and death. There was nothing to do but pretend to sleep and trust in a Being whose first law was justice. . . .

Sam would have said that the redskin bent over him for at least five minutes. Then the rancid odor went away. But even then Sam did not open his eyes or stir. The snow had been melting on his eyelids and face, and his eyes and face were wet. About four o'clock he actually sank into sleep, and slept until he heard the first movements at daylight. Chilled through and half frozen, he struggled to his feet and tried to shake moisture from his leather clothing. It was plain to him now that if he were going to make an effort to escape it would have to be in the next twenty-four hours.

He sank to the snow by the tree and waited.

23

HIS BREAKFAST was another cup of soup. He thought the scraps of meat in it were dog or owl or crow. Today, as yesterday, the redmen were all mounted, with the chief on

Sam's bay. Again Sam had to walk. This day and this night were like the former day and night. He had no chance to escape. His wily captors put the rope twice around the leather that bound his wrists, and both ends around the tree and over to the guards. His second night was ten miserable chilled hours under storm and guards.

The third day and night repeated the first and second, and Sam knew that after two or three more days like these he would be too weak to escape, or to want to. He would make a move, even if it was desperate and useless. After camp was pitched the chief came to Sam where he was tied to a fir tree and looked into his eyes. The redskin had on fresh war paint and more rancid grease on his hair; nothing about him looked human, not even his eyes, for in his hideous face his eyes could have been those of a beast. There was in them no trace of the human or the civilized—they were the hard glittering eyes of an animal looking at its prey. Sam thought the falcon must look like that when it moved to dive and strike.

He had not expected the Indian to hit him, and when, with startling swiftness, the blow fell across his cheek, Sam's eyes opened wide with astonishment. Then he looked steadily at the creature before him, telling himself that if he escaped he would never rest until he had tracked this coward down. He again made note of the man's shape, height, weight, the length of his hair, the scars, and the exact appearance of his teeth when his lips parted to snarl. Sam had no notion of why the fool had come over to strike him; years ago he had given up trying to understand the Indian male. Some infernal evil was busy in this man's mind and heart.

The chief turned to shout and there hastened over a brave who, like his boss, smelled of rancid grease and redbank war paint. The chief spoke to the brave as he came up, and at once this man stepped so close to Sam that his face was only fourteen inches from Sam's face. He looked into Sam's eyes and made an ugly sound. Sam knew it was an expression of contempt. The warrior then said, "Brave, uggh!" and again hawked the contempt up. Sam was startled; he had not known that any man in this party spoke English. "Yuh brave?" the redskin asked, and turned to spit a part of his contempt. Sam stared at the fellow, wondering if he was a half-breed. With signs and broken English the warrior told Sam that for the chief he was a coward and a sick old dog. He was an old coyote covered over with scabs and wood ticks. When the chief slapped him he had challenged him to a fight, but here the paleface stood, cowering and trembling. Were there any brave men among the palefaces?

Sam was silent. He knew that this was an Indian trick but he didn't know the reason for it. It was a preposterous lie to say that the chief would fight him, with fists, knives, or guns, or with any weapon. It was a trick. Was it some plan to cripple him, so that he could not possibly escape—to hamstring him or blind him? Sam looked up into the storm and waited for what was to come.

In his crippled English the warrior was now telling Sam that they were going to ransom him to the Crows. What the Crows would do to him he tried to suggest by stripping fir needles and pretending that they were gobbets of flesh, and by pretending with a finger to slice his nose, lips, tongue, genitals, until they were all gone. He indicated that the joints of fingers and toes would be broken, one by one; with a piece of hooked wire each eye would be pulled out of its socket; and with a string tied around each eyeball he would be led through the village, while the squaws sliced off his buttocks and tossed them to the dogs.

What purpose the creature had in mind with his catalogue of horrors Sam did not know. All the while the redskin talked and gestured, with glittering of his black eyes and guttural gloatings of joy, Sam's mind was busy. He now suspected that this band of warriors had been begging the chief to turn the prisoner over to them, and their share of the rum, so that they could torture and drink and celebrate. The animal before him had worked himself into such a frenzy of maiming and blood-letting that Sam was afraid the frenzy might prove contagious. He decided to speak. He would not speak as a normal man or in a normal voice. He would speak as The Terror, as the man of all mountain men most feared by the red people, and as a great leader and chief.

His first sound was a thunderous roar from his deep chest, and it came with such a shattering explosion that the astounded and terrified redskin almost fell backwards. The chief retreated with him and there they stood, two braves with their black eyes popped out, as Sam flung his mighty arms toward the sky and trumpeted his disdain in his deepest and most dreadful voice. "Almighty God up there in Your kingdom, look down on Your son, for he will be gone beaver before he will stand such insults! These cowards have about used up my patience! I will stand no more of it!" Now, with a deliberate effort to astound and abash them, he swiftly puffed his cheeks in and out, to make the heavy golden beard dance and quiver over most of his face; he bugged and rolled his eyes, and they shone and gleamed like polished granite; and flinging both arms heavenward, he cried in a voice that could have been heard two miles away, "Almighty Father, I wasn't born to be slapped around and spit on and the first thing I know I'll open up this red nigger and pull his liver out and choke him with it! Look down, and give me the strength of Samson!" He then burst into a crazy-man wild hallooing and exulting that sent the two Indians and the guards into further retreat, and brought into view all those in camp.

The redmen, drunk or sober, could raise an infernal racket, but such a trumpet-tongued deafening uproar of bombination and reverberation they had never heard; and while they all stared as though hypnotized the golden-bearded giant began to jump up and down and contort himself like a monster in convulsions, his voice rising to a shrieking caterwauling that set the dogs to howling and the horses to whinnying. His fires fed by enormous anger and contempt for these ill-smelling creatures who had him in their power, Sam simply turned himself loose and bellowed and howled out of him the emotions that had been filling him to bursting. All the while he was thinking of such things as Beethoven's sonatas in C major and F minor, and his own act he put on with such a shattering crescendo that even he felt a little unnerved by it. These unspeakable creatures had even taken from him his tobacco, his harp, and the lock of hair from the head of his wife; and they had fondled his revolvers and pointed them at him, and with his knife had made movements at his throat. They opened his baggage in plain sight of him and with shrieks of delight had held up to view one thing and another—his moccasins, skins, flour, coffee, cloth—until he had got so utterly filled with anger for their insolence and contempt and stinking soup that he could only unleash his whole being to the Almighty in a war song of menace and challenge, and get it out of him so that he could again breathe naturally. For a full five minutes he kept it up, his thunderous overture to the infinite; and then, covered with sweat, he stepped back and stood against the tree, arms folded on his chest with his bound hands under his chin, his eyes looking at them. Fifty-eight pairs of black eyes were looking at him. Such a tempest of rage and challenge they had never heard from man or beast and would never hear again.

It was the chief who approached Sam. He came within ten feet of him and stood like a man who thought this bearded giant might explode, as the infernal spirit regions in Colter's hell exploded. After studying Sam a full minute he summoned the brave who spoke English. But Sam had the offensive and he intended to keep it; he could tell that these superstitious children were not sure now whether he was man or some kind of god. So, with prodigious gestures of menace and challenge, and a great roaring into the sky, Sam made them understand that he would fight any five of them in a fight to the death, all of them to come against him as one man, in full view of the Blackfeet people and a hundred mountain men; and after he had slain the five, the hundred mountain men would fight the whole Blackfeet nation, the thousand of them or ten thousand, or as many as the leaves on trees and the berries on bushes. He knew that his challenge would not be accepted, or even considered; but he had in mind a plan. He went on to say that if they were no braver than sick squaws crawling in the sagebrush, or dying coyotes with their heads in holes—if they were no more than rabbits, if they were a nation of magpies with broken wings, they should take him to the Sparrowhawks and get the thing over with. But if big ransom was what they wanted—tobacco and rum and guns and beads and bullets and coffee and sugar—they should ransom him to the mountain men, who would pay much more; and after he was set free they could capture him again and sell him again. But whatever they did, they would all die like puking coyotes in their vomit if they forgot for a moment that he was a great chief and a mighty one, who wore fifty eagle feathers in his headpiece; and he was to be treated with dignity and honors; and if he was not, all the mountain men would march against them and hunt them down to the last crippled dog.

To further confuse and addle their wits he burst into tremendous song. As before, the redmen seemed hypnotized as Sam smote his breast and shot his arms skyward and poured out of his lungs the furious majesties of impatience and anger. As suddenly as he had begun he stopped, and then roared at the pidgin brave, telling him to come forward if he were not a coward hiding under a stinkbush. The man advanced, slowly and with absurd caution, as if expecting Sam to blow him off the scene. Sam told him that he, Samson John Minard, was a chief, and a bigger and more important chief than the contemptible eater of crickets who had slapped his face. Sam said to tell him that he would raise his hair and pull his scent bag off if he didn't treat him the way a chief should be treated. "Go, you quivering coyote, and tell him! Tell him Chief Samson is to be put in a tent, as befits a great one, and given his pipe and tobacco." Sam knew he would get no tobacco: once the smokers of kinnikinic and cedar bark and willow got hold of whiteman's tobacco they sucked it into their lungs day and night until it was gone. But he saw that he had aroused some of the warriors to clamorous proposals, and that the chief was talking things over with them. After a few minutes the brave told Sam that a tent would be prepared for him and he would have a robe to lie on.

A half hour later several braves came over, and untying the rope from the tree, led Sam like a beast to the tent. There he exploded in another deliberate tantrum; flinging his bound arms wildly, he said they would take the tether rope off his wrists, for did they think he was a horse to be hobbled and staked out? Hadn't they among their fifty-eight one who was warrior enough to guard an unarmed prisoner? This taunt bore results. The chief had Sam taken into one of the larger tepees, and put as guard over him one, he was told, who had made a coup when only a boy, and had more Flathead and Crow scalps than Sam had fingers and toes. Sam then repeated his proposal, in words and signs, that they should ransom him to the mountain men, and then see if they were brave enough to capture him a second time, for a second ransom.

When first made, this proposal had fired the greed of some of the warriors. Their passions had caught flame like tall dry prairie grass, as they foresaw innumerable kegs of rum and piles of tobacco. As children with little sense of the realities, they had no doubt that they could capture him a second time, or many times; and if there was to be so much firewater in the future why not drink what they had just captured? This was what Sam had hoped for. Once thirst possessed their senses there could be no prevailing against them. The chief knew that, but he was eager as any to unstop the rum and pour the liquid fire down his throat. He gave orders, and men rushed into the forest to find dead wood; other braves made ready three elk, which had been killed that afternoon. As Sam watched the preparations he tried to look sleepy and very hopeless. Five gallons might not lay them all out senseless but it was strong rum; forty pints for fifty-eight would average almost eleven ounces to the man. That ought to be enough.

The rope had been untied from the leather that bound Sam's wrists, and he had been given a small thin robe that had lost most of its hair. On this in the tent he sat and planned and waited. The brave who had been sent in to guard him was taller and heavier than most Indians: Sam thought he stood an inch or two above six feet and weighed more than two hundred pounds. He supposed that the chief had chosen one of his boldest and most dependable men, and one of the most savage, for this critter hadn't sat a full minute when with Sam's Bowie he made passes across his throat. He took from his lap a tomahawk and made movements with it to show Sam how he would split his skull. His face expressionless, Sam watched the grim pantomime; inside he was thinking: If my plan works, you dog-eater, you and me will be huggin before this night is over.

Sam was weighing his chances in every way he could conceive of. The tent was about ten feet across and about eight feet high where it was anchored to the center pole. If he were to move fast inside it, Sam told himself, he would have to bend over, for if his head struck the tent the Indians outside might see the movement. The guard sat on a heavy robe. As he faced Sam he was just to the left of the flap, which had been thrown open and back. There were three big fires blazing outside; the voices were shrill. The firelight cast flickering illuminations over the guard's face and gave a horrifying appearance of evil to his war paint. His right hand clasped the handle of the knife, his left the handle of the tomahawk. He had no gun. He was alert but tense; he had to turn his head now and then to peer out. Sam knew the man was burning with infernal thirst and was wondering if he would share the rum or be forgotten. Oh, they would bring him a chunk of roasted elk but would they bring him the water that turned a man into fire? If only he were the one who spoke some English, Sam could have talked to him and tried to make a frenzy of his resentment and impatience. As it was, he did nothing and said nothing; it would be best to look sleepy and tired. Sam was sitting straight across from the guard; their faces were only about six feet apart, their moc-casined feet only about two. Sam's face was in shadow; he

knew that the guard could not see him clearly, but Sam could
see the emotions convulsing the guard's face. That Injun's belly
was burning for rum. If they forgot him he would be mad
enough to grease hell with war paint before this night was over.

The guard made no move that Sam's lidded eyes did not see.
During the first hour he had turned to look out at least once
every ten minutes; he was then looking out every five minutes;
and at the end of an hour and a half he was looking out every
minute or less, and the way he moved showed that he was
itching with resentment and suspicion and that his thirst was
like hell's own. Nothing, Sam told himself, was more likely to
make a guard think his prisoner secure than a boiling passion
that took his mind off him and returned it and took it off again.
Alcohol could do it; a female could do it. Alcohol, it now
seemed to Sam, was the redman's curse, and woman the
whiteman's. . . .

Just itch all over, Sam thought, his bound hands in plain
view on his lap, his head sunk as though he were half gone in
fatigue and sleep. Just itch, you bastard, and keep looking. Sam
had never felt more brilliantly alert, as though all his senses and
mind and emotions shone in the full blaze of noon sunlight.
Never had his eyes been sharper. Just git yourself a thirst like
that in hell, Sam was saying inside; and over and over
calculated the risks and his chances. He figured that he had
been sitting with the guard about two hours. For nearly an hour
he had smelled the roasting flesh. He knew that tripods of green
trees had been set up and that hanging from them were the
carcasses, slowly roasting in flames and smoke. Redmen when
hungry never waited for flesh to cook but almost at once began
to hack off bloody gobbets; and by the time their hunger was
appeased there wasn't much left but bone and gristle. Before
long now these Indians would be drinking. Sam had hoped
they would drink before they ate. Once they started drinking
they would have pictures of mountain men bringing them
whole rivers and lakes of rum, to ransom the Crow-killer, so
that a second time they could capture him, for more lakes and
rivers. What dreams children dreamed!

There now came to the door of the tent a face whose war
paint had been smeared over with fresh blood. In this brave's
hands was a piece of pine bark, on which rested a pound or two
of hot elk meat. The guard set the meat by him and began to
gesticulate, and to talk in a high shrill voice ill-becoming a bold

brave warrior; Sam knew that he was asking why he had not
been fetched a cup of spirit water. The two braves gestured and
yelled at one another, and the one who had brought the meat
then went away. Sam did not move or lift the lids on his eyes,
for he knew that his moment was drawing near. Very gently he
tried to ease his cramps and relax his muscles.

In only a few moments the Indian returned with a tin cup in
his hand. Sam knew that in the cup was rum. The guard
eagerly took the cup and sniffed, and he was so enchanted that
he laid the knife on his lap, and seizing the cup with both
hands, put the rim to his lips. Sam's gaze was on the other
Indian; he was praying that the fellow would go away. He had
hoped that the guard would be alone with him when he drank
and that his first gulp would be so large it would strangle him.
Sam was to say later that both his prayers were answered. The
Indian in the tepee doorway, eager to get back to the drinking
and feasting, did vanish; and the blockhead with the cup of
rum did take such a huge mouthful that the fiery spirits choked
him. He suddenly tightened all over and was fumbling to set
the cup down when Sam moved with the swiftness that had
become legendary. In an instant his powerful hands were on
the redman's throat. Everything that he did now had been
thought through, over and over, so that there would be no false
move or wasted moment. As hands seized the throat a knee
came with terrific force into the man's diaphragm, paralyzing
his whole torso. In the next instant Sam released the throat and
his right hand seized the knife. He twisted his right hand
around until he could put the blade to the leather and sever it,
and the moment that was done, the left hand was back to the
throat to be sure it made no sounds, and the right hand was
gathering the robe, tomahawk, and piece of elk meat. He then
slipped under the back of the tent into the gray-white night.

In a flash he was gone across the pale snow and into the
trees.

24

IT WAS SNOWING hard. During the hours when he sat waiting for his chance Sam had known that he would need the Almighty's help if he were to outrun the pursuit of fifty-eight hell-fiends, and the bitter cold and deep snows of winter. His instincts told him that he was going east but he was not sure of it. During this day's march he had seen a range of mountains west of him, another north, and another east, and he had thought the range on the east was the Continental Divide. If it was, the Missouri River was only forty or fifty miles east of it, and from there across the desolation to Kate was a hundred and fifty or two hundred miles.

During his many hours of thinking and planning he had recognized that it would be folly to go south, over the trail up which they had come, or west to the Flatheads. His captors would expect him to take one of these routes. They would not expect him to go north into Blood and Piegan land, or to be fool enough to try to cross the Divide after heavy snows had come. Earlier in the day the war party had crossed a river but he did not know what river it was. He had never been through this country. He had heard that there were several rivers in this area, all of which came down from the Divide and flowed west. Up one of these rivers looked to him like the only possible way to freedom.

After he had trotted swiftly for four or five miles he stopped to listen. He could hear no sounds. He put the piece of meat to his nostrils, for he was as famished as a wolf. While sitting and waiting he had wondered if he ought to take one of the guard's thighs, but he was a sentimental man and he thought he would rather starve than eat human flesh. He had calculated all the risks and had decided that in starvation lay his greatest danger. He could hope to get his hands on little except roots along

streams, berries still clinging to bushes, a fool hen possibly, a
fish now and then in a shallow pool, rose hips, marrow in old
bones; or, if very lucky, a deer or an antelope stuck in deep
snow.

He was glad that it was snowing hard. He was singing inside
at the thought of being free. He thanked God for both and he
thanked Him for rum. He hoped that rum and rage would make
fifty-seven warriors so drunk that they would fall down and
freeze to death. He thought he had heard bones snap in the
guard's neck. If they found him dead all hell would break loose;
they would run round and round and the dogs would be baying
at their heels. But Sam doubted that they would take his trail
before morning. They would think he had gone back down the
path to the Three Forks and that they could catch him in a day
or two; or they would think he had headed for his in-laws and
would get stuck in deep snow. If it were to snow all night they
might not be able to tell by morning which way he had taken.
But the dogs would know.

There was a cold wind down from the mountains. He
listened again and thought he heard faint shrieks, and dogs
barking, but he could not be sure. His direction now was due
north and two hours before daylight he came to a river. Taking
off his moccasins and leather leggins he waded into the shallow
stream and turned up it, to the east, walking as rapidly as he
could, in water only ankle-deep or sometimes to his crotch. It
was cold but for a while it did not seem cold; his blood was hot
from exertion, his soul singing, his hopes high. He had yanked
off the guard's medicine bag and was amazed to find in it his
mouth harp. It was as if a brother had joined him, or
Beethoven's ugly face up in the sky had smiled. When first
captured he would not have given a buckskin whang for his
life; but now, with God's help, he was a free man again, and he
would remain free and alive, even if he had to live on tree bark.
The redmen might follow his path to the river but there they
would lose it, and two or three of them might go upriver but
most of them would go downriver. He could not, like John
Colter, find an acre of driftwood and lie under it for half a day
and most of a night; he could only hoard his strength and keep
going. Some of the river stones cut his feet but he remembered
that John's feet had been filled with cactus thorns; he was
starved but he told himself that Colter had lived on hips and
roots; Hugh Glass with maggots swarming in his wounds had

crawled for a hundred miles; and a man named Scott, starved and sick unto death, had dragged himself forward for sixty miles. And yonder Kate sat in the cold and sang. A man could do it if he had to. He recalled other tales of heroism and fortitude, to warm and cheer him as he struggled up the river.

Sam was not feeling sorry for himself. He was not that kind. He was not telling himself that he would perish. He was only warming himself with the feats of brave free men, his kind of men. Afraid that he was moving only about three miles an hour in his tortuous journey up the river, he looked round him but there was no other way. Until daylight he would keep moving and perhaps for an hour after daylight, for he thought it would take the redmen half the morning to find his path and follow it to the river. He would find some snuggery back under the bank—an old beaver house or a wash under an overhanging earth ledge or a pile of driftwood; and he would hole up until night came again. He could catch a few hours' sleep, if he lay on his belly, for in that position his snoring, Lotus had told him, was light. He would eat half the elk meat and all the rose hips he could find; and when darkness came he would be gone again.

What he found was a high-water eddy underwash, under a grove of large aspen; the spring torrents had raised the river four or five feet above its present level, and the high waters swirling round and round in the eddy had cut away the earth back under the trees. Sam crawled for thirty feet and after putting on his leggins and moccasins and wrapping the robe around him he cut off morsels of flesh and chewed them thoroughly. Never had elk tasted so good. Looking out the way he had come, he could see only a hint of daylight. If Indians were to wade up the river, as he had done, it was possible that they would spot his hideaway and crouch low to look back under. But they would never wade far in a river. They would think he had made a raft and gone downriver, toward his in-laws, and by the time they discovered their error he would be over the Divide.

All day until dusk he rested and slept a little and heard no Indians and saw nothing alive but one hawk. All day the snow fell. All night he took his slow way up the river. By midnight he had reached the foothills; by morning he was fighting white water. An hour after daylight he had found no hiding place, but in shallow pools he had caught a few small trout, a part of which he ate for breakfast, with a handful of rose pods. He was still struggling upward on bruised and bleeding feet when about noon he saw a cavern back in a ledge of stone. Its mouth was close to the river, with a wide shelf of spilled stones at the entrance. Leaving the river, he climbed up across talus to look in. The cavern was far deeper than he had expected, so deep in fact that his gaze went blind back in the gloom. He smelled wild-beast odors, and the odors of dove, bat, and swallow. After entering the cave he stood under a ceiling thirty feet high and looked round him. At one side he saw a smaller cave that also ran back into gloom; this he explored to find a spot where he could lie down. The animal smells in the smaller cave were overpowering. They were so heavy and so saturated with mustiness and dusts that he could feel them in his nostrils.

Returning to the mouth of the cavern, he stood by a brown stone wall to give him protective coloring and looked back down the river. The falling snow was only a thin mist now, the kind that makes way for freezing cold; he could see far down the river's meandering course and across the valley. There was no smoke from Indian fires anywhere. He went down to the river for a water-washed stone on which to lay his meat and fish. Then, sitting in the cavern mouth, he cut off about three ounces of meat and ate it, and two fish no larger than his finger. Along the riverbanks he had gathered about a quart of rose hips. How a man could live and walk for a week on nothing but these, as some men were said to have done, he could not imagine.

While looking round him he sneezed. The echoes of it startled him, for they were remarkably loud and clear. Impressed by the cavern's acoustics, he spoke, saying, "Hot biscuits," and sang a few bars of an old ballad. The echoing astonished and then alarmed him. It was somewhat like music from a great organ, rolling through vaulted chambers, with ceilings high and low. He burst into a Mozart theme, and the echoes rolling away from him into the far dark recesses sounded to him like an orchestra playing. He wondered if he was losing his mind. After he had found a spot where he could lie and try to sleep he thought of the Rocky Mountains caverns he had explored, and of the strange sculpturing that water, wind, and time had made underground. "Almighty God—" he said, and liked so well the amplified and golden-toned echo that he uttered other words. "Dear Lotus, dear son—Lotus!" he said more loudly, and from all around him back in the stone mountains the word came back to him like an organ tone.

Sam was not a man who usually felt gooseflesh in moments of danger but he had been enfeebled by hunger and want of sleep. Gooseflesh spread over him in the moment when he smelled the danger; turning swiftly to a sitting position, tomahawk in one hand and knife in the other, he saw ambling toward him not more than fifty feet away a grizzly so large that it seemed almost to fill the cavern. In a flash Sam knew that the reverberating echoes had disturbed the monster's slumber, somewhere back in the gloom, and it had come to give battle to its enemy. That it intended to give battle Sam knew the instant he saw it. The next moment he was on his feet, advancing, the hatchet ready to strike and the knife to plunge. He marched right up to the beast and smote the prow of the nose a crushing blow with the head of the axe. In an instant his arm came back and he struck again, and this time the blow fell across the sensitive nostrils. The big furry fellow said *woof-woof* and began to back off, with Sam after him, hoping for grizzly steaks; but almost at once the beast vanished, and there was only the whimpering plaintive sound of a frightened child, as the shuffling fur ball hastened back to its winter bed.

Pale from fright and weakness and breathing hard, Sam watched it disappear. He felt for a moment that he was being tested with more than he could bear. Hungry, weary to the depths of his marrow, and numbed through with cold, he would now have to leave the cavern and go. There might be a whole pack of grizzlies back in the dark; and even if there were not, the whimpering one would nurse his injuries and come forth again. Over by the entrance Sam stood a few moments, looking out. He knew by the nimbus around the winter sun that the weather was going to change. After seven days of deep storm the temperature would fall; sometimes in this area it went to thirty, forty, even to fifty below. Sometimes there were blizzards that not even the wolves and hawks could endure. There was cold that split trees open with the sound of gunfire; that froze broad rivers from bank to bank and almost to their bottoms; and the snow so hard that even the giant moose with its sharp hoofs could walk on it. It was cold that welded a man's hand to the steel of gun or knife, if he was fool enough to touch it.

After searching the valley for sign of Indians and seeing none

Sam looked up the river gorge to the continental backbone. After he had crossed the Divide the rivers would be flowing east instead of west, and he would be going down instead of climbing. With the robe flung across his left shoulder the food enfolded by a piece of it and tucked up under an armpit, the hatchet in his left hand and the knife in his right, he scrambled down to the water's edge; sat and took off moccasins and leggins and trousers; and thrust wounded feet into the icy waters. Then he waded upstream. He guessed he might as well eat the remainder of the elk and the three small fish, and keep going and keep going. After he had gone a mile or two he peeled the outer bark off a spruce and licked the juice of the cambium. It was resinous and bitter. Hank Cady had said that lessen a man has something better he kin live on it if he hafta. The cambium itself Sam found unchewable, and so peeled off strips of it and licked the juice, as he had licked fruit juices off his hands as a child. While licking the juice he looked round him, wondering if there was anything else on this mountain that a man could eat. During the long miles up this river he had seen no birds, except a hawk or two and one duck; no sign of grouse or sage hen, no sign of deer or elk trail. On the mountain slopes above him he could see no snowpaths. The untramped, unmarked snow on either side of the river was about three feet deep. He wondered if it would be less exhausting to plow through it than to fight his way up over slippery boulders, in water from a foot to three feet deep. Wading in river waters up a mountain canyon was the most fatiguing toil he had ever known; he was sure he was not covering more than two miles an hour but he kept at it, doggedly, all day long, pausing only when night closed round him.

He then searched both banks, hoping to find a shelter in which he could sleep. But he found only an arbor, under a dense tangle of berry vines and mountain laurel, over which the snow had formed a roof; he crawled back under it, out of sight. After putting on his clothes he wrapped the robe around him, and lying on his left side facing the river, he put two fish on leaves a few inches from his face, hatchet and knife within reach, and in a few minutes was sound asleep. His first dream was of his wife; they were somewhere in buffalo land, and while she gathered berries and mushrooms he cooked steaks and made hot biscuits. It was a cold night and he slept cold, but for eight hours he did not awaken. It was the first solid rest he had had in a week.

When at daylight he stirred it took him a few moments to understand where he was. Then, like Jedediah Smith, he gave thanks to God; dwelt for a few minutes on the bones of his wife and child, yonder in the winter, and on a mother sitting in a pile of bedding looking out at an empty white world; and then ate the two fish. Yes, it had turned colder. On the eastern side of the Divide would be the wild storm-winds down from Canada; there he would need more than a mouthful of frozen fish to keep him going. But he felt cheerful this morning and he told himself that he was as strong as a bull moose. He thought he was safe from the Blackfeet now. Ahead of him lay an ordeal that might be the most difficult he would ever endure, but he would struggle through it, day after day, all the way across the white winter loneliness, until he came at last to Kate's door.

"Keep a fire for me, and a light," he said, and faced into the sharp winds from the north.

25

HE HAD NO food, not even a seed pod or a root, when he reached the continent's spine and looked across a frozen white world to the thin faint tree line of a river, fifteen or twenty miles distant. Beyond the river was the wintry desolation that lay all the way to Kate's shack. The Missouri came down from the Three Forks area, and passing through the Gates of the Mountains, swung to the northeast. That was buffalo land, yonder. It was also Blackfeet land. It would be Blackfeet land all the way to the Musselshell. He could think of nothing to eat down there that a man could get hold of—even the rancid marrow in the bones of dead things would be lost under the snows.

Breaking off evergreen boughs, he laid a pile on the frozen snow and sat on the pile. Taking the left moccasin off, he drew the foot up across his thigh. The trouble with foot wounds was that they never got a chance to heal; in this foot he had a dozen wounds; during his hours of rest or sleep they tried to scab over but when he walked again the scabs softened and came off. Both feet had wounds but it would do no good to worry about them. A mountain man did not worry about small wounds, nor much about big ones. He could keep going for years with arrowheads in his flesh, or for months with open thigh or belly wounds.

Sam's problem was food. It would be a bitter irony to escape from torture and death only to fall exhausted on the prairie and be eaten by wolves. A lot of wolves and coyotes were down there and they were all hungry. They were all over that vast frozen whiteness as far as a man could see and a thousand miles beyond that; they would follow him, hoping to chew the buckskin off him, and to eat him alive when at last he fell to rise no more. The greenhorns back east told tales of ferocious maneating wolves that in lonely winter wastes of northern nights trailed helpless voyagers and pulled them down; but Sam knew of no attack of man by wolves, and the mountain men knew of none. The wolves would follow him and trot around him all night and all day; and when he slept they would steal up close to see if he had anything a wolf could eat. Hunger, if strong enough, might force them to attack a man. Hunger had made more heroes than courage.

Sam was not worried about wolves or any other beast in the area before him. He was worried about food, and the woman yonder in the bitter cold. Male and female created He them, the book said; and there sat the female, a scrawny gray creature whose whole soul and being was fixed on her dead children; and here sat the male, starving to death. His hunger pains were about what he thought he might have if two rough hands inside him were stretching his guts and tying them in knots. While examining his feet he ate snow or searched the distant riverline up and down for sign of smoke. In the southeast he saw what he took to be the Big Belt Mountains. He didn't think any mountain men were trapping there this winter. The Bear Paw Mountains were somewhere ahead of him but he didn't think anyone was trapping there either.

He found it strange that in a land where the Creator had put such an abundance of things to eat there was nothing he could get his hands on. Even if he had a gun he had seen nothing to shoot, except the bear. He thought there were buffalo along the river, and possibly deer and elk; he might find a sick or wounded old bull or cow that he could outrun and he might find some marrowbones along the banks. He had heard of men who made rabbit and bird snares but he had nothing to make .

one with. Peeling off spruce bark, he rubbed the sap into his wounds and put the moccasins on. The outside pair of the three pairs was frayed in spots and in spots worn through, and the second pair was frayed. If he made it he guessed he would show up somewhere in leather rags and tatters, fifty pounds lighter and ten years wiser.

He was on the point of rising when he decided to wash his beard. Glancing down across it, he had seen stains, and though he was not a fastidious man he tried to be a clean one. With both hands he reached into snow under the surface crust and then roughed the snow up and down through the hair and over his brows and forehead and over his head and around his neck. After a while he pulled the beard out from his chin and looked over it and could see no bloodstains from the dead Indian. He guessed blood must have gushed from the guard's nose but he had not been aware of it at the time. With the knife he sawed the beard in two close to his chin. The hair he cut off he left in a pile for the Blackfeet to find.

He rose and started down the mountain toward the Missouri. His feet hurt and the hands in his belly were tying knots but otherwise he felt pretty good. He thought he could make it to the river before midnight. Down steep ravines where there was little timber he tobogganed on the robe, using knife and hatchet to pull him along or to brake his speed. He thought snow was one of the Creator's finest works of genius and he pitied people in hot climates who had never seen it. He had heard Windy Bill say that if there had been plenty of snow in Africa there would be no blackmen with thick lips and flat noses. Bill was full of such fancies. Sam loved snow as he loved rain, winds, thunder, tempests; people who said, "I don't see how you can like snow," or, "I don't see how you can like a wind," he thought unworthy to be alive. Yonder, far south of him, were the Wind River and the Wind River Mountains, and endless miles of eroded colorful formations that winds had made. Kit Carson said that somewhere down the Colorado was an immense area of natural bridges, monuments, and stone formations that looked like old castles. For centuries, for ages, ever since the beginning, the winds had been blowing there and they certainly were a better sculptor than Phidias. No matter where a man went, from the marvels in the Black Hills to the granite faces of the Tetons, from the Yellowstone's canyon to that of the Snake and the Green and the Colorado, a man saw the wonderful parthenons that winds and water had made. "Ya doan like it?" Bear Paws Meek had said to a greenhorn sneering at the Tetons. "Wall now, I doan spect the Almighty cares too much fer ye either, so why doan ya go back to yer ma?"

Down from the mountains Sam stood on the white plains, looking through cold winter haze at the line of the river. Then he began to walk on long strides in snow above his knees all his senses alert, for he knew that moving against the white background he was as conspicuous as a black mole on the nose of a lovely woman. If there were Indians on the river they would see him coming but he had seen no sign of smoke. Dusk was filtering down from the wintry sky when the river, it seemed to him, was still ten miles away; it was two hours after dark when he reached it. There were trails in the snow but he saw no living thing and heard no sounds.

Here and there along the water's edge he found bones, and choosing a couple of thighbones and pieces from a neck, he sat hidden near river brush, while with sharpened green stick he dug marrow out. With tongue and lips he sucked the marrow off the stick. It was worse than rancid; it tasted like extreme old age, decay, and death. But it was food of a kind, it would help him to keep moving. After eating marrow until he was sickened he searched in river brush for wild rose, and gooseberry, serviceberry, and currant. He found hips and a few berries still clinging, and with a handful of them he returned to the bones. The pulpy rose pods had always tasted to him like old wood. He mixed them and a few withered currants and serviceberries with a marrow paste and devoured the nauseous mess, cheering himself with stories of men who had lived for days on such fare as this. He also chewed and swallowed some bone splinters, after he had shattered a thighbone to get at the marrow. The bones were tough to chew and had no flavor at all.

He spent about two hours making his supper. It wasn't loin steaks and hot biscuits in hump fat, or roasted grouse basted with kidney butter, but it would do till morning. After eating he bound together pieces of driftwood with tough berry vines. With his weapons wrapped in the robe, and a long pole in his grasp, he shoved the raft out into the current, and on reaching mid-channel lay on his belly, chin on his forearms, to survey the moving scene before him. Though he knew that he might starve or freeze to death, or again be captured, he could not put away his insatiable delight in the astonishing world, from the

majestic cordilleras to the smallest pouting mudpot. Under him
was a marvelous panorama of color and light. The water on the
bottom all the way across the river had been freezing, and the
ice formations down in the depths were catching the light of a
full moon and making patterns like some he had seen in caverns
in the Black Hills. Because the current was bearing him north
at about half a mile an hour the scenes under him, though
similar, were never the same. When with the pole he moved his
craft toward the eastern bank and came to a deep and gently
swirling eddy he saw three or four feet under him a multitude
of what mountain men called suckers, a species of whitefish,
with absurd little round mouths that puckered and pouted as
they breathed. If only he had a dozen of them, and his steel and
flint to make a fire, what a feast he would have!

An hour later he stood on the east bank and looked east.
Judith River and mountains were somewhere ahead of him but
he could see no sign of them in the prairie night. For a hundred
and fifty miles there might be nothing, except the wolves
trailing him. A well-armed man, well-provisioned, with a
couple of warm robes, might not have hesitated to undertake
such a journey, even in below-zero temperatures, but one thinly
clad, with one robe and no food and no way to get food, would
surely die on the way. The mountain men would have said that,
for even if he could walk thirty miles a day without food it
would take him at least five days to reach the Musselshell.

These were Sam's thoughts as he crawled under a snow-
laden shelter of willows to wait for the morning. He did not
dare fall asleep. When daylight came at last, gray and bitter cold, he searched up and down the riverbank. There was
nothing to eat but the sickening old marrow, a few rose hips,
shriveled currants on their vine. He drank a quart of river water
and he looked into the southeast. "Sam," he said, speaking aloud,
"here's where we find out if you're man or boy." He knew the
words were pure bravado. He had no reason to think he could
cross that vast white distance but there was no choice, except to
float down the river and be captured again. After he had
walked a mile he stood on a hilltop in the white waste, a hairy
giant in tawny buckskin, a robe over his left shoulder, a useless
knife in one hand and a useless hatchet in the other. Gesturing
at the heavens, with the knife flashing in pale cold sunlight, he
cried out, "Almighty Father, You have helped me this far, now
help Your son a little longer!" That was all he said; but he was

thinking of the words in Crow language: Old woman's man her children their ghosts, there, in the blackest nights they are, in the sagebrush they are crying. Yonder she was, without a fire, huddled in her blankets in ten-below-zero cold, talking to her children there in the sagebrush crying. If a woman could endure such winters, for love, could a man endure less for a dead wife and son?

Tom Fitzpatrick had said to Jim Bridger, "I've never known a man who loves life like Sam. Every hour for him is a golden nugget." That was pretty fancy talk for a mountain man but Tom had read a lot and had a way with words. Part of the force that sent Sam trudging across the white prairies was love of life, a gladness for health and youth that filled him as Mozart's gayest music filled him; and part of it was his belief that the earth on which he walked had been designed by the greatest of the artists, and that if a man had the courage and fortitude not to fail it, it would not fail him. In Sam's rough mountain-man philosophy those persons who became the wards of sadness and melancholy had never summoned for use and trial more than a part of what they had in them, and so had failed themselves and their Creator. If it was a part of the inscrutable plan that he was to live through this ordeal, and again cover the bones of wife and child with mountain lilies, the strength was lying in him, waiting, and he had only to call on it—all of it—and use it, without flinching or whimpering. If he showed himself to be a worthy piece in the Great Architect's edifice he would live; in Sam's philosophy that was about all there was to it.

He intended to call on all he had, to the last desperate gasp of it. He would walk and rest, walk and rest; and if there was nothing to eat, he would rest, and walk again. The sun's nimbus told him that the temperature was falling. Cold might be better for him than falling snow, for if he had to buck deeper snow than this he would fail fast. Nothing wore man or beast down faster than wading in soft snow, crotch-deep. As he walked Sam sighted his course on a line just a little north of what he thought was the little Belt Mountains. It was about seventy or eighty miles to Judith River, where he might find berries and bones, or a rabbit at which he could hurl his knife, or the stiff hide of a dead old bull. To appease by a little the gnawing in his stomach he now and then cut a short tassel from the fringe up and down his trousers. A man could chew a piece of tanned leather for an hour, with no result, except that it would become a soft impermeable pulp that would fill his mouth. What Sam did was to chew out the smoke and tanning fluids and swallow them. When he was far enough from the river to feel secure he burst into song; and what a picture he was, a tall tawny creature on a white map, singing at the top of his voice a Mozart aria to Lotus! He was remembering the times when he sang to her and played and the few times she sang with him. Thinking of her reminded him of their feasts together, and so next he sang the Champagne Aria. Then he sang anything he could think of that at all expressed the miracle of being alive and able to sing. There were birds that sang half their time, and there were people who complained half their time. The birds were worthy of their loveliness and their wings. There were creatures like the wolverine that never sang, but went snarling and clacking its teeth through shadow-depths all day and all night. The bull elk sang, the bull moose; and the buffalo bull was often so full of life and joy that he would paw and beller and swing round and round, bugging his eyes at the wonderful prairies and the bear grass on long stems with their domes of white blossoms. A meadow lark would sit in a tree and sing exquisite lyrics all afternoon, a wood thrush would sing the variations of its little sonata until sleep overcame it, and a bluebird through a long golden morning would sit in a high tree and empty its soul to spring. The long-tailed chat talked morning, noon, and night, and despaired in his efforts to express the wonder of it; and the incredible mockingbird filled all musicians with apologies and shame. . . .

Such was Sam's mood as he passed through ravines and over hills. The old snow down under was frozen hard but on top of it was about a foot of new snow, which was soft and nice against his moccasined feet. Now and then he glanced back at the deep trail he was making. With the morning sun filling it an Indian on a high hill could see it but he would think it a wolf path. Sam had decided to walk without stopping, if he could, all the way to Judith River, but when fifteen miles from the Missouri he saw the first wolves, and before long came to wet bones of the long-legged hare. He picked some of them up but they had been stripped clean. Even the hide had been eaten. Taking the larger bones with him till he came to an outcropping of stone, he smashed them with the hatchet and sucked up a little marrow fat and soft bone pulp.

Five wolves decided to follow him. He did not mind. Since

he was not walking like a thing crippled or old he knew that they did not expect to eat him. They were curious and hopeful. Sam supposed they wondered why he was out here in wolf land, alone, and what he intended to do. A wolf knew when a man had a gun; he was more wary then. Some mountain men thought they recognized it as a weapon; others, that they smelled the gunpowder. Even the magpie was bolder when a man had no gun.

The five wolves trailed him at a distance of about thirty yards but now and then the boldest of the five, a big fellow that would weigh, Sam guessed, a hundred and forty pounds, would come trotting ahead of the others; and if Sam stopped and turned the wolf would stop, ears forward, mouth open, and look at him. His tongue lay between the lower canines, long and curved, but because the tongue was too wide for the space between the teeth it lay up and over their points. The eyes had large round black holes for pupils, and an iris that looked pale green in the snowlight. The face did not seem ferocious but only curious, almost friendly; but Sam knew that the long gaunt body was hungry and that in its animal way the wolf was looking at him as something to eat. "I reckon," Sam said, "you'd taste a lot better than old marrow-bones and rose hips but I'll never know without you come closer." At thirty feet he thought he could put his knife in the beast's heart.

The wolf became so bold that he came within fifty feet but when Sam balanced the knife to hurl it the wolf suddenly slunk back. Once the wolf pointed his nose to the sky, and almost closing his eyes, opened his lungs to their full power in the chilling winter wolf-call. It was this mating cry that made greenhorns shiver all night. Why the Creator had designed the beast so that it mated in the deep snows of winter was another riddle; a lot of arrangements in the divine plan mortal mind could see little sense in. If, Sam thought, he only had urine from a male wolf a hundred miles away he could splash it on the first tree he came to, and this big lubber after sniffing it would go out of his senses. The city dog and the country dog on meeting acted much the same way. If he had a trap and a rabbit for bait—but if he had a rabbit he would not be thinking of wolf meat for supper.

Averaging five miles an hour except in ravines where the crust gave way under him, Sam walked all day; and when darkness fell he thought he was only twenty miles from the

Judith River. The northern foothills of a mountain range had been on his right for some time but he had seen no sign of game there or of living thing. Along the Judith, as along most rivers, there were buffalo feeding on river-bottom grasses and shrubs. He hoped to find an old or sick one. Numbed by fatigue and hunger, he kept walking. Two hours after dark, three, four, he was still walking, with five wolves trotting along behind him.

Then he came to the river, and the first thing he did was to find an open place and lie on his belly and drink. With night the cold had deepened and the frost was burning his ears. He searched up and down the river till he found a shelter he could crawl under, and with the hatchet he dug into the earth deeper than the winter chill, making a coffin area large enough to house him. He was protected by dense snow-laden brush on all sides but the river side. He had hoped to sleep but after curling up in the robe he found the earth so cold and the air above him so bitter that he sat up and considered his problem. Without food he might walk another two or three days but he doubted that he could do it without both food and sleep. The thought then seemed to him so cowardly and shameful that he tried to put it away; and while making an effort to do this it occurred to him that he ought to laugh. Wondering what he could laugh at, he thought of the fifty-seven braves rushing round and round like big red ants, or wasps, whose house had been destroyed. So he exploded a shout that could have been heard a mile up or down the river, and then burst into song: "Hey, git along, git along, Sammy! Hey, git along, Sam along Joe!" Had Hugh Glass ever laughed while crawling the hundred miles?—or Colter, as he slunk through the night, stark naked, starved, his feet soled with cactus needles?

There now rose before him, as he shivered, a vivid picture of the Indians. A brave had come with a second drink for the guard and had seen him lying there, dead, with eyes and tongue choked half out of him. Shrieking, he had run to the chief; and half drunk and stuffed with half-cooked elk meat, the redmen had rushed to the tent to stare with amazement at one of their most valiant. Then all hell had broken loose. The Indian camp must have been like an anthill after squaws built a fire around it. What odors!—of stinking war paint, fire smoke, rum, howling dogs, and rage; and what yells of fury and frustration! What wild barking from the dogs, what terrified snortings and whinnying from the horses; and then what a bedlam as fifty-seven men, clutching their guns and tomahawks, ran back and forth, east, west, north, their senses fogged with rum and their black eyes turning yellow!

Sam's idea of the scene warmed him a little. "When this ole woman she torst him come he went jumpin." Sam could imagine the chief's eyes almost down on his cheeks when, bending over in the dim light of the tepee, he could no longer doubt that The Terror had killed a mighty warrior with his bare hands. Sam snorted and chuckled and shivered. He was warming his body and warming his soul. "Me and the chief," he said, wiping a tear away, "will have a huggin match, come next summer."

He stood up and for a third or fourth time wrapped the robe around him, tugging at it as if by tugging he could stretch it, but it would reach only from his chin to his knees. Doing the best he could with it, he lay again in the coffin hole, knife and hatchet within reach, both hands clutching the edges of the robe to hold them together. It was his lower legs and feet that felt coldest. Trying again, he lay on bare earth on his left side, brought his knees up, and spread the robe over him, with the back edge tucked under his back and rump, and the front edge under his knees and hands. And though the temperature was fifteen below Sam fell asleep, with five wolves crawling close to smell him.

The wolves were bivouacked and waiting when Sam awakened four hours later, chilled through and so stiff that the only thing he could move was his head. There was no sensation in his hands or legs, and it was only with a supreme effort that he was able at last to sit up. The hunger pangs in him were as sharp as knife points when he crawled out of the shelter and rose like a huge animated corpse to his feet. As he flailed himself to drive blood through him he sensed that during sleep he had come close to freezing to death. Looking east into the gray morning, he wondered how it was with Kate.

For a few minutes he tried to quiet his violent shivering and think of things that would give him strength. There were mountain flowers—the Mariposa, caltha, and alpine lilies, the windflowers and violets and poppies, columbines and paint-brushes and whole mountainsides of syringa. It had seemed to him in times past that the loveliest flowers and the sweetest musical themes were but two aspects of the same grace; but now the relationship seemed a bit strained. He tried to hum a

Schubert song while telling himself that when spring came he would climb to the snowbanks and gather an armful of lilies to lay over the bones of his wife and son. His muscular spasms were so strong that he began to pinch and smite himself, and fling his arms wildly and jump up and down; and two hundred feet away five wolves sat on their haunches and looked at him.

26

AN HOUR LATER he looked down the Judith River, which was north, and wondered if it would be safe to ride a raft down it to the Missouri, and then down the Missouri to the Musselshell. He knew it was a stupid thought and he took it to mean that his mind was failing. After his dreadful ordeal and escape, Tom Fitzpatrick, whose hair had turned white in a few days, had said, "After a certain time the biggest danger is a man's ideas, for his mind fails and he thinks every idea is brilliant; but nearly every idea would lead him to certain death if he followed it." Yes, it was what looked like easy ways that fooled a man. So Sam looked straight east and told himself to get along, that it was less than a hundred miles to Kate's door. There was a stiff wind from the north this morning. The lands between him and Kate's shack were the winter hunting-grounds of the blizzards down from Canada. Though feeling terribly weak, Sam thought he could cover the distance in two days and two nights, if the winds did not put him down. It was the kind of land the Creator used to test His boldest children. Job he had tested one way, Sam Minard he was testing in another. The greenhorns and other weaklings, with soft useless hands, flabby bellies, and timid fawning ways, He tested by allowing them to walk two blocks to a trolley, or to fish in a hole on a pleasant stream. Sam accepted the test and resolved to survive it, but he knew that it was a test more severe than he had ever faced, with its cold and hunger, and the blizzards in which any mountain man on earth could lose his way. Somewhere yonder in the frosty early-morning haze was Judith Mountain, and somewhere beyond it was Wild Horse Lake. Not far from the lake was a sizable creek that flowed into the Musselshell. If he could see these landmarks he could find his way, even though the sun was hidden day and night.

The river before him was frozen about a fourth of the way across on either side. Sam had to find and drag across the ice pieces of log for a raft. It was when he moved to pick up the end of a log that he knew, with a pang of dismay, not only that a good deal of his strength had left him but that merely to lift sixty or eighty pounds drove sharp pains all through him. He hadn't realized that he was so weak. He spent two hours getting enough timber to the edge to carry him, and it was almost noon when he reached the farther side. It was so cold this morning that the steel of hatchet and knife burned his flesh. Deciding that he wouldn't need the hatchet, he buried it at the root of a tree; but after he had gone a little distance he turned to look back, and began to tremble, as though he were taking farewell of a living thing. He became conscious of a wish to return to it, and to take his mind off it he stared at the five wolves across the river. Then he faced the east and began to walk.

For the first ten miles it was easy walking. As he trudged along, trying to ignore the pains in nerves, muscles, and bones, there was around him only the white blinding waste, for it was blinding, even though the sun was hazed over. There was a sharp burning wind on his left, and after a while his face was so numbed by cold that there was little feeling in it. Having no mittens, he had to keep rubbing his hands or striking them against him. But it was his feet that gave him the most trouble. He now had only two pairs of moccasins and they were thin. He wondered if he ought to wrap a piece of the robe around each foot; what he did from time to time was to fold the robe and sit on it and take the moccasins off. He then rubbed his feet to bring the blood through them, and studied the sun, the sky, and the world around him. Since leaving the Judith he had seen no wolf, no rabbit, no bird. Winter cold was supreme here. He thought the temperature was about fifteen below zero, and falling. If it reached forty below could he keep going?

Of course he would keep going.

When he walked again he hung the robe over his head and down on the left side, but the wind made such frenzied efforts to tear it away that he again carried it in his arms, with his numbed hands inside it. Would Kate have a fire? Or would he find her dead? When darkness fell what a glory it would be if

far away through the cold he were to see the pale wintry yellow
of a lighted window! But there was no window, and unless she
had a fire there would be no light. He supposed that she was sitting with her knees drawn up to her belly, with all her bedding
piled under, around, and over her. It made a man mad to think
of a woman living that way, winter after winter; but her
devotion to her children was one of the great and noble things,
like Beethoven's Ninth, or a sunset, or a wild storm on the
ocean. He looked up at the frozen sky and wondered what the
Almighty thought of Kate. She was all grit and a yard wide.
What a mountain man she would have made!

Sam could guess the hour by the paler patch of sky where the
sun was hidden. It was one o'clock, then three, then five, and
dusk again closed in, and cold more bitter. He felt that he was
not walking fast or getting far; in six hours he doubted that he
had covered twenty miles. The wind became more savage after
the sun went down. Only squaws, he thought, could be as
completely wild and uncontrolled as a wind. It was absolute
raving lunacy all around him, something sent by the English
down from Canada, to terrorize and desolate American land. It
came shrieking and howling across the Missouri and then swept
across the wastes, gathering madness and violence as the night
deepened; and with his emotions as close to panic as they had
ever been, Sam sat, his back to the winds, the robe over his
back, and wondered what he could do. Job had been tested
with afflictions that became harder and harder to bear, until the
goaded and tortured man had cried out that he could endure no
more. But he had endured more. Sam grimly told himself that
he was being tested with one of the mightiest winds from the
Creator's wind chamber. He would do all that a man could do,
and then do more.

There in the deep night he sat, with the winds howling
against him, their Canada cold pouring over him like an
atmosphere of ice. He still knew which way was east. He would
rise and go again; he would walk as long as he knew the
direction and could lift his feet; and then he would make mittens of the robe and he would crawl. If he lost the direction he
would stop and dig in for the night, and in the morning he
would crawl again. The sky above him was only an ocean of
swift winds, with not a hint of moon or stars; the world around
him was riven by forces that only the strongest could stand
against. Bending to the left and into it, he went on, the knife

inside a fold of robe and one hand clasping its handle, his feet numbed; his face turned to the right and away from the driving insanity of the blizzard; his half-frozen legs stepping forward, on and on. Until the wind changed he would know which way was east, for blizzards had a way of becoming cyclonic vortexes in which all directions were lost.

Now and then he stopped, knelt, faced south, and made a hole in the snow; and he then sat in the hole so that he would not be blown away, while he took off the moccasins and massaged his feet. He tried to keep his senses alive to his physical condition, for he knew that persons could be seduced by numbing cold into a tranquil state of mind that thought all was well. He knew that he was half frozen but he could move all his toes; after vigorous rubbing he could feel a pale warmth in his feet; and moving from side to side, he could feel a little sensation in his rump. He twisted his ears and nose.

Then he walked again, struggling on through the night, as a man will when all his being is fixed on one thing; he was numbed almost to his marrow and hunger pangs were like violent massaging of his stomach and bowels; and his mind was not as clear as he wanted it to be, but he went on and on. Mountain men had tried to figure out why in a blizzard a man went round and round, while convinced that he was following a straight course. One said it was because a man was heavier on one side than the other, that if you were to cut a man down the middle from his head to his crotch you'd find one side of him five pounds heavier than the other, for the same reason that one side of his face was fuller and one ear was larger. Face a tree two hundred yards distant, shut your eyes and walk toward it, and you'd find yourself fifty feet on the right of it or the left. An obscene remark had then been made about a man's stones, and some of the men had laughed, and Windy Bill had said that might be the reason.

His eyes almost closed against the winds, his head bent, the knife now tied into a corner of the robe, his hands massaging one another, Sam went on and on, until past midnight. He knew now that the winds would howl all night and all the next day. This country from the Missouri east to the Black Hills and south to the Yellowstone was the winter playground of Canada's winds; laden with ice and menace, they came like tumultuous oceans of zero-breath, down from the great northern mountains; and after shrieking over this broad desolation they swept up the elk basins between the Bitterroot and the Bighorns, and the Bighorns and the Black Hills; and roared all the way south to the Sangre de Cristo, the great sand dunes, and the San Juans.

He guessed that was how it was, for he was forcing his mind to think and he was keeping before him the lesson of Job. His father had read this to his children. God had said that Job was a fine man, and Satan had said, Yeah, but you have built a fence of love around him and what does he strive against? God then turned Job over to Satan to test the stuff he was made of; and murderers came and fell on Job's servants, burned his sheep, and took away his camels; and then came a terrible wind from the wilderness that razed his house and killed his sons and daughters. All that was only the beginning. Me, Sam told himself, I am a wee mite hungry and a wee mite cold, so shall I shave my head and fall to the ground? Often he had heard his father utter Satan's words, "Skin for skin, all that a man has will he give for his life." Satan was a politician. A man would not give his children, his wife, his friends, his honor, or the defenseless into the powers of evil. Sam dug inside his shirt for his harp and warmed it by turning it over and over in his hands. Then, as he plodded along, he tried to play into the winds, choosing first the favorite song of Mozart's mother and of his mother. Taking the harp from his mouth, he cried into the winds, "Rejoice, O my heart!" He tried to play the finale of a sonata and a tender melody of man-woman love, while thinking of Lotus. Job, the idiot, had cursed his Creator. Job had wished he had died at birth or was sunk in eternal sleep, for there even the wicked put away their vices, and the troubled and the weary were at rest. There the prisoners lay together in peace and heard not the voice of the tyrant; the famous and the forgotten mingled their dust; and the servant leapt to his master's call no more. How his father had loved to declaim the bold words! Sam heard in the winds, "For wrath killeth the foolish man, and envy slayeth the silly one." Poor old Job, he was so tormented that he longed only for death—"Oh, that God would let loose his hand and cut me off!" For the first time in his life Sam had an inkling of what Job's cries meant; for as he staggered forward, sick with hunger and weakness and frozen to his marrow, he found himself thinking that rest was supreme among the good things of life.

He sensed the warning in time. His first act was to try to look round him but he could see only the wild gray terrors sweeping by. He might be twenty feet from trees, or miles; possibly before him there was a deep sheltered cove, full of the soft spillings from the winds. He sank to his haunches, swept the new snow away, and with the knife cut a round lid in the frozen crust. He lifted it away and plunged his arm down, and almost wept with joy when he realized that the snow here was deep. Reaching down, he pushed it back under the crust or scooped it out, until he could enter the hole, feet first. He pulled the robe after him. Then he kicked and beat at the soft snow under the crust to force it back and away, so that he could draw down out of the wind. He thought he must be in a ravine, or in a drift against trees or a bluff. On his knees he kept pushing the snow away from him and back.

It seemed amazingly warm down under the crust, but he was so sunk in weariness that he did not know his labor had made his blood race. The earth under him was not frozen; this meant that a good cover of snow had fallen, and remained, before the first hard frost. Clearing away the snow so that he could spread the robe, he sat on it, took off the mocassins, and massaged his ankles and feet. He was exhausted but he had not admitted it. More than anything else he wanted sleep but he knew that if he were to fall asleep he would never awaken. While dimly thinking of the matter he sensed that staying awake would demand more than an effort of his will. Overhead, he could hear the rushing of winds at fifty or sixty miles an hour, and when he put an ear to the earth he could still hear them, as if they were underground. They were not carrying much snow but they were filling the hole; after a while it seemed almost cozy where he sat, for no breath of wind touched him. If only he had four warm robes he would sleep for a day and a night and then walk to Kate's shack in a few minutes!

For a while he had felt warmer but actually it was below zero where he sat and slowly he was filled with chills. He had dreadful cramps in his belly; when with massaging he tried to ease them they became so severe that he almost cried out. He ate a handful of snow and it filled him with nausea. Reaching back under snow, he tried to find grass, dead bugs, or anything he could chew and swallow; but there was only the soil. He cut off a buckskin fringe and began to chew it and at once doubled over, trying to vomit. He told himself he should think of the men of whom it had been said that they lived for weeks on the stiff old hides of dead wolves, or who lived for days on nothing but grass.

He guessed he would just have to massage the numbed parts of him, think of Job, stay awake, and wait for daylight. He would also think of Kate; she was not far from him now, no more than thirty miles, or twenty. Staying awake was the hardest thing he had ever tried to do; what a tyrant it was when the body wanted rest! When twice he almost reached the point of no return he knew that he would have to set up a better watchdog. While he sat, swaying a little, his head had imperceptibly sunk, and his eyes in the same slow treacherous way had almost closed, until it had been only with a feeble glimmer of awareness that he caught himself. He tried to devise a plan whereby if he fell asleep he would sink on the point of the knife. Turning to hands and knees, he told himself that no man could sleep in that position, that if he were to fall to his belly he would awaken. But that proved to be no good either. The only way he could think of in which he had any confidence was to count to twenty, over and over, and record each twenty. For awhile he plopped a piece of snow into his mouth after uttering the word "twenty," and he thought he was doing all right until, with a start, he came awake and realized that the last word he had spoken was seventeen. Convinced that he was pampering himself, he resolved on sterner measures; he began to smite and pinch himself and to yank at his nose and ears. All this he had to abandon; the massaging and pinching filled him with a warmth that was almost the same as sleep.

"Doggone it, Sam," he said aloud, "if ye can't stay awake, then git up and go!"

He thrust up through the snow that had been blown into the hole and stood up, head and shoulders in the wind. He could see no sign of daylight. The winds seemed to be rushing by in even greater haste and he doubted that he could stand in them. To punish himself for being such a sleepy lubber he turned his head from side to side, so that the air filled with frozen crystals could smite and sting all over his face. Then he sank back under the shelter.

He was never to know how he survived this night and the next forenoon. His mind was no longer clear when at last he tested the winds and decided to go. With the robe around his back and the edges tucked in around his hands he pointed his haggard face into the east, bent forward, and walked again. He

now moved more like a robot than a man. The winds had
abated a little, a pale nimbus of light was halfway up the
southern sky, and he could see sometimes for a hundred yards,
sometimes for half a mile. For seven hours he walked, pausing
only four times to massage his feet. And at last he stood,
swaying in almost utter exhaustion, and looked at a snow-laden
riverline and knew that it was the Musselshell.

He had barely enough awareness left to know that his
journey was not over. He would have to cross the river.
Somehow he would have to determine if he was north or south
of Kate's shack. And he knew he would have to keep in the
forefront of his mind the hard and merciless fact that when a
person found his dreadful ordeal almost over his tendency was
to relax his efforts, to let go of what remained of his strength. He
tried to hum the Ave Maria while searching round him for
pieces of wood for a raft; he tried to think of a story to lift his
spirit and recalled one that Bill had told about wolves. A big
pack of wolves was running around campfires after dark,
snapping their teeth and moving in a foot or two every time
they circled the camp. At last, exploding at them in profane
rage, Lost-Skelp Dan had rushed at them with long knives,
only to see the wolf nearest him leap to his hind legs, shed his
wolf clothing, and vanish into the darkness. Before Dan could
recover from amazement all the wolves had jumped up and
fled. Sam tried to laugh at the old Indian trick but it did not
seem to be funny now, nor could he think of anything funny as
he set his teeth on the weariness and pain and dragged chunks
of wood to the edge of the river ice. The Ave Maria didn't
sound like a prayer any more. He found berry vines to bind the
logs and he got across the river but he would never know how
he did it; and he crossed the bottomlands and looked north and
south for a landmark. Seeing nothing familiar, he climbed a hill
and looked over the country up and down the river, and to the
west where he had plodded through the wild winds. He felt
pretty sure that Kate was north of him, and after he had walked
a mile he knew that she was. After two more miles and two
hours and the coming of night he looked up the hill at her cold
snow-covered shack.

In this moment, when convinced that he was looking at it,
that it was no mirage or apparition, he was overwhelmed by
sudden and awful weakness. In spite of all he could do he sank
to the earth and began to weep. The mightiest of all the

mountain men had reached the end of his strength but not of his grit. He began to crawl on hands and knees toward her door. His escape from the Blackfeet and his long journey without food through deep cold and blizzards was to become one of the legends of the mountain men, along with Tom Fitzpatrick's, Colter's, and Glass's. "He done it, he shorely did," Windy Bill would say a hundred times around the campfires. "He jist headed torst the crazy woman and clum the mountains and there he wuz. . . ."

By the time Sam reached Kate's door his hands were so nearly frozen that he spent a few minutes blowing on them, sucking the fingers, washing them in snow, massaging them, and putting them inside his clothing against his ribs. He was so weak that he was sitting, and when he saw the snowpath to the graves, and then the cairn that looked like a mound of snow, he began to cry like a tortured child. He pounded on the door planks, for the door was closed, and he said, "It's me! It's Sam!" Grasping the door with both hands, he pulled it open and back. He was straining forward to peer into the gloom when with a low cry he saw that the woman was almost in his hands. She was right by the doorway and she seemed to be sitting in her pile of bedding, but only her gray hair and a part of her face were visible. Sam put a finger up and touched her face to see if it was alive.

"It's me!" he whispered. "It's your friend Sam." He crawled over the pile of bedding and turned and pulled the plank door shut. Then like an animal he wormed himself into the pile of bedding and put an arm up and around the woman and wept quietly till he fell asleep.

PART THREE

SAM

27

SAM SLEPT THROUGH the night and into the next afternoon and when he awoke he was alone. After realizing where he was he wondered if he had hogged the bedding, and then like a beast crawled over to the north wall to paw among the cold things there. One parcel, as hard as stone, he thought was jerked venison; with his knife he peeled back a part of the skin pouch, and chipping off a small piece, thrust it into his mouth. A moment after swallowing it he turned sick and was convulsed but like a famished wolf in midwinter at a carcass he chewed and swallowed other morsels. Then, suddenly, he was seized by shudderings so strong and uncontrollable that he shook all over and moaned. He crawled over to the bedding, dragging the sack of meat after him, and with some blankets around him he sat, shuddering and wondering what was wrong with him. He drew the sack of meat into the bedding and his shaking hands tried to whittle off another piece; but he was so utterly and infinitely tired that his deepest wish was to surrender to the warmth and sleep again. And so he sank back and piled bedding around and over him, and with his arms around the pouch of venison he slept again.

It was after dark when he stirred and sat up. This time it took him several minutes to come into wakefulness and realize where he was. He was still but half awake and more than half dead. At first he had thought he was in the hole back under the snow and he listened for the winds. Then he reached around him to examine the things. On seeing the open door, the bedding, the river bottom down the hill, he knew where he was and he wondered where Kate was. He sat a few minutes, feeling more than thinking, and trying to believe that he was still alive. After a while he became aware of the bag of meat and the knife, and of the indescribable sensations of emptiness and pain in his stomach and bowels. He began to tell himself in a dim feeble way that he would find matches and build a fire and cook a feast; but when he tried to rise he seemed unable to. And so he sat, trying to think. Realization came slowly, filling him with a kind of wonder and gladness; and at last with a cry he told himself over and over that he *had* escaped, like Job he *had* endured, and here he was, alive, whole, and ready for breakfast or supper. And for vengeance, but that didn't seem so important now. What was important was that he seemed unable to move his legs, to bend his fingers, to focus his gaze; but he was alive, and with superhuman effort he struggled to his feet. Then he stood, trembling all over, and tried to imagine that he was Don Giovanni about to sing, with magnificent brio and power, to a lovely servant maid. What he did, while conjuring images of beautiful girls, was to topple and fall face downward on the pile of bedding. With both hands he reached round him and pulled bedding over him; and he was about to sink again into sleep when he began to shake with rage against himself, and again forced himself to rise.

He felt pretty weak and foolish as he steadied himself against a wall and looked out at the world. He could see or hear no sign of Kate; he hoped he had not put her to flight. By God, he had better stop acting like a sick old man, he had better get some breakfast on and be the man around the house. How long had he slept, anyway? He was not sure that he had not been asleep for a week. Where was Kate? "Kate!" he called in his weak voice. "Where are you?" He felt horrible weakness and nausea; what he wanted to do was to sink again into slumber but he forced himself to clasp the doorjamb with both hands and look out.

It was not morning, it was night, and there was Kate, the poor gray old thing, sitting between the graves with robes over her. Sam stepped outside, and moving like a feeble old man, he made his way over to her and around to face her; and in a voice that was not at all like his normal voice he told her that the Almighty had walked with him all the way from the Blackfeet camp to the Musselshell; and in more days than he could remember he had had nothing to eat; but now he was going to get up a breakfast, or supper or whatever it would be—venison steaks, roasted grouse, hot biscuits, wild honey, coffee—Did she have any baccy around?

Kate seemed to pay no attention to him. Unable to tell if she was unaware of him or was ignoring him, he told her that he would not be with her long; as soon as he got some rest and some food in his belly, and had brought in some good meat for her, he would be gone. Could she tell him where the matches were? Only a part of her face was showing; a wrinkled hand clasped the edge of the robe under her chin. Sam looked up at the sky and around at the lonely white world; and over at the cairn with its deep cloak of snow; and he wondered if he was alive after all, or if he and the woman were only ghosts, here in the winter. Turning away from her, he felt numbed with cold, half dead with fatigue, drowsy, nausea-sick, and rather mindless and weightless; but so abounding was his health and vitality that he made his way inside the shack, and sitting by the bag of venison, began to eat. Afraid that he would vomit, he put in his mouth only a thin shaving and he chewed it thoroughly before he dared swallow it; and then sat a few moments studying the sensations in his stomach before chewing again. The shavings tasted more of frost than of meat, but after he had swallowed seven or eight thin slices he felt a little better and believed he could keep them down. Looking round him in the gloom, he wondered where the matches were, the flour, the coffee. Of course she had no tobacco. When he thought of tobacco and the loss of the lock of hair, and his fine rifle and revolvers and pipes, his bitterness toward the Blackfeet came boiling up in him with such passion that he exploded and emptied his stomach. What a fool he was to act this way! But they had stolen Mick's fine horse! Oh, they would pay for it, they would pay for it! He stood up, in a childish tantrum of rage—a man only feebly in possession of his senses; and glowered round him and then went outside to look with hate at the gray wintry Blackfeet wilderness out of which he had come. He looked south, thinking of the distance between him and his nearest friend. In a few days he would head up the Musselshell to find Bill or Hank or Abner but now he had work to do.

His stomach had puked forth its shavings of meat and frost and was now growling in its pain. He thought it would be best to get a fire going and make a pot of coffee. That might settle his stomach. It might shoot warmth and aroma all through him. At the pile of wood in the southeast corner he made shavings; he dug into the stuff by the north wall and found matches, coffee, and an old coffeepot; and with a tin pail he went to the river.

There he stood a few moments, surveying the scene and looking for sign of duck, goose, or anything a man could eat. Going up the hill with the water, he told himself that Kate must have gone over this path two or three times every day since the first snows, for it was firmly packed. While the coffee was steaming he found the flour, and dipping a shaving of meat into cold flour, he thrust it into his mouth. He ground a coffee bean between his teeth. That seemed to allay his nausea; he ate a half dozen and then searched for tin cups; and when the coffee was hot and fragrant he took a cup to Kate, and knelt, offering it to her. It was hot coffee, he said; she ought to drink it. He wanted to clasp her shoulders to see how thin she was, for she looked like nothing but hide and bone. He did not know that he himself was thirty pounds lighter than he had been when he walked around the two bull elk. The past week seemed to be only nightmare: had he actually killed a man and waded up a river and fought with a grizzly and crossed a hundred and fifty miles of frozen desolation in wild winds? Had he actually lain on his belly in the night and paddled across the black cold waters? He was like a man coming out of ether; he moved more by beast instinct than by human will. But his belly was mellowing in the hot coffee and his wits were clearing. "Please drink it," he said. What were the words in Job at which his father's finger had pointed so gravely? "Lo, all these things worketh God oftentimes with man, to bring back his soul from the pit, to be enlightened with the light of the living." The temperature, he thought, was still fifteen below zero; the winds were still shrieking up the river and Canada was getting ready to dump more cyclones upon its neighbor; but Sam was warmed with hot coffee and filled with the light of the living, and neither wind nor cold could faze him now.

"All right, if you won't drink it I'll drink it."

He was astonished, as he had been in previous visits, to see how little this woman had eaten. It looked as if she lived on flour and raisins. She had never touched the woodpile. Removing all the bedding from the doorway, Sam laid a part of the fire there, to warm the earth; but at once with a sharp rebuke to himself he took the fire away. How stupid it would be to warm the earth deep, so that her bed would be cozy, and then go away and leave her to freeze to death! There wasn't much a man could do with such a woman, except leave her to God. He had learned in the past few minutes that fire wasn't good for him either; he had become so inured to cold that fire heat on his flesh was like a scalding liniment, like sunburn on his forehead and eyes. The fire was not good for the shack's cold timbers; in the heat they began to snap and complain, and moisture came out of the logs and out of the air, and stood in big drops. Smoke and heat went all through the cabin; and smoke poured out through the cracks in the walls and the doorway and the hole in the roof.

With the axe he sliced off the venison and laid the meat by the fire. Finding no grease or salt, he decided not to make biscuits until he had fresh game. While the meat was thawing he took a second cup of coffee to Kate, hoping she would drink it, and with surprise saw that she had covered her head. Again he knelt before her and told her, briefly, of his capture, escape, and long flight, but he doubted that she listened or understood. Lifting the robe from her gray head, he saw that her face was ghastly thin, drawn, haggard, immobile. Her eyes seemed to see and yet not to see. What had God done with this woman or for this woman? During her long winters here she had never had a fire or hot food but had been only a she-beast that had crawled over to eat flour and raisins, and then into her pile of dirty bedding to wait for another morning.

It was the moon she waited for but the men who knew her would never know that.

Bending low, he touched lips to her gray hair, saying, "That's for my mother and you and all mothers." He had hoped she would open her eyes and look at him when she smelled the hot coffee, but maybe smell was not one of her senses any more. Returning to the shack, he mixed flour and water and cooked the batter and called it bread. He steamed raisins in hot water until they were swollen and soft, and he made another pot of coffee. What a feast it would be! If only after he had feasted he could sit back with his pipe and think of vengeance!

Out in the frozen wastes the eyes of man or beast could have seen the smoke rising—and wolves did see it and try to smell its odors. A few of them came within two hundred yards of the shack and trotted round it, smelling the hot odors; and Sam smelled the wolves and knew they were there. He took to Kate a tin plate of hot venison, raisins, bread, and coffee, but she refused to look at it or see it. Kneeling, he held it right under her face, so that the fragrance would enter her nostrils; and he said, as if to a child, "It's hot food and you should eat it." He ar-

ranged her robes so that he could set the plate in her lap and
the cup of hot coffee at her side, and returned to the shack. He
had warmed a spot of earth for his own bed this night and he
now sat on the spot and ate, but very slowly, because sensations
of nausea filled his throat. The warmth had made him feel
drowsy and ill; he guessed that in the morning he would go out
to the hills and find a deer. Until midnight he kept the fire
burning in the shack, and Kate sat out by the graves. He went
out to tell her that if she would move he would make her bed for
her but she gave no sign that she heard him. "It's warm inside,"
he said. "Wouldn't you like to go in?" Had she forgotten what a
fire was? He seized the edges of the robes around her and
pulled. He almost toppled her over but he managed at last to
take the robes away. After holding one before the fire to warm it
he went out and draped it over her, saying, "There now, you'll
feel better." He ought to have known that she would feel worse.
To his amazement she began to cry. After staring at her a few
moments he picked her up, bedding and all, and set her inside
the cabin door. Her plate of food he put by the fire to keep
warm; and while sitting by the fire, feeling ill himself and not
far from tears, the thought came to him that this woman would
eat nothing as long as he was with her. He could no longer
doubt that she felt him to be an enemy. He fetched wood until
he had a big pile in a corner, and then, with rifle and knife close
by him, stretched out on his robe on the spot of warm earth and
was soon asleep. When he awoke two or three hours later and
looked over at Kate's bedding she was not there. He went to the
doorway and looked out. She was in the snowpath between the
graves, with bedding under and over her; and she was talking,
as if to her children. Sam looked up and saw a round frozen
moon in the sky. He went over and stood behind her and saw
that she was holding a Bible. She had her hands in a fold of
blanket which she used as mittens but he thought her hands
must be frozen, for it was a bitter night. A large robe inside the
door he thoroughly warmed at the fire and then spread it over
her and down across the book. Not once did she interrupt her
talking or praying, or whatever it was she was doing.

Inside the cabin Sam laid wood on the fire and stretched out
on his robe. When he next awakened he looked over and saw
that Kate had come inside. But at daylight her pile of bedding
was empty. Looking out, he saw her halfway to the river with
the pail in her hands; and he knew now that all winter long she

would carry water up the hill to plants that needed no water. Someday she would venture out on ice too thin and she would fall into the cold black waters and drown.

After a big breakfast he cleaned and loaded the rifle and went out to the hills for deer, elk, or buffalo. His first beast was an elk, and as soon as he had the belly open he pulled the liver out and ate most of it. This did for him what the old food in the cabin could never do: it dispelled the nausea and warmed him with vigor. He was still extremely weak; he took four journeys and six hours to carry the elk to the cabin, a chore he could normally have done in two. The hide he spread, fur side up, under Kate's pile of bedding by the door. The next day he shot two deer and brought them in, and hung them from rafters in the cabin's east end. He also ate their livers and hearts but he still felt so undernourished that he cooked one roast after another and ate them all.

The winds had gone south. The sky was frozen in gray-winter cold. After bringing in the elk Sam saw that during his absence Kate had been in the flour and raisins; he prepared plates of hot food for her but she would not touch them. To a cup of fragrant coffee under her nose she gave no response. When lying in his robe after supper, with fire snapping its flames through aspen and chokecherry and cedar, he would look over at her, sitting by the door, and he would think that she could have a little fire going all day and all night, if she would, and be cozy. He told her that he had to go south now but would be back next spring. Only God knew how many wolves had slipped up to the door to sniff at her, or whether after he had gone they would leap across her to get to the frozen deer hanging from the rafters. While making moccasins from skins he and other trappers had left here he wanted to talk to her, for he was lonely; and after the moccasins were made and laces for snowshoes he cooked roasts over two fires outside, and looked at the meat and at Kate, back and forth, and into the south and the west. He had intended to be gone before another night fell but when he looked at the cold empty world toward the Bighorns, and then into the cabin, smelling of roasted flesh and fire, he surrendered to weakness and decided to stay another night. At dusk he watched Kate move a part of her bedding outside, and a little later he looked out to see her sitting there, talking to her angels. Now and then she would incline her head, as though in assent; or seem to listen before speaking again. Down on the river was a hole where she had chopped through ice, with the impression of her knees in the frozen snow around it. He knew that she had knelt there to wash her underwear, for a piece of underwear was hanging from a tree limb, so ragged and patched that it looked as if it would fall in pieces at a touch. He would buy undergarments for her, and plenty of flour and dried fruits.

If he were to lie on his belly back in the cabin and play soft music he wondered if it would frighten or please her. He would find out. He played a hymn and then another, very low and far away, and then heard her voice. It was a soprano and it sounded cold and cracked but it was singing the second of the hymns he had played; and he went outside and stood behind her and sang with her, in a lower and softer key than hers. It all seemed to him natural and right. After five days of silence and misunderstanding it seemed proper and fitting that she should be sitting deep in bedding in zero cold, more than a thousand miles from her people, and in a thin ghostly soprano sing old hymns of hope and faith; and that behind her there should be a tall lonely man who had lost wife and son, and who now looked down at her gray hair and sang softly with her. For two hours or more she sat and he stood in the cold and they sang together. He then picked her up, bedding and all, and set her inside; gently kissed and patted her gray head; and stretched out in his robe to sleep.

He felt like a thief the next morning when he took her rifle and most of her ammunition but he told her that he would return the gun as soon as he could, and he would bring her food and clothing and anything he could think of that she might want. When at last he turned away from her, the knife in his belt, thirty pounds of roasted elk slung over his shoulder, under the robe, and the rifle in his hand, he was unwilling to go. He felt that never again would he see this woman alive. Twice before passing out of sight he stopped to look back. There it stood, the little brown shack on the hill in a white winter; and there she sat, a woman about whom he knew almost nothing, yet whom for strange reasons he had learned to love. Leaving her there, so alone and defenseless, filled him with such pangs of remorse and pity that mile after mile he strode along thinking only of her. He wanted to go back but he knew it would be senseless to go back.

A week later he skulked into a wilderness hiding place on the

Greybull, twenty miles from its junction with the Bighorn, and stood at the rickety door of a cabin even smaller than Kate's. He heard a movement inside and knew that the man there was reaching for a gun.

"It's me, Sam!" he called. "Open her up and let's have hot biscuits and huckleberry syrup."

The door opened an inch and gray eyes peered out and bearded lips said, "Sam, be it you?"

28

SOME OF THE mountain men thought Hank Cady had been baptized in the wrong vat. Sam Minard was a reticent man, but compared to him, Hank was dumb. Bill had calculated that in a year's time Hank uttered no more than a hundred words, of which ninety were some form of yes and no. No man had ever heard him talk about his childhood and his people, but there was a rumor that he had hated his mother, who had made a nursemaid of him, the oldest, and forced him to care for a dozen brothers and sisters. Bill said the only thing some kids remembered from their childhood was diapers. Unlike most of the mountain men, Hank had never taken a squaw and seemed to have no interest in women. He had a fierce brooding love of freedom, and freedom was what he had had since he came west.

After asking for and receiving one of Hank's old pipes and filling it with twist and sucking a cloud of smoke into his lungs, Sam said, "How's trapping around here?"

Hank gave him a queer look; it was not yet the season for trapping, so what could the man mean? "Tolabul," Hank said, meaning tolerable. He looked at Sam's rifle. "Hain't yourn," he said.

"Lost mine," Sam said. The strong tobacco was making him feel ill.

Hank waited a full minute. Then he said: "Crows?"

Blackfeet, Sam said.

Hank looked again at the rifle. "Whose thissen?"

"Kate's, the woman on the Musselshell."

"Yer handguns too?"

"Every damned thing but my life."

"Mick's bay?"

"Yeh."

"Whereabouts?"

"Not far from Three Forks."

Hank gave the matter some thought. Musta been Elk Horns, he said. He'd been snooping around down this way. When would the ronnyvoo be?

"When they all want it," Sam said. He wondered could Hank lend him a little baccy and a pipe till he got to Jim's?

Hank rolled over to a pile of stuff by a wall and dug in. He fetched out ten inches of twist and gravely handed it to Sam.

"And a pipe?" Sam said.

Hank again dug and came up with a corncob with a broken stem. He was a chewing man himself and smoked only the quids after he had chewed the juice out. Now, making a clumsy effort to be sociable, he emptied his mouth through the cabin door and filled another pipe with a broken stem. With their pipes burning the two men sat in firelight, rifles across their laps.

"How wuz she?" asked Hank.

Sam had been wondering if Hank could lend him a robe and if he had extra traps. Hank had been thinking of vengeance. He saw that Sam was a lot thinner and he suspected that he had endured many indignities and hardships. His handsome gray eyes, wonderfully bright and keen, had been studying Sam all the way up his frame.

"Still alive," Sam said at last.

"What Elk Horns do?"

Sam removed the stem from his teeth and seemed to be trying to remember. Well now, he had been slapped around, by both hands and tomahawk; his face had been smeared with the stuff they coughed up from their throats; and he had been starved and frozen and told what the Crows would do with him.

"They figgered ta sell ya?"

Sam nodded. On finishing his pipe he said, "Got steaks, I'm the feller can cook um." Jist roast, Hank said. After almost a full minute of silence he added, "Had supper afore ye come."

Sam glanced at the man. Henry Cady was one to have on

your side in a fight but he didn't spend much time wondering what he could do for you. A cold hunk of anything would do, Sam said; in the morning he would find something. Were they still fat around here? If he went fur enough, Hank said. He put his pipe aside and filled his mouth with twist. A part of the brown juice he spat into the fire before him and a part of it he swallowed. It was his private opinion that tobacco juice was good for a man's stomach and digestion. Bill said tobacco in his stummick gave him a hull bellyful of heartburn, and Powder River Charley said it gave him the droppins; Hank could find no words to express his scorn for such idiotisms. He now moved his bearded cheeks a little to slop the quid around in his mouth, his gray eyes looking without change into the fire. It was his way to suppose that if a man wanted food and there was any around he would find it. Sam did not mind. The smoking had appeased his hunger and he was ready for bed.

"How you fixed for buffler robes?" he asked, looking round the shack.

Hank ejected a noisy stream into the flames and wiped his tobacco-stained mouth with the tobacco-stained back of his hand. "Guess we'll hafta sleep together," he said.

After warming a spot of earth and securing the door on the inside with a stout leather thong they lay side by side on their backs, the rifle of each just under the bedding at his side. They faced the door so that on sitting up they would be ready to fire. They both snored but that did not bother them; they slept deep, without worries or bad dreams. Hank said he hadn't seen an Injun since October, or an Indian trail as far as he had gone; and becoming almost garrulous, he said the winter would be cold and the pelts good.

They were up at daylight, and Sam with clumsy tactfulness had suggested a batch of biscuits to go with their roast and coffee. Hank had merely inclined his head toward the pile of stuff by the wall. He left the cabin and before breakfast was ready brought in a beaver, from the tail of which Sam rendered out a cup of hot fat to use as butter. They ate biscuits dunked in beaver fat, elk roast, and coffee, and then sat back with their pipes. From the moment of rising Hank had said nothing; nobody could have told by his face or manner whether he was pleased with Sam's presence or wanted him to be on his way. The fact, unknown to all but him, was that Henry Cady was a very lonely man who turned warm and happy all over inside when another trapper came to visit him; but there was never any change in his gruff way. He had Sam's affinity to all things in nature; like him, he loved the valleys and mountains, the skyline's backbones, the vast black forests, the pure water and clean air and wide spaces. With gun and knife he would vanish into a mountain mass and spend days or weeks there, living on grouse and deer and wild fruits. Sam would slip up to watch a water ouzel dive deep to explore a pool's bottom, or the downy baby-heads thrusting out all around the mallard mother, or a warbling vireo hang its clever pensile nest from a tree's limb, and he would proclaim his presence with an explosion of life joy; whereas Hank would make no sound, and he might sit by a stream and watch the fish in the cold dark waters or an elk feeding in a clearing for hours with hardly a shift in his gaze.

Hank would have been happy to have Sam stay with him all winter but Sam had no way of knowing that. After bringing in a couple of deer he looked south and said it was a long way to Bridger's post but he guessed he'd better be off. It was, he reckoned, a hundred miles and more to Bill on the Hoback, another hundred to Lost-Skelp on upper Green River, and still a long way from there to Bridger's. He needed horses, traps, bedding, weapons, tobacco, and the fixens.

Hank said nothing. He figured that Sam Minard knew his own mind. But when Sam picked up only Kate's old rifle and the one robe Hank said, "Hyar now." Sam would need more bedding than that, and some baccy and a pipe, some coffee and a pot, some salt and flour. Sam knew that Hank had only one pot. Did Sam have steel and flint, or matches? Sam said he had matches from Kate's hoard. Hank hustled around in his slow way and came to Sam with a good robe, pipe and tobacco, a pound of coffee and the pot, and some flour. He tossed the robe across Sam's shoulders and said, "Worse cold to come."

Sam looked over the bedding in the cabin to see if Hank would have enough. He thought he would not. So he dropped the robe to the bedding, saying, "Might be too much to carry if I get in deep snow." Hank knew that was not the reason but he said nothing. Sam also set the pot inside the shack. He would find something, he said; maybe Bill would have an extra pot.

"Watch your topknot," Hank said.

"Watch yours," said Sam, and with a wave of his hand was gone.

Hank entered the cabin and stood a few moments in its

gloom, feeling the presence of one who had just been there. Then he turned to the doorway to look out. He looked down the river the way Sam had gone but there was no sign of him and no sign of a living thing.

29

IT WAS A LONG, cold, and dangerous journey but Sam covered it in seventeen days, stopping only one night with Bill and one with Dan. Outfitted at Bridger's and several hundred dollars in debt, he was ready to trap, but the things he had just bought did not take the place of the ones he had lost. His rifle was new and a good one but it was not the gun that more than once had saved his life. The revolver was new, the Bowie, the packgear, his leather garments, his cooking utensils; but he liked none of it. Bridger told him that his mount, a sorrel stud, was one of the finest horses from the Crow nation, but Sam knew it would take a lot of training to make it as smart as the bay. Until he stared with dismay at his new fixens he had not realized that the Blackfeet had robbed him of things almost as dear to him as his own name and honor. Wall now, as Bill had said, Sam was now the sworn enemy of two nations; and it didn't seem likely, said Jim Bridger, that he would live long. "You're a big credit risk," he had said, and he had urged Sam to trap up Black's Fork and its tributaries, where he would be safe.

Sam spent two nights with Jim and heard all the news and it was all bad news. Brigham Young and his hordes of Mormons were busy building a kingdom in the valley of the Salt Lake; and west of them, across the alkali flats and the Sierras, a million damn fools were rushing around yelling gold, and towns were springing up like the ancient Babble. There had been a town named Babble, hadn't there? Jim asked, casting an uneasy glance at Sam. The whole Western country, he said, would soon be overrun by criminals, religious blowhards, tin-cup greenhorns, and every kind of simpleton on earth; and there would be no buffalo left, no beaver, no clean spot where a man could stretch out and smell sweet earth—nothing but foul water and foul air, sewers, junk heaps, noise, and people. He was thinking of going to Canada.

Sam told him briefly, as he had told Bill and Dan, of his capture and escape. Jim had fixed on him his strange eyes flecked with tiny glittering lights and had said Sam wouldn't last long now. Elk Horns? Hank said. With Bloods and Crows after him Sam ought to get his prayers said and write a goodbye note to his mother. "I'll try and be at your funeral," Jim said.

While Sam trapped on Black's Fork news of his capture and humiliation spread over the area, from trapper to trapper and post to post; and not a mountain man heard the story but asked when the rendezvous would be. Most of them intended to be there. Those with posts, like Bridger, could not get away, or those like Rattlesnake Pete, who, thrown from a horse, was laid up with broken legs, or Bill Williams, crippled with rheumatism and holed up somewhere in the Uintahs. By the first of April it was known that the meeting would be at the Three Forks, right in the heart of Blackfeet country. By mid-April, Sam came in with two packs of pelts and settled most of his account and then headed for the Laramie post. Bridger said that unless he was plum hankering to die he had better stay out of Crow country. At the Laramie post Three-Finger McNees looked at Sam with one black eye while the other gazed off in the direction of Powder River. Doggone it, he said, he intended to be there, but if Sam was to get himself captured again and again they could not spend half their time avenging him. Hearing the words, Mick Boone came over and said surely Sam was not heading through Crow country again.

Right through the middle of it, Sam said. McNees wondered how many of the twenty Sam had killed. Mick said that not only the Crows would be after Sam, but the whole Blackfeet nation.

The humiliation of both the Crow and Blackfeet people was the chief topic of gab at the Laramie post. The Sparrowhawks, Charley said, had been aroused to insane furies on learning that their enemy had been captured and allowed to escape. The Blackfeet were not able to hide or to explain away the fact that their prisoner, defenseless and half naked, had slain one of their mightiest warriors right in their camp and that the whole fifty-seven of them had not been able to capture a man who had neither food nor weapons and had two hundred miles to go. The story of Sam's escape became embellished in the telling, by

both redmen and white, until his long trek in below-zero
weather, without food or gun or bedding, became the greatest
feat of courage and endurance in all of human history.
Mountain men with a gift of gab and invention loved to
elaborate it; they liked to describe the murderous furies of the
Blackfeet braves when, rising from their rumpots with
bloodshot eyes, they discovered that a bound and helpless
captive, half dead from hunger and cold, had with his bare
hands throttled a warrior who boasted of six coups.

At the post their efforts to lead Sam out got them little.

Zeke Campbell, who had spent the winter in the Medicine
Bow Mountains, walked around with a tin cup of strong rum in
his hand and studied Sam with the strangest eyes in the
country. Back under large, coarse, bushy brows the color of
golden sandstone were small eyes that seemed to be only two
glittering lights. He would have bought Sam a drink but he
knew that Sam did not drink. So after staring at Sam across the
top of his cup he went over to Mick Boone, one of the tallest of
the mountain men, with an abnormally long neck on the front
of which was a huge Adam's apple. Mick was a dark, watchful,
silent man, who looked slow and deliberate but was fast on the
draw. His large homely face, with its big curved nose and wide
mouth, usually broke into a self-conscious grin, even if he were
asked only an ordinary question.

The question Zeke asked was not ordinary. "For a man who
lost all his fixens he looks good, don't he?"

"He lost my bay," Mick said, shooting his brows up.

Cy Gregg came over. He had wintered on the waters of the
Belle Fourche. That was Crow country but Cy years ago had
taken a Crow girl and had paid, in the opinion of most men, a
king's price for her. He was now a Crow brother; if the Crows
did not love him or covet his scalp they at least did not molest
him. Like Bill and Charley, Cy spoke their language and knew
their ways and what they were saying and thinking. As he
moved toward the two men they fell silent, for they did not
trust him.

A moment later Jeb Berger entered the storeroom. Jeb was
the only mountain man whom no other mountain man liked. He
was a big fellow—more than six feet and about two hundred and
twenty pounds, square, deep-chested; and he was a fair shot
and a fair hunter. The thing that made men uneasy around him
was his pantomime: he was forever pretending that he was

shooting ducks or geese out of the sky or the heads off chickens; or, squaring off, that he was ready to lick the world's champion. Few mountain men were show-offs; they had courage but they did not think about it or wonder if they had it. They felt that there was something timid in a man who had to be eternally telling the world that he was an expert boxer, a dead shot, and a brave man. Jeb belonged to the boasters and braggarts, among whom in a later time a famous one would be known as Buffalo Bill. He did not really belong to the tribe of Kit Carson and Jim Bridger and Tom Fitzpatrick. He must have known that, for he seemed to be trying, morning, noon, and night, to convince other men of his skills and his courage.

Like his torso, his face was square; it was a large strong face with no weak feature except the eyes, which were the eyes of a liar. Jeb had a heavy black beard an inch long that covered nearly all his face, and in this beard his grin showed two rows of even teeth that were shockingly small in a face so large and dark. When he smiled he merely drew his well-fed cheeks back, and except for two wrinkles at the corners and his exposed teeth you saw no sign of a smile. He was proud of his beard and of the hair over his body, for he thought that hair was a sign of virility. It was his private opinion that all thin-bearded men were cowards.

Jeb came over to Mick and those with him, and when he felt that he was near enough to be cordial he grinned at them, and the next moment cut a heavy-footed caper. He shot his arms up in the position they would have taken if they had held a gun; and his deep voice said, "Boom-boom!" With a gesture he indicated that two birds had fallen. He next closed his hands and presented to Cy the pose of a boxer on guard, and did a few fancy steps. Mick was gravely watching him, his elongated skull held high, his eyes staring down his long nose. That he didn't like Jeb was plain all over his face. Mick, Cy, and Zeke were not the kind to dress down a braggart. McNees was. He came over and looked at Jeb.

"Ya heard about it?"

"Some," said Jeb, and made his mechanical grin.

"Ya kallate to be at the rondyvoo at Three Forks?"

Jeb was not a talkative man and he was never quick to reply. He loved to play the part of a deep silent person, with an extremely sensitive sense of honor and a lightning hand on the draw.

"When?" he said at last.

"About August first, ain't it?" McNees asked, one eye on Zeke and the other on Mick.

"Bout then," Mick said.

"Hey, Sam!" Sam, standing by a pile of robes and tanned skins, looked over at the men. Then he walked over, his gaze moving from man to man as he went.

"Jeb here," McNees said, "is dyun ta kill a few Bloods. Wants to know when the rondyvoo will be."

"I think most of the men want around August first."

Jeb, McNees said, was snorting like a buffler bull with a badger hanging from his balls. Jeb was looking at Sam.

"Taking a nap?" he asked.

"Just as well have been," Sam said. "Fact is, I was trying to figger out how to unhitch two bulls with their horns locked. I was about to chop a horn off when all I could see around me was the ends of gun barrels."

"Five or six?" asked Jeb, his tone saying that any man could take care of five or six.

Sam looked Jeb in the eye and said, "Fifty-seven when I left them."

"Jeb is an expert with figgers," McNees said. "How much is a third of fifty-seven?"

Jeb turned on McNees his wide unemotional grin.

"About nineteen," Mick said.

"Only three for each of us?" said McNees. "Can't we git a extra fer Jeb?"

"Jeb will want at least five or six," said Sam.

Jeb's cheeks were still stretched back in a meaningless smile. Mick's long homely face had opened in a grin that spread to his forehead. Two Blackfeet were about all he cared to tackle at one time, he said; Jeb could have one of his and that would make four for him.

Where were they to find them? asked Zeke. Anywhere, Sam said. Had they let the squaws squat on him?

"They never got that far."

McNees said: "Count on us to be there, Sam. August first." He fixed one black eye on Jeb, studied him a few moments and said, "We'll see ya there."

It was a long time till August. Meanwhile Sam had work to do in Crow country and a debt to pay to a woman, without whose food and bedding he would have died. During his second evening at the post the men sat around a big fire, a few of them drinking, all of them smoking or chewing. The talk turned to Kate. Wind River Bill had come in, and on Kate, as on most matters, he was an authority. When someone wondered if the woman was crazy or only pretended to be, Bill said he had been there six or seven times and never once had she looked at him or spoken to him. She seemed not to know that he was there, she shorely didn't.

"Did she ever know you wuz thar, Sam?"

"I never could be sure," Sam said. "I never saw her look at me."

"How long's she been there?" someone asked.

"Wall now. In forty-three I wuz on the Belle Foos; forty-four I wuz on the Tetons; forty-five I wuz on Little Powder; forty-six I wuz on Hoback; forty-seven—" The mountain men liked Bill's catalogue of places; they loved all the names. Bill searched his memory and thought he might have been on the Snake but he could be as wrong as hell, he shorely could. When was he with Abner Back? Anyway, the woman had been there a long time. She had aged a hundred years and she had grieved enough to turn a whole nation gray.

"True she talks to herself?"

Not to herself, Bill said; she talked to her children. They came and knelt in the sage bushes, or sat—he had never figgered it out; and she read the Bible to them and talked to them.

"Ya figger she sees them?"

Wall now, Bill said, and turned his face to the sky, as though to find the answer there. This here life, it was a riddle for sure, and no man had figgered it out.

"Spect she'll die there, unh?"

"Spect so." A trapper passing by someday would find her bones and would bury them between her children. Then the Injuns would burn the cabin and the winds would level everything, and there would be no sign that a mother had lived there for years, reading God's words to her angels.

A voice said, "Our mother she never loved us that way."

Not many mothers did, Bill said, for he was an authority on that matter too. He had never known a mother with such devotion as this woman's. Had they ever stopped to think that of all things there had been, or someday would be, this was the greatest? There had been only one Eve, and of all the women the Almighty had made since taking the rib from Adam

she was the one that every stud whinnied at. Waugh! There
had been only one Mary, one Cleopatra, one Elizabeth, and
there was only one Kate. He expected that God had put her
there to show the world what mother love should be. Mebbe He
had put Sam here to show what a father should be, for he had
heard that Sam took to the bones of his wife and child the
loveliest flowers he could find. The eyes of all the men turned to
Sam but he was smoking and looking into the fire and he
pretended to be unaware of them.

"Heerd say she never makes a fire."

Never, Bill said. Sam he had dragged in enough wood for ten
years and it hadn't growed none but it warn't no smaller
neither. Jeb interrupted Bill's talk to say that he had ridden
past her shack last fall. Boom-boom! Two ducks fell from the
sky. He had taken the ducks to her and a deer but she had
seemed not to want them. It was a fine fat deer. He had broken
its neck on a dead run at almost half a mile.

Some of the men glanced at one another. They all knew that
no man on earth could hit a deer on a dead run at half a mile.
Jeb's shooting was like rain on the talk. Even Bill fell silent.
Greenhorns came out from the East and boasted their heads off
about their wing-shooting of partridge and dove; but with a
Hawken rifle they couldn't hit a buffalo bull standing broadside
a hundred yards away.

McNees was the only man who had looked straight at Jeb.
When Three-Finger looked at a man he usually squirmed a little and got his tobacco smoke down the wrong hole. While one
small black eye looked deep into you the other looked off at the
sky or the mountains; and if after a few moments you swung
your gaze from the eye boring into you to the one staring at
eternity the man's head would turn and the other eye would
look into you. Three-Finger was one of the few men who kept
the hair shaved off their faces. He was a tall long-legged man
who, like Bill Williams, had always lived and trapped alone, a
hermit deep in the mountains who minded his own business
and took insults from no man. His right eye, fixed on Jeb, had
that black-bearded boaster powerful oneasy; and after a few
moments McNees said, "Heard it said you took some Blackfeet
scalps. Next August will be a great day for you." The men all
knew that Jeb had never taken Blackfeet scalps. After the
Missouri Fur Company had to abandon its post on the Three
Forks it had been a bold trapper who had ventured far into

Blackfeet land and a rare day when one took a Blackfoot scalp.

It was going to be a mighty pleasure to run that band of varmints into the ground. August first, they reminded one another the next day, and vanished in all directions from the post. Sam was again well-equipped but he missed the familiar feel of the gun he had lost, of the saddle, of the horse under him. He was in buckskin garments so new that the smoke-and-tanning smell of them was stronger than that of horse lather and tobacco smoke. It was Crow smell. After he had ridden a few hours the Rawhide Buttes were on his right, the North Platte on his left; and as far as he could see was only the pale light above the vast area between the Platte and the Powder and Belle Fourche. The Belle Fourche and the Powder were the heart of Crow country. Because of what Cy had told him Sam had decided to ride across the Sparrowhawk nation clear to the Yellowstone.

Cy had told him that the Crows were frantic with frustration and disgust. Even girls were vowing to take the warpath against him. The old chief didn't know how many of the twenty Sam had killed but a dozen warriors had been found with Sam's mark on them. As though that were not humiliation enough, the rum-guzzling Blackfeet had let him slip out of their halter and were now saying that they had captured him only to let him go so that they could capture him a second time. It was an unspeakable shame for the proud Sparrowhawks. They had not yet with their bravest men been able to put as much as an arrowhead in Sam, yet the Blackfeet had taken him, spat in his face, slapped him with tomahawks, starved and frozen him, and let him go. Cy said the Blackfeet were saying that capturing Sam had been so easy that they intended to capture him once a year as long as he was fool enough to stay in the country. They would get huge ransom, including rum, and show their ancient enemies, the Crows, that as fighters they were no better than sick old women. The Crow chief knew that there would be a vengeance wreaked by mountain men and begged for a chance to exterminate the band that had captured Sam. If denied that, the Crows would vow on their medicine bags and by all their ancestors that they would take Sam's trail and never sleep day or night till they had brought him down.

"They figger twenty aren't enough?" said Sam, grimly amused. "You say about a dozen of them are still after me?"

"They kallate."

"All the best ones?"

Oh, hell no, Cy said; Sam had slain three of the best ones, maybe four.

"And the girls are coming after me?"

"Some of them."

"Mebbe I can capture one for a wife," Sam said.

He didn't know how he would feel if he saw a girl trailing him. He didn't know how much of Cy's gossip to believe or whether to believe any of it. North of Lightning Creek in an area so forsaken that he saw no sign of any living thing he tried his new weapons; when with the rifle he was able at two hundred yards to hit an object the size of a beaver hat nine times in ten he turned to the revolver. He was not the kind of revolver shot who knocked the heads off grouse at fifty feet but he had learned during his years in the mountains that the man who saved his life in a pinch needed a cool head more than expert marksmanship. There actually had been greenhorns out from the East who at target practice could outshoot most of the mountain men but when they went out for big game and were charged by a bull buffalo or a grizzly bear their trembling hands dropped their weapons. Boom-boom! they said, when miles from danger. They had hunted tiger in India and lion in Africa (they said), but the next day they went to pieces with buck fever and shook all over when an old bull turned in the chase and looked at them with half-blind eyes.

Sam thought his weapons would do. He was not so sure of his horse.

30

THE STUD DID not fail him when a week later he had one of his narrowest escapes. He had reached the upper waters of Powder River and was in the heart of Crow land when his senses told him he was being followed. He had seen no fresh Indian tracks and no ashes of recent fires. On his way up he had rolled in sage and rubbed various plant essences over his weapons, the sad-

dle, and the horse. He had made no fires since entering Crow
country.

He looked round him and studied the physical situation.
Powder River flowed north through a lovely valley, with the
Bighorns on the west and the Black Hills on the east. It was
prime buffalo land. Except for the growth along the river there
was no heavy cover between him and the foothills, thirty or
forty miles distant. He thought of hiding and waiting and
trying to shoot the leader off his horse but his sixth sense told
him that that would not be enough to stop them. They were
desperate and they were bolder than they had been. If he were
to shoot one in a party of four or five he would then have to ride
at top speed while reloading; and all the while they would be
firing at his horse.

At the post he had been told that his packhorse was such a
well-trained beast that he could turn him loose and he would
follow. He guessed he would have to do that, for in a race for
his life he could not hang onto the rope of a packhorse. While
thinking of his problem and wondering why he was here he
kept a sharp eye on the landscape and studied the river. He
thought his best chance was to plunge into the river and cross
and flee to the mountains. A few moments later he was no
longer allowed to sit and think; a decision was abruptly forced
on him.

A mile southwest of him an Indian rider appeared on the
crest of a hill. In no time at all there were two, then three, and
four; and at last there were seven. He could tell that it was a
war party in full paint, well-horsed and well-armed. He
supposed that they were all picked warriors. Pretending not to
see them, he now followed the river path at a slow pace and
studied the river bottoms. The river along here had cut deep in
the earth and was fifteen or twenty feet below the top of its
bank. Would his horse take a leap from that height? Would the
packhorse follow? Most of his fixens were on the packhorse, as
well as Kate's rifle and food for her. The seven Indians had
disappeared. Sam would have risen to an elevated spot and
waited for them but there was none around him.

He now took a branch path leading toward the river, which
was fifty yards from him; and leaving his horses, he went back
to the main trail. When at the edge of the woods he peered out
he had a good view of the country, except the river bottoms.
The main buffalo trail here skirted the edge of the woods, with

many paths meandering through them. He knew that seven Indians would not try to approach him on horses; some would detour and come in from the north, others would come up from the south; and somewhere they would have a lookout watching the river. He still had time to plunge in and cross, while they were scouting his position, but he had never run from a fight and he didn't like to run from this one. There were only seven of them, he told himself, and Lost-Skelp would say they were only an hour's work for a boy. He was thinking bravado and he knew it. He wondered a moment if the ordeal of captivity and flight had impaired his faculties, for he didn't seem to be his usual self. Convinced that he was being stupid, he ran to the horses, led the packhorse to the edge and with one heave shoved him off. He then mounted, faced the river, dug with his heels, and with no hesitation at all the beast made the plunge to the swirling waters. The horse went under and Sam with it, except his right hand, which held his rifle high. The moment his eyes came up out of the water and he had shaken the wet off his lashes he saw something that so astounded him that he could only stare. On the high bank above him stood a naked Indian, with nothing on him but some kind of headdress, and nothing in his hands but an object that looked like a knife. If Sam was astonished by sight of the red youth he was utterly amazed by what the youth now did. He stood only an instant on the bank, tall and red and naked, when with the war cry of his people, he put the knife between his teeth and plunged in, and at once was swimming like an otter, his absurd headdress and the knife flashing above the waters. Sam's horse was swimming toward the far bank, almost side by side with the packhorse. Sam hung his rifle from the horn, swung his right leg across the beast's neck, and turned in the saddle to face the swimmer. The stud was a strong one but the Indian was gaining. As Sam watched the headdress coming closer he could no longer doubt the incredible fact that this brave, a mere youngster, was determined to count coup on Sam Minard.

Because it was not Sam's way to shoot an almost defenseless enemy he loosened the knife at his belt. He then waited, eyes staring, his mind slowly grasping the fact that this was the most spectacular act of courage he had ever seen. As the Indian came on, the black eyes never left Sam's face. Sam saw more than that. He sensed that this young one had been so outraged in his tribal and personal pride that he was resolved to prove that a Crow warrior could be a braver man than The Terror. If able to touch Sam he would in the next moment plunge the knife, and if he died in the next instant would that matter? He would be remembered by his people as the bravest warrior of them all, living and dead.

Wall now! Sam thought. Having decided what was in the youth's mind, he moved fast. If this young brave wanted a fight with knives he could have it; and so Sam slid back over the stud's rump and into the water. At that moment his enemy was no more than ten feet away. In the next moment the Indian's chest came up, like an otter's, and in a flash he flung himself on Sam. In that same moment Sam's powerful hands seized the redman's right arm and broke the knife from his grasp. The next move caught Sam unprepared. With fantastic speed the Indian came up and almost out of the water, and both desperate hands seized Sam's throat. The move had been made like a trout's, in an arc, and with such perfect timing that for a few moments as the hands closed his windpipe Sam could only bug his eyes and wonder what had happened. He was to realize later that the Indian could have seized the knife at Sam's waist and plunged it through him.

Like a horror in a nightmare of memory Sam saw the grizzly with the badger's teeth set in its nose. With all the strength he could bring to bear, from the position he was in, treading water, he took the Indian's wrists and tried to break the grasp. In that moment he was conscious of the redman spitting in his face. In that moment he caught a dreadful picture of eyes so full of hate that they were like black molten steel; and of teeth bared back into the cheeks. Sam sensed next that blackness was about to engulf him, and with the last of his sanity he did the only thing he could do: he grasped the terrible knife at his belt and plunged it deep into the Indian just under the breastbone. When the hands did not instantly relax he drew the knife and plunged it again. As he then fought to remain conscious he saw the change in the black eyes, and that change he would remember to the day of his death. He was to think of it afterward as the kind of change a father would never want to see in the eyes of a son.

Sam thought he must have been unconscious a few moments, for he had water in his lungs. Coughing, he looked round him and saw patches of red. The hands were gone from his throat, and the dead Indian was floating down the current. Putting the knife in his belt and looking at the far bank where his horses stood, Sam began to swim, keeping his head under except when he turned his mouth up for air. Once through veils of water hanging from his brows and lashes he saw his two beasts moving toward a wooded area, a half mile from the river. While he swam the thought came to him that this intrepid youngster was not one of the seven he had seen, but a lone warrior, who had left his people to count coup or die. He was as brave a man, Sam was thinking, as any he had known; and after reaching the bank, exhausted and subdued and feeling a strange shame, admiration compelled him to look down the river, hoping for a last view of this brave youth. But there was no sign of him on the slate-blue waters; he was dead and he was gone. Sam drew the knife. The river had washed it clean except for a tiny spot that had rested between belt and buckskin. With a forefinger Sam wiped off the blood smear and then touched his skin over his heart. It was the only way he could think of to salute the valor of a foe who had been more than worthy of him.

After running into the woods he turned to look back. There was still no sign of the seven. Mounting the stud, he rode at a gallop west by north to the foothills and entered a black forest. He was feeling nausea, and a sadness that was not at all natural to him. Riding by night and hiding by day, he began to wonder about a matter that only now had occurred to him. Here he was, a human male, hunted by a thousand warriors from two nations; and yonder was Kate, a female, whom all befriended and no man wished to kill. If the old Crow chief would now come to him and say that his people were sorry for the murder of his wife and child, and that the braves who killed them would be punished, he would sheathe his knife and smoke the pipe of peace. . . .

It was true (he told himself) that Kate had killed in a frenzy of hate and passion that no man could excel and few could equal but since then she had given her whole being to her children and their flowers. Sam doubted that she had killed anything, even a bug, since that terrible morning. She watered her plants, talked to her angels, and waited for the Lord to call her home; whereas he, who only now had slain a brave boy, would soon join a war party that would try to exterminate to the last man and dog an entire band.

He suspected that he was not thinking clearly. There surely were aspects of the matter to which he was blind. If the Crows had him in their hands there would be in their hearts no compassion and no mercy; and if the warrior in the river had been able to kill him he would have become a national hero, possibly the greatest hero in all of Crow history. It was an eye for an eye, the holy book said. It was not Kate's devotion to gentleness that had made her secure; it was the mountain men who had set the skulls on four stakes at the four corners of her tiny world. If the laws of life, of weakness and strength, of timidity and courage, had taken their inexorable course, with no protection of the weak by the strong, she would have been scalped long ago and her bones would now be white somewhere along the Musselshell.

Just how, Sam wondered, lying in his robe, did the Almighty want it, anyway? Throughout the Creator's world a man rarely, if ever, saw protection of the weak by the strong, except now and then in the human or in the dog family. When Sam was seventeen he had seen three bully boys tormenting a helpless youngster about their age and size, with a dozen men and boys watching the torture without lifting a hand. Sam had gone in and knocked the heads of the three together with such force that he had fractured two skulls, and had made the whole community hostile toward him. When he walked the streets mothers had come shrieking at him who had no interest, none at all, in the boy who had been tortured, but only in their own brutal hellcats. Sam had been glad to get out of the place and away from the hate in the mother-eyes. Of the mountain men he knew, he thought there was none who would take advantage of the weak or defenseless, much less torture for the hellish pleasure of it. In nature under the human level, as Sam had observed it, nothing killed except for food, or for mates, or in defense of itself or its kind. Human beings in what they called the civilized areas of life had brought killing down to such an ugly level that some men actually murdered for a handful of coins or for the simple ghoulish pleasure of it. The red people made of war a philosophy and a way of life, as the bullfighter made of bull-killing. It was not a philosophy and way of life with his country, which had recently jumped on a feeble neighbor and wrested from it half its lands, as stronger bobcats took the rabbit from the weaker. Jim Bridger said that back in Washington they were calling it Manifest Destiny. The Indians, warring against one another, seemed to be pretty well matched, man to man and nation to nation—or at least this was true of the more warlike ones. It seemed to Sam that the tribes that loved and sought war and made a philosophy of it, and killed in the full light and passion of heroism, when emotions were hottest; when a man hardly felt bullet, arrow, or knife; and, when, if mortally wounded, he broke into his death song and died in a clean way with his wings soaring—this, it seemed to him, was all right. Maybe the truth (he thought he saw it now) was that the youngster who flung himself into the river had died a wonderful death: in the last moments he had the enemy by the throat and was choking the eyes right out of his face; and his blood was boiling-hot and his hunger for glory was right at the gates of heaven. How many men in a century passed into death in such triumph? How many won such consummation of all their courage and powers in a last supreme blinding moment? All but a few of them died creaking and itching and complaining, scabbed and scarred over, half blind and half deaf, sick with loneliness and self-pity, and as remote from triumph and glory as an old robin skulking along in forest gloom with its wings dragging.

After thinking his way through it Sam felt a little better. It was pretty heavy moralizing for a mountain man, and after reaching a conclusion he felt tired. He did not perceive that his love of life was so inordinate and hungry that killing for pleasure was as alien to him as asceticism, its inseparable twin. He'd far rather sing than shoot; far rather lie on his back in a field of alpine lilies or an orchard of wild plum and syringas, breathing in the marvelous scents that filled the atmosphere and the earth, than ride away to kill some man who was coming forward with the hope of killing him. He'd rather stand on a mountain summit and shout into the heavens the concluding bars of Beethoven's C minor than follow the bugles and Zachary Taylor to Resaca de la Palma and Buena Vista.

In his moralizing Sam felt the outlines of a symphony. A day or two later he reached the core of it: he had lost a son and guessed he would never have a son now. He had lost one on the Little Snake and one in the river: Sam was unable to put away the face convulsed by passion and the black eyes hot with courage and hate; or the words which, among so many, his father had uttered aloud in troubled thought, "And where the slain are, there she is, the eagle-mother." He could not stop thinking of Kate, for where the slain were, there she was, in another world and another way. Still, he guessed there was not much difference between the eagle mother and the human mother, the human father and the wolf father. But over Kate's passions had fallen a heavenly light that was like the eyes of morning, the light of the living. It was this that perplexed and troubled him. God had said—but he could no longer remember of what or whom—that a light did shine, and eyes were like the eyes of the morning; and Job had said, "I have heard of thee by the hearing of the ear, but now mine eye seeth thee."

After a week of hiding by day and making his way north Sam felt that at last his eyes were seeing Kate, as he sat astride his horse on a hilltop and looked over at her flowers. She had quite a garden this year; he saw that she had used some of the seeds he had given her. This indicated, surely, that she knew what she was doing, or that God was guiding her hand. Approaching, he thought her flowers lovely, though he preferred the wild ones—the columbines and lilies and gilias and a hundred more. It looked to him as if she had planted a few columbines; if she had, the glory of their spurred petals would look as out of place in this arid and lonely region as the blond curls and laughing blue eyes of a girl child.

Kate now came in sight out of the river woods, the pail in her hand. While she came up the hill he studied her garden. She surely was making a loveliness of bloom and fragrance above her children, with the tallest flowers to the north and the others stepping down to the south. On the north side there was an open spot; it was there, he supposed, that she sat when she talked to her children or read from the book. When she came up with the pail he called her Mrs. Bowden and asked how she was but she did not look at him. She was like a woman who, having only a small measure of awareness, gave it all to her flowers and her children. Telling her that he had cleaned and oiled and polished her rifle, he set it by the cabin door. He then quickly framed her face and kissed her forehead, saying, "I'll get this pailful"; but when he tried to take the pail from her hand she made a wild-female movement, and Sam stepped back. He studied her as she went down the hill; each year she looked smaller and frailer and grayer. When she vanished into river brush he looked over at the cairn; then at her sage plants and flowers; and at last at the long knife and heavy revolver hanging from his waist.

This evening while smoking a pipeful he saw the moon come up; soon she would be in the garden, talking to her angels. It was too bad she didn't have some trees up there. He wondered if he ought to transplant a river willow or serviceberry or aspen. If she had a grove of aspens she could listen to the marvelous music of the leaves when the soft winds whispered over them and find the joy in their golds and yellows in the fall.

He guessed at last that he ought to go up and sit with her. She was by the flowers at the north edge, facing the sage plants, the book in her lap. Sam would have been amazed if he had known what she was thinking—for she was telling herself that not until this moment had she known how handsome her sons were, or how lovely her daughter. They had not grown at all since that night when they came out of heaven to kneel before her. But she had not thought about that. She might have said that angels did not grow but were always the same. Because the moon was full, and golden like a melon, her daughter was exquisite in her loveliness, as she smiled and nodded at her mother across the sage foliage. She wore a heavenly filmy stuff as delicate as spider gossamer, that no one had ever seen on earth, for it was not there. Kate could not see the shoulders of her sons but she knew they were gowned in a silken radiance that was not of the earth.

She read first to them Isaiah's words, " '. . . they shall mount up with wings as eagles; they shall run and not be weary; and they shall walk and not faint.' " All day while carrying water up the hill she had murmured the words over and over, for she was waiting on the Lord as well as she knew how, and she was not weary. In her soul with these words had been the others, "The wilderness and the solitary place shall be glad for them; and the desert shall rejoice, and blossom as the rose." Sam stood behind her, puffing his pipe and hearing her words: that the tongue of the dumb would sing, and in the wilderness, waters would break out and flow away into the desert. A path would be there and no killing beasts would be found there; and all sorrow and sighing would go away.

The daughter and the sons smiled at her, and all the flowers were softly nodding; and after a while the mother began to hum an old song that mothers in all lands sang to their little ones; and behind her a mouth harp was soft and low. Sam had backed away and now leaned against the cabin, his rifle at his side. Did she, he wondered, think the music was from heaven? Who could say it was not? After a few minutes he took the lead and played the simple themes that his mother had sung to her children; and in a low tired voice Kate carried the words to his music. For almost two hours he played and she sang, and not once did she turn to look at him or seem to know that he was there. He then slipped silently out of her sight.

The next day he thought to linger and play again for her but reflection told him that this would be an unkindness. If she did indeed think the music was from heaven it would be best not to overdo it, lest she find out that it was not. For the artist in him said that heaven had to be a thing that one could touch only rarely, and hope to touch once more. It would be best to slip away, for she now had an abundance of fruits and nuts, sugar and flour. He might come again this fall, after the Three Forks rendezvous, to lay in meat for the winter, and again open a heavenly window to let the music out, so that melodies of long ago could touch her soul in memory of her dead ones, hers and his.

31

THE FIRST of the avengers to arrive in the Three Forks area was Bear Paws George Meek, a big blond smiling man whom men called Bear Paws for his habit of collecting the claws of bears, chiefly of the grizzly, which he washed in urine and other astringents, and polished with clays and powders and leathers until they were as clean and gleaming as jewels. George was a happy-go-lucky fellow, or seemed to be; he had gentle blue eyes and a broad smile and pleasant words for all men, except the red, whom he despised because they had killed his brother. Under his jolly surface he was a sharp man with a bag full of tricks. He was always smiling—Bill said George smiled when he slept; and this seemed likely, for his dreams were usually of deceptions and stratagems and sharp practices, with which he outfoxed those who dealt with him. "I allus try and git the saddle on the right horse," was his definition of himself. He cut his pants according to his buckskin; he sailed near the wind; and he never waded when he couldn't see bottom. But he was a convivial cuss who didn't like to live and trap alone through five cold months, as Zeke and Hank did, and Lost-Skelp, Bill Williams, and Sam Minard. Pore ole Bill, he was dead now, and Windy was writing a poem about him:

> He chomped life down jist all the laws of God allow,
>> leastwise
>> till now.
> They ain't no longer any sign he's climbun up the hill.
>> I spect he's had
>> his fill.

He had been found down in the Uintahs, a bullet through his heart and an old Eutaw rifle across his lap. There was two feet of snow on him.

George had sometimes spent the winter with Hob Niles (dead now, like Bill), who had shared his skill with hands (they had both carved things from wood), an artist's love of exquisite detail, and tall lies around a fire. They had both preferred chewing to smoking and had brown beards on which the patches of deeper brown were the stain of tobacco juice. George had come up from Henrys River, and a few hours behind him came Tomahawk Jack, as mean a critter as ever scalped an Injun, and one of the best revolver shots in the West. Jack, like Dave Black, another expert with revolvers, was not much larger than Kit Carson, and had that man's feline instincts and small-man deadliness. If Jack or Dave had ever smiled it had been when looking at the dead face of an enemy. Thirty-five and thirty-eight the year the mountain men met at Three Forks, both were clean-shaven and rather boyish in appearance, and not much good in a fight except with weapons. Jack was almost as skillful a rider as the best of the Crows, and his Crow horse was thought by some to be the fastest horse in the mountains. That, Mick Boone had said, his large homely face cracking in a slow grin, was only because Jack was such a little man. He was bigger than Jack when he was born, Mick said. That, Bill had said, didn't mean a thing cept he'd allus been a big target.

The next of the mountain men to ride in was said by army men to be one of the three best scouts in the West. That, said the irrepressible Bill, was because McNees saw twice as much as any other man; while one eye scanned the northeast the other scanned the northwest. That he saw equally well with either eye, like a horse, was proved, Bill said, by the fact that he would look at you with either eye; and sometimes like a bird he would look at you with one and if he didn't like what that eye saw he would look at you with the other. In Roger McNees, half Scot and half German, there was no monkey business—no sense of fun and no tall tales. After he came west fifteen years ago there had been a rumor that he had slain his father and fled, but no man west of the Missouri knew if it was true and no man cared. Three-Finger loved tracking and scouting; it was said that he could stuff both nostrils with sage foliage and still smell out an Indian trail faster than a wolf pup on a rabbit track. The other men had supposed that he would do a little scouting on his way to the rendezvous, and so were not surprised by his reply to Meek's question, "Do ya know whar the varmints is?"

He knew where they were and he knew how many were in the pack. Did Bear Paws know where the sulphur springs were east of the Big Belts? "Well as my own mother's face," said George. "I been thar man an boy a thousan times." Did he know where the creek was on which Black Harris had hidden from the Blackfeet two days and a night, when they sat so close to him playing roulette that one of them touched him? "Wall, now!" said George. That was the time when Black's legs wouldn't work, on leaving the hiding place; for miles he had dragged himself along by his arms. "Allus thought that wuz Broken Hand," George said. One black eye studied George. Did he know where the Seven Mile Creek was? "Well as I know the mole on top uv my pa's nose. It had two hairs in it." Halfway between Seven Mile and the springs you turned west to the Big Belts, and in no time a-tall the camp was plum before you, as plain as the whiskers on a bull buffalo.

"Thet ain't too fur from here," George said.

"How many?" asked Jack, scowling.

If the varmints were all in camp there were fifty-eight.

One musta had a baby, said George. Sam had killed one. And fifty-eight, doggone it, wooden be three apiece. As the nigger stud said, twarn't no more than a few minutes' work.

"See Elk Horns?" asked Dave.

Three-Finger looked at Dave. "Would I count him if I never seen him?"

"Ya mean," said Dave bitingly, "ya seen his scars."

"He sees everything," said George quickly, for the two men were looking at one another.

This evening Lost-Skelp Dan and a dozen others came in. No man, not even the cold McNees or Tomahawk Jack, could look at Dan without feeling a slight chill. It was not that he was a big fellow, six feet two and all muscle and bone, with a girth of eighteen inches around his neck or his flexed biceps. It was not his big skull with neither hair nor hide on it above the ears. It was his eyes. Forty now, he had been a mountain man for nineteen years. How he lost his scalp nobody knew, for not even the snoopy nose of Wind River Bill had been able to smell out the secret. Whoever took the scalp was a greedy cuss: the knife had made the incision where the top part of the ear was fastened to the scalp but instead of pushing the top of the ear down and away the Indian had slashed across it, so that Dan was earmarked and cropped like a steer. His big gleaming skull was all hairless bone except a fringe about two inches wide across the back of his neck. Instead of cutting along the hairline on the forehead the scalper had gone halfway down to the eyes; and now almost straight across and about an inch above the brows Dan had an ugly scar that was like a welt. It seemed to fill with blood when he became angry.

Powder River Charley was speculating that if it was the Blackfeet who had scalped Dan this foray would be for him a special pleasure. Charley liked to tease a little, though he knew that teasing was for Dan like liniment in a raw wound. Dan, Bill had said, had the sense of humor of an old sick bull with a pack of wolves around it. If they all got three apiece, Charley said, they dotta give Dan the biggest one, for mebbe it could be tanned into a wig for him. Dan at the moment was puffing his pipe. He looked over at Charley, not quickly but like a man who took his time about things. His large pale-blue eyes seemed puffed softly out of his skull, like a toad's. He looked at Charley, his large strong smooth-shaven face immobile, and George decided at this point that it would be safe for him to come in with a little flight of whimsy, like a jolly sally upon a besieger; and so, rearranging his quid, he said, "Trouble is the red varmint didden leave enough hair so's we kin match it, an the hair on a man's belly is never the same color as on his head. I'll be dogged and gone iffen I kin see how we kin do it." Bear Paws looked round him, slyly, to see if his jest was setting well.

Dan now turned his cold eyes on George and went on sucking his pipe. Well, one thing you could say about Dan, Sam Minard might have said if he had been here, was that he had avenged himself on his enemies ten or twenty times. Dan had a shack far up the Madison near the headwaters, and the only time Sam had looked into it it had seemed to him that half the walls were covered with Indian scalps. Dan combed the black hair and glossed it up the way he did with beaver pelts, and as George put it, kept everything nice and purty. Once in a while, when his whole skull itched under mosquito bites, Dan would go forth to get another scalp. He always cut it across the ears and forehead and low on the neck. He was a lone and deadly killer. If Sam had been asked which of all the men he knew might give him buck ager if he had to face him in a fight he might have thought first of Dan.

The next morning there rode into camp the man whom all mountain men would have chosen by private ballot as the ablest of them all. It was not because Sam Minard was the biggest man in the West and physically the most powerful. It was not because he was the deadliest shot—there were many deadlier ones; or the most courageous—there were others more foolhardy; or that he was the coolest when faced with appalling challenge—perhaps no man on earth had nerves of colder steel when confronted by charging grizzly or redman with raised tomahawk than Hank Cady or Kit Carson, Lost-Skelp Dan or Three-Finger McNees. It was not because he was the most successful Indian fighter; in this, Kit or Dan or Jim Bridger or a dozen others were more than his match any day. It was because he had in ample measure all the traits and skills that made the superlative mountain men. There was none of Jeb Berger in him. Though Windy Bill was a brave man and a superb fighter in a pinch, there was a little of Jeb in him. Though Mick Boone would have faced any man on earth, he always felt gooseflesh when his life depended solely on his nerve.

The men who gathered here—there were twenty-three of them before they rode forth—were probably as daring and able a group of warriors, for their number, as had ever been brought together. Any one of them could be put down for two Indians, most of them for three, and a few of them for four or five. In varying degrees they were all eager for the fight. They all felt competitive, and some of them were afraid they would not get their share of the scalps. A few, like Dan and McNees and Jack, were ambitious to be recognized as the outstanding killer, when it was all over. Others—George, for one, Hobe Isham, a quiet man, for another—felt that they hadn't the killer talent to be first, and so would be content to do the best they could. A few, like Sam, David Black, and Zeke Campbell, were strategists at heart and killers only secondarily.

McNees said Scarface and his pack were encamped on a small stream against a sheer bluff with a heavy stand of timber on its crest. That was the west side. The prevailing wind when he was there was from that side but the winds in that area were like a woman's mind and changed for no reason. On the north side and back about fifty yards was dense aspen and spruce. A stream flowed past on the south side. With the men gathered round him, Three-Finger drew on bare earth a map of the area. When he scouted their position they had two sentinels out—one here, one over there, on the northeast and southeast points; and he supposed they had a lookout on the bluff above, though he had seen no sign of one. They had only seven tepees standing; he had assumed that the largest, which stood in the center and back toward the bluff, was the chief's.

It was possible that they had moved and would have to be scouted again. Looking up at a lowering sky, he said one hell of a storm was getting its belly full of water; if they could move in under thunder that would be fine.

George at last had been able to divide fifty-eight by twenty-three and now said that some of them would be cheated. There wouldn't be three apiece, all the way around. There would be three apiece for thirteen of them, two apiece for nine of them, and only one for him. Someone said that Sam dotta have an extree, since it was his huggin party; but someone else said Sam was to have the chief. A third suggested that most of the varmints should be divided equally and the remainder should be extrees, on a free range, for the men who got there first. Sam now spoke up and said one of them should be allowed to escape, to carry the glad tidings to the Blackfeet nation; and Dan said that would be fine, if he was scalped first. They would let Dan scalp him, and then give the bugger a fast horse with a cactus under its tail. "Wall now," said George. "Lotta mathmaticians here."

Some of the men talked about the imminent killing of fifty-seven Indians as if they were about to go on a buffalo hunt. Some, like Hank Cady, said nothing. For nearly all of them a redman was no more human than a blackman. "They looks a little more like a man," George had said, "but they issent when ya come right down to the marrow. When the Almighty made the

Injun he had plum run out of stuff cept ferrosities. They ain't no devil as hisses down in hell half as froshus as a red varmint."

Some of the men had come from points as far away as Bear Lake and the North Platte and felt that two pesky redskins were lean pickings for a long journey. One of them said it was like riding a hundred miles to eat two doves. If he'd knowed, Mark Hillers said, there'd be a hull army here he would of stayed home. His pa would be ashamed if he saw his son riding a thousand miles for two scalps.

"Mebbe we'd best give him three," George said. "Me, I kin stay and tend camp." Windy Bill thought that a good suggestion. Mark, he said, was plum down there torst the other side of the world, almost to Bent's Fort, and he had crossed fifty rivers and a thousand mountains to get here. Pretty soon, said George, there wouldn't be any extrees left. They'd jist hafta let the men have them who first got their knives in them.

That was about it, Zeke said; he didn't kallate any man would get his sights on anything. There would be no moon and probably no fires. The night would be so black it would be like crawling back into your ma's womb. That was right, Bill said, scanning the dark sky; they would have to tell by the feel of the skin if it was red or white. By the smell, Mick Boone said. But how was Sam to tell elk horns from wolf paws or beaver tail? It was David Black speaking, and when he spoke, according to Bill, his brain swole up like a pregnant belly.

"He will smell like a chief," George said.

Sam, Bill said, would go to Elk Horns like a calf to its mother. But what if he didn't? Dan asked. Would the man who got there first hold him by the halter and wait for Sam?

The chief, Bill said, had spit his stomach in Sam's face. He had smacked his jawbone with a tommyhawk. He had tied him to a tree and near froze his gizzard out and he had boasted and threatened almighty awful. They would have to let Sam have him. He guessed Sam would have the chief by his topknot in less time that it took a wolf to turn around.

The men spent two or three hours with their weapons. They examined the parts, cleaned and greased them, and wiped the barrels as gently as they would have touched the mechanism of a watch. Their knives they honed on fine-grained hard stones that they had saturated with goose oil, and then stropped them on soft leather. To their horses—and every man was superbly mounted—they gave a devoted care that they never gave to themselves, examining their hoofs, teeth, hams, and neck and shoulder muscles; searching under their flanks and up against their scrotums for ticks and other bloodsuckers; letting them drink only in streams clear of heavy clays and poisonous silts; and pasturing them in the most luxuriant spots. If four hundred Blackfeet warriors had moved against them their chance at life would have depended almost entirely on the strong beasts under them. A mountain man thought of his horse and his gun and knife as parts of himself—an extension of his reach and a trebling of his speed.

When the twenty-three men in this comitiva felt that no more mountain men were coming they spent another night here, waiting for storm, with sentinels in three-hour watches at the four corners. The next morning they saddled their beasts, secured their bedrolls and fixens behind their saddles, and headed north down the Missouri. Ahead of the main body went three scouts, and a mile behind it the sharp-eyed Dave Black brought up the rear. A few of them, with Dan as their spokesman, had proposed that after this band was wiped out they should push north and find another band; but the cooler heads said no, for they knew that the massacre would arouse the nation to wild frenzies. The squaws would slash their flesh and spill blood over themselves, and shriek and yell with such insane furies that the braves, like wasps spilled out of a nest, would rush around in all directions, their eyes wild for sign of something to kill. After all, Bill Williams would have said, if alive and with them, their job was to avenge the insults on the head of a mountain brother. After that they would slip silently away down the valleys and through the forests, in all directions but north, leaving the red hornets to wear themselves out in their tantrums. The important thing, they had all agreed, was to let one man live so that he could carry the news to his people. How they would shriek and gouge themselves when the lone survivor, his skull bald and red, told them what had happened!

The first night out they made camp near the foothills of the Big Belt Mountains. McNees slipped in about midnight to report that the band was still there against the bluff but showed signs of getting ready to move. Their lookouts were as before, one varmint a mile from camp on the northeast, another on the southeast, and possibly a third on the bluff. The wind was from the northwest. He kallated that it was about ten miles to the Indian camp.

The three sentinels would have to be taken out. The choice of executioners was given to Sam. He knew that it would be foolish to call for volunteers; they would all volunteer. Knowing that Dan was dying to be one of them, he assigned to him the varmint on the southeast. Because the one on the bluff would be the most difficult of the three to ambush he gave him to Three-Finger. He then looked round him at the men and thought he saw in the night gloom a special eagerness in the eyes of David Black. "All right, Dave, the one on the northeast is yours."

It was a dark night with wolves baying and the hoot owl forecasting storm. All the men lay down but they were all awake. Listening, the only sounds Sam could hear were from a night bird, a wolf, and an owl. Two hours later the party rode two thirds of the way and concealed their horses in an aspen thicket. The sky was low and dark, and huge drops of rain were falling when the men resumed their journey. How wonderful it would be, Sam thought, looking up at the dark wet sky, if at the moment of attack the Creator would fill the world with a thunderous theme of vengeance, with chords like those that opened the Fifth!

They moved forward almost as silently as the wolf, until they were met by the returning scouts. McNees had told them that he and the other two would need only a half hour. Well, mebbe, Sam thought; Dan was not as fast as the other two. They were still two miles from the Indian camp when Sam, now leading the twenty, was astonished to see a tall figure come out of night shadows, hesitate a moment, and advance toward him. It was McNees, with a wet scalp in his hand. This was not the way Sam had planned it, and he was wondering about Dave and Dan, when McNees began to whisper around the group that everything was ready for the huggin. Dan and Dave were about a mile ahead, waiting. They had found all three sentinels dozing, and had one hand over their mouth and a knife through them before they could move. The camp was sound asleep. There were dogs in the camp, McNees said; their horses were southwest around the base of the bluff and no guard was with them. They would approach from the southeast, for the wind that way would be in their faces and those asleep would hear only the hurrycane. Waugh! Sam was thinking: no wonder this man was known as one of the three best scouts in the West, the other two being Kit Carson and Jim Bridger. Still whispering, McNees said that as they approached there would be five tents in a row, facing them; about twenty feet beyond them was a larger tent, in which the chief would be snoring and dreaming of glory. Around it, on the south in a semicircle, were nine smaller tepees. Some of the varmints were not under cover, and because the rain might arouse them it was best to hurry along. By the time McNees had ceased whispering the men had in mind a map of the situation and they knew that in the five skin tents facing the east were the chief's mightiest warriors. Every man but Sam, whose mind was on the chief, hoped to be the first to reach the five tents.

They moved forward in a drizzle of rain. After a mile Dan came in from darkness and joined them. When about three hundreds yards from the camp the party halted; the men would now creep forward as silently as the wolf, for each of them wore three pairs of moccasins. Each had a revolver in his belt and a long Bowie. After fifty yards Dave Black rose as if out of the earth and slipped forward with them. When Sam and the dozen men abreast of him were about a hundred and fifty feet from the first tents they stopped, resting on one knee and a palm; and Sam looked round him at the men behind. Not even the breathing of a single man could have been heard but in any moment they expected to hear the dogs explode in alarm and fury. For another fifty feet they all slunk soundlessly forward, and then Sam straightened, a knife flashing in his hand. This was the signal. In the next moment the camp and the mountains behind it and the whole earth roundabout were shattered by a war cry that stiffened every sleeping Indian. In almost the same instant the men rushed forward at full speed and the camp's dogs came awake. For a few fatal moments the redmen were drugged by sleep and shocked by terror, and during those moments it was all over for most of them. Not one Indian in five knew what struck him.

Elk Horns knew. Sam took care of that. While the horrible cries were still echoing in the mountain night Sam in a flash was between two of the sentinel tents and over to the chief. The redman came up fast and met Sam at the flap door. While racing forward Sam had returned the knife to his belt because at close quarters he preferred to fight with his hands. At the tent door he seized the man by his two arms and wrenched him with such force that the hatchet fell from his hand. In the same moment Sam spat in his face and then flung him headlong backward across his shoulder. He swung then to a guard who had rushed out of the tent and drove his knife through him; and the next instant he seized the chief, brought him to his feet with a jolt that almost fractured his leg bones, again spat in his face, and slapped a red cheek so hard with the flat of his hand that the chief almost fell. "It's me!" Sam roared in the helpless man's face, and again uttering the dreadful war cry, he seized the chief with both hands just under his ribs and heaved him up and straight over his head. He was then on top of him, bloody knife in his hand, and while the stunned chief lay helpless Sam took his scalp.

Scalp in one hand and knife in the other, he leapt back and in morning gloom surveyed the scene. On his left he heard the footfalls of men chasing men. He heard a cry choked off in blood. Looking the other way, he saw a white man taking a scalp, and a bloody Indian rushing at him with raised tomahawk. Sam leapt, felled the man, and saved the life of Hank Cady. Hank had always been a little careless in battle. What Sam was looking for was a live Indian to send as a messenger, and when he saw a redskin leap up from a half dozen prone bodies and make a desperate spurt for freedom Sam was after him like a cougar. He overtook him in about a hundred yards and flung him down. He felt over him for weapons but this brave had none. Sam turned the Indian onto his belly, knelt on his back, and cut leather strings out of the Indian's elkskin jacket. With these he bound the man's hands behind him and was securing him to a tree when he heard his name called.

"Here I am!" Sam cried.

It was all over by then. A few wounded Indians had fled with mountain men after them, who one by one returned with their scalps. No one yet knew if any had escaped. No one knew if McNees had been right in his count. Sam and Bill and Mick walked among the dead, trying to count them; and George came up with his habitual smile and said one was dead over yonder, and another over there. Had any of the varmints got away? They didn't know, Sam said. Dan and McNees were out of sight, probably chasing someone. Had any mountain man got hurt? Well, there was Cy Gregg over there, limping like a man with a broken leg; and Tomahawk Jack, who in his eagerness at scalping had sliced most of the meat off two of his fingers; and Abe Jackson, whose collarbone had been cut in two by a tomahawk. So far as Sam knew, no white man had been killed. As for the dogs, they had all vanished into thin air, and Bill thought that some of the red devils might have taken to wings too. They'd never know until they had counted them.

In full daylight Sam and Bill and a few others tried to count the dead bodies scattered over the area but could not agree on the number. Sam then turned to the wounded. Abe had a nasty cut all right, through his collarbone and the two ribs next to it, but like all mountain men he pretended that it was nothing at all. It was because of his doggone awkwardness, he said. Some of the men chewed tobacco and gave him the quids, and Abe pushed them into the wound. Jack had made a small fire and with a hot knife point was trying to cauterize and cicatrize his wounds; and Abe, watching him, said he could use some of that medicine. Even Three-Finger had a wound, a knife-thrust in his shoulder, and into it moistened tobacco was stuffed. Zeke had slashed himself across a palm; another man while chasing an Indian in the dark had struck a tree and knocked five or six of his front teeth out. Mick Boone had torn a thumbnail off. Sam said they would examine the booty to see if there was anything any of them wanted and then they would bend the barrels and burn the stocks off the guns. He told Hank to choose five or six men and ride Indian ponies back to their horses and then go out and find elk for breakfast.

There wasn't much in the booty that any man wanted. Some of them chose pieces of leather clothing, or a tomahawk or a headdress. The rifles, furnished by the British so that the Blackfeet could wage war on Americans, were piled on a fire, and after their wood was burned off and their barrels were hot the barrels were laid across stones and a huge stone was dropped in the center of each to bend it. It was while bending a barrel that Sam was first startled and then astounded. He was busy a hundred feet from where he had scalped the chief when, glancing that way, he saw what he would never have thought could be. Elk Horns in spite of the awful drubbing he had taken was still alive. He was conscious. In fact, he was slowly and stealthily crawling toward Sam, a knife in his hand. Sam advanced on the Indian and when fifty feet away stopped and looked at him. It was the eyes that held his attention: only in the eyes of falcon, wolf, or wolverine, or of the young man in the river, had he seen such deadly hate. "I'll be doggone!" he cried, and other men came over to stand with him and look.

George said, "Sam, I thought ya kilt the varmint."

Charley said, "Is thissen the one we send to the Bloods?"

"He's tied to a tree," George said.

"Hain't no reason to send two," said Charley. "Which one do we kill?"

Bill had come over. He looked at the bloody Indian, now lying flat and staring at the men. The redman had the exact look of a wounded beast that knew all the advantages lay with the enemy yet was determined to fight for its life. He looked like a thing waiting and planning. The men saw the knife in his hand and expected him at any moment to leap up and charge.

Bill said, "Wall now, anyway he knows who done it. I figger Sam intends to send this chief and jist caught the other in case the chief doan feel up to it. Sam, be that it?"

"Might be," Sam said.

George said, "Wooden it be more insultin ta send the chief?"

"Ten times more, it shorely would," Bill said.

"Then who gits the other one?"

"He's Sam's," Bill said.

Sam was staring at the chief. He was remembering how this varmint had degraded and humiliated him and how for days he had been close to death in winter desolation; but there was something in this situation that distressed him. Perhaps it was the eyes of all the trapped and helpless or wounded creatures that had looked at him, during his years in the West, and looked at him now, out of this man's eyes. There was the blue heron. In target practice he had once shot a heron on the bank of a river, only breaking a wing. The bird, tall and stately, had come walking down the bank and right past him, with what he had taken to be contempt for him. He could never forget that experience. The bird, walking with superb dignity, had looked at him steadily with one eye as it approached and passed him and went on down the bank, its blue wing hanging.

And there was Kate Bowden.

Sam might have said, after trying to think his way through it, that in the eyes of all wounded or helpless things there was something that laid a hand on his heart. He was still looking at Elk Horns when Tomahawk Jack went over to the chief, and pressing the muzzle of a revolver against the bloody skull, reached down and took the knife from the hand. It was then that Sam saw with greater poignancy the look in the eyes that he did not want to see and was weary of seeing. Dan had been standing back, listening and watching. He now came over to

Sam and said that if the chief was to be the messenger he ought to be skelped properly—halfway down his forehead and right across the middle of his ears. Dan was eager to show how it should be done, but Sam said no, the chief had been scalped and that was good enough. If Dan wanted to scalp the other one that way and turn him loose that was all right. A bald head was a better warning than a dead Indian. They could tell them to tell their people that two messengers had been sent for the reason that it was figgered that one would be killed by the Crows on the way. Fine, Bill said; that would heap insult on two bald heads.

After thinking about it Dan said it made sense. Did he get to scalp the other one?

"Shore," said Bill, "an git it over with. We want breakfast."

As Dan approached, the Indian bound to the tree began the death song. Then the song fell silent, and so far as the men watching could tell the redman did not flinch while his scalp was taken. Half of each ear clung to the topknot. The two Indians were placed side by side before Sam, with the points of knives held against their backs. Sam studied their faces. Then Bill said, "Sam, the chief's shoulder is outta joint, it shorely is." They could all see that it was, when they looked at the position of the arm. From behind, Bill felt over the chief's torso and said that several ribs seemed to be broken. Sam must have handled him a little rough, Bill said. Both Indians were trembling with hate and outrage; all around them they could see the dead bodies of their comrades, and the pile of useless rifles. The chief was so shaken, so horribly humiliated, and so little in control of himself, that his lips were drooling saliva and blood and he was making water. George might have said that he was enough to draw tears from the eyes of a dead wolf; but Dan, McNees, Jack and a few others were looking at him as if they would have liked to skin him alive. They were thinking of the unspeakable tortures and agonies they would be put to if they were in the power of this savage. Dan would have cut his head off and hung it from a tree.

Someone asked why the varmints were not taken to camp and tied up until after breakfast. Let the red niggers think about it awhile. Sam said all right, they would do that and then send them on their way; and he turned them over to Cy and Charley, who spoke a smattering of Indian tongues. The men then mounted Indian ponies and rode to their camp; and behind them on horses, their feet tied together with leather ropes under the horses' bellies, and their hands bound, came the two prisoners. Hunters returned from the hills with the choicest portions of elk and buffalo; fires were built; and great roasts were hung from tripods, and thick steaks were laid on chokecherry limbs over red embers. Sam, Hank, and Bill were making hot biscuits. A dozen of the men were out in the vales and over the hills, gathering roots and wild fruits.

After they had eaten over a hundred pounds of flesh, with biscuits and berries, and each had drunk a quart of strong coffee, they sat back, chewing tobacco or puffing pipes. Bill took the pipestem from his teeth and, like an Indian, made a sign with the pipe at the earth and the sky. It was a cardinal's wonder, he said, that Sam didden bust the chief wide open, though as it was he done him plenty bad. He doubted the varmint would ever make it to his people; some of his innards might be split open inside. Sangre de Cristo! Jack said, and turned red with anger. Did they pet the pisened wolf because they felt sorry for him? Thar warn't no mercy in these red critters and for his own part he'd feel oneasy if this chief was turned loose. He would arouse the hull nation against them. Would the varmints figger the chief had been freed because he was a greater chief than any white chief? And Sam dotta know that if Elk Horns was turned loose he would be on his trail night and day till the last river ran dry. Why didn't they sell him to the Crows?

The proposal caught the fancy of a few of the men: Elk Horns captured Sam to sell him to the Crows and Sam had turned the tables on him. Waugh! That would larn them to stay on their own range.

For a full minute Sam puffed his pipe and considered the matter. He didn't want to offend these men who had come a long way and risked their lives for him; but he didn't want the Crows to put a wounded man to fiendish torture and death. Whether if he turned the chief loose there would be any gratitude in him he did not know. This Indian might pursue him night and day as long as he lived but Sam was thinking of the eyes of the youngster dying in the river.

"No, I guess not," he said at last. "We'll send him back and if he wants to come after me I'll be ready for him." He looked over at the two men bound to a tree. "Bring them over here."

The moment men moved toward the two Indians they began

their death song. Dan was looking at the Indian horses; he wanted the chief's horse and all the men knew it. Most of them felt that Dan should have the horse, and the chief too, because for years he had roamed the mountains and prairies with his skinned head blistering or freezing in sun and winds. The chief's horse was a handsome spirited black. Knowing how the men felt, Sam said Dan could have the beast, and at once Dan saddled and mounted him and sat proud and bone-bald and ready for war.

As the two Indians were brought to him Sam called Cy and Charley over. He told them to tell these two redmen that they would be sent back to their people; and they would tell their people that if ever again they captured or tried to capture a mountain man the mountain men would make war on them till there wouldn't be left as much as a sick old woman in all their lands. "Be sure they understand you." While Cy and Charley spoke, by turns, in signs and Indian words, Sam studied the two Indian faces. In the face of the young buck he saw only what seemed to be amazement; in the face of the chief only sick sullen smoldering contempt and hatred. Maybe he should have given him to Dan after all. Sam had been thinking that as a gesture of kindness he would put the man's shoulder bone back in its socket before sending him on his way but he now said to hell with it. A face as ferocious and evil as that deserved nothing. They were now to tell this chief that if he wanted to fight Sam anywhere any time he was not to skulk around like a cowardly coyote; he was to come out like a warrior and a brave man, into the open, where they would fight it out. Be sure that he understood it. "Tell him he's to come any day and the sooner the better." Again Sam studied the chief's bloody face. The expression now was not all sullen hate; Sam thought he saw fear, and he told himself that he would never see this chief again. The man's fighting will had been broken. What an abject pitiable thing he would be, enduring for the remainder of his life the jeers and contempt of his people. Sam guessed it would have been more merciful to have killed him.

Without knife, gun, or parcel of food the two Indians headed north, afoot, and twenty-three whitemen stood in a group and watched them go, as long as their red skulls were in sight. By noon the wolves and buzzards would be stripping the corpses. By tomorrow or the day after the largest Blackfeet village would be like an overturned wasp nest.

The men rode together to the Three Forks area and from there, singly or in pairs or threes, they went southwest, south, southeast, or east, with a wave of the hand and the words, "Watch yer topknot!" or "I'll see ye at the next rondyvoo!" Come another spring they would not all be alive, but it was that way with mountain men, it was their way of life and they would have willingly lived no other. Hank and Bill rode into the east with Sam. Bill said Mick Boone was brokenhearted because his bay had not been among the horses. Sam said he was awfully sorry about that. Maybe he should have kept the chief and traded him for the horse, and for his guns and knife, and for the lock of hair from his wife. He guessed he was getting old and foolish.

After they had ridden east a day's journey and spent a night in a thicket Sam said to Hank and Bill he would be leaving them now. They thought he intended to enter Crow country but what Sam had in mind was Colter's bilins and peace and rest.

When Sam was out of sight Bill said to Hank, "I'm awful oneasy about Sam. He jist didden act natural at all."

Hank's marvelous gray eyes were looking in the direction Sam had taken and his mind was remembering that the big man had saved his life. He spat a stream of brown juice and said nothing.

32

SAM HADN'T FELT natural since the death of the youngun in the river. He was a fighting man and fighting had been his way of life for years but he felt pretty doggone weary now as he doubled back to the southwest and headed up the beautiful valley of the Gallatin. For the moment anyway he had a bellyful of it; he had had his fill, like old Bill. Barely entering his thirties, he wondered if he was getting old. Well, he would stretch out in hot water a few days and sweat the pisens out of him; and play and sing some arias and the songs he and Lotus had sung, even the songs he and Kate had sung. It would be nice to be alone and safe for a little while. He guessed he ought to go over to his father-in-law and see if he had a marriageable daughter, for in making him for the solitary life the Creator had left something out. In his mind he now and then had a picture of red devils swarming out of the northern lands like huge infuriated wasps, their stingers hanging long and sharp. They had made the boast that the Crows were too cowardly to take him but they could take him, and they would now do their infernal best. So for a while he would live with the birds and the beasts and take stock of his resources and reduce all of living to the simplicity of bird song and hawk wing and wolf call. He had three months before the next trapping season; perhaps he should go home to visit his people. He could go by steamboat down the river but if he returned this year it would have to be overland; contemplation of a journey of thousands of miles did not fill him with joy. He wanted to see his people but he didn't want to see the kind of life they lived. He would never want to live in what was called the civilized life: "Here where men sit and hear each other groan; where palsy shakes a few last sad gray hairs, and youth grows pale and specter-thin and dies." It was something like that the poet had written. Neighbors and their children that were all energy and shrieks; debts and mortgages and policemen and funerals and taxes; out here, thank God, there were no funerals: a man died, the wolves and buzzards cleaned his bones, and that was the end of him.

Bill had brought news from Bridger's post and it had depressed all the mountain men. This magnificent untamed country was rapidly filling with people. The immigrant trains came all summer now, headed for Oregon and California; the valleys would be poisoned by smoke-belching cities, and a man wouldn't dare lie on his belly and drink from a stream. East of the Great Salt Lake were thousands of Mormons now; Bill said they professed to want only to get away from their persecutors and take as many wives as a man could use, but the basin would fill with them and overflow, and there would be only Mormon wives where today there were beaver, wild fruits, and peace. The polygamous dames would tramp down all the berry bushes and hack down all the trees; and at last all the Indians and all the elk and buffalo would be gone. There would be, Bridger said, only what was called civilization and the thought of it made him sick in his innards. How many wives did

Brigham have now? Fifty at least, and five hundred children, Jim said.

The truth was that Sam Minard had been born too late and had come west too late. He had been here only a few years when Brigham came creaking and crawling across the prairies with his Mormon hordes; and now after him came people by the thousands, itching all over to find gold or tear up the country with plows; and to build jails, impose taxes, vote politicians into office, and play like children at being elegant and civilized. Good God, he guessed he ought to push north.

In Colter's hell with its clean sharp odors of sulphur pot and steaming geyser, of vast black forests of spruce and pine and fir, Sam looked round him and wondered what it would be like after men with gold pans, axes, and plows were done with it. He tried to imagine it fifty or a hundred years hence. Why was the Creator putting so many people on the earth, anyway? Doggone it, there were hundreds of millions now; Sam thought a few hundred thousand would be enough. There were too many red people, so many that the sites of their old villages gave off foul odors for years and were stains of death on the earth. Let the red people settle for a year or two in a spot and everything under them and around them began to die and smell bad, like flowers soaked with wolf urine, until you could say, there on the Rosebud, there on the Bighorn, there on the Belle Fourche, the Chugwater, the Teton, the Snake, the Colorado, the Green—there and everywhere are the death stains where people blighted what they touched, and Nature no longer could do its housekeeping and replace stink with fragrance. There was something about people, Sam decided, and sniffed his hands. There were millions of buffalo, whole seas and oceans of them, and in twenty-four hours they dropped millions of their dung piles; but in no time at all the dung became odorless chips that were much like a handful of dried prairie grass. But a site on which people, white or red, camped for a few weeks stunk a man out of the area and over the tallest peaks. Man was, for a fact, such an ill-smelling critter that every beast and bird on earth was afraid of him because of his stink. This fancy made Sam chuckle. The Creator was slipping somewhere. To Sam it seemed that the time would come when all over the earth there wouldn't be an unpolluted stream or a fragrant dell left; or a scented thicket where a man needn't look round him before he sat; or a valley not littered and stricken with human ugliness.

Sam would have been grimly amused if told that in another hundred years there would be agitation for wilderness areas, in these very lands around him, where persons from the swarming and overcrowded masses could for an hour or two fill their lungs with clean air, hear a bird sing, sense the meaning of peace.

In the primitive edens and gardens where deer looked at him with their soft eyes, where birds peered through spruce foliage and talked to him, and the highest peaks wore on their shoulders cloaks of white that the sun never drew away; or where on the south flanks he could lie in berry thickets and spill luscious juices down his throat—where he could gather the orange radiance of thimbleberries by the double handful and feed on them while the exquisite soul-scents of mountain fruits filled his nostrils and senses; where he could gather the gold-and-bronze gum of the big fir trees and chew its wood-and-peak flavors while studhugging the tree to him, to saturate his leather clothing with its smell of mountains and eternity, drawn up from the deep earth and down from the tall skies; where he could climb with the aid of leather halters sixty feet up the golden wall of a yellow pine, taking only his rifle and harp, and find, high up, two or three big branches across which he could lie, and look up through a lacework of loveliness at pools of blue and piles of cotton, and play the waltz of the vineyard to the marvelous handiwork of God; where in a deep forest a hundred thousand or a million years old he could dig round him like a bear or badger, in the leaf- and cone-depths down through a foot or maybe two feet of it, feeling the clean earth-wonder of it in his hands and getting it all over him and breathing into his soul the earth-smells and infinite time of it, until he was filled with all the good unspoiled ancientness of the earth, forest, sky, mountains, and snows; and where he could stretch out full length in the hole he had made and cover himself over with the centuries-old accumulation of humus mold made of needles and cones and twigs, old bark, bird nests, snows, and rains, with only his face and arms out, his being enfolded by the ancientness and the peace, until at last he dozed and slept; and where with hot biscuits, an elk roast garnished with wild onions, a pot of coffee, a quart of blue-purple huckleberries he could feast not only on food that was free and divine but on the image of eternal beauty in everything around him, and then fill his pipe and smoke, and hum a few bars from Handel's "Messiah," and strain to hear a few faint notes from the infinite orchestras that he thought must be playing in the infinite blue capsule that enveloped the earth; and where at last when the day was done he could lie on the fur-soft of a buffalo robe, under the jewels that men called stars, with a cover of tanned elkskin over him, drawn up to his chin so that its scent would mingle with that of fir, red osier, mountain laurel, wild grape, and juniper smoke, and with the odors wafted in from the hot mineral pots, geyser steam, and the sky and the night. . . .

He would have remained in the haven until October if he had not seen signs of an abnormally deep winter. After years in the mountains whitemen knew almost as well as the red, or the wolf, beaver, and mourning dove, Nature's moods and auguries. Snow began to fall in the geyser basin in early September. That, for Sam, was warning enough. When a foot of snow fell in thirty-six hours he climbed the nearest peak to have a look around him, examining for omens all the things of the forest on his way up. He could not see across to the Bighorns east of him, or the Gallatin Mountains north. Where, he wondered, would he trap this winter? The Uintahs were still good but far away, and Bill Williams had been killed down there. There were spots on Bear River, the Snake, the Teton, but soon there would be ranches everywhere, and men building fences to keep their neighbors out. When there were no more open areas to go to, a man who loved freedom more than life would have to settle down, with a neighbor within twenty feet on the left, and on the right, and a whole row of them facing him across the street. Yonder, away down there, late immigrant trains were crawling along.

The next morning he packed and was off. Ten days later he again stood on a summit and looked round him; what he saw was not black forests but the plains of the upper Sweetwater where it left the mountains. He was looking at the Oregon Trail about eighty miles west of Independence Rock, and at a wagon train creaking and squealing in six inches of snow. Another batch of greenhorns would be caught in the mountains, as the Donner party and others had been caught; or they would be if the sky suddenly opened and dropped a couple of feet of winter. Was it more Mormons down there? He wondered why any man was fool enough to want more than one wife. These people were still two or three hundred miles from the polygamous saints, and a thousand from the Dalles or

Sacramento. They might have to eat their leather caps and their harness before they got through.

He felt an impulse to ride down and ask these people why they hadn't stayed back east where they belonged. Did they believe, as so many had, that out west there were gold nuggets as big as melons lying up and down the canyons and streams? And soil so rich that cabbages would grow as large as kitchen stoves? What tales the jokers had told, who had been out west and gone back east! Two years ago Sam had ridden over to a train, and a woman, sitting in a covered wagon, had wiped at her eyes with a wrist gray with alkali dust, peered at him over red eyelids, and asked if all the men out here wore skins and married squaws. None of the immigrants seemed to have the slightest sense of the kind of world this was. What they sought was not the scented valleys, the clean sky, the majesties and grandeurs, but a spot where they could all huddle together as neighbors and poison the earth. They made him think of the marching army ants and the seven-year locusts. There they had been, three hundred of them, with their beds and tables and crying children and bawling cattle, and their foolish notion that they would soon be rich and well on their way to heaven.

Astride his horse, Sam looked at the long wavering line, like pencil markings against the white. Now and then he would turn his gaze from the half-frozen beasts, the cold wagon tires, the stiff dust-saturated canvas flapping in the wind, and look north and west at the immense world of valleys, mountains, rivers, and sky. Soon there would be no trails left, no forests with berry gardens in their cool depths, no water ouzels dipping and diving at the feet of cascades, no larks singing their arias, no prairie movements that from a distance looked like dark flowing waters but were herds of buffalo, no wolf song, no cougar cry, no horn call of the loons. Over on the Big Snake not many hundreds of years ago there had been stupendous eruptions of boiling lava that flowed over the plains south and west for more than a hundred miles—a red-hot hissing and steaming death flow that had killed everything it touched, and made utter desolation, black and grotesque and dead, of hundreds of square miles. For Sam and men like him the immigrant trains were another kind of death flow: looking east, he saw in fancy a thousand miles of them, as broad as a buffalo emigration, dust-gray and plodding and exsanguine and inexorable, coming in from the east to cover the earth. He recalled what old Bill had said: "Shore as shootin they'll shove us up the peaks and offen the peaks into the ocean, and cover this whole land with their privies."

Laramie had become an expanding assemblage of log huts and tents, surrounded by piles of buffalo hides as large as haystacks. By July 5 in only one season, 37,171 men, 803 women, 1,094 children, 7,474 mules, 30,615 oxen, 22,742 horses, 8,998 wagons, and 5,720 cows had passed this fort on their way west. In the past two years scores or hundreds of people and beasts had drowned while trying to cross the North Platte in their shrunken and rickety wagon beds used as boats. He hoped the Almighty knew what He was doing. It was not for a mere man to say that a thing was good or bad, which lay farther than he could see; but men like Sam would have preferred to join an Indian tribe and move north than live where neighbors made life a hell all around them.

Leading two packhorses, he crossed the trail and rode south, but turned time and again to stare curiously at the creeping wagons, tongue to tailgate and looking like hideous monster-bugs. In fancy he imagined their sucking mouths, like a locust's; their legs like cactus spines for seizing and holding; their round unblinking opaque-looking eyes that sought in life only what the mouth could devour; and their long sandpaper feelers that nervously twitched and flicked and shook with eagerness when the creature sensed that it had touched an object that could be eaten. During the past hour he had built such a loathsome image of the immigrants and all that they seemed to hunger for that he felt a twinge of shame and was glad when the day lowered and opened its belly to spill out the big white flakes. He began to hum a Haydn theme.

A hundred and thirty miles and three days later snow was still falling when Sam sat in its lovely gloom and looked at the cabin. It seemed to him that many years had passed since he had slipped up to it to find what was left of his wife and child. His were not the kind of wounds that time could heal. Dismounting, he went over and stood by the door; and when he looked at the spot where she had been murdered he felt, with almost no loss of intensity, the deep hurt, the anger, the injustice, the idiocy in the divine arrangement and the loneliness of bereavement that he had felt when he set her skull on his palm. He had looked at the stark white of the teeth, remembering the soft ripe lips that had covered them; at the empty caves, thinking of the marvelous eyes that had had their home there. He recalled now all the lights and living things that had been in those eyes; the gorgeous mane of her hair; the whole face and the whole delightful body; and all the living wonder of her that somehow, by a will stronger than his own, had become no more than a few bones and his memory of her. It was this kind of thing that wrenched a man's heart loose and blotted the soul out of him: if only something could survive that was more than the least of what a thing had been! If, of a flower, there could be more than the dry dead petals; of man, more than bones bleaching after the wolves were done with them; of his child, some part somewhere of the brave mountain man that he would have been. Far north (it was eight hundred miles or more) he had three times removed stones so that he could reach in and thrust in an armful of flowers. Three times his hand had softly moved over the pitiable and absurd remains; and crushed petals and rubbed their essence over the two skulls. How utterly death separated the lover from the things he loved! Here by the cabin door he kicked the snow away, and sitting where she had fallen, he played a few of the melodies he had played during those few immortal weeks when they were man and wife.

33

ALL THE MOUNTAIN men had known what kind of winter it would be; it was the second most paralyzing in the memory of the oldest Indians of the north country. It set in early and deepened fast. By mid-December the Missouri was frozen across at the Big Bend, and the Yellowstone at the mouth of the Bighorn. August was feeling the chills of September when Kate saw the first blight on her flowers. She did not know that it was frost; she thought her plants needed water, and daylong for a week she trudged up the hill. By October even the late bloomers were stricken, the primroses, asters, and gold stars. The nights were cold and clear, and when the moon was up Kate sat with her children until it went down.

During her years on the Musselshell she had not been conscious of a lost husband. She no longer saw Sam striding along the spine of high mountains, or heard him filling the heavens with deep organ tones. Her life had steadily drawn in to the heart of it, until it encompassed only her children and their flowers. Except in moments of fitful sleep or when chewing at food that was old and stale and tough she gave all her time to her children and their garden, watering and weeding all day, even when there were no weeds, and reading noble verses or singing old hymns half the night.

She had been thirty-five when her family was massacred; she was not an old woman now but she looked as old as the hills around her. Bill had come by after the killing of the Indians and had been startled on finding her hair completely white. It was not gray but white, with the look of cotton. Her face was deeply seamed and the skin over it looked like leather. Her body had shrunk until she was barely five feet tall; and it was bent and misshapen, like aspens on northern hillsides after the deep snows of winter. It was not labor that had prematurely aged her but want of food and sleep: she had been so completely devoted to her children that for days on end she had not eaten, and she had slept only when too exhausted to read or sing.

During these years she had not once lain down to sleep but had sat by the door. She had so little grasp of the realities and was so far gone to heaven that she did not understand that the moon was not capricious in its appearances but came at certain hours. She got the habit of sitting by the door because she thought the moon might appear at any moment, day or night. One dream she had dreamed so many times that she had only to doze and it came again. She was in heaven with her children and everything there was inexpressibly tender and beautiful. The river of life lay clean and holy and nourishing, and away from it in all directions were gentle hillsides, abloom with flowers and redolent of orchards; and over all of it was a blue sky as impeccable as God. All the people around her were mothers with their laughing and loving children, gathering flowers, eating berries, drinking from the river, and singing glad little songs of love and thanksgiving. Kate was so happy that she gave off little laughs and cries in her sleep; and on awaking she was so filled with the glory of it that it seemed to her that all her life she had fed on the light and love of the other world. Her world, the lonely hills around her, empty but for her garden, she was only dimly aware of, if at all; for she had been approaching heaven dream by prayer and was at last on its threshold, even when awake, and was ready to enter and be with her angels.

Because she was so other-worldly in her moods eating had become wholly perfunctory; she would go to the pile of stuff by the wall and without looking at it would feel into it and around her; and if she felt something that she thought she could eat she would begin to gnaw at it, if it was old meat or hard old biscuit, or she would push it into her mouth, if it was dried fruit. The mice had worked all through her food and had spilled and eaten most of her sugar and flour. If her searching hand came to spilled sugar she would eat a little of it, or of the raw flour; or she would chew a coffee bean if she found one. Her hunger for food was on the level of her need to void and for her had no more significance. In the dead of winter when the cold was deepest and all her food was frozen and she was unable to gnaw at it, because her teeth were bad, she would suck at it. Sitting by the door with all the bedding around her and over her, she would put to her mouth a piece of old hard deer or elk flesh, and suck at it and watch for the moon.

In this terrible winter she went in December to the river for a pail of water. The river was frozen over from bank to bank. A week ago she had chopped a hole in the ice but had forgotten it; she now climbed the hill over her snowpath, to fetch the axe. She chopped until she was exhausted and found no water. This deeply troubled her, for she felt that her children's plants needed watering. The next morning she went down and chopped again. She had at last a hole eighteen inches deep, but peering down, she saw that there was no water in it. Trembling with weakness and anxiety, she enlarged it. Because most of the ice chips fell into it as she chopped she now and then had to lie on her belly and reach down for them. Then, on her knees, she would chop again. With the kind of dauntless perseverance that had put Sam across the cold white prairies she kept at the task until she could see black water, two feet down. Her hole across the top was two and a half feet wide; around it all the way down it was jutting and jagged, like a talus slope, and lying face down, she tried to smooth the wall by chipping at it. Reaching down too far, she slipped and went headfirst into the hole. At the bottom it was too small to allow her to go through, and so she stood head downward, like a cotton-wrapped stopper in a huge ice jug. But at once she began to struggle and with almost the last of her strength pushed herself up and out. Her axe was gone.

If the mountain men could have watched her now they would have spun another legend around her name. She got to her feet. Almost frozen, she rubbed her hands over each other as her strange eyes peered into the hole. She moved back to see if she had been standing over the axe, and when convinced that it had vanished into the river she did not hesitate but lay by the hole and reached into it with her right arm, and let her head and shoulders slip down little by little until her hand was in the water. She did not know that she was above an eddy whose black waters were six or eight feet deep. If she could have gone through the hole she would have entered the water to search for the axe.

After she had struggled back from the hole she was almost rigid, and hand and arm were numbed and senseless. They never recovered from the exposure. The loss of the axe was for her a bitter loss. Day and night she grieved over it and went again and again to the river to look for it, and in desperation she tried to build a fire to melt snow. Failing in this, and convinced that her plants would die, she sat, trembling and half weeping, bundled against the cold, her attention divided between the sky and the garden.

She did not know and during these years had not known the month, much less the week or day. Such things as Thanksgiving Day and Christmas she had forgotten. It was two days before Christmas in this bitter year that the second heaviest snow of the season began to fall. The first three days it was a quiet storm of the kind Sam loved, and day and night Kate sat by the door, looking up through a dusk of whirling flakes. Her path to the river was lost and all trails were lost. An hour or two each day with bare hands she pulled the snow back from her doorway and the bedding, and back from the sages where her children knelt; but she was so starved and cold and enfeebled that she had forgotten her flowers. Her consciousness was closing like a shutter but it would never close on her children before she died, or on the moon in whose light they came. On three sides of the cabin the snow at the end of the third day was over five feet deep and it was that deep on the roof. Time and again she tried to follow her old path to the river but always turned back, exhausted and weeping. Time and

again she searched through the cabin for the axe. Then memory
of it was gone too, and of the water pail, and the path, the river.
But for hunger pangs she would have lost all memory of food.

After three days of heavy snowfall the weather turned colder
and for a week the cold steadily deepened. The northern winds
came down. Sam would have said that at first they came in the
opening phrases of an overture, or in a prodigal pouring of a
dozen overtures out of the great northern ice caverns. They
would take their time about it, these winds, for they had
Beethoven's patience, and his skill in devising variations on
main themes and in building crescendo on crescendo. If Sam
had been in the Wind River country, or here with Kate, where
the winds were flinging their wild music headlong, he would
have thought that the Creator was about to use all His
instruments in a major symphony. Kate was barely aware of it.
After the snow was up to her roof and her path was lost and the
world all around her was winter white she was hardly conscious
of the winds sculpturing magnificent snow dunes. At first they
gave her only a little trouble. She daily pawed snow back from
the sages, so that her children could kneel there if the moon
came; and the first gentle winds played around the clearing she
had made and sprayed it with snow gems but did not fill it.
After the opening chords of the first movement there were cold
clear announcements from the horns, far in the north, and by
morning of the third day of winds the first movement was in full
flow. By noon the clearing round the plants had been blown
level full, but neither in volume nor intensity was the wind
more than a token of what it would be. It was a kind of molto
adagio. The second movement would be of such percussive
violence, with crescendo piled on crescendo, that her cabin
would tremble and hum in the furious winter music, and her
efforts to clear the snow away from the plants would be only
pathetic flurries in the cyclones of white that enveloped her.

But she persevered and waited for the moon. It rose, round
and frozen and wintry wan, and appeared and disappeared as
the winds hurled curtains of snow across its face. The next
morning the temperature had fallen to ten below zero, and in
the next few days it fell fast, as the second movement came in.
The first had been a vast playful statement of themes, as the
winds rearranged the snowface of the earth; and if Kate had
had any interest in the marvels of a northern winter she could
have looked in any direction and seen the buxom contoured

sculpturing of the drifts, the great massifs and mesas of winter white, as Canada hurled its insane genius over the scene. It was a world of superlative purity and loveliness, but Kate could only sit, mute, shivering, half dead; or struggle desperately with the immense drifts that had been flung against the north wall and around the corners; or kneel and dig down to try to find her old snowpath. After the cold became more intense the snow surface was frozen in jewels, and diamond-ice hurled against her face stung like flame. The winds, now denied the joy of sculpturing, seemed to put aside the softer instruments, such as cello, viola, and flute, and to bring in the horns and trumpets and kettledrums. The second movement was allegro mounting swiftly to presto: though for Kate it was only wild winter shrieking, a sharp ear could have heard delightful variations on several themes, as the winter's instruments poured their marvelous harmonies down the valleys and across the prairies and over the high white mountains. Everything in their path the winds played upon; and when they found an object such as Kate's hut, or a naked stone ledge, or a flock of tall shuddering cottonwood trees, the voices would change in both intensity and pitch, and sometimes leap up and down an octave or two, as they modeled the themes to fit the curves and contours of the world. Or when wild and high, and climbing with shrill nerve-shattering energy to the highest notes, they struck the dimples of dells and ravines, the cellos and violas would take over, the harps and flutes, and small soft melodies were played in wind eddies under overhanging snow-laden plants and in the blind stone-walled canyons. Sam would have loved it; shouting with all his being to make himself heard, he would have played one of the themes over and over in different keys, as in the third overture to *Leonore,* and imagined that his melodies were small vocal pockets riding in the winds. He would have gone singing and dancing over the earth, and returned, when weary, to eat four elk steaks and sit by the fire with his pipe and praise the Lord.

The fiercer harmonies and wilder movements, even the major themes, were not for the female, whose nest-budded instincts compelled her to seek the tranquil. By the end of the scond movement, when the temperature had sunk to more than thirty below, Kate was so numbed and lifeless that she could barely move. Hunger pains would force her, perhaps once but never twice in twenty-four hours, to crawl out of the pile of bedding and over to the north wall, where in the gloom her cold hands would feel around and over and through the things there. There was nothing she could chew, except sugar or flour, and the mice and insects had destroyed most of those. There was dried elk and deer flesh. There were raisins in skin bags, frozen as hard as stones. She would take back to the bed a little fruit and a chunk of meat; she would lay them on the hard frozen earth and after crawling into the pile of bedding try to wrap it evenly all around her; and she would then feel over the ground until her hand came to the food. She would put three or four raisins into her mouth and for ten or fifteen minutes suck at them; the meat she could neither bite nor break, and so had to put her teeth and lips over an edge of it and try to warm and soften it and suck nourishment out of it. There was no hurry; she had all day and night for this one simple task.

When dark came and the moon was there, a wan candlelight in the winds, she would again crawl out of her bedding and feel around in the pile for the Bible. She could not walk out over or through the snow, for the wind with one thrust would have put her down; and so on hands and knees she crawled until she was about where she used to sit; and there she sat, almost blown away, and stared hopefully for sight of her children. But they never came any more; the snow was deeper than the sages and there was no place for them. When her frozen body and numbed mind understood that they were not there she would turn over to hands and knees and crawl back to the bedding, and there she would sit, her ears and nose frozen, her eyes looking at the moon or down at the garden spot—back and forth through the long night, or as long as the moon was up.

Before the divine orchestra brought in its third movement Kate's right hand and both feet were so frozen that blood no longer flowed through them; and before that movement gave way to the fourth her legs were frozen to the knees. She semed not to know it. It was the seventh day of the winds and she no longer crawled over to the north wall. The temperature had fallen to more than forty below, and the instruments were now all percussive and in high keys. There was nothing the winds could do with the earth; the streams were frozen almost to their bottoms, the trees to their hearts; and in the white sculptured landscapes there was no change, no matter with what force the winds struck them. The winds were now in high piercing tones, thin and wild, and seemed to be preparing for the coda; and then, in a black evening, all the instruments built steadily to the first fortissimo, and in deafening apotheosis came roaring past Kate's door in such cyclones of sound that the sky literally was filled; and on top of it all, in frenzied explications, came the first crescendo, and on top of it the second, in such thunderous frozen magnificence that Kate was lost within the soul of it.

The next morning there was utter silence. Kate Bowden was dead. She sat there in her wraps by the door, frozen almost solid, her face toward the garden, her frozen left hand on the Bible, her frozen eyes looking up for the moon, in a temperature of fifty-two below. Two weeks later snow fell again, and for the next two months she was gently and softly buried. Snow drifted in over her and half filled the shack, until there was no sign of her, and no sign of garden or graves. Over the whole scene was spread the purest winter white.

34

ALMOST A THOUSAND miles south, where Sam had a tiny cabin back under a stone ledge, the temperature never fell to more than twenty below but he knew that it was much colder up north. He worried about Kate but told himself that she had been inured to the cold of northern winters and would be all right. He did not suspect that on the Musselshell it was so arctic that trees split open half their length, old deer, elk, and antelope frozen as hard as stone dotted the white foothills, old buffalo bulls had been blown down and covered over, and the feeblest of the coyotes and wolves had succumbed to the northern winds. It had been a good winter for Sam; the extreme cold had produced thicker fur and when spring came he had three packs of beaver, otter, fox, and mink. On arriving at his chosen spot he had moved fast to lay in a pile of wood by a ledge, and several hundred pounds of elk flesh; and each evening after supper he had honed his skinning knives, filled his pipe, warmed a spot for his bed, and slept as cozily as the grizzly in its depth of fat and fur.

It was May before he could beat a path out of the mountains.

It was the twentieth of May before he reached the Laramie post. Charley was in from the Powder, Cy from Lightning Creek, Bill from the Tetons, George from the Hoback, Hank from the Bighorns, and McNees from the upper Sweetwater. They had no news except a rumor that Abe Jackson had died of his wounds, and that the nation seemed to be moving toward a war over slavery. As for the past winter, it was the worst, Bill said, since Adam was kicked naked out of Eden and went off alone in the cold. He had wished he had a squaw, for he still loved the wimmins, he shorely did. He guessed he was getting old, for he sometimes felt queersome and had more pains than a politician had tricks. Looking in the mirror of a pool, he had seen gray in his hair and beard; and one day he had fired at an elk standing broadside at two hundred yards and hadn't even scairt the beast. "I didden even raise a hair, I shorely didden." George said he spected they should all be gittin a fambly and settlin down. Nice Californy weather and kids in the dooryard.

George couldn't have a child without help, Bill said. "He muss be as old as I am." Bill was thirty-seven and George was forty-two.

Jist the same, George said, a winter like the last one put cricks in a man's jints. Why, up in them mountains the wind like to blowed theirselves offen the earth.

"Reckon the woman on the Mussel is all right?" Bill asked.

"Hope so," Sam said. He aimed to git up there soon.

Sam bought generously for Kate. There was a lot more to buy than there had been when he came west: besides raisins there now were dried apples and peaches, as well as peanuts and hard candy, plenty of salt bacon, dried fish, rice, navy beans, prunes, honey. He bought a few pounds of each, and thread and needles and cloth, moccasins, blankets, flower seeds, a short shovel, and then looked round him to see what else he could take to her.

On leaving the post he did not for the first time in his years out west head north through Crow country. He was not running from trouble but he was not looking for it. He did not want to kill any more young damn fools bent on taking his scalp. After a hundred and fifty miles he had no doubt that he had been seen by Crows but none had taken his trail. Had they been cowed by the destruction of Elk Horns and his band, or had the dreadful winter subdued them? Whatever the reason, not a single warrior tried to ambush him or creep up on him during the long ride through the western part of their lands. Near the junction of the Bighorn with the Little Bighorn, not far from the spot where a general named Custer would make his last stand, he saw the fires of a war party that had passed; but when he stood on the bank of the Yellowstone, only fifty miles from the Musselshell, he could say that he had not seen a redman in five hundred miles.

He knew that there was a meaning in this and he felt that it boded no good. Had the Crows made a pact with the Blackfeet that would allow them to capture him again? This thought so enraged him that, sitting on a hilltop, he filled his pipe and looked south and east at Crowland, and north and northwest to the Blackfeet. He guessed that Elk Horns, his skull healed over and as bald and white as Dan's, would be looking for him. As a gesture of contempt, both for himself and for the chief, Sam decided to headlong north across the Musselshell and right into Blackfeet land. He would then approach Kate from the west, over the death trail where, nearly dead and deaf and blind, he had staggered on and on. It was in the foothills that he saw something that stopped him: a skin tepee in an aspen grove. Retreating, he hid his horses and then warily approached, rifle cocked. On reaching the tent he saw that its door flap had been sewed together with buckskin thread and that the hems of the skin had been staked to the earth all the way around. After a few moments of trying to look inside he came to himself with a violent start, and quickly looking round him, said aloud, "Sam Minard, this is jist the way ye were when Elk Horns took you!" Leaving the grove, he scouted the area in all directions but found no human prints, new or old.

Though he felt that he was desecrating a holiness he pulled three stakes and on his belly crawled under the loosened skin, rifle in hand. Unable to see anything inside, he propped the edge of the tent up, to let daylight in, and then stood and stared for a full minute. On a bed of lodgepoles two feet above the earth lay a dead warrior in full regalia, his shield of buffalo hide across his loins, his tobacco pipe, adorned with eagle feathers, across his right arm, and his medicine bag on his chest over his heart. At the head of the bed, kneeling, was a woman in what looked like an attitude of prayer. Sam knew that she was the man's wife. After carefully studying her position he guessed that she had knelt there and frozen to death. He sensed that the man was Elk Horns and he guessed that he had killed himself because his people had cast him out. Sam was deeply moved by the scene. He did not want to touch anything here, but because he had to know whether this man was the chief he gently moved her heavy hair back until he could see a part of the skull. What beautiful devotion in a wife! What a poem, what a symphony this picture before him was! The chief had been his deadly enemy but he must have had remarkable virtues to have won from a woman such love as this. Softly he put the hair back over the skull and the face. The odor of human decay had turned him sick; dropping to hands and knees and grasping his rifle, he crawled under the tent and looked around him before rising to his feet.

He guessed he had better be going. As he rode east it occurred to him that he and the mountain men had avenged not only his own humiliation but also the massacre of Kate's family, if it could be said, in earth or heaven, that a wrong so monstrous could be avenged. If Lotus had lived would she have loved him with such holiness that she would have covered his shame with her hair, and have knelt by him and died in the bitter cold? All the mountain men had been impressed by the loyalty of red women to their husbands. They were wildcats in their jealous furies, and they often killed, when they could, the adulterous husband; but they would accept floggings and brutalities that would drive white wives from the door. Covering the unspeakable shame of a scalped head with their own hair, they would freeze to death by the man they loved.

After crossing the Musselshell, Sam observed that winter had been in no hurry to depart. It was June, but on the north flank of every hill was a snowbank, molded to the hill's contours and dappled with wind dust. No river flowers were yet in bloom; he wondered if Kate's would be. He had with him twenty different kinds of wild-flower seed—enough, he expected, to sow an acre of prairie. Kate might not use them but she would be happy to have them: when building a nest, a woman, like a bird, was happiest when she had more materials than she could use. Except for the willows and shrubs the plant life hadn't put on its spring dress yet; and the river grasses were barely looking out of the earth. Everywhere were signs that the Canadian winds had been here. Cottonwood trees riven by frost now stood with their bellies open; and aspens had been snapped off by the winds or torn from the earth.

When he came to the hill where he had always paused to

look at the shack and the garden he cried aloud, "My God!" and some part of him died. He saw it instantly and knew it all. He saw the second cairn of stones, standing close by the one he had built, and he knew that Kate was dead. The grief that choked and blinded him would have been no more intense if he had looked at the grave of his mother. The sky had darkened, the earth had taken on a deeper quiet. It was all desolation now: there were no flowers—there was only an old shack with a part of its roof fallen in, and two mounds of stones.

Dismounting, he dropped the reins, and rifle in hand, approached on foot.

The sage plants still lived and for a few moments he looked at them. Then he looked at the second cairn, observing how the stones had been laid, for his first thought was that a mountain man had passed this way. He had found Kate frozen to death. But he knew it was not that. Something had caught his gaze and he now circled the two cairns and looked down at the sage, most of which had been trampled and broken, and went to the shack to peer in. The pile of filthy bedding was still by the door. By the north wall with earth from the roof spilled on it was the heap of utensils and food. Stepping across the bedding, he went over and knelt to examine it. He found an old knife but no axe. Under the bedding was the rifle.

Sam went out and looked south. Something had happened here that he did not understand. After walking twice around the cabin he knelt to examine footprints of man and horse. He went east from the cabin fifty yards. He swung north and doubled back to the south, and at the top of a hill found the incredible evidence that he had thought he might find. He knew now that a party of Indians had been here and that they were Crows. This seemed to him so utterly outside the plausible and the possible that he examined all the signs, over and over; stared again at the cairn, half expecting that it would not be there; and looked up and down the river and all around him. He knew it was true but he could not believe it, not all at once: a party of Crows had come here and found Kate in her bedding, dead, with a part of the roof fallen on her; and they had gathered stones and built a house to protect her; and they had taken none of her tools, bedding, food, not even her rifle!

How could a man believe that?

To be completely sure he searched over the area where they had hitched their horses; examined footprints of man and beast; studied from top to bottom of the cairn the way the stones were laid; found their campsite and inspected the ashes of their fire; and then for two miles followed the path they had taken eastward over the hills. The implications so overwhelmed him that after two hours of searching and study he could only sit and look and wonder. It was this way: they had come in from the southeast, perhaps looking for Blackfeet; and on the first hill from which they had a view of the shack they had sat on their horses, looking and listening. They had tied three of either seven or eight horses to a cedar and in single file had approached the cabin. When a hundred yards from it they had been able to see that most of the roof had fallen in, and that there were no flowers, no woman, no life. They had then moved nearer, and two of them had approached the door by going around the north wall. They had found her in the bed. Old woman's man her children their ghosts, there, in the blackest nights they are, in the sagebrush they are crying. . . .

Sitting by the bedding, his left palm resting on it, Sam smoked three pipes. He was trying to believe that far yonder in the pale haze in a small tent filled with death smell a wife was bowed before her man, her hair hiding his shame; and that here another wife had lived for years, alone, by the graves of her children. Greater love hath no man, but greater love hath the mother. Where was her Bible? He would know someday that they had put it in the cairn with her. Where was her axe? He would never know. Why had the Crows done this thing? It was an act of such gracious mercy and pity—or, if not that, of atonement—that he sat humbled before it.

So this was why all the way up from the post he had seen no Crow!

After the third pipe Sam patted the bedding as though it were Kate, and closed his eyes on loneliness and grief. Then he want to the cairns. On a ledge of stones shoulder high he rested his face in his arms and tried to say a prayer for Kate, or a farewell, or something. Prayers had never been a part of him, and he did not know how to say farewell. The opening of light in the last movement of the Fifth, that was prayer maybe, his kind. No matter: the Crows long ago had said the only prayer for her that need ever be said:

Old woman's man her children their ghosts, there, in the blackest nights they are, in the sagebrush they are crying. . . .

But not crying now. Not any more.

From time to time, he told himself, head bowed and tears falling, he would pass this way, to bring flowers and touch a stone. His wife and child would be here, and Kate and her children. There would be no olive-green sage plants any more, no marigolds and bluebells and gilias; no little gray woman in rags carrying pails of water up a hill all day long. There would now be only memory of her and the story of her; and after a generation or two there would not even be that. But as long as any of the mountain men lived there would be the footfalls of friends passing this way, and eyes looking over to the spot where the crazy woman lived. . . .

Meanwhile he had a job to do. Leaving everything here as he had found it, for time and God to do with in their infinite patience, he mounted his horse, drew tight on the lead rein, and set his course into the southeast, straight for the Belle Fourche and the old chief of the Crows.

35

AFTER HE HAD crossed the Yellowstone he proceeded through Crow country without his usual vigilance. He shot game, and at night he made a fire and roasted steaks. He sat outlined by flame and smoked his pipe. Though he crossed fresh trails he saw no redmen.

He decided to take the chief by surprise, and so slipped past the sentinels and sleeping dogs just before daybreak. He knew the chief's tent by the size and position of it. At the entrance he drew the skin flap aside and put an ear to the aperture. He had heard that the old chief snored as loud as a shipload of sailors, and after listening a few moments he guessed he had the right tent. Glancing round him, he slipped inside and stood in the dark. He then threw the tent flap far back, exposing to early morning a part of the interior. Because the chief was an old man he made in his sleep the sounds of anxiety and unhappiness that the old sometimes make; and so for a few moments Sam stood above him and looked at the face and listened. Then, filling his lungs, he gave the mountain-man battle cry. Instantly the chief came bolt upright, and though drugged by sleep and shattered by alarm, he reached blindly for his weapons. Sam had placed himself so that the old fellow would see his face and recognize him; he stood with a finger inside the trigger guard of his revolver and the other hand on his rifle. The chief's first recognition was that he was covered; his second, that the person before him was the dreadful killer of his people; and his third, that the killer was offering his hand and speaking.

"Thought I dotta call on you," Sam was saying. "It's morning. How about some breakfast?"

The old man rose slowly to his feet and stood, facing Sam, his eyes searching his face. He looked down at last to the extended hand. "Time we shook hands," Sam said, and seized the old hand and held it. "I figger mebbe there's too much killing in the world." Outside, the village was in uproar, with dogs howling, mothers shrieking at children, and braves racing away to their horses. Sam stood his rifle against his belly, released the hand, and drawing his knife, offered it handle first to the chief. When the old man refused to take it Sam laid his rifle on the earth, unbuckled his revolver and dropped it, and expertly threw the knife so that half the blade was buried in earth between his feet and the chief's. He offered his hand again, saying, "It's time to be friends."

The old warrior, one of the greatest his nation had ever had, stepped forward, and standing above the knife, looked into Sam's eyes. Black eye looked into gray-blue, gray-blue into black, for perhaps half a minute. Then the red hand came up to meet the white hand. Going to the tent opening, the chief called and a woman came running; he sent her for pipe and tobacco. In words and signs he asked Sam where his horses were, and sent a warrior to bring them in. Most of the braves had rushed away into morning dusk to find their horses, and now returned to stand in groups and look at the chief's tent. Word had passed that The Terror was here, to smoke the pipe of peace. As among all impassioned and impetuous people, there were young hotbloods who wanted to keep the vendetta alive, and would go on dreaming of hanging a scalp on the medicine pole, high above all other scalps there. When full daylight was on them Sam and the chief, sitting in the places of honor in the village center, smoked a pipe, as Sam looked round him at hostile faces. Never in Crow country would he dare to forget the past, for to the end of his days one of the avengers might trail him.

While the two men smoked and breakfast was prepared in the fires the chief looked at Sam with eyes almost ninety snows old and said, *"Dua-wici?"* Sam thought of Charley and Cy and tried to remember what these words meant. The chief now asked him in signs if he had a wife. Sam shook his head no.

The chief gave a signal. A little old woman, crippled by arthritis and age, hobbled over to him and bent down to listen with half-dead ears; and then hastened away, to return half dragging by the hands a frightened girl. She looked to Sam like a child but she was slender and lovely and reminded him a little of Lotus. This, the chief explained, was his youngest daughter and she was not for sale. He would give her to Sam as a guarantee of that friendship and peace that must henceforth rest between Long Talons and the Sparrowhawks. Sam was touched by the offer. He knew it was a goodwill offering of extraordinary size—to *give* to the killer of his people the only unmarried daughter of the head chief! It was almost as if George Washington had offered his daughter to Cornwallis at Yorktown.

It took Sam a few moments to sense the magnanimity of it. He then got to his feet and beckoned to the girl to come to him. She came slinking, shy and hostile, and stood before him, looking down. Stooping, Sam put his left arm under her rump and straightened; and there she sat in the cradle of his arm, her black eyes staring at him. One who read the human female more unerringly than Sam might have thought her stare a fascinated blend of hate and admiration; hate, because this was the monster; admiration, because her father had said that as a fighter Long Talons had no match in all the lands of the earth. "Wife for me?" he asked her, but she only stared. She was a little heavier than Lotus, he thought, and a little taller. He liked the womanly female of her on his arm and her pressure against his shoulder. He liked the intelligence in her eyes. He set her down but did not release her at once; with his left arm across her back and her black hair coming to the top of his shoulder, he looked round him at the braves; at the women and children in a large group beyond the braves; and at the smoke of breakfast fires. He did not want the girl but he did not want to offend his host. He now had to match the chief's generosity, and this, it seemed to him, he could hardly do, unless he gave everything he had and walked away. But then he thought of the panniers bulging with stuff for Kate. That was it! The chief would think he had bought all these things for him and his people. So with words and signs he told him that he had brought gifts to the great chief of the Sparrowhawks; and clasping the girl's hand, Sam walked over to his packhorses. There he released her and began to strip the panniers. A ten-yard bolt of cloth in brilliant colors he gave, with a slight bow, to the girl. He did not observe that she was rigid with amazement and joy. All the other things he gave to the chief, who almost melted with happiness, for he felt that at some trading post Long Talons had bought these things for him.

During the hours spent with the chief not a word was said about Kate Bowden. But the chief knew that Sam knew what had been done, and Sam knew that he knew it. The Indian male was in fact a sentimental soul, but from early childhood there waited for him a pattern of life in which he would be brave, daring, ruthless, and conquering. The chief wanted to know if the pale people from the rising sun were going to keep coming until they overflowed the land and drove the red people out. Sam said he would fight for his red brothers before he would see them robbed of their ancient lands. That pleased the chief, and so they smoked another pipe. Sam had given him four pounds of tobacco, and to the young warriors around him he promised tobacco and rum. The chief said they were all friends now. His people had enough trouble fighting the Blackfeet and the Cheyenne; he wanted only peace with the mountain men.

While Sam took breakfast with the chief the daughter stood back, her black eyes studying the whiteman. Perhaps she was trying to imagine what life would be for her as his wife. The Crow women were menials but they seemed fairly contented with their lot, and they boasted louder of their lords and masters than any other women Sam had known. This girl, he supposed, was thinking that she would gather the wood, set the fires, cook the food, tan skins, sew and mend garments, find forage for horses and berries and roots for her man, while in fringed and beaded buckskin he rode arrogantly away to kill an enemy or a bull. So far as Sam knew, no Indian girl had ever preferred a whiteman to a red. He didn't know whether he would ever come back to claim her or ever want another wife. If he could be at peace with all the tribes around him he would have the life he wanted—the free wide world of valleys and rivers and mountains, of natural odors and natural music, where the black currants and red chokecherries and red plums bent their boughs toward him, and his drink was pure water and his bed was the earth. If he were not slain by man or beast, someday he would be old, and like the old bull he would go off somewhere and be alone to wait for death.

But he had before him, he hoped, twenty or thirty years of full living and millions of square miles to live them in; hot steaks and bird throats singing to him and mornings as fresh as the first alpine lily, and evenings as deep with peace as the earth under them. Turning on a hilltop, he looked back at the thousand Sparrowhawks watching him, and made a sign which said that he would come again someday; and then he galloped off into the southwest and a brilliant Rubens sunset. Maybe he would go down to see Jim Bridger, who was having trouble with Brigham Young and his Mormons.

When a few days later he came close to the Oregon Trail he paused, as in former times, and looked at the scene before him. There they were, hundreds or thousands of them, as far back as he could see in clouds of dust, and as far ahead—a long gray line of bawling beasts and squealing axles and creaking wagon beds that hadn't a drop of moisture left in them. There they were, pushing on and on like the armies of red ants; and behind them were other thousands, on their way or getting ready; and in the future their children's children would swarm over this magnificent land, chasing to their death the last elk and deer, shooting the last songbirds, trampling the last berry bush; there and everywhere with their houses and hotels and saloons and gutters, their towns looking like gigantic magpie and crow nests; there and everywhere, proliferating, crowding, and making untidiness and stench of everything, a people bumping and stumbling to get out of one another's way. Every Indian tribe was becoming more restless as the hordes poured in, and before long there would shorely be bloody war between the red and the white. During the hour that he watched the slow dust-saturated serpentine crawl of a wagon train four miles long there filled him the realization that his way of life would someday be no more. For a little while there would be patches of it left up in Canada but here it would all be what Jim Bridger said it would be, swarming human masses, with the effluvium of their body smells and city smells and machine smells rising to fill the heavens and wash away the blue. Sam didn't know if the Creator had planned it this way or if it was only the blind way of the blind. He remembered what a musician had written after hearing the *Don Giovanni* overture: that he had been seized by terror as there unrolled the ascending and descending scales, as answerless as fate and as inexorable as death. Sam guessed he wouldn't go on to Jim's post now but would turn back to the bird wings and giddy roadrunners and bluebirds, spilling lyrics out of the clean blue loveliness of their souls. He would go back to the Breughel mornings and Rubens evenings, and see what Bill was doing and what Hank was doing; and he would find a bushel of wild flowers and lay them gently over the bones of two mothers and one child.

And so after a last long look at the immigrants he turned and headed straight north, back into the valleys and the mountains.